MAISEY YATES

Part Time
Cowboy

CONTENTS

Shoulda Been A Cowboy

CHAPTER ONE

JAKE CALDWELL HAD most definitely improved with age. It really didn't seem fair. Rather than gaining five pounds around his hips like she had, his chest and shoulders had grown broader, his waist trim, his stomach washboard flat. It almost, *almost*, made her rue her addiction to the loganberry tarts she stocked in the pastry display at The Grind. Almost.

Cassie Ventimiglia slowly sank down behind the counter, putting Jake, who was outside dismounting his motorcycle, out of her sight. She didn't need to spend any more time looking at him. She needed to take inventory of her soy milk. She opened the mini fridge that was built into the counter and began to dutifully do just that.

Her soy milk supply was sufficient. Which was good to know. Important. Much more important than taking in the view outside.

Cassie rose again slowly, eyeing the small dining room. Most of the women in it were casting subtle glances outside. And

Cassie figured they weren't checking out Copper Ridge's main street.

Jake had that effect. But he always had. Even back when he'd been that dark scowling boy with perfect hair and wicked blue eyes wandering the halls of the high school, tattooed and bad news, and everything that kept mothers of good girls awake at night. And ensured that the fathers of good girls kept their shotguns close by.

Actually, that was probably why he had been so fascinating. As far as Copper Ridge, Oregon, went, he had been universally disapproved of. And what was more attractive than that, when you were seventeen and just starting to figure out that there was more to life than what your parents had told you? Nothing. At least not as far as she'd been concerned.

Of course, she had actually gotten to know him. Had seen beneath some of his tough exterior. Had bothered to see him as a human being. For all the good that had done her. She'd just ended up with a crush wider than the Columbia River Gorge. And before she'd been able to confess that, before she'd been able to tell him just what she wanted from him, he'd left.

She seemed to have that effect on men. But she wasn't going to think about that right now. She was going to think about muffins. She could inventory those next. So hooray for that.

Anyway, she had no reason to be…staring at him, thinking about him, drooling after him. He'd given no indication at all that he was interested in her as anything other than a tenant he happened to live near. He was aloof to the point of being cool. That was something that had changed.

When he'd been a teenager he'd had an air of intensity, anger and restlessness about him. Now he just seemed… Well, he seemed almost bored to be here. Like he was looking through things.

Like he was looking through her.

The little bell above the door chirped and she looked up just in time to see Jake walk in. He had been here for more than a week. Back in town, staying in the apartment next to hers. It was a complicated situation, really.

Jake's father had owned the building that housed her coffee shop and the apartments above it, in addition to a couple of other properties in town and a ranch just outside of it. That meant Jake was the owner now. And effectively her landlord.

At least he hadn't changed much since he'd arrived, with the exception of inhabiting the neighboring apartment. She only hoped he continued to not change things.

He came into the coffee shop every day and ordered an Americano and a muffin. Which meant that she should be used to him by now. It meant that her stomach should not go into a free fall, her heart should not skip several beats, and her palms should most certainly not get sweaty.

In addition to the fact that his presence was old news by now, she was thirty-two. She was, in the immortal words of *Lethal Weapon*'s Roger Murtaugh, too old for this shit.

And yet the second he'd walked in each morning, her heart rate had indeed increased, her stomach had plummeted, and her palms were definitely starting to get a little bit damp.

She forced her breathing to slow as he approached. He was holding his bike helmet beneath his arm, propping it against his hip. There was something epically badass about him when he stood that way. It was as appealing now as it had been fifteen years ago. And she had no idea why that was. He'd never been a good idea for her, never been a logical match. Her hormones had never registered that fact.

He laid his helmet on the counter and pushed his hand through his dark hair, drawing her eyes to the tattoo of dark evergreen trees that wrapped around his arm. They started at his wrist and extended up to his elbow. His tattoos fascinated her, now and always, because she'd never been able to imagine voluntarily undergoing something so presumptively painful.

That he'd been willing to do it only added to his mystique.

Oh, shoot. She had a feeling her internal monologue had been running for quite some time, and it was very possible Jake had been standing there for a little longer than she realized.

"The usual?" The question came out a croak, and she was none too impressed with herself.

Jake lifted one broad shoulder, not sparing her a smile. Smiling did not seem to be a part of his emotional vocabulary. That much she had learned over the past week. "Sounds good."

"The only kind of muffin I have left is blueberry."

"That's fine." He shifted his weight from one foot to another and for some reason she found it fascinating. "Every muffin you've ever served me has been delicious."

Cassie nearly choked. "I'm glad you like my…muffins." For some reason it all sounded dirty. Maybe her mind was in the gutter by default because he was here.

Maybe it didn't even have anything to do with him. Maybe it was her. After all, it had been three years since her divorce and even longer since she'd made skin-to-skin contact with a man.

That was a long time. She hadn't been conscious of just how long until Jake had blown back into town.

"There's nothing to dislike about your muffins."

She sucked in a sharp breath and choked on it, coughing violently. She turned her head to the crook of her elbow, trying to suppress it. "Sorry." She patted her chest as she grabbed the portafilter from the espresso machine. "Swallowed wrong."

She went over to the grinder, ignoring the heat in her cheeks as she turned it on, putting the portafilter beneath it and releasing enough grounds to produce a double shot. She tamped them down and went back to the machine, fitting the portafilter back in and pressing the button, counting the seconds on the shot as it filled the little tin cup she had placed beneath it.

It was a nice distraction, and once again she felt justified in her selection of a manual machine versus an automatic one. She emptied the completed shot into a paper cup and then poured hot water over it, putting the lid on and setting it on the counter. Then she reached into the basket and pulled out the last remaining muffin.

She extended her arm to hand it to him, only realizing her mistake when the tips of his fingers brushed hers and the shock of pure electricity ran through her body, immobilizing her for a moment.

She looked up and compounded her mistake as their eyes clashed and she was hit by a second bolt of lightning. And for just one nanosecond, she saw something flash through his eyes, too. Something not entirely cool and neutral.

She took her hand off the muffin and it went flying over the edge of the counter and onto the floor somewhere around his feet. She wasn't sure exactly where, because she was too horrified to look. "I thought you had it. I'm sorry. I'm sorry. No charge. Nobody wants a floor muffin."

He arched a dark brow, bending down and retrieving the muffin before standing back up and holding it out. "It's still wrapped. I'm sure it's fine."

"No, really. I insist. Everything is on me." Because, if she charged him, she would have to take his cash and if that happened they might touch again.

"All right, I'm not going to argue with that." He took his helmet, the muffin and the coffee and turned away, giving her a half wave with the hand that was clutching the coffee cup.

He walked outside again and rounded the back of the shop toward the exterior stairs that led up to his apartment. Cassie let out a breath she hadn't been aware she was holding.

She really needed to get it together. Yes, Jake Caldwell was back. But now, just like back in high school, there was no point in lusting after him. Nothing had happened then, and nothing was going to happen now. End of story.

And she had more inventory to take.

JAKE SET THE muffin and the coffee down on his counter and jerked the fridge open. It was early, but he was going to go ahead and grab a beer rather than that afternoon caffeine hit he'd been looking forward to.

Because he didn't need to be any more amped up than he already was. Something about this damn town screwed with him. Always had. Foolishly, he'd imagined that after so many years away the place might have less power.

Nope. Between the afternoon he'd spent at his dad's place clearing junk out and that little interaction with Cassie down in the coffee shop, he needed to cool down, not rev up.

He wasn't the same man he'd been when he left town. So what was it about this place that made him feel like he hadn't changed all that much? Still not quite able to handle all the shit at home. Still finding himself drawn to the kind of women he shouldn't be allowed to touch.

Cassie Ventimiglia was one of those nice girls. Caring, way too sweet for her own good. She'd been one of the few people who'd spoken to him back in high school. They'd been thrown together, part of a tutoring program to help his delinquent self get it together and get his grades up.

She'd been tempting, inexplicably. Because she was not the kind of girl he would normally look twice at. But she'd looked at him like she'd seen him, and he'd...

Well, it was just a damn good thing for her he'd left when he had.

But even now, when he'd come back to deal with selling his family's properties, she'd been first in line to welcome him back, even if it had been unintentional.

By default, he owned the building her business was in, and the place she lived. Going over his dad's paperwork he could see that before Cassie the building had been out of use for years, and bringing no income in. And while Cassie was getting a better deal than was reasonable, her being in the place was preferable to it sitting there bringing in no revenue at all.

Yeah, Cassie was definitely not the kind of woman for him to go messing around with. Probably he was looking at celibacy for the duration of his sentence in Copper Ridge. He had a history with too many of the women here. Either they'd already been with him in high school, or they hadn't wanted to be for very specific reasons.

Plus, a one-night stand would be almost impossible here. The odds of you running into each other the next day on the street were way too high. Just another reason Seattle suited him a whole lot better than this place.

A little anonymity was much better for a guy like him.

And possibly right now a cold shower would be the thing for a guy like him. Dammit. How long had it been since he'd gotten hard over brushing fingers with a woman? Answer: fifteen years.

He thought again of his last night in Copper Ridge. Sitting in an empty library with Cassie, all of his focus zeroing in on her lips. He'd been saying something about his family and she'd reached out and put her hand over his.

A caring gesture. One that had sent a rush of heat straight through his body and he'd wanted... He'd wanted to close the distance between them then. To kiss her. Deep and hard. To make that connection he felt with her real, physical.

He shook his head. What was it about her? What was it about *here*?

He grabbed the bottle opener off the fridge and popped the top on his beer. Taking a sip, he turned to look out the window. His view was of Old Town's main street. Painted clapboard buildings, with red brick interspersed. An American flag rising up above City Hall. And beyond that was the ocean. Without seeing it he could still picture the coastline. Evergreen trees, yellow bursts of Scotch Broom, and weedy blades of grass with edges sharp enough to cut into your skin.

Across the street, behind the apartment building he was currently residing in, was a long stretch of winding highway, forest and ranches. Yeah, he knew all of that, could picture it all without having to look.

Copper Ridge hadn't changed, but he had. He wasn't the same Jake Caldwell he'd been.

He wasn't a juvenile delinquent who couldn't do a damn thing right to save his life. Hell no. He managed a successful business in a very competitive environment. His boss trusted him, and he had done everything he could to earn that trust.

Unlike his old man, his boss actually believed he could do things right.

Which made him wonder yet again why he was here and not back in Seattle in the mechanic shop.

He sighed heavily. That was all because of John, too. The older man, who was, unquestionably, a mentor to Jake, had told him he had to come back and handle his family affairs himself. He'd said that was what a man did.

So he was here, handling his family affairs like a man.

And there would be no handling of pretty female tenants while he was at it. So his body was just gonna have to calm down.

He had a feeling this was going to be a long couple of months.

CHAPTER TWO

WHEN CASSIE FINALLY made her way back up to her apartment she was exhausted. She also had no fewer than three missed calls from her mother. She kept her phone on vibrate during the workday, which probably gave her mom fits. But then, her mom was the main reason she kept it on vibrate.

Work hours seemed to mean nothing to the woman.

Cassie was about to call her mother back when the phone started to shiver in her hand, the screen lighting up and her mother's picture appearing on it.

Cassie groaned and hit "accept."

"Hello?"

"Cassie, I've been trying to get a hold of you all day."

"Yeah, Mom, I've been working all day."

"Did you just get home?" The note of worry in her mother's voice did not inspire any warm fuzzy feelings in Cassie. Not at this point. Not considering Cassie lived directly above her workplace. Her commute was a staircase. "It's late, Cassie."

"I know, Mom. But such is the hazard of running your own

business. Anyway, I walked back up to the apartment using the interior stairs. Nothing is going to happen to me between work and home."

"But you work too much. How in the world are you supposed to meet anyone when you're working all the time?"

Ahhh, and here we came to the bottom of Mama Ventimiglia's worry. Not so much for Cassie's safety, but for her singledom.

The guilts would come next. They were her mother's specialty. A single mom, she'd always been hyperinvested in keeping her daughter from making the same mistakes she had.

The biggest mistake being getting pregnant without securing a man. Cassie was always thrilled to be numbered as one of her mother's mistakes, even if the other woman didn't really mean it that way.

"You know, Mom, I serve people coffee all day. I talk to people all day. I meet new people every day."

"But I bet you're going to tell me you can't date a customer."

Cassie sighed heavily. "You never know. Never say never. Never assume windows are locked when doors are closed, or something like that." What she really wanted to say was absolutely *no*, never, no. But she knew that would only keep her mother on the phone longer. And it wasn't like she didn't enjoy talking to her, sometimes. Her mom was nothing if not well-meaning, but when it came to the topic of Cassie's love life, or lack thereof, Cassie would rather she left well enough alone.

"I worry about you. I don't want you to end up like I did."

Alone. With nothing but a daughter and no man. "I know. But I'm fine. I really am. I'm happy."

"I don't see how you can be happy, losing Allen like you did."

Cassie fought the urge to scream and hurl the phone across the room. "I don't feel like I lost much of anything divorcing him. He was a dud. Better to have no potato chips than broken potato chips, or something."

"It's still a potato chip, Cassie."

Cassie sighed. Hoisted by her own bad analogy. "Right. Well, I'm on a diet."

"Do you still have the meals I sent for you in the freezer?"

"Yes, I do. I'll have one of those, thank you."

"I only say these things because I worry. Because I love you."

"I know." Cassie sighed again, heavily. "I love you, too. I'll talk to you later."

"Talk to you tomorrow."

Cassie disconnected the call and flipped it from her hand onto the couch, walking through the open-floor-plan living room and into the kitchen to rummage around for dinner. There was meatloaf in the freezer. Along with frozen mashed potatoes all portioned up for her already, and cooked with love by her mother. So yeah, she could be a bit overbearing, but there were some things Cassie really couldn't complain about.

She put the plastic container in the microwave and started it, then wandered over to the couch and flopped down. The couch butted up against the connecting wall to Jake's apartment. She heard a squeaking noise, then the sound of running water and realized it was the shower. She and Jake must typically run on different schedules, because she hadn't heard his shower noises before.

She'd never lived in this place while someone else lived in the adjacent one. It had originally been open space, and at one point in time, both units had been rented out. Then it had sat empty for ages before Cassie had rented it from Dan Caldwell, and until now, she'd never realized how thin the walls were.

And now she was terminally distracted wondering if Jake had taken his clothes off yet. Realizing that he was naked just on the other side of the wall. She jumped up off the couch and scurried back to the microwave, tugging open the door and closing it as loudly as possible in a vain attempt to drown out the sound of running water.

She pulled the lid off the Tupperware and grabbed a spoon, stirring the potatoes with much more vigor than was necessary.

Taking a bottle of wine and a glass out of her cabinet, she poured herself a generous amount. The wine would help. It would dull her senses. Hopefully make her slightly less edgy, and slightly less aware of what was happening in the apartment next door.

She took a sip of wine, and eyeballed the couch. That was usually where she ate but she wondered if she was inviting disaster by moving back over there.

But then the alternative was huddling in a corner of her kitchen just because she couldn't get a handle on her hormones. That was ridiculous.

She sniffed and collected her dinner, walking back over to the couch and setting the plate on her coffee table. She startled when she heard what sounded like his shoulder bumping up against the shower wall. It sounded very slippery. And solid.

She took another gulp of wine.

She found herself thinking back to the last conversation they'd had before he'd left town. The one that had made her realize she had to tell him how she felt. She'd been tutoring him. Meeting with him twice a week after school in the library to go over math.

She'd been the only one to volunteer for the job—at least, the only one who'd been qualified to do the job who had volunteered for it. It had been intoxicating to be near him finally. And something else entirely to actually spend time talking with him. She'd been certain that there hadn't been more to the guy than everyone thought he was.

Yes, he'd been into some trouble. There was no denying that, and he didn't try to. But there was more to him than that, and she'd seen it clearly.

It had been an unseasonably warm day in Copper Ridge. The sun taunting them as they sat inside, beneath stale fluorescent lights. But Cassie hadn't been sad to miss it. Because looking at Jake for an hour or two during their study sessions had quickly become the highlight of her week. They had been the only two students left in the library, and she'd been able to see his stress written in every muscle, every tendon in his body.

He'd actually been picking up on all the math really well, but that day he hadn't been able to concentrate.

She'd asked him what was wrong.

Just family shit.

He hadn't said anything else, but she hadn't been able to stop thinking about it. About him. And for a moment she'd been overcome by a sense of longing that was much stronger than fear. She put her pencil down, and her hand over his.

That had been the first time they'd touched. The second time had been today, when she'd brushed his fingertips handing him a muffin.

Fifteen years between those touches and both had affected her much the same. Electricity that shot straight down to her bones.

She'd jerked her hand away then, too. But she had decided that night that when she saw him again she wouldn't pull away. Because they had a connection, she had felt it.

She'd been an idiot, which was basically her track record with men, as she knew now. But she'd been so innocent then that she hadn't realized she could be so wrong about another person.

Jake had been her introduction to that. Jake should've served as a warning. Because the next day, Jake had been gone. And the day after that Jake had still been gone. And the day after that.

He had never come back. Hadn't graduated. At least not at their school. His father was still in town, but Jake was gone. The older man had never reported him missing, so she'd assumed he knew where he was.

But she hadn't.

She hadn't seen him after that day in the library until last week when he'd come riding back into town, but that didn't mean she hadn't thought about him in the years between.

She'd thought about Jake Caldwell far more often than was reasonable.

And she was still thinking of him, though it was sort of hard not to when the man was showering just on the other side of her living room wall.

She heard another thump, followed by a very male sound, something that verged on a grunt. She froze, her wineglass touching the edge of her lip.

She shouldn't be listening to him. It was a violation of his privacy, and there was no excuse for her to be sitting there trying to work out exactly what was going on.

But then, in her defense, this was sort of an invasion of her privacy, too. She was a hostage to the noise. Yes, she could move farther away from the wall. And yes, she did not have to lean in closer to it, or hold her breath so that she didn't miss anything, but this was her home and if she wanted to sit at an awkward angle and listen intently to the activity happening next door, she had every right.

She heard another sound, similar to the first and heat flooded her face as realization crept over her. She suddenly had a guess as to what exactly was happening in the shower. That realization should have sent her searching for a pair of earplugs. Instead, she set her glass of wine down on the coffee table and, biting her lip, leaned even closer to the wall.

Unbidden, her eyes fluttered closed, images filtering through her mind. His muscular body, water sluicing over his bare skin, and his hand wrapped around his—

She swallowed hard.

Her heart was beating in her ears, and she willed it to slow down so that it didn't block out any of her auditory entertainment. Guilt played companion to the tightening ball of adrenaline in her stomach. But it wasn't enough to stop her.

It had been a long time since she'd felt like this. A long time since she felt that sweet anticipation, that low-level hum of excitement that ran along every nerve ending, shooting sparks through every vein.

She was unwilling to let it go. Unwilling to do anything that might break the spell she was under.

She heard one more sound, a short, harsh groan and a curse, then the water shut off and she was left feeling unsatisfied, hollow and unsteady.

She picked the wineglass back up and gulped the rest of the contents down. She was going to need another glass to forget the sound of Jake's self-administered pleasure. Another glass to soften the need that was currently cutting into her like a knife.

The temptation to take her own shower and indulge in exactly the same activity was almost overpowering. But she was going to see him tomorrow. She was going to have to look him in the eye and make his coffee, and it was already going to be nearly impossible. If she thought of him while doing...that... it would be the most terminally uncomfortable moment in the history of mankind.

She was going to drink another glass of wine, watch reruns of *Gilmore Girls* and forget that this ever happened. It shouldn't be too hard.

She ignored the fact that the moment when she'd put her hand over his fifteen years ago remained one of her most vivid memories. Ignored the fact that that probably meant tonight would be burned into her brain forever.

Because there was no point in dwelling on Jake Caldwell. None at all.

CHAPTER THREE

JAKE WAS SO caught up in the hell that had been his day that it wasn't until he was inside the coffee shop and in front of the counter, that he remembered.

Then, as his eyes connected with Cassie's, it all came flooding back.

His shower, and exactly what had gone through his mind when he'd jerked off in what had proven to be a futile effort to get sex off his brain. All he'd wanted was a little relief, but inescapably that moment when her fingers had brushed his hand kept playing through his mind, and then he would picture her face. But not looking uneasy, or blank and carefully professional as she usually did. No, he'd imagined her brown eyes clouded with desire, her full lips pink and swollen. Her dark hair out of its usual ponytail, and spread out over his pillow.

Yeah, he'd pictured that. And now he was standing in front of her in The Grind, those images intermingling with reality. It was official, this place regressed him. He needed to get out.

If hours up to his elbows in mud and sheep shit hadn't proven that, his reaction to her certainly did.

He turned his head at the sound of the bell above the door. A man in a uniform, whom he recognized from high school as Eli Garrett, walked in. Eli was as clean-cut as ever, tall, dark-haired and smiling. Also fully able to beat the ever-loving shit out of someone should the need arise, Jake had no doubt.

Anyone in a law-enforcement field tended to make Jake nervous. Even though he hadn't been arrested since high school. And even then, no charges had ever been formally filed.

He deserved it, at least in one case. Stealing money out of the register of the Farm and Garden where he worked had been pretty low. Especially considering how nice the owners had been. But while he'd been cuffed and taken down to the station, in the end the owners had said there must've been some mistake. A little scaring him straight combined with some mercy he knew he hadn't deserved.

Cassie looked past Jake and smiled. That was not a smile he'd ever seen directed at him and he found himself feeling annoyed that the other man was on the receiving end of it. "Hi, Deputy Garrett. The usual?"

"Yes, Cassie, thank you."

"Of course. Deputy Garrett, do you remember Jake from high school?"

Great. Now he had to be friendly. He took a breath and turned so that he was facing Eli, then held out his hand. "Jake Caldwell. Back in town for a bit." He didn't need to be intimidated. And he didn't need to stand there feeling ashamed of who he'd been.

"Yeah," Eli said before accepting Jake's offered hand and shaking it firmly. "I remember you."

"That might not be a good thing."

"Do any of us really want to be remembered for who we were in high school?"

That was a bit more kindness then Jake expected. "I don't guess."

"So, what brings you back into town? Moving home?"

Jake bristled at the description of Copper Ridge as home. "My dad died. He left me his estate. I'm just back to get the ranch and things into shape before I put it on the market."

"Sorry about that."

"It wasn't unexpected." Which was sort of an odd response, but he wasn't going to stand around and pretend to be grieving. Not considering that he hadn't even seen his father once in the fifteen years since he left. No one was more surprised than he was that the old man had left him the place.

He nearly snorted. The place and all the shit in it. Junk on the front lawn, stacks of paperwork he would need six months to get through.

"Even so," Eli said, "sorry to hear it." Cassie handed a cup of coffee back to him and Eli handed her a five dollar bill before nodding once. "See you around." He turned and walked away.

"You make a practice of serving customers in front of the line last?" Jake asked, directing the question a Cassie.

"No, it's just that Deputy Garrett is a busy man."

"You don't think I'm a busy man?"

Color flooded her cheeks, and he couldn't deny that he took a small amount of pleasure in having rattled her. "I'm sure you are. Speaking of busy, you must want your muffin."

"I would. I would like my muffin." He didn't really care about the muffin.

"And your coffee?"

"You can't eat a muffin without a coffee. I'm not a barbarian."

"No, I daresay you aren't. In fact, a lot of people would say muffins are quite civilized. Not really a manly food."

"Muffins aren't manly?"

"Well, I don't get a lot of men in here ordering them."

"Well, screw that. Muffins are delicious."

She lifted a shoulder. "Fair point. Delicious blueberry or delicious chocolate?"

"Do you even have to ask? If there's chocolate, the answer is always chocolate." Other than securing the rental of the apartment this was the most talking they'd done since he'd come back.

"On that we can agree." This time, she put both the muffin and the coffee on the counter, rather than handing either directly to him. He was weirdly disappointed by that.

"Since you didn't drop the muffin, I insist on paying for it today."

"I suppose I won't argue with you on that, either."

"Still cash only?" he asked, tugging his wallet out of his pocket. She was not the only business in Copper Ridge that didn't take debit or credit yet.

"Yeah, for now. I'm getting one of those things for your phone that lets you take credit payment, but I haven't done it yet."

"How long have you had this place open?"

"Two years."

Which explained what seemed to be a bare-bones staff and the very late nights she put in. All the hallmarks of a business that was still trying to get on its feet. "Well, good for you. It's a lot of work running a business."

"Do you run one?"

"Not really. I manage one. But I don't own it. The owner is a friend of mine, and he's semiretired." He'd be all retired soon, and Jake was poised to take over. If he could shake off the bonds that held him here. "The friendship part is just one reason I was able to come here and settle my father's estate." Calling that dilapidated piece of property—and the vacant building downtown and this place—an estate was almost laughable, but he wasn't sure how else to phrase it.

"When you say settle it, what exactly do you mean?"

"What it sounds like. I don't have anything keeping me here. I'll be going back to Seattle as soon as I can."

Cassie drew back as though she'd been slapped. "Oh. Will you have a property manager, or…?"

"No. I won't need one. Because I won't have property here anymore."

Her dark eyes widened and she shot a quick look out to the dining room, before looking back at him. "You mean you're going to sell?"

"Yeah."

"All of it, though? Not just the ranch?"

"Yeah, did you think I was planning anything else? I'm not going to stay here and play cowboy. It's not my thing."

"Well, I thought you might make your intentions explicit considering you own the building I live and work in."

"I'm a little ways off from listing it, and I had intended to offer the place to you."

"I can't get a loan for it."

"Then you can continue to lease it from the person who buys it for me."

"You're assuming that the person who buys it from you will allow me to continue leasing it. And that they won't raise the rate."

Jake rubbed the back of his neck. This was not the kind of complication he needed. If he had a hope in hell of buying John out eventually like he was planning, he needed to offload these properties. He was in a decent financial situation, but buying a very successful business wasn't cheap. And sure, he could keep the properties and lease them, but that would rob him of money he could use as a down payment, and land him with a bigger mortgage than he was comfortable with. In addition to that, he would have to get someone to manage things in Copper Ridge for him, and all of it would just keep him tied to a place he had no desire to be tied to.

And he felt sorry for Cassie, he did. But warm fuzzy feelings weren't going to get him where he needed to go.

"Well, we have some time to figure it out." Even though he

knew he would arrive at the same conclusion regardless of how much time passed.

"I'm not sure I like that."

"What?"

"That non-answer. It might be easy for you to just leave things up in the air, because you have all the control. I'm the one whose livelihood and home hang in the balance."

"Look, I really hate to be a jackass about this, but it isn't my problem. My problem right now is getting all of the shit off my dad's property. Because if I don't do it myself it's going to cost me a crapload of money that I don't want to spend. And trust me, coordinating the removal of rusty cars, old toilets and fucking chickens is not as much fun as it sounds."

"It doesn't sound fun at all."

"I know, that was kind of the point."

"You're removing chickens and helpless coffee shop owners. Big week for you."

"I'm re-homing them. And I'm not doing anything with you. Yet."

"As you make your decision, remember, you owe me for yesterday's muffin."

He frowned. "It was on you. Because you dropped it on the floor."

"That was before I knew you were intent on throwing me out onto the streets."

"I am not throwing you out onto the streets."

She lifted her hands and then slapped them down against her thighs. "You might be. You don't know. You're going to wash your hands of me. And leave me to be devoured by the winds of fate."

"That is…just a little dramatic, don't you think?"

"It's not dramatic at all! You are talking about selling my building out from under me. I don't think there is an overdramatic where that's concerned."

"If that were the case. But nothing has been decided, there

is no specific buyer threatening to take anything from you, and I am not paying you for the muffin."

"You know what? That's just petty, is what that is. You were going to pay me for the muffin, and then I told you not to, but now I want you to, and you won't."

"That's because you're being retaliatory. And I think it's small." He was more amused by all this than he should be. More amused by her than he should be. But she was quick, and she was a lot more fiery than he remembered her being in high school.

"Oh, so now I'm small? Yeah, I'm small. That's what I am. A small-business owner. And I'm being crushed by The Man."

Jake had never been accused of being The Man before in his life. He didn't exactly have the look for it. "I am not crushing you. And I'm going upstairs now. Where I can eat my muffin without being abused."

"Abused? I would've thought you were a bit sturdier than this, Caldwell."

"I'm very sturdy. I promise you that. I just also happen to have an aversion to histrionics."

He turned and headed back toward the door. He didn't have the luxury of worrying about Cassie Ventimiglia and her coffee shop. Yeah, it would suck if whoever bought the place took it out from under her. But he was sure there were terms that could be worked out. And yeah, maybe her rent would go up, but she was underpaying. He also knew she didn't have a predetermined amount of time on her lease. So she didn't have any protection in that manner, either.

And sure, it made him feel bad. But not enough to willingly submit to holding on to a piece of Copper Ridge. Not enough to submit to holding on to a piece of the Caldwell family.

There was a reason he had left all those years ago. And the reason was as valid today as it had been then.

Cassie didn't know. Nobody did. And that meant the way he handled things was nobody's damn business but his.

CHAPTER FOUR

CASSIE HAD SPENT the rest of last night feeling incredibly annoyed, and stirred up, and like her entire life was being upended yet again. She felt like she'd already had enough upheaval for one lifetime. Yes, it had only happened once. But once was enough. She did not want to start over again. How many times was a woman supposed to reinvent herself?

She, of course, had not found that answer while pacing around her apartment growling. And today, the answer continued to elude her as she sat in the driver's seat of her car, unable to get it to start. The hits just kept on coming.

She cursed and got out of the car, fighting the urge to kick her tires. She had errands to run, and this was one of her only days off. So, of course, the car that she rarely used refused to perform its function.

She released another growl into the universe and slammed the door shut, stomping around toward the front of the coffee shop. She was going to have to call her accountant and let her know she was going to be late. Liss would do her best to reschedule her, but Cassie hated to put the other woman out.

Just as she was about to go inside The Grind, Jake appeared from around the back of the building. She froze, feeling slightly sheepish about the way she had behaved toward him yesterday. She was justified, but she'd been childish. And she really could've been a little bit more mature. If only because she imagined having him feel positively toward her was better than having him angry with her. All things considered.

And she wasn't usually one to make waves, but then, Jake had always brought out feelings in her that were less than typical.

"Good morning." There, she had greeted him. And she hadn't even spewed any fire and brimstone in his direction.

"Good morning." He raised his brows, clearly just as surprised as she was that she'd managed to be civil.

"I hope you slept well." She hadn't heard him showering last night, so thank heaven for small favors.

And that was not what she wanted to think about right now. Not when she was annoyed. Not when she was looking at him, and would probably start blushing.

"Yeah, I slept fine."

She bit back a rude comment. "Well, that's good."

"You sound thrilled. You don't work this morning?"

"No, I have the day off. Which means I have to do the business things I can't do while I'm in the shop."

"Exciting times in Copper Ridge."

"You aren't lying."

"So where you headed?"

"My accountant's. To drop off financial stuff."

"Ahh, I see. As opposed to dropping off badger-related things at your accountant's."

"Charming. Now, while you do a very good impression of the sarcastic jerkface, I am in a bit of a rush, and having car trouble so..."

She couldn't really figure out why Jake made her feel so damned obstinate, only that he did. And that she didn't really mind. To the contrary, she sort of liked it.

He gave her something to kick against when she generally felt like she was simply drifting downstream.

"I'm going to ignore the fact that you called me a name I haven't heard since I was in elementary school. What kind of car trouble are you having?"

"I don't know." She hated that feeling of not knowing. Or more accurately, of knowing she was in over her head, and that she needed help, but didn't have it.

Frankly she couldn't afford to get the car repaired, and she had no idea how to replace anything herself. Her husband had done that stuff, and these were about the only times when she felt his absence. Most of the time she felt like she was better off without him—enriched even. But when the drain was clogged, a car needed repairing, something heavy needed lifting, or a jar lid was being particularly stubborn, she really missed the bastard.

"Well, if you show me your problem I'm sure I can tell you what it is."

"The thing is, I'm late to meet Liss."

"Where is her office?"

"It's up the road about five miles, not something I can sprint. Even if I started walking now, I would still be late."

"If you wait down here for a second I can come back with a solution to your problem."

She blinked rapidly. "Well, that sounds…almost too good to be true."

"I promise you it's not." He turned and walked back around the building and she just stood there gaping. And staring after him. Because even though she was officially annoyed with him, he was still nice to look at.

Something about being exposed to Jake was a whole lot like jumping from a sun-soaked rock into a freezing river. For the past five years she'd been comfortable. Comfortable right where she was, finding her feet again, letting go of a marriage that had lasted eight years instead of a lifetime. Once she'd done that she'd settled in and found purpose in her new life. She hadn't wanted what she'd lost again.

Jake made her want things. Not love and commitment-type things, other things. Naked things. Sweaty things.

It made her feel a little bit flushed just thinking about it.

And right on cue, just as her face was overheating from her libidinous thoughts, Jake reappeared, holding a motorcycle helmet.

"I'm not sure what you think you're doing with that." She eyed him suspiciously.

"I'm offering you a ride." He extended the helmet, her face reflecting in the shiny black surface.

She looked up from her own wide-eyed stare, and presented it to him. "I don't ride on motorcycles."

"Well, you can start today."

"I think you misunderstood. It's not that I've never had the opportunity." But she hadn't. "I don't ride on them because the idea is about as appealing as inhaling dandelion fluff and then licking a pig's foot to get the taste out of your mouth."

"Evocative."

"I'm trying to get my point across that I don't find the idea very appealing at all."

"Yeah, I actually got that out of your simile," he said.

"Wow, you even knew it was a simile."

"I had a good tutor back in high school."

SOMETHING ABOUT BRINGING the past into the present made Jake's chest tighten. He didn't like to think about the past and he had good reason. But Copper Ridge made it impossible not to.

"I tutored you in math, not English. I was not the one to teach you about similes."

"Maybe I just absorbed some of your intelligence."

"See, you think I'm intelligent. Therefore, my concerns about riding on a motorcycle are probably valid."

"Probably. But then, I've been riding on one for about seventeen years and I seem okay."

"Okay, I don't have time to stand here quibbling with you about this." She snatched the helmet from his grip and put it down over her head, so that only her nose and eyes were visible, a strand of dark hair hanging down the middle of her forehead and disappearing beneath the face mask.

"That's a good look for you, Cassie."

She blinked, and he was suddenly very aware of just how long her eyelashes were, and how very attractive that was to him. Seriously, the brush of her fingers against his and her eyelashes. He needed to get a grip. And not the type he'd gotten in the shower a couple of days earlier.

"It doesn't surprise me that badass biker chick is kind of my thing."

"Speaking of," he shrugged off his leather jacket and held it out toward her, "You need to complete the look."

"What about you?"

"We'll be driving through town, so I'll go slow. But I would still feel better if you wore the jacket."

She took the jacket and shrugged it on, the sleeves hanging over her hands and the bottom extending to midthigh. There was something sexy about that, too. And he was just done questioning his sanity, because it was clear the question was answered. It was gone, and he needed some kind of sexual release.

But not with her. Maybe he would drive up to Tolowa and look for someone to hook up with. One-night stands weren't really his thing these days, but exceptions could be made.

At least with someone he would never see again.

"Okay." The word was jittery, and so was she, her fingers trembling. At least what he could see of them peeking out from the jacket sleeves. "Let's do this, I've got an appointment."

"And you have all your paperwork?"

"Yep." She tapped the large purse that she had slung over her shoulder.

"All right then." He walked over to his motorcycle and put on his helmet then got on, waiting for her to do the same.

"So I...just get on behind you."

Oh, shit. He'd sort of overlooked this part. "Yes," he said, conscious of the roughness in his own voice.

She took a tentative step to the bike, then disappeared from his field of vision as she moved behind him. He felt a light touch on his shoulder, which was quickly taken away.

"It's fine, you're going to have to hold on to me anyway." Sexual tension was making him testy.

Two hands gripped his shoulders, and he felt her settle in behind him. Her thighs rested on either side of his.

"You need to put your arms around my waist." Yeah, this was going to kill him.

She complied, her grip so tight around him it was like she was attempting the Heimlich. "This feels slightly unstable," she said, her voice in his ear, muffled by the helmets between them.

"It's not, I promise. As long as you're not going to let go of me suddenly."

"Yeah, it's safe to say I'm not going to be doing that."

He started the motor. "Good. Are you ready?"

"No."

"We're going anyway, okay?"

He felt her nod against his back and he smiled, putting the bike in gear and moving forward, careful to take off gradually so that he wouldn't terrify his virgin passenger.

He gritted his teeth. All things considered that wasn't a very good descriptor. It stuck his mind straight back in the gutter.

He did his best to keep all of his focus on the road, on the passing scenery. Belatedly, he realized he hadn't exactly gotten directions from her. But he figured he would keep going straight until she gestured wildly.

In his defense, he had been distracted. By trying not to be distracted by his attraction to her.

Maybe that was the real issue. Maybe his attraction to her

was an attempt at distracting himself from other problems. From the ranch, and all of the ghosts that it held. It was strange seeing it now, fallen into such dilapidation. In order for the excuse to wash, he had to ignore the attraction he'd felt to her back in high school, but for the sake of his sanity he was willing to do that.

The ranch had never been a mansion by any stretch but it hadn't been run down like this. But his mother had been gone for more than twenty years, and Jake himself hadn't been back in fifteen. From all accounts, his father had been in a home the last two years of his life and not living out on the property.

Someone must've been taking care of the animals because they were still there, but no one had bothered to do any upkeep on the house. If he had ever had any affection for the place, the disrepair would have made him sad.

They drove past the collection of tourist shops, which were one major change from when he lived here as a kid. This street had mainly been deserted, and there had been very little value in the properties. Which was, he assumed, how his father had managed to end up with a few of the buildings. And why he had never been able to do anything with them. The place had been a near ghost town back then.

From what he'd gathered since coming back tourism had started to build in the past ten years, along with the restoration of Old Town. Brick that had once been crumbling and run-down was now charming and quaint. Buildings that had been peeling and splitting were now restored, painted bright whites, pale blues and deep reds. Fish shacks that had only ever been for locals were now obviously designed to bait out-of-towners with promises of the freshest seafood.

One little building that he'd remembered as being empty was now covered in wind chimes, flags and things made of driftwood. It was amazing what paint, new signage and some landscape could do.

He took the main road up out of Old Town, away from the beach. As the road curved inland the pine trees thickened, casting dusky shadows over them, golden sun filtering through the trees and bathing everything in a glittering haze.

Objectively, Jake had to admit the place was beautiful, which was a tough thing for him since it also created a knot of tension in his chest that refused to ease. He managed to find beauty in Seattle, though it had taken a few years of living there to get used to all of the glass and steel. As cities went, there was a lot of nature. And the ocean was still nearby. He didn't think he could live anywhere that wasn't by the ocean.

It wasn't that he spent a whole lot of time beachcombing. He wasn't big on the sand between his toes. It was a feeling of freedom the ocean afforded. He had a vague sense that as long as it was nearby there was an escape. The idea of being land-locked unsettled him. It was akin to being trapped in his mind.

That was one of the reasons he'd always ridden his bike. There was something about it that felt like flying. That felt like escape. What he wasn't used to was riding with another person, and interesting that Cassie's arms tight around his waist didn't feel like restraints. They felt warm, they felt secure.

And it felt like they were escaping together.

Though what Cassie Ventimiglia might have to escape from he had no idea. It struck him then that he knew nothing about the life she'd led since he'd left. He knew that she had opened The Grind two years ago, and that was the beginning and end of his knowledge.

It made him feel like an asshole to realize that. Seemed like he should've asked.

But it wasn't as though she'd asked about him. As far as she knew he had ridden off one day, then ridden back. And nothing had happened in between. In some ways, he was content for people to think that, and in other ways not.

Because he had spent a hell of a lot of years trying to escape the man he'd been. And he sort of wanted people to know he had.

That was the most sobering thing about becoming an adult as

far as he was concerned. Riding out of town in a rage, angry at himself, angry at his father. And later realizing that a lot of the shit that had come down on him was his own fault. Of course, the reason he'd been stirring shit up in the first place did come down to his old man.

There'd been no way of pleasing the bastard. So Jake set out to do just the opposite. But that last screw-up had been too much for either of them to overcome. That final altercation breaking bonds that had already been brittle. Shattering them beyond repair.

Cassie suddenly squeezed him tighter, and he looked to the left, spotting a new little row of businesses set back in the trees. Copper Ridge Business Park, as the sign deemed it, was new, or at least less than fifteen years old, which for a place like this meant new. It was almost laughable to call it a business park in his opinion. A row of five businesses that were all connected, and fashioned to look like little white clapboard houses. There were even roses climbing up a freaking trellis. The place was like Mayberry. Again, had he had any attachment to the town, it might've made him smile.

He slowed the motorcycle and turned in, figuring if this wasn't it, he could at least get directions from her here.

When he killed the engine, Cassie got off, tugging off the helmet and shaking out her hair. He couldn't help but admire the way the dark strands shimmered in the sunlight. Yeah, there was no doubt that, physically, at least, where Cassie was concerned he was a goner.

"Thanks." She handed the helmet back to him.

"I take it this is the place?"

"Yeah, this is it."

"How long is it going to take?"

"It shouldn't be long. I just have to drop this stuff off and sign a couple of things. I can get a ride home from Liss. It won't be a big deal."

"I'll wait for you."

"Don't you have things to do?"

"Yeah, honey, I've got a ton of things to do, but leaving you stranded here is not one of them. I'm not in any major hurry."

"Honey, huh?"

"I'm sorry, does the endearment offend you?"

The corners of her mouth turned down. "I'm just not sure what I did to earn it."

"Did you need to earn it?"

"Back in high school you just called me Cassie," she said. "That worked for me."

"Well, I can go back to calling you Cassie if you like."

"It would be for the best."

She turned and walked into the little building, and he crossed his arms and rocked back on his heels. Watching her walk away was not a hardship. There was no doubt that Cassie had an ass he could stare at for days. He wondered idly if she'd had that back in high school, and if he'd just been too much of an idiot to notice. More than likely, though, the years had enhanced her shape.

The Cassie he remembered had been a bit too skinny, but still cute, with large brown eyes that had looked at him like he mattered. Just another reason he'd never gone there back then. Just another reason he couldn't go there now. Hell, he was actively moving toward ruining her life. Which was no surprise, because that was pretty much what he did. Whether he meant to or not. He ruined things. He ruined people.

He could remember sitting in the library with her, studying subjects that made his head hurt, that he didn't care about. But she'd made him want to try, because she'd seemed to believe he could do it. Nobody else had had that kind of confidence in him. Not teachers, not family. And so he had tried for her. Mainly because when he got something right she didn't seem surprised. She just seemed to accept it, accept that what he was doing was simply living up to his abilities. It had been a hell of a thing for a kid who had lived most of his life feeling like everything he did fell short.

He could also remember wondering sometimes, after a word of praise had come out of her mouth, what it might be like to kiss that mouth. What it might be like to kiss a girl who saw more than his bad attitude and motorcycle. A girl who might be into him, not because he was all wrong, but because something about him was right.

He'd dismissed the thought almost immediately. Kissing a girl like her would ruin her. No doubt about it. Not because of who she was, but because of who he was.

Revisiting it now was pointless.

A part of him was afraid that his seventeen-year-old self had had a bit more restraint than his thirty-two-year-old self where she was concerned.

That was sobering.

Cassie appeared a few moments later, a smile on her face when she exited. A smile that faded slightly when she made eye contact with him. Dammit.

And dammit that he cared.

"Okay, I'm ready," she said.

"You have any more errands you need to run?"

"Well, I was going to head over to the Farm and Garden to get some plants for the front window box at the shop. But it's not something I *need* to do today."

"It's not a problem, I'll take you by. I'm assuming it's the same Farm and Garden that's always been here."

"The very same."

He knew the place well, seeing as he'd worked there. Seeing as he'd stolen from the people who owned it. Damn, he had been an asshole. There really was no two ways about it. But he had changed. And maybe it would be a good thing for him to walk in there and let them know that. He felt like he owed that to Mr. Travers.

He wanted him to know that letting a juvenile delinquent

off the hook had mattered. That his kindness had amounted
to something other than more arrests. Because Jake had gone
on to make something of himself. No, there was no pretending
he was some kind of tycoon, no pretending he was a million-
aire. But he was successful, he owned a house. He was aim-
ing to buy John's mechanic shop. He was responsible, and he
had done the right thing since leaving town. It was because of
people like Travers that he'd managed that.

He realized just then how grateful he was. He tried so hard
not to think of Copper Ridge that he often forgot the good things
that'd been hidden here, tucked away behind all the bad stuff.
Like light breaking through the trees.

"Put on your helmet. Let's go," he said.

"Are you sure?"

"Seriously, it's no problem. Unless you're afraid of the bike."

A faint dusty rose color darkened her cheeks. "The bike
was fine."

"Good to know I didn't scar you for life."

That earned him a smile, and it was genuine. And he felt like
the sun had peeked out from behind the clouds. Dammit again.

"Come on, Cassie, let's get your flowers."

CHAPTER FIVE

THE ENTIRE FRONT of Cassie's body tingled. And it showed no signs of stopping. She could blame some of it on the rumble of the bike. On the vibrations of the motor moving through her for the ride out to the Farm and Garden. But intellectually she knew better. The real cause of the tingling was Jake. Was having her legs all wrapped around him, and her breasts pressed against his back while they drove through town.

Really, it wasn't fair. She hadn't had this much contact with a man in too many years and suddenly she was being pressed up against one. A hot one. One she had heard touching himself only a wall away from her just a couple days ago.

There was no way a mere mortal woman could withstand such temptation. And she was sadly a mere mortal, as she was discovering.

She dismounted the bike and took the helmet off, surprised at how comfortable she was with the whole thing already. It really wasn't all that scary. But her mother had drummed into her that motorcycles were vessels of death and if she were to ever get near one she would surely burst into flame.

But it turned out if she *were* to burst into flame it would be because of Jake, not the motorcycle.

Jake took his helmet off and followed her into the store this time rather than waiting outside.

"I thought I might get some petunias." She realized that she was making inane conversation, and she couldn't even stop herself. If it wasn't muffins, it was flowers, and she had a feeling the guy didn't really care about either.

Well, that wasn't true. He'd had some pretty strong things to say about muffins.

"Man, I haven't been back to this place in fifteen years. Which is kind of an obvious statement," he said looking at her, "since I haven't been back to town in that long. And you knew that."

It appeared that Jake was making inane conversation, too. And that gratified her more than it should.

"You used to work here, didn't you?"

"Yeah, for a while. Before I screwed it up. Like I did everything else back then."

"What happened?"

"I stole money from the register. Because I was an asshole." He didn't make eye contact with her when he said that, his expression granite.

"Oh," she said, feeling her heart sink. She didn't know why that bit of information disappointed her. It had happened forever ago. But for some reason, she'd never believed he was as bad as people had said. And she only realized just now that that meant she had thought he wasn't bad at all.

"Are you actually surprised?"

"Okay, I confess I am. I kind of thought your infamy was exaggerated."

"I wish it was. But the fact is I was basically a ridiculous little cuss. And I deserved most of what came to me."

"I never saw that in you."

"I put on a pretty good show for you. Mainly because you

smiled at me, and at that point there were very few people in town who did."

A dark head popped up from behind the counter, and the salesclerk flipped her braid over her shoulder and turned to face them, smiling broadly. "Cassie! What can I do for you today?"

Cassie offered Kate Garrett a smile in return. "I was thinking flowers, Kate. Thank you for asking."

"Who's this?" Kate asked.

Kate wouldn't remember Jake because she would've been a kid when he left. It was easy to forget just how much younger than her brothers she was.

"Jake Caldwell." He extended his hand and Kate shook it. "Currently from Seattle, previously from Copper Ridge."

Kate's dark eyes widened. "Oh! Welcome back, then."

"It's only temporary."

"Well," Kate said firmly, "enjoy your time here anyway. You're visiting Cassie?"

"Not really."

Tension thickened in the silence and Cassie didn't really know what to say. "Just petunias would be great."

"I can grab those for you," Kate said. "How many you need?"

"A couple of flats. Pink and purple."

Kate disappeared out the back, leaving Jake and Cassie alone again. It was no less awkward with Kate gone.

"I'm not even sure if I should be buying flowers."

"Why is that?" he asked.

"You know, just in case I don't end up keeping the shop."

"Cassie, it's not like I'm selling your business. The building eventually. But you're acting like I'm stripping you of your livelihood or something."

"You might be. You don't know. You don't know what's going to happen."

IT STRUCK JAKE then that he was standing there being the bad guy yet again. He didn't like it, but it was a necessity in many ways. It had nothing to do with Cassie personally, and everything to do with him simply wanting ties cut cleanly. He hadn't asked for this. Hadn't asked to have all of his dad's stuff left to him.

He was too smart to do anything but make the most of it but he was hardly going to fall on his sword for anyone. He wasn't fit to play the role of martyr.

"No, I don't know what's going to happen. And neither do you. This isn't personal, Cassie. I came into all this property unexpectedly and I have no desire to hold on to it. I have a life away from here. And I deserve a little payment for the time I served on the Caldwell family farm." *Do you?* He ignored that thought. He deserved it if he thought he did, right? For all his sins, and yeah, he'd committed them, his dad had plenty of his own.

Jake gritted his teeth and fought against the rising tide of guilt. Guilt over Cassie. Guilt that was as old as the day he left.

Hell, he had a feeling a lot of his guilt was as old as he was.

"Right, fine. I get it, Jake. Things were hard and you don't want to own a piece of this place, and I can understand that. But I do. The Grind is all I have. The Grind and that tiny little apartment above it. I don't want to lose another planter box."

"What do you mean by that?"

"I've already done this, Jake. I've already invested my sweat and energy into a place only to have it taken from me. Those were my flowers, dammit! And he kept them. And she just let them die."

"What are you talking about, Cassie?"

"I spent eight years working on our house. Working on our marriage. And in the end it wasn't permanent. The one thing that was supposed to be permanent and it wasn't."

"You're married?" A flash of heat, of anger, unwanted if not entirely unexpected, shot through him. On the heels of that came the biting realization that the marriage she was talking about certainly wasn't healthy. And a part of him decided very quickly that he didn't much care if she had a husband or not.

Shades of old Jake, and it shouldn't be too surprising considering this place seemed to bring that out in him. Seemed to bring out the worst.

"No. Not anymore. I took my name back and everything, seeing as he had the house."

"How did he end up with it?" He knew it wasn't any of his business, most especially since they were standing there arguing about whether or not he was ruining her life. He had no right to ask for details. No right to get protective and proprietary since he could neither protect her nor keep her.

"We didn't have kids. I didn't have a job. My name wasn't on it."

"Your name wasn't on it?"

"I didn't have credit. He started the process of buying it while we were still engaged. Then of course in the end I was really screwed because I didn't earn any credit over the course of the marriage. I had to move back in with my mother when we divorced. Until I got The Grind and the apartment above it."

"And how did you end up with that?"

"The building was empty, and I noticed. I had gotten a job at Rona's Diner waiting tables so I drove by every day. And every day I imagined making it mine. It isn't like your dad was a mentor, or even a benefactor. I tracked him down and asked him if he needed it for anything and he said it was just sitting there costing him property taxes. So we worked something out that seemed fair. Something I could afford, but that would give him income. It was all sort of unofficial, but at that point he was—"

"In the assisted living place."

"Yeah."

Kate walked back into the room a moment later with a couple flats of flowers on a rolling rack. "Do you want me to just put this on your tab, Cassie?"

"Yeah, that would be good." Cassie wasn't looking at him

at all now. He wasn't sure why. If it was because of the whole thing with the coffee shop, the discussion about his dad, or the mention of her divorce. Possibly all three. That would figure, seeing as he couldn't seem to puzzle out how to talk to Cassie.

"Oh," she said, and then she did look at him. "Are we going to be able to get these on your bike? I guess I should've thought of that before we came in."

"We can figure it out."

"Oh don't worry about it," Kate said. "I'll drop them by The Grind on my way home."

"You don't have to do that," Cassie said.

Kate tugged on the end of her braid. "Seriously, no big deal."

"You're too generous, Kate," Cassie said.

"Not even a little." The other woman grinned. "I'm going to expect a coffee for my efforts. Possibly a muffin."

Jake shot Cassie a look, and her mind must have gone to the same place, because she was staring at him, eyes wide, clearly remembering earlier muffin-related innuendo.

Cassie looked back at Kate. "That seems fair."

Jake hesitated for a moment. "Hey, Kate, is Jim Travers around?"

"No, he and Margie are in Hawaii. They come back over the summer. But otherwise they are usually at their house in Maui these days."

"Can't really blame them for that," he said. He ignored the tug of regret in his stomach.

"Definitely not. Someday I'll go to Hawaii and confirm my suspicions that it's paradise. Until then I'll take their word for it." Kate shoved the rack back behind the counter, then grabbed a piece of paper and a marker and scribbled Cassie's name on it, sticking it on the flats. "I'll be by later."

"Thank you," Cassie said.

"Not a problem. See you later."

"Come on," Jake said. "I'll take you back."

"Thanks," Cassie said. "I suppose it was the wrong time for

me to rake you over the coals about selling the building. Seeing as you're helping me."

"If you ask me, there is no good time to rake me over the coals. But I might be biased on that score."

She turned and pushed the door open and both of them walked outside into the cool morning air. The wind was just starting to kick up, blowing sea salt and sand in from the beach, mixing with the aroma of pine and bark that surrounded them.

"Possibly. Just a bit." Cassie stuffed her hands in her back pockets and arched her back, the leather jacket parting as she did. His eyes were drawn, helplessly, to the curve of breasts pressing against the thin fabric of her shirt.

He looked away, turning his focus to the thick grove of trees across the road, the ruffling of the pine branches in the wind. "All right, let's go. I have my own work to get to." And he knew he sounded grumpy and ungracious, but he couldn't take the time to rectify it. Because if he did, she might smile at him again. And if that happened he might do the thing he'd been thinking about for days—he might lean in and kiss her. And that wouldn't be good for anyone.

Most especially her.

CHAPTER SIX

JAKE COULDN'T EVEN find respite in the privacy of his apartment. Mainly because he was discovering the apartment wasn't all that private. Oh no, to the contrary, the walls were paper thin and he was very aware of the movements that Cassie was making on the other side of them. He could tell when she was getting into the shower, when she was walking across the living room, and whether or not she was wearing shoes. He found he sort of liked it when she was barefoot, if for no other reason than it meant she was wearing less.

Worse, he was getting attached to the sounds that she made. To not being alone. His house in Seattle was nice, in a quiet neighborhood, with quiet neighbors. He didn't share any connecting walls. And no one ever stayed the night. When Jake hooked up he preferred hotels, and when that wasn't happening he made it so they ended up back at her place. They rarely seemed to mind, and if they did, he just went and found someone else. Clingy wasn't his thing. Sharing space wasn't his thing. Because feelings weren't his thing.

He prized his control far too much.

But there was something comforting about hearing another person moving around so close. Comforting and at the same time disturbing. Especially since what he really wanted to do was storm over to her apartment and eliminate all the space between them. No walls. No clothes.

He hadn't had it this bad in longer than he could remember. If ever. When he wanted a woman he had her, and he never wanted a specific someone enough to cause this kind of trouble. Notable exception: Cassie back in high school.

He had a feeling that was the thing messing with him right now. All that unspent, long-buried desire.

Because right now Cassie Ventimiglia was obsessing his mind, and his body. And it was pretty damn stupid.

Even as he thought of his neighbor, he heard the sounds of her moving around, and then a sharp, shrill squeak. He jumped up from his couch, and ran to his front door without even thinking about it. Probably she had seen a spider. Or something similarly innocuous. But the desire to fulfill the fantasy that was turning over in his brain, combined with the protective instincts Cassie seemed to bring out in him, had him halfway down the stairs before he could even think about it.

He called himself ten kinds of stupid while he walked around to the other side of the little entryway in the back of the coffee shop, and up the stairs that led to Cassie's apartment.

Yeah, he had enough self-awareness to realize that he was looking for any excuse to knock on her door. Which was crazy considering that she didn't like him, she made him feel like an ass, and he knew he couldn't touch her.

His instincts, or his dick, didn't seem to care. Because before he knew it he was standing in front of Cassie's door pounding on it as hard as he could. He heard a strange thumping sound and then the door swung open and he found himself facing Cassie, who was standing on one foot and holding the other one.

She squinted. "Yes?"

"You sounded like you were in distress."

"Oh. I stubbed my toe." She winced and squeezed her foot then set it back down and straightened. "Did I disturb you?"

"Not disturb per se, but the walls are kind of thin. I don't know if you noticed."

Color flooded her face. "Oh, yes, I have noticed."

Interesting that she blushed when the question came up. It made him wonder if she was thinking the same things he was. It made him wonder if maybe she was listening to what he was doing. If she had been fantasizing about the very thing he was. Tearing the wall down and tearing each other's clothes off.

That was probably wishful thinking. He'd always had Cassie pegged as being a little bit more cautious than that. He'd put her in a box in his brain that was labeled Nice Girl. Whatever *that* meant. He didn't have an exact definition handy, but he vaguely thought it might mean she wasn't the type of girl whose clothes you just ripped off.

"I hope I haven't been too…disturbing," she said, blinking rapidly.

"You aren't that bad." The color in her face intensified. Very interesting, indeed.

"It was really nice of you to come check on me. But I'm fine. I don't think I broke anything, and there's no blood. Just a coffee table that I moved a few days ago. And now I'm not really familiar with exactly where it is. So the leg got my toe."

"You were rearranging furniture?" He was asking stupid questions now, because he was reluctant to leave.

"Yes. I did a little rearranging." She was still blushing and now he was dying to know why. He wanted to push, and hell, if it was anyone else, he would push. So he was going to push.

"Feng shui?" he asked.

"What…like making a money corner and stuff?"

"Something like that." Except feng shui didn't make you blush.

"I'll have to get a lesson from you in the future, since you seem to know all about it. But in this case I just was moving my couch, so it seemed like moving the coffee table was the thing to do."

"Just looking for a change?"

"Why are you giving me the third degree about the location of my furniture?"

"I'm not trying to."

"If you must know, it's because I can hear you showering when I'm sitting on my couch. And it bothers me." A jolt of something hit him square in the gut.

"You can hear me showering?"

"Yes." She swallowed hard, hard enough that he could see it and hear it. "And I can hear the things you're doing in there."

Heat assaulted him, his face burning so hot he was sure it must be red. Blushing wasn't his thing, but hearing her say that, knowing exactly what he'd done in the shower a couple of days ago, had him feeling like he'd stuck his head into a bonfire.

"Oh." That was all he was capable of saying. He couldn't remember the last time a woman had made him blush, or the last time one had rendered him speechless. But so-called Nice Girl Cassie Ventimiglia had managed to do both.

She tilted her chin up. "Yes, I heard you doing…things."

He cleared his throat and tugged on his shirt collar. She made him feel like a naughty schoolboy. He couldn't remember actually feeling that way when he'd been a naughty schoolboy. "Things?"

"Yes, things."

And then a switch flipped inside him, and he remembered who he was.

He was Jake Caldwell. He wasn't a teenager. And neither was she. He was a guy who got shit done. He didn't blush. And when he wanted a woman he damn well had her. No, he *shouldn't* have Cassie, but there were a lot of things he shouldn't do. And at the very least, he was going to win whatever game they were playing here.

He wouldn't touch her. But he wasn't going to let her direct things, either.

"Honey, I would be very careful about where you take this conversation."

"Would you?" She arched her dark brow.

"Yes, I would. Because if you're implying what I think you are, then you're taking us into dangerous territory."

"I'm not implying anything. I'm saying it."

"You are not saying it. Your voice is thick with meaning, but you said nothing."

She crossed her arms beneath her breasts. "I heard you... I heard you..."

"I'm waiting, babe. Because for all I know you heard me singing 'I Dreamed a Dream.'"

"Do you even know that song?"

"Yeah, I do. I have culture." And he had heard it played over and over again on a movie trailer.

"Well that isn't what I heard. And I think you know it. Otherwise you wouldn't be daring me. Don't deny it, either. I know that's what you're doing."

"Yeah, I'm daring you," he said, taking a step closer to her. "You're right about that. So if you want to have this discussion, let's have this discussion."

"Why?"

"You're turning red, baby. I think you bit off a little more than you can chew."

The color mounted in her cheeks, and he had a feeling that this wasn't a blush. He had a feeling he was witnessing Cassie Ventimiglia entering a full-blown rage. Perversely, the thought pleased him. "All right, Mr. Tough Guy. I moved my couch because I can hear you showering. And I could hear you pleasuring yourself while you were showering." She was breathing hard when she finished, and she was so red she looked a bit like an overstewed tomato.

He gritted his teeth and tried to look casual. "I'm a guy. I'm not going to say I don't do that in the shower."

"Well, I don't need to hear it."

"It bothers you?"

"Of course it bothers me! It would bother anybody. Nobody needs to hear that."

And then, just because he wanted to go to her, just because he wanted to get her to give something away, just because he wanted her to be in hell the same as he was, he pushed further. "It only seems fair that you had to hear it. Seeing as I was thinking about you."

Her mouth fell open and then closed, and then open again. She looked a little bit like a guppy that had been yanked out of the water. A very cute guppy, but a guppy nonetheless. "I can't believe you just said that."

"Offended?"

She blinked a couple of times. "No," she said, standing stunned. "No, I'm not."

"You aren't?"

"No, I'm not offended. I'm not offended at all. In fact, I would go so far as to say I was intrigued."

"You're intrigued. By the thought of me touching myself while thinking about you."

"Yes, I find that very intriguing."

Jake crossed his arms over his chest, all the better to keep from reaching across the empty space between them and hauling her to him. "You really need to be sure this is where you want the conversation to go, baby. Because I have a feeling it could get out of hand very quickly."

"Maybe I want it to get out of hand. And trust me, Jake, no one is more surprised by that than me."

"I don't think you really want what you think you do."

She took a step backward, deeper into the apartment, and

he found himself following, like a dog on a leash. He stepped past the threshold, and inside. And he knew that he had made a very grave mistake. His dick, on the other hand, was rejoicing at what it was certain would be a victory.

"If you push me, you might find that you don't like the results."

She lifted her hands. "Or maybe I'll find out I *love* the result." She balled her hands into fists and pressed them against her eyes. "Jake, all my life, I've been a good girl. I know you have no idea what that's like, all things considered."

"Probably not, considering I have a penis."

He was certain that if she had possessed the physical capability she would've blushed even harder. As it was she seemed to have reached maximum capacity. "Oh yes, I'm aware, as we've established. But I didn't mean the gender part. I meant the well-behaved part. The good part. You were always so wild, and you just did what you wanted. You didn't seem to think what anyone else thought mattered. I, on the other hand, am crippled by what everyone else thinks."

Something in his stomach twisted. He didn't like the direction this conversation was going. It was cutting a little bit too close to the bone.

Cassie continued. "You with your tattoos—tattoos when we were in high school. Badass. You and your motorcycle when I didn't even have a car. I just couldn't help but admire that in some ways. I still do. Because I did everything I was supposed to, *everything*. Got married to this guy who was supposed to be great, and we were supposed to have kids. My mother was thrilled with the decisions I made. The guy wore a tie to work. I still didn't win, Jake. I didn't win. Because Allen left me. Or rather, he kicked me out. But either way the end result was the same. He never had kids with me, he wanted to wait. And then he got remarried eight months after the divorce was final and by the time that happened they already had one on the way.

Good behavior did nothing for me there. Nothing at all. And right now I'm standing here asking myself what this good behavior has *ever* gotten me."

He'd underestimated her again. He always had. It hit him then the Nice Girl label he'd slapped onto her was just as limiting, just as much a simplistic lie as the Bad Boy label was on him.

She'd been hurt. Badly. And standing here facing that he had no clue how to handle it.

He cleared his throat. "I thought good behavior was supposed to be its own reward."

She exploded, her tiny frame turning into a ball of energy as she paced around the apartment. "Where are my rewards?" She swept her hand around in a half circle. "Do you see them anywhere? I don't see them. I live in an apartment that I don't own, that's going to get sold out from under me, and when that happens I'll probably lose my business, too. I don't have a husband, which frankly is fine, because a bad husband is worse than none at all. But ultimately my life isn't anywhere that it was supposed to be." Her dark eyes locked with his. "I'm tired of being good. I don't want to be good anymore."

"Then what is it you want, Cassie?"

"I want to have fun. I want to be bad. I want the one thing I was too afraid to go after when I was in high school."

"I think you need to spell it out for me, just in case I'm misunderstanding."

Cassie took a deep breath. "I want to be bad, Jake. I want to be bad with you."

CASSIE WAS SHOCKED to the point of being horrified by her own actions. But things had been set in motion, and even though she felt like she was having an out-of-body experience, watching herself say these things, hearing the words come out of her mouth, she didn't seem to be able to control them. She was like a snowball that had started rolling down a hill, picking up momentum, picking up weight. And from her vantage point she could see that she was moving toward destruction and death. But there was no way to stop. Avalanche Cassie was firmly in motion, and she would not be deterred.

This was not her. This was far too bold. But she wouldn't take it back now. Not even if she could.

"Let me get this straight, Cassie. You want to slum it with me?"

Her face burned, her heart pounding so hard she could barely breathe. "I don't really like the way you put it. And sort of."

"You object to me telling the truth?"

"I don't consider you beneath me. So I don't think the term *slumming it* applies. But I do think you're what I need. You're the kind of guy I need."

"Okay, Cassie, let's talk about exactly what you want." Something had changed in his expression, his eyes becoming sharp, dangerous.

"I want… I want you." She could not believe those words had just come out of her mouth. More to the point, she couldn't believe how true they were.

She was a good girl, which she meant in that old-fashioned way her mother would use it. The way that was supposed to keep you out of trouble. Out of a situation like her mother had found herself in.

The truth was Allen was the only man she'd ever been with. And they didn't even have sex until they were engaged. So obviously she had never solicited a guy she barely knew, much less a guy she knew things wouldn't work out with. A guy she wasn't even looking for *things* with. Not things other than sex, anyway.

"What, you want me to bake you a pie? You want me to pay for that last muffin? What *exactly* do you want, Cassie?"

He wasn't going to let her get away with pushing the decision off on him. He wasn't giving her a chance to blame him later, to say it was all his idea. He was making her say it. Making her claim it.

"Sex," she said.

His expression hardened further. "Say it all."

Oh boy, he wasn't going to make this easy.

She took a deep breath, trying to hold on to her nerve. Although there was something to be said for losing her nerve. If she lost her nerve, she could back out. She wouldn't have to tell him what she wanted; she could pretend this had never happened. And she could go back to being the very good, very sexually frustrated Cassie Ventimiglia, who had never once propositioned a man and never would.

The Very Good Cassie Ventimiglia who'd been celibate for three years, and would probably be celibate for three more, and on into eternity because her business ruled her life and she was gun-shy about relationships. Thirty-two, divorced and sexless for the rest of her life.

Either that or she could go play the slots at the nearby casino. Pick up on guys putting nickels in the machine.

Holy hell, if she wasn't careful she wasn't going to turn into her mother. She was going to turn into her grandmother.

Yes, she *could* lose her nerve. But then nothing would change. She would continue to be the same person she'd always been. She could stand on the other side of life's raging storms, and look back and see herself walking through unchanged, unruffled and the same Cassie she'd always been.

But she had to wonder what the point was of going through a major life crisis if you didn't let it change you for the better. There was none. It was as pointless as being good with no reward. It was as pointless as living what amounted to a nearly spotless life and still having your mother despair of you.

It was as pointless as finally getting up your courage to tell the hot tattooed boy you tutored that you had a crush on him, only to have him disappear the next day.

Cassie had had enough of that kind of pointless. But she

wasn't going to change without making the decision to change. And she wasn't going to get her reward if she didn't reach out and grab it.

She was damn well going to grab it.

She took a deep breath. "I want to have sex with you."

He crossed his arms over his broad chest, and her eyes were drawn back to those tattoos on his forearms. They flexed and changed with the tensing of his muscles. Fascinating. And very, very sexy. "Are you sure, baby? You haven't even kissed me."

She swallowed hard. "Well, maybe we should change that."

"You don't even like me."

"Do I have to like you to want to kiss you?"

He reached back and slammed the door shut, walking all the way into the apartment with a determined look on his face.

"Now that you mention it, honey, I'm not sure that it does matter." He approached her, his expression transformed into that of a lean, hungry predator. And she was trembling like prey. But she didn't even care. She didn't want to run. Not even a little bit. She wanted to stay exactly where she was, so that he could catch her.

It hit her then, she would make a terrible gazelle, since she was just standing there waiting to be eaten. But she was wondering right now if she might be a half-decent temptress.

It was total craziness. Utter insanity. And she didn't even care. In fact, she felt like it was her due. She felt like she deserved a bad decision mixed somewhere in the middle of all her extremely logical choices.

Because the simple fact was that though she had made technically right decisions, they had very much turned out to be the wrong ones. Things that had been intended to bring her happiness had only brought her pain. And if things were going to be upside down like that she might as well get an orgasm out of it.

He hooked an arm around her waist and pulled her against his chest. He was hotter than she'd anticipated him being. He was hard, too, a solid wall of muscle, nothing like any other man she'd touched.

Her ex-husband had been thin to the point of being weedy. And bones were hard, but they were most definitely not muscle. She had already learned something new after five seconds in Jake's arms. All male bodies were most definitely not created equal.

He lifted his hand and touched a strand of her hair, winding it around his forefinger. It was a nonsexual act. But there was something about the movement that was more sensual than anything she could remember before.

Another learning experience just two seconds after the first. A touch didn't have to be under the clothes to be sexual. And when a man looked at you the way that Jake was looking at her, it was almost better than skin-to-skin contact.

She was certain of one thing already: this was going to go far and away beyond her level of experience. This was the kind of thing that would change her irrevocably. She didn't have a string of lovers in her past, so there was no way that Jake would blend into the masses. There were no masses. She had a feeling that even if there were she would be facing down the same problem. Jake Caldwell would be unforgettable whether there had been one lover or one hundred. And she had to decide whether or not she wanted Jake to be unforgettable.

Silly girl, he already is.

She knew her smug inner voice was right. Because for fifteen years she had remembered him. Had remembered that touch in the library. Had remembered the way she'd felt when he'd looked at her. For fifteen years she had remembered him and he had never given her reason to.

Tonight he would give her the reason. Tonight he would give her a memory that would make her tremble every time she thought of him.

Yes. No matter what, Jake Caldwell would always be unforgettable. But the question was, would she always remember Jake as the one that got away, or would she remember him as the best sex of her life?

She looked at his face, at his dark blue eyes, his sensual mouth. The square jaw rough with dark stubble. He was incredible. He was a mistake any girl would be lucky to make.

Some people went out and got bad haircuts. Not her. She was going to get Jake.

There was no question about how she wanted to remember Jake Caldwell. She wanted to remember him as the only man to ever make her knees shake.

So there would be no losing her nerve.

He released his hold on her hair and moved his hand to cup her cheek, sliding his thumb across the ridge of her cheekbone as he continued to look at her intently. He was the most beautiful thing she had ever seen. More beautiful than the sun setting into the ocean, or a view of the mountains on a clear day. He was more beautiful than a chocolate cake with birthday candles. And that was saying something.

"Are you just going to look at me? Or are you going to kiss me?" She was starting to wonder if Jake was losing *his* nerve. But that didn't seem possible. She doubted Jake was afraid of anything.

"Getting impatient, honey?"

"Yes. I'm a little worried that you aren't."

"I am. Trust me. It might surprise you to know that I've thought about kissing you for a while now. To be honest, I've wondered what it would be like since I was seventeen years old." He brushed some of her hair away from her eyes. "I knew it would be wrong. Because you were a good girl. A smart girl. You were helping me with my math homework, for God's sake. But that didn't stop me from thinking about it. I thought about what it would be like to lean in and kiss you, right there in the school library. We were the only ones there except for the librarian, and I bet we would've turned her hair a few shades grayer. But it would've been worth it."

"You thought about kissing me?" Cassie couldn't breathe. Couldn't even process what he had just said.

"I thought about it quite a bit. And I'm thinking about it now. But I find the anticipation makes it sweet."

"What, fifteen years isn't long enough?"

He chuckled, the sound rolling over her. "You may have a point." He spread his hand on her lower back, squeezing her tight as he tilted her chin up.

She let her eyes flutter closed and she held her breath, counting down in her mind. In some way she felt like there had been a countdown running on this since they were seventeen. And now it was finally winding down, fifteen years later. And now at three, two—and then his lips met hers.

There was nothing in her imagination that could've prepared her for the reality of Jake's kiss. It was quite simply too far outside anything she'd ever experienced before. His lips were hot, testing for a moment. He simply pressed them against hers and allowed the sensation of touching him in this way to bloom over her. To let the feelings slide over her like melting butter. Slow and warm, growing more liquid with each passing second.

Then he tilted his head, parting his lips, and she followed his lead. He took advantage of the improved angle and slipped his tongue along the seam of her lips. A shiver started at her core and radiated through her entire body. Her knees were already shaking, and they hadn't even gotten to the good bits. Or rather, she was just going to have to modify what constituted the good bits in her mind. Because not a single part of this had been bad. Not a single part had felt like filler, while he was simply waiting to get to the rest. Every movement was intentional, every one something he seemed to be savoring. She felt desired in a way she hadn't ever experienced before. She felt wanted. She felt needed.

It turned out Jake's lips could say a whole lot when he wasn't talking.

When they parted they were both breathing heavily.

Blue eyes burned into hers. "Tell me again why you want me." It was not a request, but a demand. There was something dangerous in his expression, and she couldn't quite translate what it was. What it meant. She only knew that there was a wrong answer. And that she was afraid she might give it.

"I want you because… Because if a girl can have a wild time, you seem like the kind of guy to give it to her."

"What is this, some bad '50s musical? Find a guy with a leather jacket and he'll show you a good time?"

Her stomach twisted. "Don't be like that, Jake. You know your reputation."

"Yes, I do know my reputation. But I sort of figured you knew more than that."

"Well, I thought maybe I did. But it turns out…"

"I took the money out of the register," he said, his voice rough.

"I'm not upset about that. It was forever ago." She had the strange feeling she had chosen poorly. But what had he wanted her to say? Had he wanted her to say that she wanted him because he was special? Because she'd had a crush on him since she was seventeen and this was wish fulfillment in a way he couldn't possibly understand? Because from the first moment she'd known sex was a thing, she'd wanted him to be the one she had it with? He wouldn't want to hear that. That would send him running screaming from the room. That was the kind of thing that sounded a lot like commitment. Neither of them wanted that.

"So you want a bad boy, is that it?"

She bit her lip. "If you want to put it like that. Sounds a little bit cheesy."

"Why don't we just go with it." There was a hardness to his

tone that disturbed her, but the heat in his eyes overtook any misgivings she had.

"I'll go with anything you want to give me."

"Now I like when you say things like that." He rubbed his thumb along her lower lip, then leaned in and traced the same path with the tip of his tongue before dipping it inside her mouth again. The motion was hot, slick and it sent a wave of longing through her that she couldn't control. Didn't want to control. Her stomach tightened, wetness pulling in the center of her thighs. She couldn't remember a kiss ever doing so much for her. In fact, she was sure one never had.

She wanted to tell him that. She decided she would tell him that.

"I've never kissed anyone who is quite so proficient at it." *Great, Cassie. That's how you talk dirty. Throw in some three syllable words.*

A wicked smile curved his lips. "I'm proficient, am I?"

"Well… And sexy. So sexy."

He chuckled, and she felt the weight lift off her chest. Maybe she hadn't made him angry after all. "Just be you, Cassie. I don't want you to be anything but you."

"I don't know if I want to be me. I don't think she really knows how to do this." She laughed nervously, hoping he wouldn't hear just how shaky her voice was.

"You seem to be doing just fine." She tried to look away, and he gripped her chin again, turning her face toward his. "Look at me, Cassie."

She obeyed, keeping her eyes locked with his. "Good girl." He leaned in, and she watched him, watched the intent in his eyes, the desire there. He angled his head and kissed her neck, kissed along the line of her jaw, to the sensitive skin of her throat. She was going to melt. She was going to melt in between all the cracks of the wooden floor, and when he went to sell this place, he wouldn't be able to get a very good price because there would still be particles of melted Cassie lingering in the wood grain.

"Oh, oh, Jake..." She was panting, saying his name, powerless to do anything but beg. Because she was about ready to come just from a few kisses. And that was not like her at all. She was more of a dim lights, flowers, roses, romantic music, forty-five minutes of foreplay kind of girl. She was not an argument, three kisses, climax kind of girl.

Although Jake made her feel like she might be.

Jake made her feel like something entirely new. Jake made her feel like she was drowning. But in the best possible way.

He moved both hands to her waist, tugging her more tightly against his body, the warmth of his touch seeping through her shirt. It made her feel impatient. Impatient for his skin against hers. And that bit of contentment she felt simply luxuriating in the moment passed. Suddenly, she just wanted it all. Wanted him pressed tightly against her with nothing between them.

She wanted to feel for herself just how different he was in every way. Wanted to feel every inch of his skin, wanted to know if he had chest hair or if he was smooth. She found in that moment she didn't really care what the answer was, only that she got the answer. Because everything about Jake had been perfect so far, and she knew she wouldn't be less disappointed with his body once it was bared to her.

She swallowed hard, and told herself that this was the last of her nerves. If she was going to have one night with Jake Caldwell, the hottest guy she had ever known as a teenager or an adult woman, she wasn't going to waste a moment of it acting like a terrified virgin. She knew the drill. She knew what went where. She'd taken the plunge, and he had said yes. He was kissing her. There was nothing to be nervous about.

"Take your shirt off for me, Jake."

"Getting demanding, are you?"

"I plan on making quite a few demands, actually. I hope you don't mind."

"Not a bit." To prove his word, he gripped his black T-shirt, tugged it up over his head and tossed it onto the floor.

Her heart pumped hard against her breastbone and she had to fight to catch her breath. She had been entirely unprepared for the beauty that was Jake. Yes, no lie, all men's physiques were not created equal. She really hated to do a comparison between Jake and her ex, if only because she hated to think of her ex in this moment. But it was impossible seeing as it was the only other male body she'd been this close to.

Where Allen had been pale, and a bit freckly with ribs instead of abs, Jake was tan and beautifully muscled. He had, to answer her earlier question, a fascinating smattering of dark hair over said muscles. It made her mouth go dry, made her fingers itch to touch.

And so she would. Because tonight wasn't about restraint. It wasn't about sparing herself from embarrassment, or making anyone proud. It was about pleasing herself. And touching Jake would please her in more ways than she could count.

She put her hand flat on his chest, her breath hissing through her teeth as she did.

"See something you like?" he asked.

"Oh, I see so much that I like." She let her fingertips trail over his muscles, relishing the combination of rough, hot and hard. "I used to think about this."

"Did you?"

"Well, kind of. I mean, it's not like I knew very much about this sort of thing back in high school."

"I think I knew too much about it."

"That doesn't surprise me."

"Oh, right," he said, grabbing her wrist and tugging away from his chest. "Because I'm such a bad boy."

"Because you're hot. Unlike me, I'm sure you had a lot of dates."

"Not dates exactly."

She had a feeling the subtext was that he hooked up. If she'd known that back then it would've made him even more impossibly dangerous. It probably would've made her even more attracted to him. Because teenage girl logic. Actually, her adult woman logic, too. Maybe something in her had just snapped. Too much good, too much people pleasing. His entire life was her own personal porn.

It was forbidden, something she would never do. And that was what made his life philosophy so appealing. Human nature. To want what you couldn't have. To be enticed by things you shouldn't be.

"Well, I didn't date, either. Though I mean that in a much less roguish and charming way than you did."

"I'm not sure I was all that charming."

"I beg to differ." She stretched up on her tiptoes, and pressed her lips to his again. She didn't want to talk anymore. She didn't want to do anything but kiss him. Okay, that was a lie. She wanted to do a whole lot more than kiss him. "You charmed me," she said, her lips against his.

"I don't think this is charming. I think this is seduction."

"Either way. Works for me."

She put her hands on his biceps, the utter solidness of him shocking. Without thinking, she patted one of his arms. She felt him smile against her mouth. "What are you doing?"

"I've never felt muscles quite like this before. I like it." Her face heated. "Sorry, I don't think I'm very good at this."

"You are very good at this. I don't think my ego—or my arm—has ever been stroked so thoroughly."

"I'm not very experienced."

"That probably shouldn't turn me on. But it does."

"Well, at this point I don't really want anything to turn you off."

"No chance of that, baby."

He slid his hands down to her hips and around her backside, a bolt of heat spearing her straight to the stomach as his touch moved lower, as he squeezed her gently. An inelegant groan escaped her lips, and she didn't even care. How could she care? Nothing was more important than what she felt right now. Not pride, not ladylike noises.

It suddenly occurred to Cassie that he was doing all of the exploration. And that she was wasting an opportunity. She moved her hands to his back, fingertips tracing a path along the line of his spine, and down to the curve just above the waistline of his pants. She decided not to hesitate, and simply followed her instincts. She pushed her hand just beneath the denim, bare skin making contact with bare skin. She felt him jolt, felt an immense amount of satisfaction as he did.

That she could have such a strong effect on a guy like him was fuel enough for her own ego. Which admittedly at this point was a little bit bruised. Years of indifference would do that. Years of feeling the disconnect between yourself and the person with whom you were supposed to be the most intimate.

It hit her then how little she felt like she had. She hadn't truly had a claim on her husband. Hadn't owned the house. She didn't own the apartment she was in now. But right now, with Jake reacting to her touch the way he was, it felt very much like having something of her own. It felt very much like ownership. And even if it was only temporary, it made her feel anchored in a way she hadn't in years.

He gripped the hem of her T-shirt and tugged it up over her head, leaving her standing there in her plain black bra, the air suddenly feeling slightly cold against her skin.

He cursed, short and sharp and yet more satisfaction bloomed in her stomach. He wanted her. He wanted this.

She made him cuss. That was...immensely satisfying.

"All of it." That was all he managed to get out, the desperation evident in those words fueling her fire even more.

Without pausing to think she reached behind her back and unclasped her bra, throwing it on to the floor before shoving her yoga pants and underwear down, too, leaving her completely naked in front of Jake.

No time for nerves now.

She pressed her body back up against his, luxuriating in the feel of her bare breasts against his chest. His chest hair was rough against her nipples, the contact sending slow waves of pleasure through her, her internal muscles contracting in time with the throbbing of her pulse.

"Jake," she said, barely able to force the words through her constricted throat. "I want to see you."

He released his hold on her and took a step back, his hands going to the snap on his jeans. And she watched, her attention completely rapt as he pulled the zipper down, then pushed his pants and black boxer briefs down his lean hips.

Cassie's eyes went wide, and she knew she was absolutely telegraphing her thoughts straight to him. But she didn't care. This was for her, after all. That meant she wasn't obligated to pretend to be more experienced than she was. Wasn't obligated to pretend to be blasé as she was looking at the most beautiful man she could've ever dreamed up.

He was incredible, his thick erection enticing in a way she'd never imagined something like that would be. Sure, she knew women giggled about big penises, and size mattering and all of that. But sort of like big boobs, she'd never figured it was something that might really matter.

She was changing her stance on the subject.

Of course it wasn't only his blatantly male member that had her dying to touch him. It was everything. Muscles, tattoos, chest hair, even his thighs. She had never given a whole lot of thought to a man's thighs before. But Jake's were worth thinking about.

"Are you just going to stand there staring all day? Or are you going to touch me?" he asked, his voice rough.

"Oh, I'm going to touch you."

She closed the scant distance between them, placing her hand on his chest, feeling his heart raging beneath the surface of his skin. She took an extreme amount of satisfaction in that. In the fact that she had affected him so strongly. The fact that all of this seemed to matter to him, almost as much as it mattered to her.

She moved her hand down to his arousal, wrapping her hand around him and squeezing gently, watching as his mouth tensed and his eyes closed, as he let his head tilt back. She watched the tendons in his neck tighten. She could see his pulse pounding, hard and fast at the base of his throat, and she leaned in and flicked her tongue across his skin, tasting his need. The desperation that matched her own.

She flattened her hand over his length, exploring the shape of him, testing his hardness.

"Be careful," he said, his voice a growl, "or this is going to be over a lot quicker than I want it to be."

She moved her hand away from him. "Well, we don't want that." Sure, a small part of her would take pleasure in the fact that she had challenged his control like that. But most of her would just be disappointed to have things end prematurely.

She hadn't had sex in three years, and she was not missing out on it now.

Speaking of that…

"Oh, shit!"

Jake's eyes widened. "Well, that's not something I'm used to hearing at this stage."

"Condoms." She was starting to feel slightly panicked. No, there was no need to panic. There was a store within jogging distance. And her pride honestly had no place in this. She would do a condom dash. She would.

"I've got one," he said.

"Only one?"

"You sound disappointed."

"I haven't had sex in a very long time."

He chuckled and tugged her against him, kissing her deeply.

When they parted they were breathing hard. "Why don't you wait and see if you enjoy this time? Then we'll worry about getting more."

"Oh, I am not concerned. About the enjoyment."

"Good."

He leaned in and kissed her neck, then moved lower, kissing the curve of her breast before sliding his tongue down to her nipple, tracing a circle around it. Her hands flew to his head, gripping his hair, holding him to her as he continued to lavish attention on her body.

He parted his lips and sucked her deep into his mouth, an answering pull of sensation echoing in her midsection. He lifted his hand and cupped her other breast, teasing her with his thumb before pinching her lightly. She tightened her hold on him, lowered her head and rested her cheek against his hair, hanging on tight as he continued his sensual assault. He had her shaking, whimpering, begging... If she hadn't been so lost, she might have been embarrassed.

He raised his head, a slash of darkened color bleeding over his cheekbones, betraying just how affected he was by all of this.

Then his lips crashed down on hers, the kiss deep and hard, his tongue sliding against hers. He gripped her thighs and tugged her up, wrapping her legs around his waist, bringing the damp center of her into contact with his length. She arched against him, trying to ease the ache that was building there. But it wasn't enough.

"Which way to the bedroom?" he asked, his words labored.

"No time. Couch."

He carried them over to the couch and set her down, settling between her legs and kissing her as he slid his hardness through her slick folds. His eyes locked with her own, and a whimper escaped her. He lowered his head and kissed her, taking her lower lip between his teeth and biting her gently, the sensation combined with the motion of his hips sending a white-hot flash of pleasure through her.

"Now. Please now."

"Not yet." He pressed a kiss between her breasts, then one to her stomach. It took her a moment to realize what he intended to do, but when she did everything in her seized up. She had never done this before. But she had fantasized about it.

Oh, had she ever.

He kissed her inner thigh, his wicked blue eyes never leaving hers as he moved closer to the center of her need. He flicked the tip of his tongue over her clitoris, and her hips bucked off the couch. He took that opportunity to reach around and grab her by the hips, pulling her hard against his mouth and deepening the intimate kiss.

"Oh! Jake!" She threaded her fingers back through his hair, not caring if she hurt him. Which seemed a little barbaric, perhaps. But the pleasure he was giving her verged on pain, and somewhere in her muddled mind she thought maybe if she gave him pain, it would verge on pleasure.

He growled roughly as he continued his exploration of her, adding his fingers, sliding two deep inside her, working them in time with his magic tongue.

She wasn't going to last. And if she couldn't, she knew she wouldn't come again. For a moment she felt slightly wistful about the fact that it was about to be over for her. But only for a moment. Because the spiral of need in her was so tight that she knew it had to break. Otherwise she would.

He used his fingers to stroke her in time with the motion of his tongue, and sent her over. Hurtling down into an abyss. For a moment everything was blank, weightless, all of her senses sacrificed on the altar of the pleasure that was coursing through her. There was nothing but this, nothing but what he made her feel.

It was incredible. Beyond a simple climax and into something entirely different. Something that consumed her in a way nothing else ever had. Right now there was no worrying about whether she pleased anyone.

Because she herself was so wholly pleased, she simply couldn't care.

He abandoned her for a moment, leaving her lying spent on the couch, electricity buzzing over her skin. He returned a moment later, and she realized he had gotten the condom and had already seen to protecting them both. He joined her again, kissing her deeply, his hands going back between her thighs, stroking her. She was almost too sensitive, but she didn't want to tell him to stop, either.

Finally, he positioned himself at her entrance, the blunt head of his arousal testing her before he slid in the rest of the way.

She gasped as he filled her, stretching her. It wasn't painful. Not at all. A feeling of complete satisfaction overwhelmed her. He fit so perfectly. He felt so amazing she could think of nothing else.

And she didn't want to.

She cupped his face and kissed him and he began to move inside of her, each measured thrust pushing her back toward the edge. An edge she hadn't thought she would reach again. Not so soon. But this was nothing she'd experienced before. This wasn't just sex, this was Jake. And she should've realized by now what that meant. That none of the previous rules applied. That none of her previous experiences meant anything.

His control started to fray, his movements becoming harder, faster, amping up her excitement to an impossible degree. Each thrust brought his pelvis back against her clitoris, pushing her closer, until she was arching up to meet him, desperate for release.

A second wave broke over her just as he stiffened above her, a hoarse groan on his lips as he shuddered out his own release.

As they lay there on the couch, in the quiet of her apartment, no sound beyond their shattered breathing, three things kept going through her mind.

She'd just made love with Jake Caldwell. He had in fact managed to make her come twice. And she would never be the same again.

CHAPTER SEVEN

OKAY, SO HE was kind of a dick for leaving in the middle of the night. But he had to be out at the ranch early the next day. Or rather, he supposed he didn't have to be, but it made for a nice excuse in his head. And he really needed a nice excuse.

That much was true.

Because without the excuse, he had to face the truth that he needed to leave because he was feeling too many things. Too many damn feelings. He didn't do feelings. He knew madness lay on the other side of his feelings. He wasn't being overdramatic, it was just the truth.

He scrubbed his hand over his hair and grabbed his leather jacket off the hook by the door, pausing and looking at it, thinking about Cassie wearing it yesterday. How it had swallowed her tiny frame and made her look even more petite than she was. And he was done thinking of that. There was only madness on the other side of that, too. He would be redirecting his thoughts now.

He put the jacket on and continued out the door, walking

down the stairs and stopping when he reached the landing and saw Cassie standing there at the bottom of her stairwell, looking slightly lost.

"What are you doing here?" he asked.

"I was about to ask you the same question. Since I was looking for you."

"You were looking for me?"

Cassie shifted, her expression adorably sheepish. And when the hell had he ever thought of a woman as adorable? "Well, I've never exactly woken up alone after having sex with a guy."

"Right, well, I didn't have…anything, and we didn't have any more condoms so…" *Right, way to be an asshole, Caldwell. Tell her you couldn't have more sex with her so you left.*

The thing was, he'd needed space. Because while they'd been getting it on he'd been fine. But as he'd been laying there holding her in his arms he kept replaying what she'd said to him over and over again.

He kept hearing her say that she wanted to make a mistake. That she wanted to be bad. And that bothered him in a way he couldn't quantify.

Or hell, maybe he could. Maybe it was because he'd always imagined that Cassie saw more to him than that. And now he could see she was just like every other woman he'd ever screwed. Into the tattoos, into the motorcycle, into the idea that he had some kind of secret bad-boy magic hidden in his wang.

Not that he was complaining, since that got him so laid it was ridiculous, but as he seemed to be getting feelings all over this little interaction with her it was more disconcerting than usual. Again, it was this place. This place and this woman, and all of it made him feel like what he really needed to do was get the hell out of Dodge.

Which was why he'd left her apartment this morning, really. He'd been running. Because he was a coward who'd gotten his feelings hurt. And it was not a nice look on him.

"Sure. Right, condoms." She tucked a strand of hair behind

her ear, then clasped her hands in front of her, looking a bit like a nervous little mouse. "Very important. Seeing as I'm not on the…pill. Because of things. Reasons. Celibacy mainly."

"Were you looking for me?"

Cassie bit her lip. "Yes, I was looking for you. Because I don't really do the sex-and-dash thing. And I've decided it's not my thing."

He crossed his arms over his chest. "Then maybe I'm not your thing."

She wrung her hands. "I wouldn't go that far."

"*You* said you wanted to screw around with the bad boy, Cassie. And if there's one thing bad boys are good at, it's a fuck and run. So if that isn't what you want then maybe you need to revise your idea of how you want to conduct your little rebellion. Maybe carrot cake with raisins is more your speed."

"First of all," she said, drawing up to her full height, which put her just beneath his chin, "raisins are awful. A rebellion should be about having fun, and there is nothing fun about eating the lowest form of dehydrated fruit. Second of all, I did say that I wanted a bad boy. But I lied. I think I'm naive, and my idea of what a bad boy is is somewhat skewed. Or maybe I was just being flippant. You're not an asshole, Jake, no matter how much you might pretend you are. Sorry, I guess now your secret is out."

Jake felt the shock of her words all the way down to his toes. "What is it you're saying exactly, Cassie?"

"I don't know!" She threw her hands up above her head. "I don't know, Jake. The thing is, I feel like I said the wrong thing to you last night. I'm afraid that's why you left this morning." She put her hands back down to her sides, her breathing hard and uneven.

"What, you think you hurt my feelings?" Even as he said the words, dismissive, like they were crazy, he wondered if they might be true. Or maybe hurt feelings was a step too far. But it was just too close to the bone, all things considered.

"Look, whatever I said…"

"Cassie, don't worry about it. This place messes with my head. I was pissed at myself, because I shouldn't have touched you. Nothing can come of this so there's really not much point in continuing, and you said yourself you're inexperienced. You haven't been with anyone in a long time and I took advantage of you."

Her dark eyes flew wide. "Don't feel like that! I mean, I wanted you, I wanted this. I don't want you to go regretting it now because you think somehow I didn't know what I was getting into. I was married for years. It's not like I don't know about sex."

"I know you know about sex, it's this part you obviously aren't too familiar with."

"Maybe the problem is that we're not at the part you think we are."

"What do you mean?"

"I mean, maybe we aren't at this kind of awkward morning-after-we-shouldn't-be-speaking-of-this-let's-never-talk-again moment you think we're at."

"Are you telling me how to do one-night stands?" he asked. "Because I'm more familiar with those than I would like to admit."

She took a deep breath, her eyes going particularly wide. "Last night was really special to me."

"Cassie…don't do this." He wasn't trying to stop her from talking so she wouldn't embarrass herself. No, he was trying to stop her from talking because he was afraid of what she might say. Of what it might make him feel.

"No, you do not get to tell me to stop it! You do not get to control this."

He had never seen Cassie so worked up before. And here she was, all worked up over him. He shouldn't like it, but he did.

"Do you have any idea how long I've lived my life for other people?"

"Probably about as long as I've lived life for myself."

"If not longer! Jake, last night was special to me. Because you're special. When I said I wanted a bad boy, I didn't mean to insult you. I meant that you amaze me, the way that you just did what you wanted. The way you left Copper Ridge because it was the best thing for you—"

"Whatever you do, whatever it is about me that you like, don't let it be that. There was nothing admirable about the way I left."

"What you mean?"

He let out a harsh breath. "Did you think I just left? Did you think I just got it in my head that it was time to skip town, so I did?"

She lifted her thumb to her mouth and started gnawing the nail. "I guess… I guess I sort of did."

"Well, that isn't what happened. I did something really stupid. Like really stupid. Illegal. I am not some kind of figure for you to pattern your rebellion after. You shouldn't admire anything that I did."

"Jake…"

Before his brain could reason it out, his mouth made a decision. "Why don't you come out to the ranch with me?" he asked.

Cassie nodded slowly. "Okay, I can do that."

"I'll just get your helmet from my place."

Jake turned slowly and walked back toward his apartment. He wasn't in a hurry to get to the ranch. After this she would understand who he was, and why he'd had to leave. And anything admirable she had seen in him would be destroyed. And no matter how much he knew it had to happen…he was in no rush.

CASSIE LEANED AGAINST Jake's back as he maneuvered the motorcycle over the back roads that lead to his father's property.

Last night had been a revelation for Cassie. She had felt uninhibited in a way she'd never felt her entire life. She hadn't done anything to please anyone but herself. And still she'd somehow managed to please Jake.

Waking up and finding him gone had put something of a dent in that confidence. But regardless of whether he'd been able to establish a physical distance, there was no emotional distance. Not really. There was a bond between them, no doubt about it. No matter that he'd shown up to Copper Ridge without so much as a smile for her, from the moment she'd seen him again she'd known it was still there.

It was a strange sensation to be so certain of something. To feel like she wanted to hang on to something. She'd realized something this morning as she was lying in her empty bed, missing Jake and wishing he hadn't left. She'd realized that she had never fought for anything. Lord knew why. But she hadn't. Maybe it was because of the way things had been with her mother.

She hadn't felt like she had the right to fight with her, because she'd always known that her existence had made her mother's life difficult. Oh, Maria Ventimiglia would never say that, and she never had. But she implied it in new and interesting ways all the time. From the time Cassie was about six years old she could remember the story of the one man her mother had loved. The story of how he had wanted her to choose between having a child and having him. And Cassie had always known what the choice had been. Because she was with her mother, and her mother didn't have a husband.

That was why her mother had always put so much importance on making sure she got married before she got pregnant. Why Maria had always put so much emphasis on the need to find a husband. Because when you were a working single mom finding one was nearly impossible. When you'd had your heart ripped out by the father of your child, who wanted you to make an impossible choice, you knew how precious that relationship was.

So Cassie had felt obligated to make her first relationship work. To give it the respect her mother wanted her to give it.

Her mom had been instantly attached to Allen, and in fact still was. Cassie had never felt like she had any other option but to follow that relationship to its conclusion down the altar. And she could see now what a mistake it had been. But she had simply gone along with the path it was easiest to walk.

And when Allen had wanted a divorce, she had complied. She hadn't even fought for her damn house. Who did that? Eight years of marriage, and she had simply walked away. She hadn't asked him for counseling, hadn't asked him to keep trying.

The sad part of that was that she had loved him enough. But she was starting to wonder if she had loved herself enough.

Spending a few years alone was an interesting thing. She'd had the benefit of starting a business, of fighting her way through financial uncertainty, of making things happen for herself. Of being with a man simply because she wanted him, not because he was an ideal prospect for future husband, or someone who would make her mom proud.

Those experiences had changed her, and were changing her still.

And when she realized all of that this morning, she had also realized that she was prepared to stand and fight for Jake.

Because she wanted him, because the feelings that she'd always had for him had never truly gone away, but had only been dormant.

And he had brought her out here to discourage her. Of that she had no doubt. But he was about to discover that she was a lot stronger than he was giving her credit for.

She hoped she was about to discover that she was a lot stronger than *she* had ever given herself credit for.

It occurred to Cassie as the motorcycle pulled into the property that she had never been to Jake's family ranch. By the time she had started doing business with his father, the older man had been in a nursing home. So she wasn't certain what exactly she had expected. But it wasn't what she saw. The house was run-down, old cars, tractors and other farm implements littering the lawn in front. Slowly corroding, halfway between a man-made creation and dirt at this point.

There were wire fences, with chickens running through gaping holes, and goats wandering around in the muddy enclosure. All of the foliage had been stripped within a two-foot radius around the fence, compliments of the voracious hoofed creatures.

"Wow." She tugged off her helmet and dismounted the bike.

"Yeah," he said, following her lead, his boots sinking into the mud. "It's basically a shithole."

He sounded almost ashamed, and she didn't want him to. She wanted to make it better. "It's really not."

"No, Cassie, it is. You don't need to be nice. It wasn't all this bad when I was growing up. But things have really fallen apart since."

"I just imagined, since your father owned other properties in town…"

"Yeah, you imagined that this would be nice. That we had money or something."

"I'm starting to realize how little I knew about you."

"Which is what I've been trying to tell you."

"Well, stop *trying* to tell me, and just tell me." She looked at the man who last night had become her lover. She felt inextricably linked to him, and she would be lying if she said it was because of the sex. Because she had felt inextricably linked to him since she was seventeen years old.

He had always been there. In her heart, in her mind. She had always been drawn to him, fascinated by him. And now that they'd slept together that pull had only grown stronger.

She looked around, searching for something to say, since he was not responding to her prompt. "So, you've been fixing the place up?"

He chuckled. "Why? Can't you tell?"

"Not really."

"It's a testament to how bad it looked before. I don't really know who was taking care of the animals, but obviously someone was. Now that I'm here they seem to have stopped. So I've been managing them."

"This is where you grew up?"

"Yeah, unhappily." He put his hands on his lean hips and looked around. "I never missed it. I never missed it once after I left."

"And you were going to tell me why you left." She took a step out of the muddy patch and to the side. She fixed her eyes down on the green, stepping on a weed that popped, a milky substance oozing out of the stem.

"Yes, I guess I was."

"Are you still going to tell me?"

Jake was silent for a moment, then he took a deep breath. "Look at me again."

His request was firm, loud in the otherwise silent front yard. She obeyed. "Why?"

"Because I want to see you looking at me one more time before you lose your respect for me."

"Jake, being perfectly honest, you've come here, endangered my livelihood, had sex with me and left my apartment before I woke up. If that hasn't damaged my opinion of you, I think it's safe to say nothing will."

He looked away from her, a muscle in his jaw ticking. "You say that, but you don't know."

"No, I don't know. So stop with this mysterious crap and just tell me."

"It's in the bad-boy handbook. We're supposed to be mysterious and brooding."

"Yeah, well, knock it off. We both know you don't particularly like the label, so stop living up to it."

"I haven't lived up to it. That's the thing. I'm not the same person I was when I left here. I've gotten a handle on my shit. I'm not just going off half-cocked, letting my anger bleed out on everything. That's what I was doing back then. My version of managing my temper was to release it and let it savage whatever got in my way. There's nothing sexy about that. Nothing attractive about it. I needed to get punched in the face, I did not need to get blow jobs as a reward for my bad behavior."

Heat prickled her face. "Get a lot of those, did you?"

"A few," he said, deadpan.

She cleared her throat. "You've got a handle on your anger now," she said, looking at him, at the rage that was evident behind his blue eyes. It was funny he was saying that, because she felt like he was still angry. Felt like there was an endless well of it inside of him that he'd simply covered up. But it was leaking out, escaping, maybe because of where he was, or maybe because she had gotten too close to his emotions. For whatever reason she was more conscious of it now than she ever had been.

"Yeah, I've had a handle on it. I got out. I did what my father said I could never do. I got a job, I kept it. I earned the trust of the owner of the business. I learned a skill. I'm a mechanic, and I'm a damn good one. I know that for a lot of people that wouldn't seem a big achievement, but for a kid who was told he would never do anything but serve jail time? It's huge. When I left, I found something I could do. I found a way to be constructive. There's a whole lot of power in learning a skill."

"I imagine there is. I own a coffee shop, I'm not going to look down on you because you're a mechanic. I respect it."

"Yeah, *I* respect it. I don't especially need anyone else to. My dad never would have, he owned land. That was somehow better than anything I could ever live up to."

"What did your dad do to you?"

Cassie thought of her own mother, of how fraught their relationship could be at times. Though she had to admit, her mother probably wasn't aware of how difficult it was. Her mother excelled at manipulation, at guilt, and creating a running tally of debts owed. She rarely shouted, but she would cry, get upset. And for Cassie that was a lot more damaging than a screaming match.

"Doesn't matter. After my mom died I just don't think he

could figure out what to do with me. I was about twelve when that happened. I'd never been close to my dad, but it only got worse. We didn't grieve together, because he didn't grieve. And as a result neither did I. At first he just stopped paying attention to me, so I would do stupid shit to make him look in my direction. And eventually the neglect turned into resentment. I couldn't do a damn thing right in his eyes. Not my chores, not my schoolwork. And I admit, I didn't do any of it particularly well. I had a hard time in school, I was never going to graduate at the top of the class—you've seen my work so you knew that."

"It isn't that you weren't smart, Jake. That stuff just isn't easy for everyone."

"I know that, objectively. Now, as an adult. But as a kid? I just believed him. I was dumb, but I couldn't do anything right. And since I could never do anything right anyway, I decided I might as well embrace it. So I was always pushing things. Always trying to make him angry, because he was always angry anyway. The more I pushed it the angrier he got, the angrier he got the angrier I got. And eventually I stopped trying to control it. So we would have shouting matches, and that never ended well. Usually with me getting punched in the face."

"Jake," she breathed, feeling like all the air had gone out of her lungs. "That's not okay."

"I know it. I know." Cassie's stomach tightened, anxiety coursing through her, pain wrenching her chest. "What happened, Jake?"

"The night after you and I studied in the library, I came home. He was pissed about something, something I had done wrong on the ranch. Something I had missed because I had gone to get some extra tutoring, because I was failing school. Which was just typical. Because I couldn't do anything right. I couldn't do the chores right if I was trying to do school right, but if I was smarter I would've been able to just do school, instead of needing all that extra help."

Jake shook his head. "I was so angry. So fucking angry. I

couldn't do a damn thing right for him. He told me to go out and check on the wheat field. So I did. I went out there with my lighter and my cigarettes, and I thought to myself it would be so easy to just smoke the place. To make all my problems go away. Because if the ranch wasn't there, I wouldn't have to take care of it. I wouldn't be able to fail it. And I just did it. I didn't have any control over my emotions. I didn't have any control over my impulses, and I threw the lighter and the cigarette down the field. I watched it burn, Cassie."

Cassie put her hand over her mouth, careful not to interrupt him. Careful not to make a sound.

He continued. "I regretted it pretty quick, but by the time I tried to put it out, it had gone too far. There was nothing I could do. Nothing I could do but watch my anger burn out of control. I didn't leave. I was thrown out. My father told me he never wanted to see me again because of what I'd done. So I got my bike and I left. I never came back."

Cassie pictured Jake as he'd been. The long, lean boy she'd known, with a chip on his shoulder and a reputation she'd always assumed was misunderstood. And she realized that she had been doing him just as much of a disservice as everyone else. Other people had written him off, while she had been looking at him through rose-colored glasses. Both things had prevented people from seeing what was actually going on with Jake. Some people had made him a villain; she had made him a fantasy. And all the while no one had seen the boy as he was. No one had seen that he needed help. That he was drowning, in hurt, in grief and in rage.

"Oh, Jake, I'm so sorry."

He took a step back from her. "Why are you apologizing to me?"

"Because I should've seen, I should've asked you. Should've talked to you. I was so busy fantasizing about making out with you that I never stopped to see you as a person. And I did the same thing last night. You're not just a fantasy, you're a human being. And I didn't see that." She took a deep breath. "I didn't see past myself. What I wanted."

Jake laughed, the sound bitter, echoing off the canopy of trees. "Most men wouldn't complain about you seeing them as a fantasy, honey."

"But you know what I mean, Jake."

He looked down. "I guess I do."

"I'm sorry."

"Don't apologize to me. What I did was inexcusable. I cost my father Lord knows how much money, unless he got the insurance to cover it. But probably not, seeing as it was arson."

"You don't even know?"

"No, I don't know. I left, and I never came back."

"Because he told you to."

"Yeah, and I was looking for any excuse." He let out a long breath. "Don't try to make me the victim here. I was the bad guy."

Cassie scrunched her nose. "It's funny, I thought of us as opposites all this time. I looked at you and I saw a guy who had the kind of freedom that I envied. My mother always made me feel guilty. Like she had sacrificed everything to have me. And she did, Jake. In fairness, she did sacrifice to have me. So I felt like I had to live my whole life to please her. On the surface we seem different, but if you really look closely I think we're the same."

"Why? Did you set your mom's kitchen on fire?"

"We both had people who wanted something from us we didn't know how to give. I changed myself. I did everything I could to be the person my mom wanted me to be, even if I didn't want the things she wanted. I wanted to own a business, I wanted to go to college. But my mom made me so conscious of the importance of finding a man and getting married, and not ending up like her, that I did that instead. Without even realizing that was what I was doing." She was only just now fully realizing it.

She bent down and picked a dandelion, snapping the heavy yellow head from the stem before she continued. "But it wasn't me. It wasn't right. I don't even think I loved him. Not really. I loved the idea. I loved the idea of finding someone, and having this idyllic family life that my mother had always wanted, but couldn't give us. I wanted to give that to us. And then when push came to shove and he didn't want to be married anymore, I didn't even know how to fight, because I had always just gone along with what other people wanted for me. Then I was standing there, a failure in my mother's eyes. And it didn't even matter what I thought, how I saw myself, because it had never mattered to me before. I think we are just the same. Your father wanted something from you, but instead of bending over backward to try and do it like I did, you flipped him the middle finger and did everything you could to rebel against him."

"That's basically us being opposites."

She laughed even though she didn't find any of it particularly funny. "Except, if you think about it, both of us were just living for other people. Neither of us were doing what we wanted. We were reacting to the things other people told us. What do you want, Jake? What do you want from life?"

He rubbed the back of his neck before dropping his hand and making eye contact with her again. "I have what I want. At least I had it. I just want to go back to Seattle, I want to buy the mechanic shop, and I want to keep living." He took a deep breath. "I've got a handle on everything now. Coming back here just stirs it all up."

"Probably because you don't actually have a handle on it."

"I do. I just need to get away from this place."

"And what would you do in Seattle, Jake? Once you have your mechanic shop, then what?"

"What kind of question is that, Cassie? What will you do? Are you going to keep living to please your mother? Are you going to run your coffee shop and try to find a new husband? What are your goals?"

"My goals? I'm good with figuring out who I am. Apart from all of this. Apart from expectation. I've already started. I have my business. Right now, I have you."

"Not for long."

Okay, so she'd overstepped here. She'd been feeling…brave. Not herself. And she'd said something dumb. Damn, that hurt. Even if it was true. And she knew it was. She didn't expect this to be a forever thing. She knew she couldn't keep him for very long, but that didn't mean she wouldn't miss him when he was gone.

"I know that, okay, Jake? I've been married before. I don't really want to go there again. Not just now. Now when I'm still getting everything together."

"Is there a point where we're supposed to have it together?" he asked. "Because if so, I seem to have missed it."

"I intend to someday. I'm tired of settling. I'm tired of settling for my mom's dreams. I'm tired of just accepting what gets lobbed at me. I think I deserve more. Don't you?"

"Do I think you deserve more? Hell yeah. Do I think I do?" He squinted and looked off into the distance. She wondered if he was looking toward the field he'd lit on fire. "I think I deserve what I worked for. I don't really think I deserve much else."

And she could tell the subject was closed now. That she'd pushed things much further than a one-night stand should be allowed to.

"Do you want to show me around?"

"That is kind of why I brought you here. I was going to show you the field I burned. He never grew anything in it after that. At least, it doesn't look like it. Still a bunch of ash." He swallowed hard. "Sometimes you just can't undo stuff. Sometimes you can't fix it."

"Do you wish you could fix things with your dad?"

"I don't know. Our relationship was what it was. I doubt he ever changed."

Her heart felt like it was splintering, for him. For the rift he would never have the chance to heal.

He walked up the porch steps, and she watched one of them bow beneath his weight, and she followed carefully to avoid the one that was compromised. He unlocked the door and she trailed him inside. The inside of the house smelled stale. It looked clean enough, but as she walked across the wooden floor she could see that there was a film of dirt on the wood, could see where Jake had walked when he'd come in on previous visits.

"Are you going to clean all this yourself? Are you going to get someone in to help you?"

"I don't know. I'm trying to find the line between how much work I can miss, and how much money I want to fork out. Basically, I'm sacrificing vacation days that I never take to be here. So at this point I'm not losing money. But I'd really like for this venture to be an asset, and not a drain. So there's only so much I'm willing to invest."

"That makes sense." She thought about their previous conversation. "And you want to use the money you get to buy the mechanic shop you work at."

"Yep."

"Why is that so important to you?"

"Because it's what I've been working for."

"And you only want what you worked for."

"Makes sense, right?"

"I suppose so." She stuffed her hands in her back pockets and walked deeper into the room, looking at all the furniture, the dusty Afghan laying across the dusty couch. It was such a quiet space. And she had a feeling it hadn't been when Jake and his father had lived here. "Is it weird to be back?"

"You have no idea." His voice was rough. And all she wanted to do was reach out and touch him. Offer comfort. But she didn't know if she should. Didn't know if he would feel like she was invading his space. Or take things further than he wanted to.

"So you've never thought about staying?"

"I can't stay here." Blue eyes clashed with hers. "There's nothing for me here."

I'm here.

She left that unsaid. Because hadn't he just told her that she wouldn't have him for long? He made it very clear that this wasn't permanent. One night hardly meant forever. And she knew that intellectually, but it didn't stop her from wanting more. The ache that was building in her chest wasn't based on logic. It was based on that connection that had always been there. That had never been uprooted, no matter how life had tried to dig at it.

"Well, did you ever wonder why he left it to you?"

His hollow laughter filled the room, and he put his hands in his pockets and leaned back against the wall, resting his head against the cracking plaster. "I've done nothing but wonder that since I came back." He cleared his throat and lowered his head. "The old man told me never to come back. So why the hell would he leave it to me? I would've thought he'd be more likely to leave it to you. Or to some vagrant. Or a drinking buddy." Jake shook his head. "I have no idea why he picked me. No fucking idea."

"Do you think the reason is important?"

"I've never treated anything the old man did like it was important. Why should I start now that he's dead?"

"I suppose that's a good question. You know, I never knew my dad." She didn't know why she was telling him this. She didn't waste a whole lot of time worrying about her dad, or lack of one.

"I suppose that means you're going to tell me I should appreciate the one I had."

"No, I don't think that at all. I just think crappy parents have a lot to answer for."

He laughed again, and this time it was much more genuine. "Now on that I absolutely agree with you."

"So, can I help you today?"

"It's your day off, Cassie. I hardly think you should spend it scrubbing out this place."

"I want to. Jake, let me do this for you."

"Why do you want to do anything for me? I thought I was just your rebellion."

"My rebellion can take a backseat. For today I can just be a friend helping another friend. Two people who have something in common hanging out together."

"Is that something in common that they really like getting in each other's pants?"

She had a feeling he was trying to be offensive, but instead she was flattered that he wanted to get into her pants again. "Sure, that. And the fact that we're both trying to make lives for ourselves outside of what people told us was possible. Outside of what people told us we should want."

"All right, Cassie. I'll accept your help. But only because I'm in no position to do otherwise."

"You flatter me so. Now where can I find a mop in this place?"

BY THE TIME Cassie was done cleaning she could hardly say the place sparkled. If anything, the house seemed like it had been brushed over with a patina, leaving a dull, well-worn look to everything. But it couldn't be helped. In some ways it was charming, especially now that there wasn't a layer of dust covering every available surface. Baby steps.

Jake had been outside all day, throwing junk into a Dumpster that he'd had the disposal company bring out to the property, and making arrangements for the bigger things to be hauled away. He was also working on finding homes for the animals. By the time they got on his motorcycle and headed back into town, they were both on the brink of exhaustion.

About halfway there, it started to rain. The sky seemed to break apart as cold water poured out over everything, fat drops hammering the two of them as they rode on.

By the time they reached the apartments, they were both soaking wet, and Cassie was saying a prayer of thanks for face guards. They dismounted the bike and she tugged off her helmet, shaking out her hair, the damp ends splattering the leather jacket.

Jake turned to face her. "Thanks for your help. I really do appreciate it. I know sometimes I have a hard time showing it. But I think now I'll go ahead and pay for that muffin you dropped on the floor."

A crack of laughter burst from her lips. His displays of humor were so rare, so few and far between that they always shocked and delighted her. "Well, your generosity is appreciated. I fear the lack of revenue from that muffin was really going to affect my bottom line for the month."

"Hey, the hazards of owning a small business."

She smiled at him, and he smiled back. Such a simple thing, but it made her heart squeeze tight. Made her stomach flip over. "We're still standing in the rain," she said, her words sounding a little dazed. Because she was a little dazed. By this. By him. By whatever was happening between them.

He looked up, raindrops falling on his face, rolling over the bridge of his nose and down his cheeks. "So we are."

"Do you want to go inside and get dry?"

"Just a second."

JAKE DIDN'T OFTEN act on impulse, not anymore. But something about Cassie seemed to bring out a side of him he had long repressed. And tonight, he was acting on impulse. Again.

He wrapped his arm around her waist and tugged her against him, relishing the feeling of her soft breasts pressed against his chest. Then, before he could think it through too much, before she could protest, he brought his lips down on hers and kissed her.

Her lips were soft, wet from the rain, tasting like salt air, sex and Cassie. He dipped his tongue into her mouth, sliding it against hers, feeling her shiver beneath his touch.

She was so hot. So perfect. Everything he could ask for in a woman, and then some. He had never wanted like this, or if he had, he certainly didn't remember. And if he couldn't remember, the feeling couldn't have been this strong.

Because this kind of desire would stay with him, just the way a rainy afternoon in the library studying math had. Memories like that should've faded, and yet they hadn't. Cassie was too vibrant. When he was touching her, when he wasn't touching her. It was like holding life in his hands. Not just something alive, but the very essence of life. Warmth, beauty, air. Everything a person needed. Everything they could possibly want. And he knew without a doubt he didn't deserve to be holding her. But he was. For now, for as long as he could, he would.

And it didn't matter that it was raining. Or maybe it did. Maybe it was the rain that made the two of them together feel possible. That made this feel fresh, and new. Maybe it was the rain made him feel different, like he could have this. If only for a moment.

He wanted to push her up against the side of the building and take her there. Right there on the main street of Copper Ridge. He wanted to stake a claim on her, when he had no right to do that. He wanted to shove his control to one side and simply do as he pleased.

Dangerous. Those thoughts were dangerous. And right now, he didn't even care.

He managed to wrench himself away from her, his body protesting, his brain driving the boat for a moment as he tried to convince himself that they needed to move this somewhere a little more private.

"Let's go back around to my door," he said.

He didn't want to walk through the coffee shop with her, not now. That desire was in complete opposition to the one he had only a moment ago. To the fantasy he'd had about taking her outside so that everyone would know she was his. In reality he knew he couldn't do that to her. He couldn't link her that closely with him in public.

Because in the end, he would be leaving. And Cassie had to stay. Cassie was the one who would have to deal with the fallout of having a fling with him. And he wouldn't do that to her.

He had a feeling he wouldn't be able to leave her entirely unscathed, but on this score, he would protect her.

"Okay, I'm not going to argue."

He grabbed hold of her hand and started to lead her to his door, fumbling for the key and opening it as quickly as he could, his fingers clumsy, numb from the cold rain.

He waited for her to walk inside before he slammed the door shut behind them, making sure it was locked. Then he turned to her, his heart pounding heavily. "My hands are cold."

She pulled her shirt up over her head and gave him a defiant look. "I don't care."

"Maybe we should go upstairs instead of standing here in the entry. I don't have condoms."

"Well, the condom thing I do care slightly more about. But, happily for you, and for me, I was not actually just getting out of bed this morning when you ran into me here."

"What were you doing?"

"I was coming back from the store. Where I got these." She dug into her big purse and produced a box of condoms. "Which is…you know, a lot of them. Slightly ambitious. Especially considering you disappeared on me after…but I thought just in case. I'm an optimist."

He laughed, completely amazed that he was able to be both this turned on, and amused. "A little bit. But I like it."

"I'm glad. Because I don't think I'm going to suddenly transform into a smooth-talking siren."

"I wouldn't like it. Because then you wouldn't be you."

Her dark eyes, which had been sparkling with humor, suddenly took on a glossy sheen. "I don't think anyone's ever said anything like that to me before."

"Anything like what?"

"Like… Anything that made me feel like being me was an asset."

His heart squeezed tight, and he hated those who had come before him. The people who had been in her life before this moment, for having her around all those years and never saying just how special she was. And then he hated himself, for realizing it back when they had been in high school, and never saying it then. Because someone should have. This woman should know how special she was.

"I need you to be you. I don't think you can possibly know how much." He shouldn't have said those words. And yet, he couldn't keep them to himself, either. She needed to hear them, but it should be from a better man. From a man who wasn't going to leave her, who wasn't going to put her business up for sale to serve his own interests.

Are you still going to do that, you prick?

He didn't really have a choice. It had nothing to do with her, it never had.

But everything right now was about her. Everything. He felt like he was being kept alive by her very presence, which was a strange and terrifying sensation. And also one he didn't particularly want to lose.

He didn't understand it, either. But what he did understand was the hum of sexual attraction that burned beneath the feelings that were swelling in his chest. He couldn't do anything with the feelings even if he'd wanted to, so he figured he would just follow the sexual attraction. That he knew. That he could deal with.

It was all they could ever have.

And since she'd been forward-thinking enough to buy condoms, they could have it right now.

He took her into his arms and kissed her deeply, gripping

the clasp on her bra and undoing it with one hand before moving deeper into the entryway.

She pulled away from him, her eyes wide. "You're very good at that."

"I've honed some very specific skills over the years. If your transmission needs replacing, I'm your guy. If your bra needs removing... I'm pretty good at that, too."

She blinked rapidly, a smile curving her lips. "What else are you good at?"

He pushed her back against the wall, kissing her neck. "What else?" he whispered. His lips were close to her ear, so close he couldn't resist biting her gently. "I've been told I really know my way around a woman's body." He lifted his hand and cupped her breast, squeezing her nipple between his thumb and forefinger. And suddenly, thoughts of all of his previous experience fled from his brain. The words he'd been about to say drying up on his tongue. Because no other women mattered. "I suppose that doesn't matter. The only thing that matters is that I know my way around your body."

"I don't have any complaints."

"What do you like?"

"You."

He kissed her cheek. "I'm flattered by that, honey. But I really do want to know."

"I... I liked what you did in the apartment last night. No one has ever done that for me before."

"What? No one has ever gone down on you before?"

Color flooded her cheeks. "Well, technically now someone has. But before that..."

"How long were you married to that asshole?"

"Eight years."

"Something was seriously wrong with him."

"Didn't really think much about it. That's the hazard of inexperience, I suppose."

"It's not a hazard of inexperience, it's the hazard of sleeping with assholes."

She wrapped her arms around his neck and kissed him, tugging at the waistband of his pants. He helped her get his jeans and underwear off, then ripped his shirt over his head when he realized he was standing there in nothing but a black T-shirt, probably looking a bit like a dick.

She didn't seem to mind.

He unsnapped her jeans and made quick work of the rest of her clothes. Then he stopped for a moment, trying to get a handle on his breathing, and just enjoyed the feeling of being skin to skin with her, every inch of him touching every inch of her.

"There is something I do have experience with." She met his eyes, a determined glint in them.

"Oh really?"

"Yes, and you asked me what I liked. Well, I can't say I've particularly liked this in the past. But I'm feeling inspired. And I think we should follow bursts of inspiration."

"Do you?" he asked, arching one eyebrow upward.

"Sure. If I hadn't followed my inspiration for this coffee shop I would still be living with my mother. Inspiration is a good thing." She extricated herself from his hold and lowered herself to her knees in front of him. He felt like he'd been slugged in the stomach. The vision of Cassie, kneeling before him, her brown eyes locked with his, was something out of the fantasy he'd never even dared let himself have.

"Cassie," he said, his voice rough.

But whatever he had been about to say was cut off, lost to him completely when she wrapped her hand around the base of his cock and leaned in, flicking her tongue over the head. She tightened her grip on him as she took him more deeply into her mouth, the edge of her tongue sliding down his length.

He laced his fingers through her hair and fought the urge to let his head fall back. He wanted to watch her. Wanted to watch this. The sight of her lips around him was enough to push him over the edge now.

And if that wasn't enough, the physical sensation had him ready to beg for more. Her heat, the slickness. But it was only an echo of what he really wanted. Where he wanted to be.

"Okay, Cassie, I'm going to need you to stop now." He could barely force the words out through his tightened throat.

She moved away from him, her eyes glassy, her expression dazed. "Did I do something wrong?"

"No. You're doing it a little bit too right. And I don't want this to be over yet."

He reached into her purse and pulled out the condom box, tearing it open and pulling out a plastic packet that he made quick work of. While he rolled it on to his length she stood, her eyes fixed to him, like he was a particularly decadent dessert.

He couldn't say he'd ever had a woman look at him quite like that before.

Part of him wanted to stand there and enjoy it. But a much bigger part of him wanted to be inside her thirty seconds ago, so he decided to forgo the pleasure of being stared at.

He pressed her against the wall, gripping her chin and kissing her deep while he took hold of her thigh with his other hand and tugged it up over his hip, opening her damp center to him. He pressed the head of his cock against her entrance and tested her before sliding the rest of the way in, gritting his teeth in a valiant attempt to keep from exploding.

"Fuck." He said the word more like a prayer than a curse.

He flexed his hips, thrusting hard, and a rough sound escaped her lips.

"Too hard?" he asked, concerned that he was asking too much of her.

"No." She put her hands on his butt, encouraging him to keep going. "If you stop, I might kill you."

"You wouldn't."

"I will poison your muffin."

"You're ruthless, baby."

"I am now. Ruthless about what I want. And I want you."

He withdrew from her, then thrust deep. "The feeling is mutual."

And then talking was impossible, because he was lost in the sensation of being inside of her. Lost in his need. His need to be consumed by her, to consume her. His need to have everything. All of her.

He buried his face in her neck, bracing himself as his climax started to build, as it began to overtake him. He didn't want to finish first. The other selfish guy who took what he wanted without a care for her satisfaction. He wanted to be different. He wanted to be better. He wanted to wipe all the memories she had of her husband away, and replace them with memories of him. Of course, he needed to be worthy of that, and he wasn't certain he was.

His limbs began to shake, his blood roaring through his veins. He slipped his hand between her thighs and rubbed his thumb over her clit, desperate for her to find her release. He stroked her, once, twice, and felt a shudder wrack her body, felt her internal muscles pulse around his cock.

That was all he needed. He let go, her name on his lips as he found his own release, as it overtook him completely.

He rested against her for a moment before withdrawing, looking around the small entry area. "No trash can?"

"No." She laughed.

"What's so funny?"

"Nothing is funny, really. Just...great."

His heart started thundering faster in his chest, a feat he hadn't imagined possible, considering it was still raging from his recent orgasm. "I am going to need a trash can, though," he said looking down.

"Oh! Of course. Well, you can come up to my place and use mine. And we have a few uh...left, and we can use the rest of those."

Heat streaked through him. "You're very ambitious."

"It's a new thing I'm trying. High standards."

"I like the way you think."

"I'm glad. Because I don't just set goals, I meet them." She smiled at him, her determination and enthusiasm infectious.

He marveled at the difference in the way they approached life. She was breaking free. Uncovering all of the things she had kept buried for so long. In contrast, when he had left town, he had foreclosed on his feelings. Boarding them up, and leaving them vacant. Making sure he couldn't access any of them again.

Because when he opened himself up, bad things escaped. He envied her in some ways. Most of all he regretted the fact that she needed a man who was open to her, too. And he could never be that for her.

But he could be with her now. And if that was all he could get, he would take it.

CHAPTER EIGHT

CASSIE HAD NEVER been so happy in her life. She was just focusing all her energy on not facing the fact that that happiness was a fantasy, and not reality.

Because Jake wasn't going to stay in Copper Ridge. Jake wasn't integrated into her real life. Her freedom was confined to the bedroom.

Well, that wasn't strictly true.

They had thoroughly explored their chemistry in several different rooms. Kitchen, living room, her bedroom and his. Not to mention the entryway to their apartments, which she could no longer walk through without remembering what it had been like to be pinned up against the wall by Jake while he thrust into her, hard and deep.

She smiled happily and put the lid on a paper cup, turning and handing it to Lydia, the president of Copper Ridge's Chamber of Commerce. The other woman was on her phone, but offered a broad smile and a finger wave as she took her coffee and walked back out of the café.

Suddenly, Cassie was overwhelmed with a feeling of sadness. Which was strange considering just how happy she'd felt a moment before. It was something to do with standing here in the coffee shop, not knowing how long she would have it. Not knowing how long she would have any of the things that meant the most to her. Jake among them.

He really was important. He was becoming essential.

But it was different than things had been with her husband. With Allen, it had been about maintaining a certain type of life. It hadn't ever been about him specifically, and she was sort of ashamed to realize that. To admit it to herself.

Being married to him had been about realizing an ideal, an ideal she realized...well, hadn't been ideal. At least not for her. It hadn't been about love, it had been about changing herself so she could be more acceptable to the people around her. And being with Jake wasn't like that. She didn't care what anyone thought about her and Jake. Granted, no one knew about her and Jake yet, but she already knew she wouldn't care.

But if she wanted Jake, in any capacity besides the temporary, it wasn't going to be a smooth path. It was not going to be the path of least resistance, nor one that earned her approval.

She didn't care. She realized right then that being with Jake was going to mean sacrificing that sweet, nonconfrontational comfort she prized. Interestingly, she didn't think anything she'd ever done had been sacrificial. Yes, it had been to please other people, but it had been about her own comfort. Not just about theirs.

She was afraid of confrontation, afraid of making people angry at her, because then they might not want her anymore. She'd gotten angry about losing her house. Her flowers. Her husband. But she hadn't fought for any of it. She hadn't even tried.

But Jake was changing that, had been from the moment he'd come to town. She'd pushed against him almost immediately. Had fought back, had demanded what she wanted.

And she liked that. Wanted to keep doing it. Wanted to keep being strong.

The revelation was shocking enough that it took her a few minutes to realize she was staring straight through Ace Coleman like he wasn't even there.

"Oh." She blinked. "Hi, Ace. Did you need your Red Eye?"

"Yeah, late night last night. Another late night tonight."

"The life of a bartender." She started a double shot of espresso and filled up a medium-size coffee cup while the shots were running. Then she dumped the shots in the cup and put the lid on. "Here you go."

She took his money and made change on autopilot, still considering what she might be willing to do. What she might be willing to sacrifice.

She looked around the coffee shop, weight settling on her chest. She knew everyone in here. Knew everyone by name. And when tourism picked up later in the spring there would be strangers for her to meet.

She would miss the building if it were sold. But it occurred to her that without a doubt, she would miss Jake more.

And just like that she realized that her decision was made.

WHEN JAKE GOT back from the ranch that night he had a surprise waiting for him on his doorstep. It was his very favorite kind of surprise. A Cassie-shaped surprise.

Over the past two weeks she had become an essential part of his day. He didn't leave at night anymore after they were finished making love. He stayed. Mornings had become something wonderful, instead of something to be dreaded.

Because he no longer woke up to a blaring alarm clock, cold sheets and bone-deep exhaustion. No, he woke up to a blaring alarm clock and the warm, curvy woman in his arms.

And now she was here waiting for him when he was ready to drop dead from exhaustion after working on cleaning up the junk around his dad's old property. She was here, looking like home, and rest, and everything he needed right in that moment.

She had a habit of doing that. Looking at him like he was important. Like she saw all kinds of good things that no one else ever had. She smiled at him when she was helping him deal with ranching responsibilities—and when he was helping her bake scones for the coffee shop, because it really was the least he could do with all the help she'd given him.

Not a reserved smile, either. A real smile. One that made him feel like he could do no wrong.

He didn't think he deserved it, but he'd damn sure take it.

"Well, aren't you a sight for sore eyes."

She smiled, and he felt like it was a tally in the relatively vacant win column on the score sheet he kept of his life. "Am I?"

"Very definitely." He stepped past her, leaning in and dropping a kiss on her lips before unlocking the front door. "I need to get cleaned up a bit, though. Then maybe we can have some dinner."

"Okay." Cassie was vibrating with energy, even more than usual. It was one of the things he liked best about her. She had a lot of enthusiasm for what she was doing with her life, for life in general, and it only seemed to be growing.

He stripped his shirt off and threw it on the floor, wandering into the bathroom and removing the rest of his clothes before turning the shower on. It was an interesting thing having someone waiting for him when he got home. Something he hadn't ever missed, because he never had it. Something he realized now was most definitely missing from his life.

Don't go getting attached to it. He turned the water to the shower on and waited for it to get warm before he stepped inside.

He heard the bathroom door open, and saw Cassie's silhouette through the textured glass. He could tell that she was naked, and immediately his cock started getting hard.

"I figured, seeing as you have me now, I would make sure

you knew you didn't have to pleasure yourself in the shower."
She opened the shower door and stepped inside, all smooth skin
and gorgeous curves.

"Pleasure myself, huh?"

"Well, what would you call it?"

"Nothing fancy. Just a little jacking off."

She worried her bottom lip, looking like she was considering the words very carefully. "Jacking off. Serviceable. Definitely descriptive."

He wrapped his arms around her and kissed her nose. "I will
never understand how you can make my cock so hard it hurts
and make me laugh at the same time."

"I don't know. I can only say that I'm honored." She kissed
his lips. "Honored both to make you laugh and to make your
cock hard."

"Nice girl Cassie Ventimiglia, talking dirty to me in the
shower."

"Nice girls know how to have fun, too."

"Yes, we're smashing stereotypes all over the place lately."

"No more talking." She kissed him again, this time deeper,
moving her hands over his chest and around his back, down
to his ass.

"Demanding."

She nipped his bottom lip. "What did I just say?"

His erection pulsed, arousal flooding through him. If she
wanted to play this game, he was not going to stop her. She
moved away from him, revealing the condom packet in her
hand. She opened it slowly and positioned it on the end of his
length, rolling it on.

"Foreplay is great," she said, "but we don't need any of that
right now."

He was not going to argue. He reversed their positions, pressing her against the wall as he thrust deep inside of her. He kept
his eyes open, trained on hers. It was a surreal thing, being here
with her now, when just a few short weeks ago this had been

nothing but a fantasy. It had been his own hand on his cock, not her tight, slick body.

It was real now, she was real. And it was better than he ever could've imagined.

Need built between them, each thrust bringing them closer and closer to the peak. She clung tightly to his shoulders as he rode her hard, and when they reached it, they reached it together.

They stood there, sated, and he didn't want to move away. He wanted to stay inside her. Wanted this moment to last.

"Oh, Jake." He loved it when she did that. When she said his name like that, like it was her own personal revelation. "Oh, Jake, I love you."

CHAPTER NINE

WOW. SHE HAD really said it. She meant it, so she didn't regret it. But she did sort of regret that Jake was looking at her like she'd grown another head. That was not the typical postcoital expression she was used to getting from him.

"Aren't you going to say something?" she asked.

They were still standing underneath the water, reminiscent of that day in the rain. But she didn't feel triumphant right now; instead she felt a sense of foreboding.

"What is there to say?"

"Well, *I love you, too* is typically the desired outcome of that kind of declaration, but I can't say I was really expecting that. Though I was expecting a little bit more than the angry face you're giving me right now."

Jake opened the shower door and got out, grabbing a towel off the rack and running it over his chest. "You knew this wasn't permanent."

"Yeah, I knew it. But I decided to go full rebel and not play by the rules. I fell in love with you."

"How is that even possible?"

"How is it not possible, Jake?" She followed him out of the shower, grabbing the towel out of his hands and running it over her own body, leaving herself mostly damp.

"I don't even know how to answer that."

"Well, fair enough because I don't know how to answer your question."

"I feel like I did a pretty good job of making a case for the fact that I'm kind of an asshole."

"I have yet to see a whole lot of evidence of that." She should've known he would be like this. Really, she should have.

"Did you miss the part where I burned down my father's fields?"

"Nope. Fresh in my memory."

"Then you must realize that you don't make any sense."

"Okay, so let's just stop this right now. I love you, and you're not talking me out of it. So you can stop trying."

He picked his jeans up off the floor and put them on, zipping them carefully. "Did you forget one little problem?"

"What problem?"

"I'm going to sell your coffee shop. I'm endangering your livelihood." He stared at her hard, and she didn't say anything. "I'm not staying here."

"I know. I thought… I was thinking that if you want to, I mean, that is if you want me to, I would go back to Seattle with you."

His face went blank, his frame stiff. "You want to come back to Seattle with me?"

"Yes. I do."

"What the hell is wrong with you? You're just going to drop everything and come with me?"

"It isn't like that." Cassie took a deep breath. "I was thinking about it and I realized that the worst thing I do, and I do it over and over again, is play it safe. I do things that make other people happy so that I don't have to take chances. I don't have to make mistakes, or struggle. And I especially don't have to deal with the consequences. Because it's all someone else's fault. Well, I'm tired of that. I want to take a chance. And I want to take it with you."

"Are you sure you aren't just changing the narrative so you can revert to type?"

That barb hit its intended target, sent a bit of insecurity running through her. "I'm not." And she knew she didn't sound all that confident. But she wasn't used to this. Wasn't used to confrontation, wasn't used to holding her ground.

"You sound real certain."

"Well, what's the point either way?" She was feeling angry now. "I mean, you're going to put me into a precarious position anyway once you leave. I might as well take a chance on this."

"Oh, so you want to come with me because I'm forcing your hand? I've never been so flattered."

"That isn't it. You're just making me mad." She swallowed hard. "It's always been you, Jake. Always. Back in high school and now. I almost took a chance then, but I missed it. I missed my chance. I knew I couldn't miss it this time, not because I was afraid. I started to say something that night in the library and I changed my mind, I let fear get the best of me. And I lost my opportunity for fifteen years. I was not going to lose this opportunity, too."

Jake turned away from her, his broad, muscular back filling her vision. Then everything blurred, tears filling her eyes. Because she knew this was the end. She knew he wasn't going to soften, wasn't going to make his own declaration of love.

Declarations of love didn't go this way.

"I'm not sorry I said it." She wouldn't be sorry. She would not be sorry for her existence anymore. For taking up space. For being the choice she often feared her mother wished she hadn't made, for being a disappointment to her husband. "I'm glad I said it. I'm glad I took the chance. And I hope years down the road when you look back on this you'll wish you'd taken the chance, too. You'll wish you were as brave as I was. Tough, tattooed Jake Caldwell, too afraid to take chances."

Jake turned around, his expression fierce. "You think that's it? You think I'm afraid to take chances? Maybe I'm just too damn smart to make the same mistakes more than once. I know what happens when I give free rein to my emotions. Shit burns, Cassie. And so do all of my relationships." He pushed his hands through his hair. "I am not the guy you give things up for."

"Maybe not. But I'm the woman who takes chances for herself. Because I deserve to try for happiness. I thought I deserved to try for this."

"You deserve a hell of a lot more than me."

"Only because you don't really see yourself, Jake. You were so angry because all anyone ever saw you as was a bad boy. A screwup. But you don't see yourself as anything more. You're your own biggest enemy."

"Maybe so. Or maybe I just see myself clearly."

"I've never fought for anything before. I just kind of let things happen. I'm fighting now. I want to fight for you. I love you, Jake. There, I said it again. I officially have no pride."

"I can't love you back."

Cassie's eyes filled with tears, her chest so heavy she thought she might fall to the ground, thought she might never be able to get back up again. So she took a deep breath, used all her strength to stay standing. "Okay, then."

"Cassie…"

"There's nothing you can say to make it better. So don't even try."

"I wasn't going to."

That almost made her laugh. "Of course not. Were you going to rub it in?"

"I don't know. I don't know what I was going to say."

"Well, I'm going to say goodbye. There's only so much my ego can take. This was a great growth experience but I can't say I'm eager to stand around and marinate in it. Please don't come buy your muffin from me tomorrow. I hope wherever you do buy one, it has raisins in it."

She put her clothes on as quickly as possible, not looking at him again. Ignoring the fact that her T-shirt was sticking to her wet skin. Then she walked through the apartment and stormed out the door, only then realizing that she'd left her shoes there. Oh well, it was too late. Those shoes were dead to her. She would have to get new shoes.

A sob wracked her chest, and tears started spilling down her cheeks. She scrubbed her forearm across her face, but it didn't stop the tears from falling. She had a feeling nothing would.

She felt like the world was ending, and she hadn't felt that way when she got divorced. But then, she'd already known this was different.

Because Jake was her choice. Jake was the one thing she'd stuck her neck out for. Jake was the one thing she'd taken a chance on. Jake had been her decision, and her decision alone. And the failure of that was all hers.

The heartbreak was all hers, too.

She knew from past experience that what-ifs could consume you, could keep you up at night with the possibilities of what might have been. But, standing here, with absolute certainty, didn't feel a whole lot better right now.

She only hoped it would take fewer than fifteen years to get over Jake this time around.

But she wasn't overly optimistic.

BY THE NEXT morning Jake had two things: a hangover and a plan.

He was a little bit happier with the plan than he was with the hangover, but he imagined it was par for the breakup course. He wouldn't know; he didn't think he'd ever been involved in a breakup before. Not calling a woman you were sleeping with the morning after didn't count.

This was more like an official breakup. He could tell, because he felt like wolves had burst through his chest in the night and savaged his innards. He'd felt a similar pain at other times in his life. When his mother had died, and when his father had made him leave the ranch. Heartbreak, maybe. Or just plain old grief.

Either way it sucked.

But he couldn't ask Cassie to give up her life here for him. He'd lied to her last night when he told her he couldn't love her. But he'd told her the truth when he said he wasn't the kind of guy worth giving up a life for.

All he had to do was look at the evidence of his past to prove that. He'd never done anything but screw things up, had never done anything but give the people he cared about grief. He'd never been able to be good enough for his father. Disappointment was all he ever saw reflected in the old man's eyes.

It would kill him to watch the love in Cassie's eyes transform into that. Slowly, over the course of years, he was certain it would. Because his relationships had never gone any other way.

So it was decided. He was going to leave. He would turn over the cleanup of the property to someone else, and he didn't care if that cut into his profits. The other thing he was doing was signing the building that housed the coffee shop over to Cassie. He wouldn't be out anything. Not out of pocket anyway. Sure, he would have to get a bigger loan to buy the mechanic shop, but that didn't matter. The building only had value because of Cassie's business. It only had value because of the work that had gone into restoring Old Town. He hadn't been a part of that. But Cassie had been. She was the one who deserved to reap the rewards.

He was back out at the ranch for one last visit. One last time to look around. To yell at some demons. To rage at things that couldn't be fixed.

That was how he found himself standing at the edge of the field. The dirt in front of him was still a mix of ash and soil, and nothing more. Unsurprisingly, there were no answers here. He didn't know why he'd bothered. He didn't know what he'd

been looking for. Or maybe he did. He'd been looking for answers, but there was nothing here but ghosts. Nothing here but
memory.

There was nothing new at all. The time for getting answers
was over. His father was dead; they could never reconcile. Jake
could never scream at him and ask why nothing he'd ever done
had been good enough. Jake could never say he was sorry.

The time for all of that had passed. And he'd been hiding.

So many things left unsaid.

That made him think of Cassie again. Mostly because everything made him think of Cassie, but partly because of what
she'd told him about that night in the library. And how she'd
almost said something to him then. That was the night he'd almost kissed her. But instead it was the night everything had
gone to hell.

Yes, his past was littered with things left unsaid. Kisses left
ungiven.

You're just doing it again. Repeating the cycle.

No, it wasn't the same. He was making a conscious decision
to turn away from her, because it was the best thing for her.

Maybe you could stop running?

He was ready to kick his inner voice in the balls. He didn't
have anything for himself here. Nothing but shitty memories.

He turned away from the field and headed back toward the
house, walking up the porch, purposely stepping on the board
that flexed beneath his weight. He pulled open the screen door,
and went inside.

He wondered what other people felt when they came home.
If they felt a sense of belonging. If they felt happy. All he felt
was like he was being crushed beneath something. Beneath too
many words that could never be spoken. Beneath the mistakes
he could never fix.

He walked up the stairs, each one creaking beneath his feet.
They had always done that. In a weird way it was kind of comforting. Familiar.

There was a stack of papers on the desk in his dad's room that he wanted to grab before he left. Just in case it had personal information..Here there were some report cards and other personal documents of his and he didn't really want to leave them behind for whoever ended up inhabiting or cleaning the place.

Their existence was as inexplicable as the old man's decision to leave him the property. He didn't know why his dad had kept them. He'd thrown Jake away quickly enough. Why not the papers documenting his life?

He pushed open the door and picked the papers up from his father's desk, shuffling through them. He'd meant to do this weeks ago but he'd simply looked at it all and taken the first few sheets off the pile, then left it.

He sat on the edge of the bed, kicking up a cloud of dust as he did. He flipped through documents, absorbing himself in the past. In receipts and shitty grades. In notes from teachers.

And then, somewhere in the middle, was an envelope with his name on it. Another report card maybe. He tore the envelope open, his stomach tightening when he did.

It was a letter.

Jake,
If you have this letter I'm probably dead. No getting around that fact. I started a few of them years ago and never sent them. So I imagine the only one you'll end up with is one you find.

I wasn't a good father. But you know that. I'm not good at apologizing, either, but I owe you one.

I'm sorry. It doesn't seem like enough. Because I said a lot of other things when you were growing up that should never have been said. And *I'm sorry* doesn't take them away.

I can't think of a better way to show you that than to leave everything with you. I know I said you couldn't handle it, but I was wrong. I don't know what you've been up to all these years but I know you did good.

Dad

Jake's hands were shaking when he put the letter down. There was no explanation there. No grand answers. No declaration of familial love, but then, that just wasn't in his dad's nature.

But there was something better than that.

His dad had trusted that he'd turned out okay. Had trusted that he could leave all of his properties with him, and that he wouldn't make a hash of it. Had trusted he wouldn't burn anything down.

He looked around the room, and things suddenly seemed different to him.

He wished his dad had sent the letters. And Jake wished he had come back at some point while his father was alive. But he'd been afraid. He had been afraid that he wouldn't be able to fix it. Afraid that no apology would ever be enough. It would've been. He realized that now. On both sides, *I'm sorry* would have fixed a lot of things. Talking would've fixed a lot of things.

He had been planning on riding out of town today. Had been planning on leaving today much the way he'd left fifteen years earlier.

But he wasn't going to do that now. He wasn't going to leave things unsaid. Not again.

Fifteen years ago he'd been nothing more than a scared boy. Running away from mistakes he'd made, letting someone else's words dictate how he felt about himself. Dictate who he was going to be. He'd spent all that time away licking his wounds and trying to become worthy of something. Anything.

And he'd come back trying to show them. Show them all that he'd changed when what he'd really done was hide.

But he had someone who thought he was worthy already. And that was worth more than a mechanic shop in Seattle. It was worth more than anything. And if it wasn't too late, he had to see if he could prove that to her.

Something Cassie had said was moving through his mind, over and over again. She hadn't been brave enough to fight. Because she'd been too afraid to fail. And that was what he'd been doing, for the past fifteen years. All under the guise of being a better man. He had convinced himself that what he was doing was protecting the world. From his anger, from his emotions. But what he had really been doing was protecting himself. Selling himself short.

Well, he wasn't going to do that anymore.

He wanted Cassie Ventimiglia, and while he wasn't entirely certain any man could be worthy of her, he was going to go and get her.

Because without her nothing mattered. Without love, nothing mattered.

CHAPTER TEN

CASSIE WAS EXHAUSTED by the time her shift ended. Emotionally and physically. She loved working in the coffee shop, and the only thing she ever would have traded it for was Jake Caldwell, but that didn't mean it didn't take its toll.

Making coffee with a broken heart was especially taxing.

She walked out from behind the counter and was about to turn the sign in the window when she saw a very familiar figure walking toward the door. She froze, unsure of whether she should scamper back behind the counter and hide, or if she should jerk the door open and fling herself into his arms. Probably she should find a middle ground. She wasn't good at middle ground with Jake.

No, considering they'd gone from bickering to her telling him she loved him in the space of only a few weeks, it was pretty clear middle ground was not a place they could inhabit.

Since she couldn't decide on a course of action, she was sort of standing there staring like a deer caught in the headlights. And it did not take long for him to notice her.

"Crap crappity crap," she said under her breath.

And Jake just kept moving closer. He pushed open the door and came face-to-face with her, his blue eyes intense.

"I have something to say to you."

"I hope it isn't more mean things," she said. "Because I'm kind of over that."

"No, and I'm sorry there were mean things. Any mean things. You didn't deserve mean things."

"I know," she said, her heart thundering heavily.

"I think I had a revelation."

"Well, this should be interesting." She crossed her arms beneath her breasts, trying to stay immune to his apology, trying not to melt. Trying to look casual, and not like she was dying to hear the words he was about to say. Really, when people had news to deliver, they should just get to the point instead of making a big song and dance about it.

"I went back to the house this morning. I was going to leave. I had made my decision. I was going to pay someone to finish cleaning up the property, and I was going to leave this building to you."

Shock speared her in the chest. "Jake, I never wanted charity. I never wanted you to give me the building. I wanted to buy it."

"I know. I know you didn't want anything unreasonable. But I wanted to leave it to you. Because this is your blood, sweat and tears. This is all your work. The reason the building matters is because of what you've done. You should be proud of yourself."

She felt a warm glow in her chest. "I am."

"Good. I'm glad about that. But I changed my mind."

"Jake, this is pretty close to being mean. You said you weren't going to be mean."

"You can still have the building. It's just that I decided not to leave."

"What?" The warmth was growing now, spreading through her, and it felt an awful lot like hope.

"When I went back to the house today, I was going through

some paperwork that I knew I needed to take care of before I let anyone else in. I found a letter from my dad."

All of the breath rushed out of her body. "What did it say?"

"The long and the short of it? He apologized. And I realized that we could have been spared a lot of years of hurt, if we hadn't been such idiots. There are a lot of mistakes that can't be fixed, a lot of hurts that can't be erased completely, but *I'm sorry* is a pretty good Band-Aid. I wish we would've at least tried to put it on there."

"I don't need an apology from you, Jake."

"Well, that's good, because I don't want to give you an apology. Well, I do. But that's not all I want to give you."

She took a deep breath. "What do you want to give me?"

In response, he took a step toward her, gripped her arms and pulled her toward him, dropping a kiss on her lips. It was deep, hard and short. Over way too soon.

"I'm a little confused now," she said.

"I love you."

Her mouth fell open. "Say it again."

"I love you, Cassie. I did last night when I sent you away, when I told you I couldn't love you. I was lying because I was afraid. And like you said, because I didn't think I was worthy. I'm still not sure I am, but I want more. You're the bravest person I've ever known. You're overcoming things instead of letting them own you."

He took a deep breath. "I thought if I left Copper Ridge I would escape all of the bad shit in my life. But all of my demons came with me because they weren't really about this place, they weren't really about my dad. They lived inside of me. I've spent a long time just trying to get by. Protecting myself from wanting anything too badly. Because I didn't want to be hurt again. I loved my dad, and he rejected me. I messed things up. And I've spent all these years afraid that I would do something like that again. Afraid that if I ever loved anyone all it would do was push them away. That they would find out I wasn't good enough. And Cassie, the last thing I wanted was to see your love for me turn into indifference, or worse, contempt."

"That's never going to happen." She hurt for him, for the pain he'd been through. For the pain they both had been through. "I saw you. Even then."

"I think it's kind of amazing that you did."

"We've always had a lot more in common than we realized."

"I don't want to be safe anymore, not if it means being alone. Not if it means not having you."

Cassie looked into his eyes, at the sincerity there, at the love. No one had ever looked at her that way before. Like she was everything they could ever want. It was exhilarating, and terrifying. And she wanted it to last more than anything. "What about your mechanic shop? I don't want you to give up anything for me. I know what it's like to be responsible for crushing somebody's dream. I worry that my mother always regretted choosing me over the man she was in love with. I don't want to be in that position with you."

"First of all, you're the only choice. That's all there is to it. Second of all, I can open a mechanic shop anywhere. It was never about that, really. That was a thing that I could pour myself into, that didn't cost me very much in terms of my emotions. I wanted it, I worked for it. But it only mattered because it gave me something to do that wasn't dealing with my shit."

"I can kind of understand that."

"Well, it would figure. Since you were about as emotionally messed up as I am."

"Hey, I've been working on myself for a couple of years now. I'm a little more advanced than you are."

He laughed. "I suppose you are."

"What are you going to do?"

"I figured we could break down the partitions between the apartments. Live up there. You could continue to run The Grind. I could assist. I've learned how to make scones. Maybe I'll open a mechanic shop. Right here in town. And if your car breaks down, I will be here to help."

"A live-in mechanic… That is tempting, Jake, I won't lie."

"I thought it might be."

She chewed her thumbnail. "Are you worried about your reputation? About what people will think of you? I mean, we don't have to stay here. We can go anywhere you want."

"No," he said, his voice firm. "This is your home. And mine. I want to stay here. Anything else would be running. And I don't really care what anyone else thinks. I have changed. And I can prove it to them. I'm not afraid to do that."

"I'm so proud of you, Jake. I really am."

"Are you afraid of what people might think of you being with me? Of what your mother might think?"

She laughed. "Unfortunately, it's not even a very fair test. My mom will just be happy I'm with someone. As far as she's concerned relationships are the holy grail. And as for everyone else? They'll learn to love you. Otherwise I won't serve them coffee. And I'll save all the muffins for you. All your detractors will be muffinless."

"That's a pretty intense threat."

"And I mean it. You're mine, Jake Caldwell. You aren't a bad boy, you're my man. My very good man. And I'm proud of you."

"And you, Cassie Ventimiglia, are most definitely your own woman. And I wouldn't have you any other way."

"I love you, Jake."

"I love you, too, Cassie." He took her into his arms and kissed her, long and deep, the kiss they should've shared fifteen years ago. "Even if it came a little late, I'm glad it happened." He had obviously been thinking the same thing.

"Maybe it didn't come late. Maybe it came at just the right time."

"That's right. I think maybe we both had to go on a journey before we were ready to meet here."

"If that's the case, then you're just in time."

He brushed his hand over her cheek, and she went ahead and let herself melt. She wasn't going to hold back. Not with him. "That's good to know. I don't have a white horse. I have a Harley and I'm not exactly a white knight…"

"I'm fine with that. I like you with an edge. I'd never ask you to be anything different."

He tightened his hold on her, his blue eyes intent on hers. "In that case, are you ready to ride off into the sunset with me?"

Cassie leaned in and kissed his cheek. "I'm ready to ride with you forever."

Jake smiled, a true smile that she felt all the way down to her toes. "Forever sounds just about right."

EPILOGUE

PEOPLE HAD BEEN complimenting Cassie on her engagement ring all day. It wasn't getting old. She doubted it ever would. This time around was so much different from the first time she'd gotten married.

Because this was Jake, and there was no one like Jake. And because Cassie finally felt like herself. Which was a much better place to be in when you were pledging yourself to someone forever and ever.

The past six months had been the best of her life, no question. Business at The Grind was booming, they'd set a date for their wedding, and Jake was about to open his very own mechanic shop.

Happily, it hadn't taken any time at all for the citizens of Copper Ridge to accept that Jake Caldwell was most definitely good people. If her stamp of approval hadn't done it, Jake's work ethic most certainly had.

Well, and some of it probably had to do with the fact that he was smoking hot. Even though he was taken, it didn't mean that the women in town didn't enjoy getting their car worked on by the best-looking mechanic in a hundred-mile radius. Possibly in the entire world. But she might be biased.

Though she didn't think so.

The door to the coffee shop opened, and a familiar but elusive face walked in. Unlike his brother Eli, Connor Garrett was rarely around these days. He rubbed his hand over his beard and approached the counter, stuffing his hands in his pockets. He looked like he had lost weight.

It was no secret that the past couple of years had been rough for him.

"Hi, Connor, what brings you in?"

His gaze landed on her left hand. "Engaged?"

Classic Connor, not very talkative.

"Yes, recently."

"Congratulations. Nice when you find that special someone." His voice was gruff, definitely not projecting much joy. But she couldn't say she blamed him.

"I would say so. What can I get for you?"

"Just a coffee. I'm meeting Liss here in a little bit to discuss some business things."

"Oh, she helping you with some accounting for the ranch?"

"No. If everything goes smoothly, we're going to be renting out one of the houses on the property to be used as a bed-and-breakfast."

The idea of more lodging right near town definitely appealed to Cassie. The Garrett Ranch was a couple of miles inland, but it was close enough that a B and B on the property would probably benefit The Grind.

"That's a great idea, Connor!" She handed him his coffee and he took it with a curt nod.

"It's not a bad one." And she had a feeling that was the friendliest remark she would get out of him.

He turned and walked to a table, taking a seat and busying

himself by staring fixedly at the table's surface, not making eye contact with anyone.

The door opened again and Jake came in, covered in grease and wearing a broad smile.

Cassie leaned over the counter. "Kiss me, but don't touch me."

"You don't ask for much, do you?" He leaned in, careful to let only their lips touch and nothing else.

"I do. I ask for a whole lot. At least I do now."

"And I'm so glad you do. Because if you hadn't, Cassie, I would've let you get away. You were the braver of the two of us. You have no idea how happy I am about that."

"And you have no idea how happy I am that you are ready to stop running."

"That's right, honey. The only running I'm going to do from now on is going to be to run toward you."

She'd always lived in Copper Ridge. From the moment she was born, and she couldn't imagine ever living anywhere else. But it was Jake that made Copper Ridge truly feel like home.

Because he was here. And he had her heart. Now and always.

* * * * *

Part Time Cowboy

Dear Reader,

I chose to set the little town of Copper Ridge up in the northwestern corner of Oregon because, to me, it's got some of the most beautiful scenery in the world. Mountains, evergreens, ranch land and the ocean. A little bit of everything lovely.

Of course, after choosing the setting for a series, populating the town is next. With shops and homes, with people to live in them and work in them.

I love stories that center around family, particularly groups of siblings, and the first family that came to my mind were the Garretts—a group of siblings who have supported each other through great times and bad times, who still get together every week for dinner, conversation and the chance to insult and encourage each other.

The first Garrett you'll meet is Eli, the upstanding brother who takes care of everyone, not just in his family, but in the whole community. And I hope you love him as much as I do.

I hope you enjoy their story, the Garrett family and the town of Copper Ridge.

Happy reading!

Maisey

To Haven. I've dedicated a lot of books to you,
but in truth, you deserve them all. You're the
reason I get anything done, and the reason I
believe in love and happily-ever-afters.
I'm so grateful that I've got you.

CHAPTER ONE

WHOEVER SAID YOU couldn't go home again had clearly never been to Copper Ridge. The place hadn't changed. Not in the ten years before Sadie Miller had left town, and not in the ten years since. It probably wouldn't have changed much in another ten years.

Well, it would change a little bit now. The population sign would increase by one, adding back the resident she'd taken away when she'd left town at eighteen. And it would also contain at least one more bed-and-breakfast.

So, in an unchanging landscape, she would be responsible for two changes in a very short amount of time.

She deserved a medal of some kind. Though she doubted anyone in this town would ever give her a medal. She was just the wild child from the wrong side of the tracks. Not many would be welcoming her with open arms.

But that was fine with her. She wasn't here for them. She was here for her.

She looked across the highway, at the ocean, barely visible

through the trees on her left. She could remember walking there as a kid. A long hike in the sand, through gorse and other pricklies, around the lake and across the road.

A walk she and her friends had always made without their parents. Because the main perk of getting out for an afternoon was getting away from their parents, after all. At least it had been for her.

It was strange to see something familiar. She'd spent so many years moving on to the next new place. She never went back anywhere. Ever. She went somewhere new.

This was the first time she'd ever been somewhere old. And she wasn't sure how she felt about it.

She looked at the gas gauge on her car and sighed. The little yellow light was reminding her that she hadn't made a pit stop since she'd gone through Medford, nearly three hundred miles ago. She was going to have to stop somewhere in town before she went out to the ranch. She wasn't exactly sure where the Garrett ranch was, just that it was on the outskirts of Copper Ridge.

She'd never been invited onto the property before.

The fact that she was leasing a business on it now would have been funny if she didn't just feel horrible, stomach-cramping nervousness.

But then, she figured facing past demons was supposed to be scary. She wouldn't know for sure since she'd spent years avoiding them. Six months ago, that had changed.

Working with people dealing with grief and loss was always impacting—there was no way around it. But one very grumpy older woman who'd lost the house she'd been in since the 1940s had forced her to think about things she'd always avoided.

"Home is wherever you are," Sadie had told her.

Maryann, whose every decade on earth was marked clearly in her snow-white hair and the deep lines etched in her face, had scowled at her. "Home is where I raised my children. Where my husband breathed his last breath. I don't know who I am outside those walls."

"You're still you. I've spent a lot of my life moving from place to place, and I take my essence, my soul, or whatever you want to call it, with me wherever I go."

The other woman had waved her hand in dismissal. "You can't know, then. You're a vagrant in your own life. If nothing matters to you, how can you sit there and tell me that something I poured the past sixty years of my life into is meaningless?"

And that was when she'd realized...as a crisis counselor she'd helped so many people deal with loss. Either the loss of a loved one, the loss of a marriage or, very often, the loss of a home, and she'd realized that all that advice had been thin. Rootless, because she was.

Because nothing was permanent in her life. Because not one thing had the kind of deep resonance and meaning for her that Maryann's home had for her.

She'd never before been quite so conscious of the transient nature of her life. But in one blunt sentence her patient had reduced the past ten years to a tumbleweed in her mind's eye, while Maryann's own past had risen up like a redwood. Towering, significant. Rooted.

After that she'd felt so aware of how alone she was. That she'd let every friendship she'd left behind wither on the vine and die, that she'd done a crap job of making new friends since she'd moved to San Diego. That her last boyfriend, Marcus, hadn't been missed from the day she'd rolled him out of bed and out the door for the last time.

Those revelations had led to online perusals of Copper Ridge. Which had led to an ad she hadn't been able to get out of her head.

Long-term lease. Perfect for a private residence or bed-and-breakfast.

From there, she'd examined her savings, done estimated profit and loss based on exhaustive research of similar businesses, and before she'd quite realized what she was getting herself into…she'd committed. Committed to leaving the career she'd spent more time in school for than she'd spent actually practicing.

For the first time in ten years, she'd agreed to an extended time frame in one location. And for the first time in ten years, she was headed back to the one place she'd ever called home.

Of course, now she felt like she was approaching doom. Which she didn't think was at all dramatic. Since she was never dramatic.

Except for when she was dramatic.

From the backseat, she heard Tobias, more commonly known as Toby, let out a plaintive meow. The entire road trip had been endured with growing indignation by her cat. But then, she paid the rent, so he had to deal.

"Sorry, bud," she said. "I have the thumbs, I man the can opener. That means you have to stick with me. And if that means moving up the coast, it means moving up the coast. At least I didn't fly and throw you into cargo." Which, during their many moves together, had been a necessity on occasion. Toby wasn't a fan of air travel.

The cat didn't respond to her attempts at mollifying him. Which didn't really surprise her. In many ways, she was much more dependent on him than he was on her.

Sadie looked out at the expanse of evergreen trees that lined the road, a rich, velvet green that she hadn't found anywhere outside of Oregon. California was sun and palm trees, deep blue ocean and heat. It was beautiful, but in a different way.

Copper Ridge was all majestic mountains, shades of green and steel-gray sea. Not the kind of beach you hung out on in a bikini unless you were a local. The wind was cold and blew the sand up hard and fast, the grains biting into skin like little teeth.

It was its own kind of beauty, that was for sure. She'd been all over the United States. From the Deep South to the East Coast and back west again, and nothing had ever been quite like this. She'd never thought she'd be back.

But she was. And the dread was ever encroaching.

Suddenly, the car engine started to growl, and she pushed down the gas pedal, hoping to feel it rev again, only to be disappointed.

"Oh, frickety frick," she muttered as she pulled to the side of the road and the engine went totally silent.

Gas had apparently been needed sooner than expected.

She leaned forward, pressing her head against the steering wheel. "I knew it was doomed. I knew I was doomed!" She straightened up and looked backward at Toby. "Don't start. Don't get judgey."

Toby did nothing but stare at her with green eyes that were extremely judgmental despite her command. "You suck, cat," she said, reaching down and digging for her purse, then feeling around for her phone.

She pulled it out and saw one bar of service. Oh, right. Because that's what you got for moving away from civilization and settling in the absolute sticks.

She tapped her fingernails against the side of the phone and contemplated who to call. She didn't really know anyone in town anymore. Her own parents had moved away ages ago, and she wouldn't call them even if they hadn't.

Thankfully, she could get roadside assistance, but what a freaking pain.

She pulled up the browser on the phone and typed *tow trucks* into the search engine, then grimaced as she watched the little wheel up in the top left-hand corner of the phone spin, and spin and spin while it tried to grab hold of a satellite signal for long enough to pull up some results.

"Oh, Copper Ridge, you've bested me before, you aren't allowed to do it again." She kept her eyes on the phone and then growled at it, setting it on the passenger seat while she leaned over and pulled a stack of papers out of the glove box. She had to have a number for her insurance on hand at least.

Somewhere. It had to be somewhere.

A loud rap on the glass behind her shot a shock wave through her and she whipped around, releasing her hold on the stack of papers, sending them flying through the car, where they settled in both the front and backseats.

She looked around at the mess, then at the knocker. On the other side of the glass was a man in a tan uniform, a gold star on his chest, sunglasses over his eyes. What she could see of him was...well, hot. Which was the last thing she expected, because she'd been living in San Diego for a few years, the land of the beautiful, and rarely, if ever, was she so overcome by a man's face that all she could think was "hot." But maybe that had to do with the recent startle. She was just a little dazed, that was all.

He pointed downward, an authoritative gesture that took her a minute to attach meaning to, mainly because something was pulling at the back of her brain. A memory that was attempting to come to the forefront.

She blinked and tried to get herself together, tried to get herself back into the present. She pushed the button on the door and the window slid down, removing the barrier between herself and Officer Hottie.

"Hi," she said. "I'm out of gas. But I have roadside assistance so... I mean, I'm okay. Except I don't have very good cell service. So I was looking for... Well, anyway, did you stop for a reason?"

"To check on you," he said, the expression on his face strange. He looked like he had a memory tugging on his brain, too, and that made her own memory pull even harder.

"Yes...because...distressed motorist." She looked around at all of the scattered papers. "Right. But I'm not really distressed. I'm fine."

Wow, but he really was hot. Chiseled jaw, short dark hair. He created a response, low and deep in her body, that felt familiar in a very disquieting way.

He bent down in front of the window and she caught the name on his badge.

E. Garrett.

Oh, no. No no no no. There were not enough swearwords in the English language to express all of the bad in this situation. She was stranded on the side of the road, and she'd just encountered one of the chief demons from her past. In a uniform. The welcome committee from hell. Not that she'd imagined she'd be able to avoid him forever, considering her B and B was situated on his family's ranch, but she'd imagined she might avoid him for at least ten minutes after hitting the city limits.

She was not in the mood to deal with him. She was revising his nickname. Not Officer Hottie. Officer Stick-Up-the-Ass. That's who he was.

Not only that, he was a reminder of a whole host of things she would rather just forget.

And then his expression changed, and she knew he was catching up.

"Sadie Miller," he said.

"Well, damn." She smiled at him as best she could, but her palms were starting to sweat. Authority figures did that to her in general, and authority figures who had once fingerprinted her were an even bigger issue. "You do have a good memory."

"You never forget the first woman you put in handcuffs," he said, his voice low and firm, giving zero impression of a double entendre, and yet, it hit her that way.

Hit her and ricocheted around to parts inside of her that had gone ignored for a long time.

She cleared her throat and straightened her shoulders, trying to look arch and serious, and everything she'd spent the past ten years turning her life into.

Eli Garrett wasn't allowed to make her feel like a scroungy teenage girl, because she was not a scroungy teenage girl anymore. Similarly, he was not allowed to make her feel hot and bothered like he'd done back then, either, because…well, because she wasn't the same person she'd been then.

"Indeed," she said.

"What brings you back into town?"

He didn't know? She looked at him, studied him. He didn't know. Well, that was just peachy. Connor Garrett had neglected to tell his brother that he'd offered her the lease on the house. She had a feeling that was going to go down with Eli like a live leech in his breakfast cereal.

"Am I, um…am I being detained?" she asked, fidgeting in her seat.

"No," he said.

"Then am I free to go?"

"Where? You're out of gas."

Point to Officer Garrett. "Yes. I am. Maybe…maybe you could help me with that?"

His lips, which were far more interesting than they should be, didn't smile, didn't lessen their tension. They simply remained in a flat line. Uncompromising. Unfriendly. Like the man himself. "Just a second." He turned and walked back toward his squad car and she started picking up the papers she'd strewn all over the car.

Her heart was beating so hard she thought she might have a medical event. What were the odds that he was the first person she saw when she came back to Copper Ridge? It was a bad omen. A very bad omen.

Of course, her first thought, still, was that he was hot. She'd thought that at seventeen. But then, to a rebellious kid with an affinity for underage drinking, a man who was part of the sheriff's department was sort of the ultimate fascination. The ultimate no-go. So of course, even when she'd resented his presence, she'd gotten a little kick out of checking him out.

She let out a long breath. She'd sort of hoped that he'd gone on to law enforcement in another town. Or that maybe he'd given up wearing a uniform altogether and discovered a passion for pottery…maybe in the south of France.

But no. Eli Garrett had done what most people from Copper Ridge seemed to do. He'd found his place in the little community and stayed in his carved-out niche.

You should judge. Since you're back and all.

Yes, she was back.

At this point in the game, Copper Ridge had seemed as good a place as any to give her demons the big middle finger.

And hey, she was facing one of them a little bit early. But, considering he had a gun strapped to his lean hips, she thought maybe giving him the finger wasn't the best idea.

"I put a call in for you," he said from over her shoulder.

"Gah!" She startled. "Could you not sneak up on me like that?"

"Do I make you nervous?"

"No. Why would you make me nervous?"

"Criminals *do* seem to get nervous around the badge."

She frowned. "I am not a criminal. I am a licensed therapist in eight…no, *nine* states."

"With a criminal record."

"I was a minor."

"No arrests since then?" he asked.

"I ask again, am I being detained?"

"No."

"Then… I'm free to go."

"Except that you're out of gas," he pointed out. Again.

"Well, *you're* free to go, then."

He lifted a shoulder. "Yeah, I could. But I feel like it's my mission to make sure you don't get into any trouble. Or light anything on fire."

"Okay, look, I didn't light anything on fire on purpose. I knocked over a lantern."

"Which is why arson wasn't on the list of things you were arrested for."

"Do you forget anything?" she asked.

"Public drunkenness. Disturbing the peace, resisting arrest. Not arson, though. And that's not even mentioning the number of times we had to come and ask you and your friends to leave a store, or stop loitering where you didn't belong."

"Good lord, what a sad small life you must lead to remember my rap sheet. *I* barely even remember it."

"As I said, you don't forget your first."

She screwed up her face. "That sounds possibly more sexual than I think you mean it to."

"How does it sound sexual?"

She squinted. "Really?"

She waited for a full four seconds while it registered. She could see when it did because his humorless, impassive face had a slight shift before going back to being total granite. He still had his sunglasses on, so she couldn't see his eyes, only her own reflection. Which looked flushed and flustered. And not from heat, that was for sure.

"Why are you here?" he asked.

"I didn't say," she said.

"I know. I tend to remember conversations that happened less than five minutes ago."

"Yeah, well, I don't see how that's any of your business, since I'm not being detained for questioning."

"For someone who hasn't been arrested more than just the once, you have the lingo down perfectly."

"I'm a therapist. I work with some troubled souls. I've seen more than one arrest."

"Hmm," he said. A noise halfway between a word and a grunt.

"What?"

"I'm surprised you became a therapist, is all."

"Why?"

"Because."

She knew what that because meant. *Because you're such a*

mess. That was what it meant. And she was not a mess. She wasn't perfect, but she wasn't a disaster, either. Anyway, thankfully, having your crap together was not a requirement for being able to help others get their crap together. So there. She didn't say that last part, though. Because...well, gun. Badge. Handcuffs.

"I like to fix things," she said. That was honest. "To fix people, actually. I don't just arrest them and throw away the key. I try to make an impact on people's lives."

"Well, it takes both types, I guess," he said.

"Yeah. So anyway, don't you have some teenage miscreants to harass? I seem to recall that being your MO."

As soon as she said it, an old red pickup truck eased into the space in front of her and an old man, one who looked familiar, got out, holding a gas can the same color as the truck.

"Well," the other man said, a smile on his face, "if it isn't Ms. Sadie Miller."

Apparently she was wrong about not having anyone in town who still knew her. It was like these people had nothing better to do than remember every single soul who was born in this burg. For all eternity.

In fairness, though, she remembered Bud, too. She had no idea what his real name was. Or if he had one. Hell, that could be it. There was more than one Bubba in town, and they went by it completely un-ironically, so there really was no telling.

"Yes," she said. "Yes, it's me."

"What brings you back to town?" he asked. "Your parents aren't back, are they?"

"No," she said. "They're still down in Coos Bay." Not that she spoke to them. For all she knew they could be somewhere else entirely by now, but she didn't care. Not anymore.

She couldn't watch their dynamic, not now that she had a choice. She'd moved away from her father's rages. She wasn't going to expose herself to them again.

And her mother wouldn't leave. No matter how many times Sadie begged, her mother wouldn't leave.

"I see. Well, it's good to have you back." He put his hand on the bill of his ball cap and tugged it down sharply before heading to the back of her car and opening up the gas tank.

Just like that. Like her presence mattered. Not like she was some hooligan who'd accidentally started a little barn fire and gotten herself arrested. Not like she was the child of a wife-beater or a disturber of the peace.

Like he was happy she was there.

Darn. She felt a little emotional now.

She unbuckled and got out, standing next to the car and watching Bud, bent at the waist and pouring gas into her car. "Hey, whatever I owe you, I'll bring it by the gas station. I don't have cash, but…"

Bud straightened. "Don't you worry about it," he said. "Consider it a welcome home."

She couldn't fathom why he was being so nice. She'd barely had any interaction with him. Back when she'd been a kid she would often go into the store that was adjacent to the station, after she and some friends had gone swimming in the river, and buy candy bars for fifty cents. Shivering in wet bathing suits in the cold, air-conditioned building.

But she hadn't really thought of him as someone who would know her. Or…care. "I appreciate that." But she would still be going down to the gas station to pay him back as soon as she could.

Maybe even before she went to the Garrett ranch.

"Thank you. Both." She wasn't going to let Eli Garrett get to her. She wasn't going to let this stand as some sort of sign of how the rest of her venture here was going to be.

Nope. Just because it began with a vehicular disaster and Eli Garrett did not mean it would continue on that way.

Her eyes clashed with Eli's and she looked down at the ground before realizing that was more awkward than just looking at him like he was a normal person. And not like he was a very handsome person who had once handcuffed her.

Even though he was.

She cleared her throat. "I'm going to go now. I have…places to be." Eli would find out what those places were eventually, but hopefully that didn't mean they would have to actually see each other.

She got back in the car and shut the door, and saw in her rearview mirror that Eli had done the same. Good.

She took a deep breath and started the engine, then put the car into gear. She was on to new things, reclaiming an old past and stealing its power.

And a little run-in with Eli Garrett wasn't going to change that.

CHAPTER TWO

THE CATALOG HOUSE was even more beautiful than advertised. Rough around the edges, yes, but Sadie had been warned about that.

The lawn needed replanting. Or sod. But she wasn't sure she had the budget to lay down a grass carpet. Which meant she might be stuck with seeding, and patience. She hated being patient. She didn't like sitting around. And she had never waited for the grass to grow.

She leaned back against her car and studied the house. From the rocks that went halfway up the facade, to the solid, original wood paneling and the cut-glass windows, it was something that spoke of a different time.

It was hardly a rough-hewn cabin. It was almost too elegant to be out here, buried in the trees at the base of the mountains. But she knew, from what Connor had sent in his email, that the house was one his great-great-grandfather had ordered for his wife from a Sears and Roebuck catalog around 1914. Something to make the wilderness of Oregon seem a little less wild, compared to their old home in Boston.

Sadie imagined that, in a land of log cabins, this had been the most modern dwelling in the area.

Not so much now, but it had charm. And really, that was what a bed-and-breakfast needed. Connor had said renovations would be up to her, but she had permission to do what she wanted to the place, so long as she paid for it and—per her lease—left it in better condition than when she came. Which meant, according to him, "no stupid shit like shag carpet."

She took in a deep breath, let the smell wrap itself around her. The sharp tang of salt from the sea, wood that was heated by the sun, and pine all lingered in the air.

It was familiar, but different, too. She'd been away from this air for a long time, and when she'd left, there was nothing about Copper Ridge that had felt special to her. She hadn't been able to see the beauty anymore. It had all shrunk down to a little house on the wrong side of the highway, and the smell of dirt, blood and booze.

There hadn't been a lot of moments where she'd stopped and smelled the forest. If she'd ever gone into the forest it had been to hide out, in a little alcove not far from the Garrett ranch, and smoke a cigarette. Which sort of negated the fresh clean air aspect of it all.

It struck her then that she was within walking distance of the place. That if she wanted to, she could leave her half-unpacked boxes and see the haven she'd gone to with her friends all those years ago.

A strange ache filled her chest, a feeling of longing and homesickness that was unfamiliar to her. There was weight in that clearing. Roots. And, she strongly suspected, a high probability of ghosts of bad decisions past.

She and her friends had been nothing more than children then, angry at life. Determined to do whatever they could to take back some control. Which had taken the form of drugs, alcohol and sex. Because those little rebellions felt like an achievement.

But she was an adult now. And she had the control. The life she made here would be hers. More than just a reaction to what was happening in her family home.

She didn't need to see the clearing. And there were no ghosts.

With that final thought, she picked up Toby's pet carrier and strode up the front porch and lifted the lid on the mail slot by the door. Connor had said he'd put a key in there for her. She had the impression he intended to interact with her as little as possible.

Which suited her just fine. She had the money she needed to do the remodeling on the house, and she was sort of looking forward to spending a few weeks in relative solitude handling all of it before she got things up and running.

Maybe then she'd look up her old friends. Or not. That would be…well, it would be too close to revisiting times that hadn't been fun for anyone. Maybe she would meet a guy. Go on a date.

Lately she'd been out of the habit of both dating and making friends.

The moves made it hard. And if she was honest, starting fresh was her preference. She didn't like bringing old places with her into the new ones. Not that there weren't friends and boyfriends she had cared for. She had cared. She did. It was just that she liked them as happy memories. She didn't like letting a relationship stretch on to the point it started to show wear and tear.

She pulled the brass key out of the box and put it in the matching lock, turning it hard before it gave. "All right, Toby," she said. "Welcome home, whether we like it or not, because we can't back out of the lease, and after I remodel this place, we'll officially be broke."

She walked them both inside and looked around. It was dark, but it was clean. The wood floors were definitely in need of polishing, but nothing was seriously wrong with them. There were some threadbare rugs that needed replacing, light fixtures that needed updating. But it didn't smell like mold or anything, so that was a bonus.

"It really does have to work out," she said, setting Toby's carrier up on the kitchen table. "Because otherwise you'll be reduced to standing on a street corner and offering kitty head scritches for money. And none of us want to see you stoop that low."

She opened up his cage and he wandered out, looking around and sniffing the air, his tail twitching. She ran her hand over his gray striped fur, then scratched him behind his ears. "Really, though, you could charge for this service," she said. "You give me instant Zen."

Toby just looked at her, as though to say he would be much more Zen if they were back in their bright, white apartment in sunny San Diego.

But then, Toby was used to following her around at this point, so she knew his indignation would be brief.

First order of business was to get Toby's litter box out of the car. The second was to start making this place habitable.

Like it or not, ready or not, she'd made a five-year commitment, and she had to see it through.

"All right, Toby," she said. "It's time to do this thing."

"THERE WAS A CAR over at the Catalog House. I saw it when I pulled in," Eli said.

"Yeah."

Eli glanced at his brother, who was at the kitchen table looking more sullen and antisocial than usual. Which was saying something.

"And there was a light on," Eli continued, pushing for an explanation.

"Yeah."

"You don't sound surprised."

"No shit. I thought you were the law enforcement around here. You'd think you could put two and two together."

Eli was tempted to hit Connor over the head with something, but it was June. And June was a bad month for Connor, since it was his anniversary month. But then, March was a bad month for Connor, too, because it was Jessie's birthday. And April was a bad month because it was the month she'd died three years ago. August was when they'd started dating, ten years ago. December was when they'd gotten engaged.

So basically, there were a lot of bad months for Connor. And Eli got it, and he hurt on his behalf. But it didn't mean he didn't want to hit his brother for his obnoxious surliness sometimes.

"Would you care to explain?"

"Sure. We need some more revenue. I leased the house. Long-term."

"What? Don't you think we should have talked about this?" he asked.

"No," Connor said. "Because while I respect that this ranch is yours, too, you have to respect that it's more essential to me. It's my only job, Eli. You and Kate have work outside this place, but I don't, because someone has to run it full-time."

"I know that, but you didn't think about telling me you were going to lease out a house on our property?"

"I did think about it. I decided against it. Because I thought, at the end of the day, it was my damned decision."

"Dammit, Connor, I say this with love, please get drunk and pass out. You're impossible when you're like this."

"I'm always like this," Connor said.

"Yeah, and you're always impossible."

"Why are you all growling in here?" Kate, the youngest of the Garrett clan, walked into the kitchen, her dark hair in a low ponytail. She looked like she'd been working hard all day, and it was probably because she had been.

"Because Connor's in the room," Eli told her.

Kate smiled and crossed to Connor, planting a kiss on his cheek. Connor grunted.

"I love you, too," she said. "Did anyone make dinner?"

"No one made dinner," Eli said. "We all have jobs. But I did bring a pizza, just in case." Eli turned and put the box of pizza on the granite countertop. Kate started getting plates out of the cupboard.

This was Connor's house, the main house on the property, which he'd shared with Jessie during their years as a married couple. He stayed because this was the family ranch, going back generations. Because he was the one who worked the land, and the one least likely to leave. This was his rightful place.

But Eli often got the feeling he hated it.

"I will take a beer now," Connor said.

"Get it yourself," Kate suggested. "I'm already dishing up your dinner, and I am not a waitress."

"You wouldn't get a tip if you were one," Connor grumbled, getting up from his spot at the table and wandering to the fridge, jerking it open.

Eli noticed that there wasn't much in it beyond beer and cheese. He wasn't sure he liked what that said about his brother's mental state. Or maybe it was just that Connor hadn't had time to go shopping recently. That could be it.

"You should get a housekeeper," Eli said.

Connor grunted, which was something he seemed to do a lot lately. "I don't want a stranger rifling around in my stuff."

"Then hire someone you know."

"No."

Eli took a piece of pizza out of the box and set it on a plate, doing his best to ignore Kate, who wasn't using her plate, but was standing, arched over the bar, dripping sauce onto the otherwise clean surface.

Eli didn't like that. He liked things in their place. He liked things clean. He'd spent too many years putting things in order to let them slide now.

When they'd been kids, cleanliness hadn't just been a preference, it had been survival. Connor keeping things going on the ranch and Eli making it appear that there was a functional adult managing the household had been the only way to keep Child Protective Services away.

Order had been the only thing keeping them all together.

"So, Connor was just telling me about our new tenant."

"We have a tenant?" Kate asked, her mouth full.

"Yes, we do."

"Get me a beer, Connor," Kate said.

"Do I look like a damned waitress, Katie? Do I?" he growled, while he stalked back to the fridge and got out two beers, handing one to each of his siblings.

"Guess so," Kate said, taking the bottle and popping the top on the counter.

Sometimes Eli wondered if Kate had suffered a bit for having nothing but men in her life. But if he mentioned that to Kate she would probably spit on him. Which just proved his point.

"So," Eli said, leaning against the counter. "The tenant."

Anything to get his mind off the events from earlier today. Sadie Miller. He remembered her as a little blonde ball of trouble. Dressed in all black, ripped jeans, she'd been a stereotype of social rebellion. His least favorite kind of brat to deal with. She'd also been feisty as hell. Resisting arrest was putting it mildly. It had been his first summer with the sheriff's department, and they'd broken up a big party in an empty barn. Drunk, freaked-out teenagers had made the whole thing a nightmare. Basically, all hell had broken loose.

And he had ended up handcuffing and booking seventeen-year-old Sadie, making her the first person he'd ever arrested. Though ultimately she wasn't charged, as he'd said, with ill-advised word choices today, you never forgot your first.

"I drew up a long-term lease so that the Catalog House could be used as a bed-and-breakfast," Connor said.

"A what?" he and Kate asked the question in unison.

"You heard me. With the renovation of Old Town, and the fireworks show on the ocean getting bigger every year, tourism is a big deal. And I want in on that industry."

"How is your going behind our backs us being 'in on the industry'?"

"Income from the lease, and a small percentage of profits. And like I already told you," he said, directing his words at Eli, "some of us only get money from the ranch, so the more profitable I can make it, the better."

"And you're sure that your lessee isn't going to destroy the place?"

"She's a local. Or at least, she was."

The hair on the back of Eli's neck stood on end. "Is she?"

"Yeah. Younger than us, older than Kate, so I don't think any of us would have known her in school."

He would have laughed if there were anything remotely funny about it. "I have a good guess about who it might be," he said, setting his beer on the counter. "Sadie Miller?"

"Yeah. How do you know her?"

"I arrested her once."

Connor's eyebrows shot up.

"Well, damn, I didn't know she was a criminal."

Eli let out an exasperated breath. "She's not a criminal. At least, I don't think she's a career criminal. Granted, she committed a crime, that's why I arrested her, but she's not going to make a skin suit out of anyone."

"Bleah." Kate stuck out her tongue.

"I'm just saying. I arrested her for being drunk and disorderly about ten years ago. It wasn't exactly organized crime. And before that she was the kind of kid you'd see wearing too much eyeliner, smoking cigarettes and looking angry at the world. A bigger danger to healthy lungs than to society at large."

"Well, that's comforting," Connor said.

"I take it you didn't do a background check?" Eli asked.

"I did. But apparently not a thorough one. Credit check, though. Because her rental history reads like an epic novel. I needed to make sure she wasn't dodging. But she wasn't. She just likes to move."

"Well, I can't have any of this interfering with my campaign," Eli said.

He'd thrown his hat in the ring to run for the position, with the blessing of the current sheriff, who was now retiring. And since he'd decided to do it, it had become more and more important daily. Especially after he'd won a top two spot in the primary, his lead over the other man running substantial enough that a win in November looked almost certain. But that didn't mean he was resting on his laurels. No.

There were spreadsheets. Lots of spreadsheets. Because he couldn't help himself. Anything worth doing was absolutely worth doing right.

"It's not going to mess with your campaign. She's going to run her business, and you'll take care of your business. While I increase some of my profits."

"So how long do you think she'll stay here?" Eli asked, hoping the answer was "not long." She disturbed his sense of order. All of this did, but the fact that Sadie Miller was involved only made it more disturbing. And he did not need disturbing. Not right now. Not ever, really.

"She signed for five years."

"Five years?" he and Kate spoke together again.

"Will you stop repeating my answers back to me in question form? Yes, five years. It's going to take time to get a business going. There's some updating that needs to be done on the house. She's agreed to pay for it, and orchestrate it all."

"You're crazy. You're going to let someone else, a stranger, live on our property for five years without even…meeting her first?" Eli asked.

"It's over. It's signed. I'm not discussing it any further," Connor said.

Eli leaned back against the counter and took a long drink of his beer.

Kate shrugged. "It might be nice to have a woman around again."

"She's not going to be around," Eli said. "She's running a bed-and-breakfast, apparently. There's a difference between that and her being around. This is a big property."

"I was just saying. And maybe I'll go visit her," Kate mused.

"Eli's right, Katie," Connor said. "Everything is going to be kept separate."

"That's fine." Kate picked at the top of her pizza. "But I do think it would be nice to bring her something. A housewarming something. Foodstuffs. Small-town hospitality in action and all."

"Feel free to deliver foodstuffs," Connor told her. "I don't give a sh—"

"Yeah, yeah, I know," Kate said. "You don't. About anything. I get it. You're a grumpy codger and you aren't going to be sociable. Ever. Again. I won't make you."

"Good," he said.

Kate turned to Eli, her brown eyes wide.

Eli put his hands up. "Don't look at me," he said. "I'm not joining your small-town welcoming committee."

"Fine. I'll be the representative for this family. And try to prove we weren't—" she took a bite of her pizza and spoke around a mouthful of cheese "—raised by fucking wolves."

"Well, we'll leave that up to you," Eli said. "I have faith in you."

"Gee, thanks."

"I'm going to head home," Eli said. "I'll leave the pizza."

That earned him a thanks from Kate and a grunt—no surprise—from Connor.

"I've got the afternoon off tomorrow," Eli added, "so that means I'll be by to help out. Do you have anything big going?"

"Not a lot. We have to tag the calves this weekend, though. Are you free?"

"Yeah," he said. "I'll be around for that."

He was in law enforcement by choice, but he was a rancher by blood. He, Connor and Kate all did some local rodeo events now and then, too, though Kate was by far the most successful and was looking to turn pro when she got the chance.

Of course, the fact that he was either working for the county or working on the ranch was a big part of why he had no social life. But he didn't really miss it. Unless he was horny. Then he kind of missed it.

"Great," Connor said. "See you tomorrow, then."

"See ya." He turned and walked out of the kitchen, through the entryway and onto the porch. He stood for a minute and looked out at the property, and at the light in the distance. The light that was coming from the Catalog House.

Sadie Miller was in there. On a five-year lease. Damn it all, it didn't get much more disrupting to his sense of order than that. Of course, the past couple of years had been one big, giant disruption for their family.

They all felt the loss of Jessie. And they all felt the hole that her death had carved into Connor. He wasn't the same. He never would be.

But then, that was the way this place was. Or at least, that seemed to be the way love was for their family. You got it, you lost it.

It had started with the first generation of Garretts on this land. His great-great-grandfather had ordered that house and had it built. His great-great-grandmother had lived in it for only two years before getting pneumonia and dying.

Then there were his great-grandparents. His great-grandmother had died in childbirth, leaving her husband a shell of a man, barely capable of keeping the land going, and not entirely managing to keep track of his children. His grandfather had run off with a woman from town, leaving his grandmother to raise her kids alone. And then there were his parents.

Their mother had gone when Kate was a toddler. Off to God knew where. Somewhere warmer and sunnier. Somewhere with men in suits instead of spurs.

A place without needy kids and the smell of cows.

But it had left her husband to sink into a mire of alcoholism and despair.

It had left Connor to grow up at fifteen. And for Eli to follow right along with him.

And all that pain had started in the house that now sheltered Sadie Miller. It seemed fitting in some ways. Since she was a pain in his butt.

He walked down the steps to the driveway, then headed down the path that took him the back way to his house.

Sadie Miller wouldn't be a problem, because he wouldn't let her become one.

He was the law around here, after all.

CHAPTER THREE

SADIE WOULD VENTURE down into town today at some point. Grab some supplies. After she'd taken inventory, of course. She knew there were some tools in the shed, per the typed-up—and very brief—note Connor had left on the kitchen counter.

But until she had some clue about what sort of work she might need to do, the tools were fairly useless. She had some basic information on the minor flaws in the house, but there were other things she wanted to tackle.

Most of the place had the original wood paneling. Wainscoting that went halfway up the walls, which were painted a deep cream. The wooden detail was echoed on the ceiling, crossbeams forming a checkerboard over the plaster ceiling.

It looked like the crown molding in a few of the rooms had been replaced at some point, and it didn't match. Which meant she was going to need to take it down, and then mount some new stuff.

That wasn't a part of her original plan, but she had a little cushion for some surprises. And money set aside for some major projects, like the addition of a back deck. And since structural issues were Connor's problem, she didn't anticipate running into anything that would absolutely kill her budget.

Some people might call her a flake, but she was a well-educated flake with a basic understanding of money management.

She walked into the kitchen, and to the walk-in pantry that was larger than some bedrooms she'd had in her years of apartments. The solid wood shelves had a fine layer of dust over them. A mop and broom standing in the corner were the only residents, except for a few daddy longlegs hanging on the ceiling.

She made a mental note to take care of those guys later and walked back out into the kitchen, opening up cabinets that were mainly empty. There was one cabinet filled with mismatched teacups, and she counted that as a good find.

A quirky touch to add to the place. As inspiration went, it was a good place to start.

She wandered back through the dining room, which was nearly dominated by a large wooden table that was scarred from years of use. Refinishing that would go on her list of to-dos, but not for a while. She'd throw a tablecloth on it for now.

Out in the hall, the old wooden floor squeaked under her feet. Weirdly, she liked the sound. Liked the reminder of the age of the house.

The boards on the stairs were the same, her fingertips leaving a light trail on the banister as they cut through the thin film of dust. The house had obviously been cleaned when the previous tenant had left; it had just been a couple of years since anyone had been back inside.

She walked down the hall and pushed open the doors to each of the four bedrooms. They all had gorgeous four-poster beds. They would need all-new linens and drapes, but she'd been expecting that. The two bedrooms on the backside of the house faced the thick, undeveloped forest, and the other two provided views of a bright green field, dotted with cows.

All the rooms needed blinds to block the light so guests could sleep as late as they liked, and do whatever they wanted with no privacy concerns.

Two rooms had private bathrooms, while two others had to share one in the hall—not ideal, but given the age of the house, that it was as well-appointed as it was was sort of a miracle.

All it would take was a bit of scrubbing, polishing and the addition of matching molding. Also, some knickknacks, new furniture and a carload of linens.

The shopping would be the fun part. She would try to keep it local so that the finished product reflected Copper Ridge. She was really getting into this whole concept of community.

For now, she was going to go and hunt for those tools Connor said were in the shed. What she would do with them was up for debate, but she had a kind of driving need to do whatever she could.

Sadie tromped down the steps and into the yard, the bark-laden ground soft beneath her tennis shoes, dew from the weeds flinging up onto her pant legs and sending a chill through her.

It wasn't warm yet this morning, but the wind was still, the trees around her seeming to close in tight, sheltering her and her new house from the outside world.

She whistled, the sound echoing off the canopy of trees, adding to the feeling of isolation. She liked it. And even more than that, her guests would like it.

Well, they'd better, anyway, since she was committed to five years here. Claustrophobia's icy fingers wound their way around her neck when the thought hit. Five years. In one place. In Copper Ridge, no less, the keeper of her hang-ups and other issues.

You're confronting your past. It's what you'd tell a patient to do.

Her inner voice was right. But her inner voice could go to hell. She wasn't in the mood to confront things. She was just… trying to feel a little less wrong. A little less restless.

A little less like she was a rolling tumbleweed. Or a running-at-full-tilt tumbleweed.

She'd given so much advice that she'd never once followed. Facing fears, facing the old things that held power over a person. Going back to a point of trauma and seeing that it held no magical properties.

Well, she was following it now.

She zipped up her hoodie, fortifying herself against the general dampness that clung to the air, and walked down the path that should lead her to the shed.

An engine roar disturbed her silence, and she turned to see a black truck barreling down the long, secluded drive that led to her house.

She stopped and watched, trying to catch a glimpse of the driver. She failed, but she figured it was too grand an entrance for someone who wanted to Freddy Krueger her, so she was probably good.

She shoved her hands into the pockets of her hoodie and headed back to where the truck had parked. "Hello?"

"Hi."

The feminine voice that greeted her wasn't what she'd been expecting. Neither was the petite brunette who dropped down from the driver's side, wearing a flannel shirt and a pair of Carhartts. Her braid flipped down over her shoulder as her boots hit the ground, and she looked up and smiled.

Sadie vaguely remembered that there was a female Garrett, but she'd never known her. Unsurprising, really, since this girl looked wholesome and shiny, and all the things Sadie had never been.

"Kate," she said, extending her hand. "Kate Garrett. The sister."

"Nice to meet you," Sadie said, shaking the other woman's hand.

"I didn't want to drop by last night because I thought it would be rude, but I thought I'd stop in today just to say hi. And to ask what all your plans are."

There was something wide-eyed and sweet about Kate, something that stood in contrast to her firm handshake and confident manner. She was strength, and openness, and for a moment, Sadie envied that. The bravery it must take.

"Well, I have plans to turn the house into a B and B that will hopefully be ready for guests in about a month and a half." She put her hands on her hips and let out a long breath. "Enough time to get things arranged, and to settle in, hopefully."

"If you need any help, or anything, I'm happy to give it. I work at the Farm and Garden, and I know a lot about plants, animals, general repair stuff."

It stunned her, yet again, how nice people had been to her— exception being Eli—since she'd shown up. She'd imagined… she didn't know. She'd turned Copper Ridge into such a dark place in her mind that she'd been sure people would all but greet her with torches and pitchforks. And yet, no one had.

Facing your demons, and finding out there aren't quite as many as you thought?

"That's really nice, but I don't want to take any of your time," Sadie said.

"Really, I don't have a whole lot happening right now. Just work. And it's very male around here, so it's nice to have a more feminine influence."

It occurred to her then that it was time to stop resisting connections. *Five years, remember?*

"If I need something, I'll take you up on that," she said. "You'll be better company than a random hired hand."

Kate laughed. "I try. What are you after today?"

"Trim. Light fixtures. I might look at new hardware for the cabinets."

Kate wrinkled her nose, then looked at the house, and at Sadie's car. "If you have renovation stuff to buy, you aren't fitting it in there. Ten pounds of potatoes, five-pound sack. But if you want, you can come in with me and use my truck to make deliveries back to the property. You just need to be able to pick me up at closing time."

Sadie hadn't had a firm plan for the day, but she couldn't deny that the use of a truck had a very high chance of coming in handy.

Her immediate gut response was to say no. Because accepting help meant the possibility of needing to pay someone back. Sadie was fine giving help, and expecting nothing in return. But she'd always been afraid of leaving town owing a debt.

But you're staying here. At least for a while.

"Thank you, Kate," she said. "That's so nice of you. I would really appreciate your help."

"WELL, SHIT," CONNOR SAID, looking around the field. "I think we missed a calf."

Eli straightened and wiped the sweat off his forehead. It hadn't seemed too hot earlier, but now the sun was high in the sky, beating down on them. The middle of the field provided no shade, and the work they'd been doing wasn't easy.

"You think?" he asked, looking around the field and spotting a red angus, one of the few reds who had ever popped up in their herd, who he knew full well had been ready to birth a while back. "Oh, yeah. She calved already."

"And I don't see baby. Which means she's got him hidden somewhere, or he's dead."

"Dammit." Eli tugged his T-shirt up over his head and mopped the sweat off his chest before chucking the shirt on the ground and getting up onto his horse. "Let's go find him."

Eli spurred his horse on. "Got her number?" he asked, meaning the identification number on the mother cow's ear.

"Yeah, I know it."

"I'm going to guess he's under the trees somewhere." Eli gestured to the back of the field that led toward the houses. It was still heavily wooded, providing the herd with a place to escape the weather.

Connor followed him, the horses' hoofbeats the only sound as they galloped across the field. Eli kept an eye out for a carcass in the grass, but the absence of crows and buzzards had him feeling optimistic.

Death was a part of ranch life, but it wasn't one he enjoyed.

Sure, they raised cattle for beef, but they took care of them. They had value to his family that ran deep. It was hard to explain to someone outside of the ranching community, but those in it understood the connection without him having to voice it.

Hell, with a job this demanding, you had to love all the elements of it, or you'd never choose to do it. It was really why he chose to do it only part-time. Maybe that made him a fairweather cowboy, but he was okay with that.

He still got his job done. Both his jobs, in fact.

He tugged his horse's reins and slowed her down when they got to the edge of the trees and Connor dismounted.

"Oh, great," he said, looking back. "We got mama's attention. But then, I guess that means we're close."

But the last thing they wanted was to be on a twelve-hundred-pound mother cow's radar while they tried to run down her three-day-old calf and give him a piercing.

Eli got off his own horse and followed Connor under the trees. "Okay, Con," he said, "make this fast because I don't want to deal with mom cow's attitude, all right?"

Then he saw it, spindly and wobbly, under the trees. Black as night, obviously not inheriting his mother's coloring.

"Okay..." Eli said. "Let's do this thing."

Connor crossed his arms over his broad chest. "Get in there, part-time cowboy. You're on shift." He handed Eli the applicator, which was already clean and ready.

Eli took it, then flipped Connor his middle finger before wading into the foliage.

He looked over his shoulder. The mother cow was jogging

now, heading toward them, not happy to see them getting closer to her baby. And they couldn't blame her. But he needed to get the baby's tag on so they could match him up with his mother later. Easy enough to figure it out now, but harder later in a field of black calves.

"Hurry up, man!" Connor called.

"Right," Eli said, tossing the word over his shoulder as he battled through the brush, sticks breaking beneath his boots as he headed toward the calf, who was attempting a getaway. "I'll just speed this along."

"I don't want you to get your ass trampled."

"Well, neither do I," Eli growled.

Eli lunged for the calf, and as he did, the mother started to charge in their direction.

"Hell!" Connor dodged to the side and the mom nudged at him with her head, bellowing and generally trying to intimidate him. He sidestepped her next attempt at butting him.

Eli turned his focus back to the calf and grabbed him, fitting the applicator to his ear and punching as hard and secure as he could, holding the animal's neck and head still with one arm while he finished the job with the other.

"Got him!" He released the little black calf, who now had a yellow tag on his ear and seemed none the worse for wear.

"Then haul ass," Connor said, moving through the trees and back to his horse. Eli did the same, and fortunately the cow was now just focused on her baby, who was making a low bawling sound.

"He's playing it up now." Connor wiped his forearm over his brow. "Trying to make his mom even madder."

"I don't think she could possibly get much madder," Eli said, trying to catch his breath.

"Probably not. I'm going to ride back out for a minute," Connor told him. "Just to check everything over. You want to meet me back at the barn?"

"Yeah, sure."

Eli mounted his horse again and rode back toward the barn. One of the ranch hands, a high school kid Connor had hired to help with menial stuff, looked up from mucking stalls as he entered.

"Hey, Mike," Eli said. "Mind taking care of Sable for me?" He got off the horse and patted her neck.

"Got her," Mike said.

"Great, thanks." Eli walked around the barn, Connor's most prized acquisition. They'd poured all the money from their father's life insurance settlement into it.

Eli braced one hand on the solid wood wall, arching backward. Damn. He had a hitch in his back. He was too young to get old.

And he had to work a shift for the force in the morning, which meant he didn't have time to be sore. Double duty was a bitch. But he couldn't ever give up either job.

Connor lived and breathed the ranch, but Eli appreciated the break.

Because, when it came right down to it, he'd rather chase bad guys than be chased by a damned cow.

Though, being sheriff potentially meant doing a lot more paper pushing, and a bit less bad-guy chasing. But it also meant the chance to effect some good change in the county. Sure, some of it was down to the fact that he was a control freak, and the chance to take total control of the filing system was almost irresistible, and some of it was even ambition, but mainly he wanted to be sheriff because he loved Copper Ridge and the surrounding areas. And serving in law enforcement was the best way he could think of to show that love.

He heard a loud crash, followed by several more crashes and a shrill curse word. He started toward the noise without even thinking, because that was what he did. If there was something wrong, he went toward it, not away from it.

He walked down the path toward the din. Toward the Catalog House. And he already knew that whatever he was going to find there was going to make him very, very grumpy.

When he came through the trees he saw her, across the driveway in front of Kate's truck. Sadie was standing at the end of it, holding a bundle of crown molding or trim of some kind that had to be ten feet long at least. And in front of the tailgate, down by her feet, were various pieces of hardware and what had probably been a light fixture before it had met an untimely demise on the gravel driveway.

And here was the distraction he just didn't need.

"What are you doing?" he asked.

"Oh." Her head whipped up, her blue eyes wide for a moment, before they narrowed, her expression turning into a scowl. "You have to stop sneaking up on me. I've been in town less than twenty-four hours and I think you've scared a grand total of twenty-five minutes off my life."

"Somehow I think you'll be fine without them."

"Says you. That's an entire sitcom's worth of life you just cost me. Now my plans of watching one final episode of *Friends* before I go to meet my maker are completely dashed."

"Do you need help?" he asked patiently.

"Do you ever laugh? Because that was funny."

"Rarely. Not as rarely as my brother. But rarely."

"Maybe it's a male Garrett thing. Your sister is more fun than you are."

"So much fun that you stole her truck? Are you already adding to your list of felonies?" Eli asked, making his way over to the truck and surveying the small disaster around Sadie's feet.

"You of all people should know I was never charged with a felony, Deputy Pedantic, so let's not be dramatic."

"Just looking out for my sister." And he meant it. Because Kate was too sweet. Too trusting. And Sadie was someone he couldn't predict. The combination made him nervous.

"Kate stopped by and offered her pickup truck. Because she's very, very nice."

"Too nice," he said, still looking over the items that had spilled out onto the ground. "And you figured you'd unload this all by yourself?"

"Well, the trim isn't heavy. It's just unwieldy. But I didn't realize the guys had packed my bags up against the gate, and they had one tangled in the trim and… Anyway, I had a momentary disaster, and I have a broken pendant light. But it will be okay."

"I could help."

"Helping me wouldn't make you burst into flame?" she asked.

"Depends. Are you planning on lighting something else on fire?"

She let out a growl. "I told you. I did not light anything on fire. I knocked a lantern over. There is a difference."

"You started a fire. It was an accident, but you did, in fact, light an entire barn on fire."

"I feel like intent should matter here."

"All right, then, I intend to help you. Maybe you could stop trying to make everything so difficult and let me get to it."

SADIE WATCHED, AND TRIED not to let her mouth hang open, as Eli came closer, shirtless and muscular and just im-damned-possible not to stare at. He had dirt on his chest. His hairy, masculine, muscular chest.

He'd looked so clean in that uniform of his. Like he ironed it directly onto his body so that it would form straight to his physique and never wrinkle. And he looked good in it.

But never had she imagined that there was something so raw and manly underneath it all. He was downright…rough and uncivilized beneath all that law and order.

She suddenly realized she was staring. Pretty much at his nipples. It didn't get more horrifying than that.

She cleared her throat and looked back up at him. Met his brown eyes, which was the socially acceptable thing to do.

"Thank you," she said.

And all her good intentions fell like a Jenga tower when he

grabbed the middle of the trim and crown molding bundle she was holding and lifted it up, out of her hands, to hoist it over his shoulder.

"Where do you want it?" he asked.

Her brain was taking in too much stimulus to compute the exact question. He was standing there, every muscle outlined to perfection by the stance and the weight of the items he was holding. He just looked so damned capable. Standing there and holding things that had been almost impossible for her to manage, like they weren't anything at all.

Actually, that part was really freaking annoying.

But it looked great. And she couldn't refrain from letting herself have a little moment. One where she admired the strength in his chest, the sharp, defined lines in his stomach. And down beneath those abs, a perfectly flat plane with deep grooves on either side of it that disappeared beneath the low-slung waistband of his jeans.

She almost had to bite her own fist to keep from whimpering.

What the hell was wrong with her? She didn't lust after guys she didn't like. Anymore. Sure, she'd lusted after him—mildly, until he'd arrested her. But she'd grown up since then.

She liked it simple, she liked it happy. She liked nice men who wanted a sweet, easy relationship, and when that wasn't easily available, she did without.

She'd been without for a while, so she was clearly just having a weak moment on the physical desire front. And hey, that happened. But that didn't mean she was going to do anything about it. Most especially not with Eli Garrett. No, thank you.

She wasn't a fling girl anyway. Mainly because the idea of getting naked with a total stranger was not at all appealing. She always got to know a guy before she hopped into bed with him. And getting to know the guy made it not a fling, but a relationship.

And if relationships were not, at present, a happening thing, flings weren't a happening thing ever. Ergo, sex was not a happening thing for her.

Ergo his abs had just killed 65 percent of her brain cells.

"Just…the porch is good," she said, walking backward, her eyes still trained on him. She grabbed one of the plastic bags, which was lying, tipped and spilled, on the tailgate, and bent, her eyes still on Eli as he turned and started walking toward the house.

His butt.

Oh, my.

Yep. She'd just crossed over into shameless ogling and she didn't even care. Didn't mind even a little bit that she didn't even like the guy.

Why not look at him for a minute? The fact was, thrills were few and far between for her. Connor might be just as hot. She might ogle him next.

But he wasn't here. So for now she would just take a moment to note the way the denim cupped Eli's muscular, rounded…

"So…you gonna nail this up or what?"

It took her a full second to realize "nail this up" wasn't a euphemism for a sex act.

"The molding?"

"Yes," he said, setting it down across the porch.

She scrambled to pick everything up, avoiding the broken pendant light and gathering the rest of her odds and ends. "That was the plan. There's a nail gun in the shed. At least, I think Connor had that on the list. He left me a list."

"Decent of him."

"He's been sort of the invisible man since I arrived. He left instructions, but I haven't seen him."

"Yeah, well, he's like that. Actually—" he bent down to straighten up one of the trim pieces and she cocked her head to the side and watched the muscles on his back shift and bunch "—he didn't tell me anyone was coming to rent the place." He straightened. "Let alone signing a long-term lease and spending the next five years running a bed-and-breakfast on my damn property."

"It's sort of a shared property. If you want to be technical." She scurried up toward the porch, her bag in hand.

"Right. So how is it you're going to install all this? And why are you installing all this?"

"I want the trim to match. Obviously over the years some things were replaced at different times and some of it doesn't match. The wood in here is beautiful and I don't want anything detracting from it."

"But even the replacement molding is older than...we are. It might as well be original."

"Well, no, it might as well not be, because if it were, it would match. It gets accolades for age but I'm still replacing it."

"So you're going to put this cheap-ass stuff in there?"

"It is not cheap-ass! Look at how much of my budget is devoted to this and you will see just how not cheap-ass it is. It's very nice, actually. And if all you're going to do is insult my molding, then...get off my porch."

He crossed his arms and leaned against the railing. "I don't think I will. It's my porch. You're just leasing it."

"I have rights!"

"It's a bed-and-breakfast. What if I want to make a reservation?"

"It's not open yet."

"It could open faster if you didn't want to replace perfectly good molding."

She sputtered, her comebacks all jumbled around because... biceps. And forearms. And things. Why was he so distracting even while he was annoying? Why did it seem like the annoying only made it all more interesting?

She had no idea what was wrong with her. She needed some wine. A bottle of wine. And for him to go away. She was done with her thrills. She was on thrill overload. She was clearly giddy with the thrills and had crossed over into crazy town.

"What else do you have in the bag?" he asked.

"Things," she said.

His dark eyes narrowed. "What kinds of things?"

"Things of a home-improvement nature. Which I will use to improve this home."

"What the hell does it need improving for?"

She huffed and stalked to the front door, fishing the key out of her purse before pushing the door open. "Come in and see for yourself."

She walked in ahead of him, trying not to be overly conscious of just how big and masculine and *there* he was.

"Look," she said. "And by that I mean really look, like someone who's never seen this place before, and not like someone who loves it because it's sentimental."

"Who said it was sentimental?"

"Obviously it's sentimental. You're attached to molding."

"I just don't like change," he said, the words coming out stilted.

"Oh, really?"

"There's an order to things," he muttered. "It's easier to keep track of them that way."

She waved a hand. "Well, I love change. It's what makes life interesting."

"Which begs the question why you're back here. Committed to five long years…"

"Because there's no place like home. I've been all over the country and I've never been anywhere that felt like Copper Ridge."

He paused, studying her far too intently for her liking. "How long did it take you to get that response down so perfectly?"

Anger sparked through her. Because he had her number. "Are you saying my response seems rehearsed?"

"Yes. Very. Why are you really here?"

Oh, damn him. "Because. It was time. Because… I was tired of feeling like I was running away."

"From?"

She lifted a shoulder. "Things."

"Same things you got in that bag?"

"Yep. Nuts, bolts and other assorted crap."

Toby chose that moment to come padding down the stairs and into the kitchen.

"You have a cat," he said, "in the house."

"Yes," she said. "Where else am I going to keep my cat?"

"The barn."

"You don't keep a friend in the barn. Well, maybe *you* keep your friends in the barn. That could be why you don't have any friends."

"I have friends."

"I haven't seen any."

"You've seen me at work and at home."

"And I've seen nary a friend. Are they in the barn now?" She made her eyes round and looked at him in mock horror.

"None of my friends shed. And they don't leave dead animals on your carpet."

"Neither does Toby. I don't think he'd kill a mouse. He's too civilized for that."

"A cat that won't kill mice? That just sounds worthless to me."

She shot him a dirty look and scooped Toby up from his position by the table. "You can't have it two ways. Either it's bad for him to leave dead animals lying around, or it's bad for him to not kill things."

"I like it when cats kill things. Outside."

"Then have your cats the way you want them. I'll have mine the way I want him. And I will have matching molding. We're just going to have to disagree on the fundamentals of life. Big surprise there, right?"

"Good point."

"Well. Good. Glad we've come to that…conclusion." She set Toby on the table. "So…now I need to get back to work."

"You honestly think you're going to do all this alone?"

"Yes. I am. I'm a hard worker and I'm not afraid to get my hands dirty."

"I thought you were a therapist."

"Was."

"Didn't you listen to people for a living?"

She blew out an exasperated breath. "Listening is hard work, I'll have you know. It's why so few people do it. And anyway, I have the desire to finish all this work, and one thing you should know about me is that when I set out to do something, I get it done, okay?"

"Well, I'll look forward to seeing you get this done."

"Yeah, well, I look forward to you putting a shirt on," she said.

The words hung between them and she tried not to pull a face and reveal just how embarrassing they were to her. Because, damn it all, she was trying to pretend that she hadn't noticed. And she was pretty sure she'd been managing to hide the whole I'm-helplessly-checking-you-out thing from him, too. Except now she'd gone and shown she was disturbed by it.

Bah.

He cocked his head to the side. "This bothers you?"

"No."

"Then why did you say…?"

"Because. Because this is a place of business."

"I thought you weren't open."

"I'm not, but…still."

He leaned in and she caught his scent—sweat and skin. Man. And the want, the need, grabbed her around the throat and shook hard, unwilling to let her go. She should move. She should stop breathing him in.

But she couldn't think about what might come next. Because her brain was totally blank.

All she could do was stare. At his lips. At the square cut of his jaw. It was dusted with stubble now, not clean like it had been yesterday. Yes, today he looked more out of order in every way, and she had to admit, it was interesting. Fascinating. Dangerous.

Something crackled between them, and he seemed to feel it, too. Because his expression wasn't granite like usual. There was heat there. Even fire. It flickered, quick and hot, in his dark eyes, and then it was gone.

"I think I've imposed on you a little too long," he said. "I have my own work to do."

"Right," she said. "Go on, then."

"If you need anything…"

"I'll call Kate."

"Call Kate." His words came at the same time hers did.

"Right," she said. "I'll do that. I'm picking her up…soon, actually. So. Okay, then."

He ran his hand over his hair, and she felt a little zip of attraction hit her low as the motion highlighted his biceps. Yet again. There was something wrong with her. It must be all this fresh air.

"I think we'll be okay, Sadie," he said, his voice rougher than it had been a moment ago.

"You…do?"

"Just stay out of my way, and I'll stay out of yours. And try not to change too many things."

CHAPTER FOUR

SADIE MILLER, IT TURNED OUT, was incapable of following orders. She'd done nothing but change things in the two days since she'd breezed onto the Garrett family ranch, and she showed no sign at all of stopping.

First of all, she'd had a crew there reconditioning the wood, stripping paint. Then she'd followed behind, repainting trim. She was like a little blonde windup toy, and every time Eli drove on the road to Connor's house or the main part of the ranch, he caught glimpses of her working outside the house. He could always resolve to hole up on his end of the property. The road to his own house ran the opposite direction, but that would mean no visiting with his family, and no ranch work. And he wasn't that desperate to avoid her.

Still, he didn't want to catch glimpses of her. He didn't want her there. And dammit, even he knew that verged on curmudgeonly. But he couldn't be bothered to care. He had things happening in his life. Important things. And he didn't need her wandering around the place like a breeze-blown hippie.

Shit, he was uptight. But even so, he hated the feeling of an interloper on Garrett land, and yeah, dammit, he was totally a curmudgeon. There was no denying it. But it just felt...invasive.

He didn't like change. He didn't like people crowding. It was a habit from childhood. They didn't have friends over, well, friends other than Jack Monaghan, and they didn't invite company in past the front porch. They didn't let them see what was inside. They didn't let anyone know the extent to which things had fallen apart.

It was a habit that died hard. Or not at all.

Eli pulled his car past the Catalog House, determined not to look again. Determined not to care. He'd promised Connor and Jack an evening of poker and beer and he planned to deliver. Connor would probably be happy as hell if they canceled, which was one reason he was determined not to.

He parked in front of the porch and looked up at the house. When Jessie had lived there, it had looked nicer than it ever had in Eli's memory. And everything had slipped since losing her.

Connor's muddy boots and other random castaways from a day's work were spread out on the wooden deck, which was in bad need of staining. The windows, vast and prominent, were spotted with water drops and splattered with dirt. Even the door had dirty handprints. Like a very large child lived here. A man child who'd crawled down into a bottle of whiskey the day his wife had been put in the ground.

A man who echoed their father a little too much. Not that Eli had a right to judge, considering that he'd never loved anyone. Not the way Connor had loved Jessie.

He'd never lost like that as a result, either, and he planned to keep it that way.

He got out of the car and noticed Jack's F-150 was already parked in the muddy driveway—which badly needed to be graveled, Eli would handle that—and he walked up the steps, knocking his boots against the top stair to get some of the mud off before pushing the front door open.

He could hear Jack's voice already—animated, loud, the same as he'd been since they were a bunch of skinny preteen boys. Jack was a year younger than Eli, but had always been close to both Connor and himself. If Eli had gotten in trouble as a kid, Jack was the reason. As much as Eli liked order, Jack liked disrupting it. Eli couldn't help but foster a strange admiration for Jack's total disregard for rules.

He couldn't partake, but he could admire. From a distance.

"The police are here," Eli said drily, walking through the entryway and into the dining room, where Connor and Jack were already seated, a stack of cards and poker chips in the middle of the table.

"Sadly," Jack said, "we haven't had the chance to do anything illegal yet."

Connor just sat there looking long-suffering. It was painfully obvious they were trying to pull him out of the pit he was in, and as always, he was so damned aware of it that he'd dug his heels in and was clinging to rock bottom for all he was worth. Stubborn ass.

"And now you won't get a chance. Are we ready to play? And drink? Thankfully, I'm within walking distance so sobriety is not a necessity."

"Public drunkenness?" Jack asked.

"Private property."

"Fair enough."

"Liss is coming," Connor said.

"Then why isn't she here?" Eli asked.

"I invited her," he ground out. "But she's not off work yet."

"So now we have to wait, I take it?"

"She's bringing the good alcohol," Connor said.

"Well, in that case," Jack said, relenting.

"Where's Kate?" Eli asked.

"Home, I expect," Connor told him.

Kate lived in another house on the property. It was small, and designed for two people at most, but it was perfect for her.

"Does she know Liss is coming? She might want to see her."
Liss was one of Connor's best friends, and had been a very
close friend of his and Jessie's, both before and during their
marriage. And Kate seemed starved for female companionship,
as evidenced by her obvious desire to wrap Sadie Miller up in
a blanket like a little stray kitten. But he was not having that.
There would be no adopting of Sadie Miller.

He grabbed a beer from the center of the table, out of the
bucket of ice emblazoned with the Oregon Ducks O on the side,
and popped the top off.

"We don't really need Katie hanging out and listening to us
talk," Jack said.

"Don't call her Katie," Connor said. "She hates that."

"You call her that exclusively," Eli reminded him.

"Yeah. I'm her older brother. I can." He jabbed a finger in
Jack's direction. "He can't, though."

"Oh, for God's sake, Connor. Isn't it hard work being this
unpleasant all the time?" Jack asked.

"You're still here," Connor said. "The door is open. There
are plenty of other men for you to play cards and drink with.
Though they'll never satisfy you the way I do."

Eli almost choked on his beer. "You have to warn people
before you break out random acts of humor, Connor. It's unexpected."

"I hate to be predictable."

"Yeah," Jack said. "You also hate puppies, rainbows, and I'm
pretty sure if compound bow season ever opened on unicorns
you'd be first in line."

Eli heard the front door open, and the sound of feminine
shoes on the hardwood floor. Which meant it wasn't Kate, because she wore boots, just like the rest of them.

"I'm here!"

It was Liss. She breezed into the room, tugging her auburn
hair from its bun and shaking her head. "Gah. Nightmare of a

day. Going through financial records for…a place. Confidentiality, sorry."

"Yeah, I know something about that," Eli said.

"I'm sure you do. But accountant work doesn't show up on a police scanner." She set a brown bag on the table. "I come bearing Jack. Daniel's, that is."

"Then you can sit down," Connor said, already reaching for the bag.

Liss frowned.

"Stop it," he said. "Don't give me the sad eyes." He looked around. "This isn't an intervention, is it?"

"Does it need to be?" Eli asked.

"No. I'm fine. Let's play cards."

"Strip poker," Jack said. "Because Liss is here."

Liss looked him over, then looked at Connor and Eli. "I'd win that game, Jack. No matter how you cut it."

"No strip poker," Eli said.

"You're just still mad because the last time I talked you into taking your clothes off, when we were about twelve, I think, we ended up getting caught skinny-dipping by that group of high school girls," Jack said.

"And that was the day I quit listening to you."

"Less talking. More betting," Liss said, pounding the table.

"Fine. Fine."

There was a knock at the door that sounded borderline frantic. And Eli knew that Kate wouldn't knock.

Connor got up. "Just a sec."

He walked out of the room and they all watched after him, listening. "Oh! Thank God you're home." A woman's voice.

"I'm always home," Connor said, his flat tone carrying into the dining room.

Connor. Full of charm as always.

"I'm having a slight disaster." Oh, no.

"Come in." Damn.

More footsteps, then Sadie Miller walked into his brother's dining room.

She was a mess. Her hair was wet and hanging in twisted, yarn-like strands over her face and down her shoulders. She wore a baggy gray sweatshirt that had damp spots spreading wherever her hair touched the fabric. "I'm having a problem," she said a little bit sheepishly, looking around the table at everyone.

Jack and Liss both looked confused.

"This is Sadie Miller," Eli said. "Our new tenant in the Catalog House."

Liss's eyes darted from Connor back to Sadie. "Oh. Hi. You're the one doing the B and B?" For some reason, her friendliness sounded forced. And of course Liss knew about the bed-and-breakfast. In fact, Eli had a feeling she'd been involved somehow.

"Yes," Sadie said. "That would be me. Though, right now the B and B is doing me. So to speak."

"What happened?" Connor asked, crossing his arms over his chest.

"Pipes. Burst. And I was trying to—" she brushed wet hair out of her face "—stop it. To a degree. But I couldn't. So I...uh... wrapped the pipes as best I could and changed and came here. I'm not sure where this falls under our tenant agreement. Technically this had nothing to do with my renovation and everything to do with me trying to shower in the upstairs bathroom."

Connor's brows locked together. "Well...hell if I know. I didn't really anticipate having to be involved."

Sadie blinked. "Well, we signed a whole...agreement. And there are certain things...as the...the landlord...and..."

Eli sighed. "Would you like me to go and take a look, Connor?"

Connor nodded once. "If you don't mind."

I mind. I mothereffing mind. "Nope," Eli said, sliding his beer toward the center of the table and pushing his chair back to stand.

Sadie was eyeing him warily. "Thank you," she said, and he could tell she minded about as much as he did. But she had no place to be irked in all this. She was the one who'd chosen to rent a place on his family property.

She was the one with really quite nice breasts, thank you very much, that were causing him some problems currently.

Getting laid in a small town was problematic. Which made breasts that were actually probably no better than average more noticeable than they should be.

She didn't look hot right now. She looked like a wet hen. He should remember that. He sent a meaningful message below his belt, but he had a feeling it was going to get lost in translation.

Mainly because his body never seemed to want to translate those kinds of messages. But then, what guy's did?

Especially not when the only company said body had enjoyed for the past six months was that of his right hand.

"All right," he said, "let's go check out your disaster. I'll sit this round out," he told Jack.

Jack swept the deck of cards to the edge of the table and leaned back, shuffling expertly. "All right, kids, get ready to lose your hard-earned money."

"Sorry," Sadie said, as they walked out of the room. "Obviously I'm interrupting."

"It's not a big deal. It's a thing that happens a lot. Poker. I'm not going to miss one game. And the sad fact is, Jack's right. We're all going to lose our hard-earned money to him. And he'll continue the grand tradition of having non...hard-earned money."

"I bet there's a story there," she said.

"Isn't there always?" he asked.

She nodded. "Yeah, in my experience, there is. Speaking of—" she pushed the front door open and he followed her onto the porch "—what's Connor's story?" The end of the sentence was hushed.

He closed the door, feeling a little uncomfortable having a stranger digging for information. Mainly because he was so used to family junk staying in the family. Because it was still ingrained in him. To keep the exterior looking shiny, no matter how bad the inside was.

But Connor's deal wasn't really a secret. A cursory visit to Copper Ridge's cemetery would tell his story in full.

"I don't know if you remember Jessie Collins."

"Vaguely. I might. Did she work at the Crow's Nest?"

"I think so," he said, trying not to picture his sister-in-law too clearly. Because it was too sad, even for him.

"Well, she was Jessie Garrett for about eight years. But, uh… she was killed in an accident."

It was a night Eli would rather forget. He could remember the scene clearly. A dark two-lane highway, and a car wrapped around a tree. He'd known it was too late for whoever was inside. That it had been from the moment of impact. He'd seen too many accidents like that, and not enough miracles.

The car had been so messed up he hadn't recognized the make or model. Hadn't realized it was Jessie's until one of the volunteer firefighters, who'd been first on the scene, had come charging back from the car yelling at him not to come closer.

They'd been trying to spare him because of who it was. But in the end, he'd looked. Because he had to be sure.

And then he'd been the one to officially notify his brother. And nothing in all of his life, in all of his training, had prepared him to stand on the front porch in his uniform and tell his older brother that his beautiful wife wasn't coming home. Not that night, not any night after.

Damn trees. Damn road. Two people they'd loved lost that way.

Though in their dad's case, he'd been at clear fault. Alcohol had caused his crash. Jessie had probably swerved to miss a deer, but they'd never know for sure.

"Oh," Sadie said, her voice muted.

"So he comes by his attitude honestly," Eli said, walking down the stairs to the driveway. "You want to ride in the patrol car?"

She looked at him, a brow raised. "It's a short walk. Anyway, I don't want to have any flashbacks."

"Emotionally traumatized?"

"Completely."

"Good. I probably kept your ass out of trouble."

"Ugh," she said. "Do not act like you did me any favors. What helped was getting the hell out of this town."

"Is that what helped?"

"Yeah. There's not enough options here. And there's way too much free time. I badly needed to escape."

"So why are you back?"

She sighed loudly. "Can I get away with repeating what I told you earlier?"

"No."

"Well, fine. That is just a damn good question." She took a big step and her foot landed in a pile of sticks that crunched loudly beneath her boot, before she shifted, her other foot making contact with soft dirt as she continued on toward the Catalog House.

"And you don't have the answer?"

"You know…you have to live somewhere. And I've had a hard time finding a place that didn't…suck. So I'm back here. Because—" she turned partway and offered him a shrug and a sheepish smile, the setting sun igniting a pink halo around her pale hair "—well, I am. And currently, all I've achieved is drowned-rat status."

"Don't go near the barn. Connor has rat traps."

"And cats, I hear," she said, tromping through the tree line and into the driveway of her…his…house. He followed, frowning involuntarily as he caught a glimpse of the bare flower beds. Sure, all that had been in them before was overgrown weeds, but she had them completely stripped now.

"Those are the rat traps I was talking about."

"Don't talk about cats that way in front of Toby. He's sensitive."

"He's probably been talking to you about his feelings too much."

"Was that a therapist joke?" she asked, moving ahead of him and up the stairs to open the front door.

"Yeah, it was. Excuse me, I'm out of practice with jokes."

"Obviously."

Her cat was there, on the kitchen table, looking at him pointedly. As if he sensed that Eli had absolutely no use for him, and he was greatly offended by it. Except Eli knew that wasn't it because it was a cat, and cats had no higher consciousness, as evidenced by their reaction to string.

He stared back at the cat.

"He is unimpressed with you," she said.

"The feeling is mutual. Now hang on a second while I try to figure out where the water shutoff is."

"That would be helpful," she said. "Water shutoff valves would be helpful."

"Connor should have left you a list of that stuff. Where it all is. Fuse boxes and water mains. Though I'm betting he doesn't even know where it is here."

"How long has it been since anyone's lived here?"

"A couple of years. An older lady rented it for about ten years, until she died."

"This place is kind of full of sad history," Sadie said.

"Yeah. Welcome to the Garrett Ranch, where the motto is, if it doesn't kill you…just wait."

"That is distasteful. I'm sure."

"Completely, but also the story of our lives. Now, I'm willing to bet your shutoff is somewhere inconvenient, like…maybe the shed outside?"

"I haven't looked."

"All right, come on. If we find it, I can show you how to shut it off."

"Maybe I know how to shut it off," she said, following him back out the door and down the stairs. "Maybe I'm a water-valve expert."

"But you aren't," he said, opening the door to the shed.

"Fine. I'm not. But I usually have nearby landlords who… do this for me. Which is sort of what's happening now, except you're involving me. Although, I have to say, I have never had a pipe just…explode all over me before. Not a euphemism."

"How could that be…?"

Her eyes widened and she looked at him meaningfully. "Pipes…burst…liquid all over the… Oh, wow. Think about it. Please don't make me say it. And I'm going to stop talking now. Please shut my water off."

Suddenly, he got it. Heat shot from his face down to his groin. This was what happened when he spent six—okay, honestly, it was closer to seven—months without sex. His mind was completely void of anything that went beyond boobs and the innuendo that had just popped up. So to speak. It was enough to… well, as she'd put it, *explode his pipe*.

He did not have time for this. He didn't have the patience for it, either.

"Fine," he growled, stalking to the pipe that was sticking out of the ground in the back of the old building, wrapped in a thick swath of insulation. He reached down and pushed the valve up. "So now your water's off. Direct me to your flood and I can see if there's a quick fix that won't require you to go without water all night."

"It's in the upstairs bathroom. So…back to the house. And I hope you're enjoying this tour of…things that are not finished in the yard," she said, leading them both back to the house.

"What are you doing with the flower bed?" he asked, looking at the bare dirt.

"I don't know... Something. I was hoping someone could tell me which plants you...plant here this time of year. I don't know anything about flowers or grass or... I'm going to do some investigating tomorrow."

"Haven't you planted flowers before?"

She shrugged. "There's never been any point. I leave before anything grows. Or...when I was in San Diego I had an apartment and I had, like, a little pineapple plant in a pot. But some asshole stole it off the balcony. So I figured unless I wanted chains on my potted plants I'd just forget it. This is nice. I don't have to chain things to the porch." She opened the front door and walked in, then paused at the base of the stairs. "Up that way. The one off the master bedroom."

He sighed and walked upward, toward his watery doom. Or something like that.

He could hear her following behind, her footsteps softer and off rhythm to his own.

He walked into the bedroom and saw a few damp footprints on the wood floor, then he looked into the bathroom, where there was a sizable puddle by the sink.

He sighed heavily and got down on his knees, the water seeping through his uniform pants, then he opened the cabinet doors. "What the...hell?"

"I had to improvise," she said, her voice small.

He leaned in and examined the makeshift stopper she'd wrapped around the pipes. A shirt, a pair of sweatpants and...a black lace bra winding it all together.

"I was about to get in the shower, so I was already naked, and then there was water and so I had to stop it, and then I had to...tie it off. With something. I think that bra is toast."

He cleared his throat. "Probably." He reached out and started unwinding the bra, and tried not to think about how this was

the first time he'd touched a woman's underwear in seven—
okay, maybe it was more like eight—months.

It was Sadie Miller's bra. He should focus on that. On the
fact that he remembered what a gangly, hissing little miscreant
she'd been back when she was a teenager. All long limbs and
blond shaggy hair, smelling like booze and cigarette smoke as
she kicked at him while he'd tried to put her in handcuffs without breaking her slender wrists.

Sadie Miller's bra should hold no interest for him. And neither should her breasts. Or her innuendos.

ELI UNWOUND THE STRAP a little bit more and the rest sprang
free, spraying his face with water.

Sadie bit her fist to keep from whimpering as she watched
Eli Garrett, on his hands and knees, fiddling with her bra. She
was so mortified she wanted to flush herself down the toilet. It
would be preferable to this nightmare.

She was just one giant explosion of embarrassment after the
other tonight. The whole pipe euphemism? What was her problem? Why did she say things like that around him? Good gravy.

She was good at talking to people. She did it for a living.
Spoke with calm authority and with self-control, and with carefully chosen words.

And here she was pointing out every innuendo and dying a
million tiny deaths—not in the good French way—like some
extra awkward high school geek she'd never been.

What was it about Eli that caused regression? It was a mystery to her. He made her feel flaily. And kind of...horny. And
that was just stupid. Cracking lady-wood over a cop said nothing good about her deep emotional issues. She was a therapist.
She really should have a better handle on this.

Though she wasn't really a therapist at the moment. She was
a bed-and-breakfast owner who was sinking her life savings
into a place with leaky pipes, populated by grumpy, muscular
men. Who said she didn't make good life choices?

He unwound all of her clothing—thank God she hadn't used her panties. She was just really, really thankful. Then he stood up, the sodden garments in his very large hand, his dark brows drawn together. "This isn't a quick fix. You will need a plumber. Which my brother will pay for."

"He said he wasn't sure where all that fell in the agreement." She reached out and took the ball of clothes, water dripping onto the floor.

"But I am," he said, his voice hard. "It's BS to act like he won't pay for a burst pipe. Obviously that had nothing to do with your improvements. My brother is just being a lame landlord. Trust me, he's not doing it on purpose. He's just…non-functional right now."

Sadie's heart squeezed tight. "I'm sorry about his wife. I… If he ever needs to talk…"

"He would rather shove barbed wire under his fingernails. And I'm being literal."

"Okay, then, so maybe vouchers for my services wouldn't go over well in exchange for this debacle."

"Connor isn't a talker," Eli said.

"Well, big surprise," she retorted, dumping the wet clothes into the sink and walking out of the space that really was way too small to be sharing with a man of his stature.

"What is that supposed to mean?"

"It just seems like it runs in the family, that's all."

"Meaning?" he asked.

"You're a little uptight," she said, walking near the bed and feeling a sudden surge of heat and self-consciousness. Dear Lord, it was like she wasn't even an adult anymore. Internally jittering because she was standing near both a man and a bed and they were alone.

"If by uptight you mean responsible for a shit-ton of stuff, sure," he bit out, "I'm uptight. Do you need water?"

"I have some," she said. "All over my floor."

"That isn't what I meant," he said, his civility clearly almost at an end. "You're going to need…coffee in the morning at least, I assume, and you need to shower."

She lifted a shoulder. "It wouldn't hurt."

"Either Connor will get his ass in gear and try to fix this tomorrow, or we'll want to call out a plumber. Either way you don't have water tonight, because the main has to stay shut off since the pipes are so old. And it means you don't have water until midmorning tomorrow. So, would you like to come to my place and shower and get a couple gallons of water?"

She blinked. "I…uh…"

"It's a simple question."

"I just didn't expect you to extend me hospitality," she said.

"I'm not a complete asshole."

"Oh. Okay."

"You say that like you don't believe me."

She shrugged. "I don't know, Eli, but whenever you're around I get a tension headache. Or I end up in handcuffs. So, suffice it to say, I'm not entirely convinced that you aren't a total asshole. Sorry."

And she also wasn't convinced she wanted to go to his house and get naked when he was in a nearby room. And run her hands all over her wet, slick skin, which would inevitably feel really good. And with his image so very large in her mind…

Yeah, well, again, she regressed in the company of this man. What grown woman worried about this stuff? It was…prurient. And juvenile. And things.

She needed both a shower and some water and the man was offering. So she should stop sweating, and stop insulting him, and just go with it.

"That would be great, actually," she said. "And I'm sorry about the asshole thing."

He put his hands on his lean hips and she took a moment to admire him. His uniform conformed to every muscle in his body; the tan shirt and dark brown tie, along with the gold-

star-shaped badge honest-to-coffee did things to her insides
that were unseemly.

Obviously she needed to buy batteries for her long-neglected
vibrator. Dammit, how sad was it that her *vibrator* was neglected. A sex life, sure. People had crap to do. Who had time
to go around hooking up and sweating and making walks of
shame? She certainly didn't.

But she barely took the time to orgasm anymore. And when
she did, she had to kick Toby out of the room, because it was
awkward, and then it sort of felt like she was announcing her
masturbatory intentions to her cat, which felt even weirder.
There was something unspeakably sad about the whole thing.

But that was the reason Eli's presence had her so shaken.
That was her story, and she was sticking to it.

"Whatever," he said. "Come with me."

He certainly didn't make a big song and dance about gra-
ciousness. He almost seemed burdened by inescapable chivalry,
which was sort of hilarious, or would be if she wasn't so busy
marinating in her embarrassment.

"Let me get some clothes," she said. "You can wait downstairs." Because she would probably fizzle into an ash ball and
blow away in the wind if he watched her pull a new bra out of
a drawer.

"Fine," he said, walking out of the bedroom and swinging the
door partway closed. She waited until she heard his footsteps
on the stairs before rummaging for new clothes. She pulled out
a long-sleeved thermal shirt and a pair of black yoga pants, and
a new bra and panties. And then she got a duffel bag to con-
ceal it all in.

She stuffed the clothes inside and walked downstairs to
where Eli was waiting, standing there staring at Toby, who
was still on the table, looking defiant.

"I'm ready," she said. "Do you have jugs at your place?"

"Yes," he said. "We always save a bunch for target practice,
so that won't be a problem."

Holy hell, she really wasn't in San Diego anymore. She was in Oregon, no question at all. "I should have guessed."

"What's that supposed to mean?" he asked, holding the door for her.

"Nothing. I just forgot the kinds of things you good ol' boys get up to in your spare time. I've been living in a city, if you recall."

"You've been gone for how long?" he asked, walking down the front porch steps. She followed him closely, clutching her bag to her chest. Looking at his dark brown pants, which seemed to be giving his butt a hug while shouting, "Look at it! Look at it!"

"Ten years."

"And where have you been in those ten years?"

"Polite conversation?" she asked.

"Why don't we try it?"

"I'm game if you are. Okay, I went to three different schools in four years. I started in Tampa, because, parties and the beach. Which is nothing like the beach here. Turns out, I hate college parties and breathing in Florida is like inhaling soup. So I lasted a year there. I basically toured the South." She increased her pace to keep up with Eli's long strides, following him down the darkened driveway. He pulled a flashlight off his belt and used it to light up the bark-laden ground. "Louisiana, North Carolina, and after I graduated I went to Texas, which you really don't want to mess with, just ask the locals."

"After that you went to California?" he asked.

"Nope. After that there was New York, Chicago and Branson."

"Branson?"

"Missouri. It's Las Vegas for families, Eli. Incidentally, I also lived in Vegas, but not for long. Then I went to the Bay Area and quickly discovered I couldn't afford to live there unless I wanted to donate a kidney to science, and then I went to San Diego. And now I'm back…here."

He stopped walking, the flashlight beam still directed at the ground. "I can't imagine picking up and moving that much."

"No?"

"I've got too much to pack up and bring with me. You know, Connor, Kate, all their stuff. The cows. Plus, there's this land. Our family land."

"Yeah, well, it's just me and Toby. We travel light."

He started walking again, continuing on straight down the drive. "I'll regret asking this, because... I shouldn't care. But what the hell did you expect to find moving from place to place?"

She lifted a shoulder. "I don't know. Everywhere is so different. I managed to trick myself into thinking that I'd find a place that made me different. And to a degree, it's true. Every place changes you a little. When I was doing therapy, I was a crisis counselor, so I always dealt with people going through the worst things possible. Every patient I spoke to changed me in some way. Every home I lived in, every restaurant I ate at... But...the one thing I've never done is go back to a place. I've only ever gone somewhere new. I thought I would see what it was like."

"And?"

"No magic yet. But I do think I've finally realized that it doesn't really matter where I live. I'm not going to find a perfect place that makes me perfect. So I figured I'd come back here and wrestle demons."

"What kind of demons are you wrestling?" he asked.

It was said drily. Insincere. And yet she found she wanted to answer. She found she wanted to talk to him about the demon she'd met head-on the night he'd arrested her. The night she'd nearly been killed.

She didn't blame him for that. Not really. She knew dimly that some people might. But she'd never put her father's actions onto Eli Garrett's shoulders. Because it had started long before then. Because she had a feeling that night was inevitable. Regardless of what date it fell on, regardless of what triggered it.

And it had been the reason she'd gotten into her car and driven away. And never once looked back. Until now.

"This way," Eli said, pointing his light toward a cluster of pine trees off to the left. "We can cut through here. It's faster."

She followed him through the trees and into a clearing. There was a house up the hill, surrounded by trees, the porch light on as if someone inside the two-story wooden cabin was waiting for them. Wide steps led up to a wraparound deck with a glass door, and large windows dominated the front of the place, making the most of the location, set deep into the trees and far away from any roads.

"No wonder you've never left," she said.

"Well," he said, "not much point when you have a house ready and waiting for you, is there?"

"Sure there is," she said. "If my parents had given me their house I still would have run. Happily for me, they never offered. I think the house ended up with the bank when they went to Coos Bay." She felt like the statement was a little more revealing than she might have liked, but oh well.

"Well," he said, obviously uncomfortable. And obviously unwilling to say more, even though the *well* held a wealth of meaning. He was really, at his heart, a decent man, even if he was reluctant in his decency.

"Well," she said, matching his tone, "my parents' house was essentially the crap cherry on top of a landfill, so for that reason alone I wouldn't want it. Thank you for being too nice to say that." She hopped over a tire rut that was filled with muddy water and continued following him down the road.

"I wasn't thinking it."

"Bull, and ten points if you can guess the word that follows."

"I wasn't, Sadie. I've been to a lot of houses like that. I've seen a lot of things. People have hard circumstances. And I don't like to think of their living situations that way."

"Why not?" she asked. "They do. Trust me. I mean…we do. We know."

"I don't judge people based on where they live."

"Is that honestly how you feel? Or are you just throwing out some…good-guy line?" she asked, as they came to the end of the road, where it narrowed and led up to his house.

"Honestly?" he asked, turning to face her. "I care about this place. I care about Copper Ridge. And I care about Logan County. This is my home. And the people here are my responsibility. It's not my job to look down my nose at anyone. It's my job to protect the people here." He continued walking, turning away from her again, his broad back filling her vision.

Her heart jammed up against her sternum. Anger mixed with a strange kind of longing that she didn't want to apply to him. That she didn't want to apply to anything or anyone, really.

"And you do a damn fine job, I'm sure," she said, following him up the steps and waiting for him to unlock his door. The man locked his door. In Copper Ridge. Dear Lord.

"I know," he said. "I haven't exactly been hanging out for the past ten years so my first arrest could tell me that, but now that you have, it's sort of nice and circular. I could use it for my campaign."

"Hold up," she said. "Campaign?"

"Yes. I'm running for sheriff." He bit the words out as if sharing them with her was a monumental task.

"Oh, really?" she said, eyes widening. She couldn't help but be…intrigued by that. Maybe *intrigued* was the right word. Because Eli Garrett seemed to be a few things to her, and none of them were overly diplomatic. And it seemed to her, not that she was an expert, that a person running for any sort of elected position needed to behave, at least some of the time, like he didn't have a stick lodged in his rear.

But that was just her take on it.

"Yes," he said. "Really."

"Well, color me intrigued. What all does this entail?"

"Right now? I was the top finisher in the primary, and the final election is in November. My lead was pretty strong, but I still need to keep campaigning. Make more signs. I have a few months to prepare for a community Q & A," he said, pushing the door open. "This is the house." He swept his hand in a broad gesture across the living space. It was open, and neat, very different from his brother's place, which had an air of sad neglect about it, every bit of dust and dirt a fingerprint of grief. Eli's home had no fingerprints at all. Which, in and of itself, she found fascinating.

"Wow. Connor should hire you," she said.

"Because I'm not at all busy," he said. "I mean, obviously I'm not. I'm here getting water for you and letting you use my shower."

"Because you care for the members of the community," she said. "Which I am, at this moment, grateful for. Much more so than that time you cared for the community by handcuffing me and putting me in the back of your patrol car."

"That seems to come up a lot."

"It's our cute meet, meet cute, whatever they call it. It's part of our story," she said, watching the tension between his brows intensify with each word. There was no doubt, she disturbed him. And he was growing even more disturbed having her in his house.

"Right. So, the bathroom is upstairs. Feel free to take as long as you need in the shower. I'll get the water ready for you to take back."

She cleared her throat, annoyed with herself for finding sincerity so hard. She was a basket case. Why anyone took her advice on anything was a mystery to her, particularly when she acted like this. "Thank you. Honestly. I know that I've sort of crashed into your life sans finesse here, and I appreciate you… well, I'm glad you haven't found a reason to arrest me again and I'm very grateful for the chance to shower."

He nodded slowly. "You're welcome."

"I'm going to go and…shower now." And she was going to hope that she could do it without thinking too much about his proximity. Or without thinking about him at all. Yes, not thinking about Eli Garrett at all—in the shower or out—would be the ideal thing.

If only she could manage it.

CHAPTER FIVE

ELI GRITTED HIS TEETH and hunched his shoulders, trying to ignore the sound of the running water. Trying to ignore any and all thoughts of Sadie in the shower.

It was hard, no pun intended, because there hadn't been a woman in his house, in his shower, in…possibly ever. It had been so long since he'd had an actual relationship, he couldn't remember. Longer still since a relationship had mattered, since every actual girlfriend he'd had sort of faded into the distant past like a soft hazy dream.

The kind he had no desire to revisit. Because girlfriends were a whole level of responsibility he didn't want or need. At this point, with Kate still unsettled and Connor deep in his grief, Eli couldn't fathom taking on much more.

Which is why it's obviously the best time to increase your workload.

He pinched the bridge of his nose and took a deep breath, before dropping his hands back to his sides and stalking to the fridge. He was going to drink a beer. And he wasn't even going to bother to go back for the poker game. They'd all do fine without him.

He pulled a cold bottle out from the back and popped the top off with the magnet opener he kept stuck to the freezer.

Yeah, it was a terrible time to take on more. Connor needed help on the ranch, and he always would. It was their legacy, and Eli had to take part in it. Then there was the emotional aspect of dealing with his family.

On top of that, Sadie being in residence was adding another layer to his to-do list that he did not need. Because for all Connor said he was going to handle it, here *Eli* was, freaking handling it.

Not a huge surprise and not much he could do about it, either. Five years. Five years of Sadie and foibles that would undoubtedly be similar in nature to this. Sometimes he wondered if he'd been an ax murderer in a past life and he was destined to spend this one atoning.

But then he remembered reincarnation was bullshit and took another drink of his beer.

And reincarnation was not the only thing that was bullshit. That there was a naked, wet woman in his house whom he could not and would not touch was also bullshit.

He'd had a permanent frown etched into his face since Sadie had shown up. He didn't even feel like trying to fix his attitude. It was just one more thing to add to his list of things to worry about. One more thing that he had to add to an increasing, unwieldy pile of Things For Eli to Manage.

Things he knew without a doubt wouldn't get taken care of if he didn't do it. Because that was life. It was his life.

Which he was normally not so bitter about. But something about the addition of a woman whom he wasn't allowed to touch, a woman he shouldn't even want to touch, naked in his house was like jamming an injured thumb into the center of a lemon. Grabbing two empty gallon jugs from under the sink, he began to fill them for the woman he was trying not to picture naked.

He heard soft footsteps on the stairs and turned to see bare feet come into view. Bare feet with shocking pink nails. Followed by baggy black pants and a very soft-looking shirt, molded to breasts that he should not stare at—but did anyway—and then the rest of Sadie appeared.

Her blond hair was wet and piled on top of her head, tendrils falling down the sides of her face, her cheeks flushed from the hot water. Her makeup was gone. Lashes that had looked dark and heavy were now spiky and pale.

She looked damp and warm and he had no business wondering about her body temperature, or her level of dryness.

"Thank you," she said, her feet hitting the floor. She walked to the kitchen counter and slung her bag, and her shoes, onto the granite surface. "I feel more like a human and less like a mole person, so that's always good." She was smiling now, effortless, friendly.

As if she hadn't been pissy and sulky with him only a few minutes ago. As if they had no history between them whatsoever.

Fine, it didn't matter to him. She was just a problem to check off his list. He was not going to waste time overthinking her. He didn't have the time to waste.

"Shoes," he said, the muscles in his back tensing from his belt line to his shoulders.

"What?"

"Take your shoes off my counter, please."

"Sorry," she said, pulling them from the surface that would now have to be disinfected.

"Yep," he said. "I'll grab your jugs for you."

Her blue eyes rounded. "Oh, really?"

"What?"

"You're going to…grab my jugs for me… I don't… You've *had* sex before, right?"

Heat assaulted him, starting in his face and burning a line

straight down his chest to his cock. "Yes. What does that have to do with anything?"

"You seem to be operating on a frequency wherein sexual innuendo doesn't exist."

Jugs. Suddenly an image of him putting his hands over her breasts and, well…grabbing them…flashed through his mind. "Because I'm not a fourteen-year-old boy," he shot back. "And I don't call women's breasts jugs." He said the last part through gritted teeth, trying to figure out how in the hell he'd gotten into a conversation about breasts with the woman whose breasts had been tormenting him from the moment she'd crashed back into town like a blonde tornado.

"Well, that's mature of you. I don't typically call them jugs, either. I prefer 'the girls' or 'sweater bunnies,' but even I went there."

He about choked on the sip of beer he was trying to take. "Don't you have work to do back at your place?"

"Nothing pressing," she said.

He gritted his teeth. "Do you want a beer?" He didn't want her to stay for a beer. Why was he so compulsively appropriate? Especially when she was standing there talking about *sweater bunnies.*

"Thank you," she said, "that would be good."

He laughed, even though he found nothing about any of this funny, and turned back to the fridge, tugging another bottle out, and opening it before sliding it across the counter toward her.

In spite of himself, he found he was curious about her plans for the Catalog House. Because maybe if he knew about the changes, they wouldn't feel quite so invasive. A long shot, but worth a try.

And anything was better than talking about her breasts.

"What's next on your list for the place?" he asked.

"I have to make the downstairs back bedroom livable. That's going to be my room. It's small, and part of an addition. So it's a little damp and chilly, but with caulking and some oil heaters I won't die. And since we're headed into summer it won't be bad at all. Then obviously I need to make sure the plumbing is better than it is. Flower beds are a priority, and linens and blinds. And after that, barring menu creation, I should be good to start advertising and getting special events scheduled."

"Wait...special events?"

"Yes! I thought it would be fun. Ranch tours. Picnics. And I'm thinking on Independence Day a community party would be great."

"People. Here?"

"Yes, people. I'm opening a bed-and-breakfast, for people and not, despite what you may have thought, cats. And if I want to attract people, it seems like bringing visibility to the place is the way to do it."

"What's the point of attracting locals?"

"Uh, locals go away on romantic weekend getaways to local places. And also, their family members come and visit. And people from surrounding areas might come to the parties and think of me. And honestly, maybe they'll think of Garrett specifically when they go to buy beef."

"How do you know about what we do on the ranch?"

"I Googled it. Because I am interested in helping you. And me. It's all...symbiotic helpfulness. And what's wrong with that?"

He felt like he was losing control. Like she had come along, grabbed his control and was running around holding it over her head, laughing maniacally as he tried to reclaim it.

"What's wrong with that is you're proposing to turn this place—*my* place—into a fun fair. We live here. We work here. This isn't a carnival."

"I never said it was! But what's wrong with a few special events? It's not like I have to take over the barns. I mean, I would, but I can keep it contained."

"Have you run any of this past Connor?"

She shrugged. "Not...specifically, but he did agree to let me bring a certain amount of the public onto the property when I initially sent over my business plan, so I didn't see why this would be a problem."

"You didn't see why it would be a problem?" he asked.

"No. I didn't." She took a drink of her beer. "I'm running a business, and it benefits Connor, benefits Kate and you. I have a five-year lease agreement, and it seems to me that we should all be into ideas that will make things more successful. Right?"

"Not ideas that include my ranch crawling with a bunch of random people. I don't like that kind of disorder."

"You are the singularly most frustrating, uptight, obtuse... No one makes me mad, Eli. No one. I am not an angry person. I like to smile. And every time I'm around you, no matter how cheerful I determine to be, I end up irritated."

"That's funny, Sadie, because I feel like I end up irritated every time I'm around you."

"I just think your irritation is contagious," she said.

"Maybe you're so irritating you irritate yourself."

"Oh! Bah! What are you, twelve?"

"I thought you were the one acting like an adolescent boy, not me."

"No, I am the one acting like I have a sense of humor. Because I do. And you," she said, drawing her beer against her chest, "are ridiculous. And humorless."

"If you think that barb is going to wound me, you obviously don't know me very well."

"I don't know you very well. And I'm content with that. I think I will spend the next five years not knowing you very well." She grabbed her shoes from the stool and plopped onto it, bending over and fidgeting while she put them on her feet. She straightened, a clump of wet hair falling out of her bun. "I'm going to go now. And I'm taking the beer. And the water. Thank you. Again. I'll try not to bother you anymore."

He snorted. "Good luck."

"Oh, I don't need it. I don't mind bothering you. You are

clearly the one who is bothered by being bothered. So...you're the one who needs the luck, not me."

She stood up, collected her bag and managed to grab the water jugs as well, then turned on her heel and stormed out toward the entryway, out the front door, slamming it shut with her foot and rattling the windows.

She had no right to be angry. He was the one who had every righteous reason to be pissed. She was a tenant, not a part owner. She had no right to be making decisions that affected his life and his business.

Tomorrow, he was going to talk to Connor about her. And very definitive boundaries. After he was done with work anyway. He groaned and shoved his beer back. It was officially getting too late for him to stay up and drink. Sadie Miller had ruined his entire evening, and now he was going to have to go shower in a shower still wet with water that had been on her body. And then he was going to have to sleep with visions of sweater bunnies and strangers doing the hoedown on his porch dancing in his head.

Which meant he was better served getting on the computer and working on campaign plans. At least planning would help make him feel like he had some control.

Yes, tomorrow, he would talk to Connor about what needed to be done.

And tonight? Tonight he would just have to deal with his annoyance. At least annoyance was better than sexual frustration.

ELI TOOK A SIP of his coffee and walked out of Copper Ridge's coffee shop, The Grind, and onto the main street. Connor gave him endless grief about the fact that he cut his coffee with steamed milk. And that he ordered lattes. But he wasn't a fan of the black sludge his brother poured down his throat all day.

Eli needed caffeine, and he would get it in the way he found most palatable, even if his older brother called it Bitch Coffee.

Besides, he needed his coffee extra bad today because of his encounter with Sadie last night.

He'd been so annoyed that he'd barely been able to sleep, thanks to the images of his property being overrun with civilians. And he knew that it shouldn't bother him. But he also knew that if it really did happen, he would be putting caution tape all around his portion of the property and shouting, "Get off my lawn!" to anyone who got too close.

Old habits died hard, and things like that.

Anyway, that kind of behavior wouldn't be good for his campaign. And he had to think about that kind of thing now.

He let out a breath and headed toward the crosswalk. He waited for the signal to change, then started to cross, heading back toward his patrol car. A breeze came in off the waves. Salt, brine and moisture filled his lungs.

He needed to get his head on straight and stop worrying about Sadie. Though if there was a magic way for him to just stop worrying he would have found it a long time ago. But it seemed like the day his mother had walked out the door, she'd taken his stability and shoved a knot of anxiety straight into his chest that he'd never been able to get rid of.

He put his uniform on every morning and took it off at night, and the worry didn't go on and off with it. It was in him. Part of him. He'd more or less accepted it. And accepted that the only way to really deal with it was to make sure things were taken care of.

"Deputy Garrett!"

He looked to his left and saw Lydia Carpenter signaling him. He really didn't have time to field any issues from the Chamber of Commerce today. Lydia always had something to talk to him about. From obtaining proper licensing for an event, to dealing with complaints from home owners about "noise pollution" during one of her carefully planned summer concerts.

Everything in him screamed, *Not my problem*, but on the outside he just smiled and nodded. Because, most especially, when someone was hoping to gain the good favor of the voting public, one had to be pleasant.

"Ms. Carpenter," he said, "nice to see you. I'm on patrol so this has to be quick."

"Oh, fine, fine, fine," she said, tucking a strand of dark hair behind her ear, spitting the words out rapid-fire. "It will be. I just wanted to tell you I had a chance to meet with Sadie Miller today."

"You what?" he asked.

"Sadie came by the Chamber with a list of ideas for community events hosted on the ranch."

"She did what?" he asked, the words coming out a bit terse.

Lydia didn't shrink under his terseness. She didn't react at all. Her petite frame was unshaken, her smile firmly in place. She was young to be in the position she was in, possibly a bit younger than he was. And when he thought about it, he had to concede that the woman must be almost entirely composed of efficiency and stubbornness to achieve what she had, even in a town so small.

Her smile broadened, which he would have thought was impossible. And he had to admit that she was actually very pretty. But it didn't make this less annoying.

"She stopped by and we had a lovely chat, Eli." Suddenly he was Eli and not Deputy Garrett. "Her ideas for the Independence Day community barbecue are so good. She's talking about canvassing all of Logan County with flyers. I suggested we get it listed on the nightly news Community Chalkboard and on the Chamber's website. I think it's the kind of thing that could really benefit Copper Ridge. The coastal fireworks on the Fourth are already such a big draw, adding events that extend tourists' stays will only be good for everyone."

He was afraid, honest to God, that a blood vessel in his eye was going to burst. Sadie'd circumvented him and Connor, and now he was effectively roped around the balls by the president of the Chamber of Commerce.

If he tugged too far the other way, he could find himself neutered. And if not anything half that dramatic, he could at least find himself out of the running for sheriff.

"Thank you, Eli, so much for allowing this to happen on the ranch. I can't think of a better place, or a better man to host. All things considered, I mean. I'd love to help with anything I can," she said, looking at him with large eyes. "I can help plan games. I could come by your place and look at different areas that might be of use for the event."

He cleared his throat, hoping it would help dislodge the rage ball that was blocking his ability to breathe. "I'll get in touch with you, Ms. Carpenter," he said, very purposefully not using her first name, because for some reason he just had a feeling that was asking for trouble. "Now, if you'll excuse me, I need to get on with my day."

He turned around to face his patrol car, which was parked against the curb, to see Sadie two blocks down, exiting one of the little shops on the corner, a small paper bag in one hand and a coffee in the other.

Before he could even think through his next move, his feet were propelling him toward her. And he was pissed.

She lifted her head and froze when she saw him walking toward her, her eyes widening, before she schooled her expression into an easy smile. "Why, hello, Officer Garrett," she said.

"Deputy," he bit out. "And do not give me that overly innocent face, Sadie. I know what you did."

"Do you?"

"Yes, I spoke to Lydia just now," he said.

"Ah," she said, nodding, "Yes. Lydia. She was so excited about the ideas that I had. And very keen to come over and help me get everything in order. And very, very excited to talk to you about it."

"What does that have to do with anything? What does it have to do with the fact that you have, yet again, overstepped?"

"Nothing. I was just making an observation that you have a big fan there."

"What?"

"She likes you," Sadie said, taking a sip of her coffee. "A lot. And I'm not really sure why, but I sort of assumed you have to possess something that looks like a personality when you're not around me, or you wouldn't have half the people in your life that you do. Which leads me to the conclusion that you just don't like me. But back to Lydia… Yeah, she likes you."

"What the hell do you mean she *likes* me? Who says that anymore?"

"Fine. She wants your body. Do you approve of that assessment?"

"No," he said, frowning. "No, I don't. She's just friendly because she's president of the Chamber of Commerce, and it's her job to be friendly."

Tourism was an emerging industry in Copper Ridge, and it was quickly becoming the heart and soul of the town, which was, in his opinion, the jewel of this section of Oregon coastline. The coastal Old Town section had been totally revamped half a decade earlier, and what had once been dilapidated was now made charming.

With that had come vacation rentals, small motels and a smattering of bed-and-breakfasts, similar to Sadie's.

In addition there were now candy stores, boutiques and shops specializing in crap made of salvaged flotsam that were destined to collect dust on mantelpieces up and down the West Coast.

The rest was mill and timber towns, run-down fishing communities, all banded together under the header Logan County, so named for its surplus of loganberries that lined the highways and tangled around the trees in the forest. All his responsibility. A responsibility that was starting to feel a little more burdensome just at the moment.

"Sure. I'm not going to argue the point with you," Sadie said. "But…you're a little oblivious."

"I find that ironic coming from a woman who seems oblivious to the fact that I don't want to host a community barbecue…picnic…pie eating contest or whatever the hell it is you're—"

"Oh! Pie eating! That would be great!"

"Sadie," he said, his tone warning.

"What? You're being a stubborn cuss," she said. "I am working hard to establish my B and B as something special. Yes, there are several in town, but they're just that—*in town*. Which, I grant you, provides the ocean view, but if you want solitude, a chance to be surrounded by the mountains. To just…be on a ranch? Well, that's what I provide. I want people to come and see it. I want people to *want* to be there."

"And you're going to accomplish that with pie eating."

"Argh! I genuinely don't understand what your issue is."

"Because I didn't tell you what it is," he said. And he didn't plan on it. The bottom line was, he was uncomfortable opening the ranch up to the public, and that was all she needed to know.

"Well, maybe you should."

"Do you want me to talk about my fucking feelings?" he asked, the language, in this context and while in uniform, not something he would normally use. But the woman was standing on his last nerve and grinding it beneath the heel of her impractical sandals—and yes, he'd noticed them, since the top of her head was now just above his shoulders, rather than at the middle of his chest. "Because we're not in your office, and I would not pay for that level of torture."

"I would refer you to someone else," she said. "A specialist of some kind. And anyway, I'm not practicing here. I'm just opening a bed-and-breakfast and trying to bring cheer—and pie—to the community." Her pale brows locked together, a slight crease forming between them. "Do you hate pie and cheer?"

"I like both, in the appropriate place, at the appropriate time. I assume you still haven't run any of this by Connor."

"Not as of yet."

"Well, his *hell no* will be even more emphatic than mine."

"What about Kate?" she asked.

"If you use my sister against me I am throwing your cat out into the barn with the rest of the rat traps," he said.

"Okay, then, note to self, speak to Kate about this, because she will clearly side with me."

"I have work to do," he said. "Work that does not include playing house on someone else's property. We'll have to resume this at another time."

"Okay," she said, lifting her chin in the air, "we will."

SADIE WATCHED ELI'S retreating back and fought the urge to throw her coffee at him. She imagined it, though. Imagined the cup landing smack in between his broad shoulders and spraying that uniform with dark brown liquid.

She would mourn the loss of such a gorgeous, well-fitted garment, but it would be a small price to pay for how satisfying it would be in terms of venting her frustration.

No, she hadn't talked to Connor yet, but when they'd discussed the agreement—granted, over email—and come to an understanding about the percentage of her income he would be entitled to, they'd also discussed taking steps to ensure that it was a very profitable venture.

Connor wasn't the friendliest guy, even via email, but one thing he had talked about was the ranch, and why he was interesting in leasing the house. Ranching was hard and increased restrictions made it even harder. Selling their product wasn't as simple as it had been when the ranch had first started, and the cost of getting cattle to official USDA stations wasn't negligible.

One thing she'd picked up about Connor was that the ranch was the most important thing to him. And she felt like he would be on board with her plans when he saw the merit in expanding what they used their property for.

Of course, the chance remained that he was as unreasonable as his younger brother.

She huffed and headed down the street, the opposite direction from Eli, toward the Farm and Garden, where Kate Garrett was currently working her shift. And no, Sadie was not above using the youngest Garrett in a bid to get her way.

She pushed the door open, a bell tied to a string resting above the entryway signaling her presence with a soft, pleasant sound.

Being back in a small town was jarring and strange, but comforting in a million little ways she hadn't let herself imagine it might be. From gas station attendants who knew your name—and pumped your gas for you, welcome to Oregon—to little bells in doorways.

"Hi, Sadie, what brings you in today?"

Sadie smiled at Kate, who was behind the counter, her dark hair in a simple braid, her figure disguised by a plaid flannel shirt that was tucked into a pair of tan Carhartts.

The urge to strangle your brother is what compels me today, thank you very much.

"Flowers, actually. I need to get the front flower beds in order and I know absolutely nothing about anything leafy or petally."

"Well," Kate said, coming out from behind the counter, "you've come to the right place. Because I know a lot of things about plants."

"Good. So…you sort of know where I'm talking about, right?"

"Just the boxes in front of the porch?"

"Yeah, um…what can I plant there?"

Kate laughed. "I'll help you out. Just come out to the back with me."

Sadie tucked a strand of hair behind her ear, adjusting the paper bag she was holding as she did so, then took a sip of coffee as she followed Kate out through double, automatic glass doors to the back patio. Plants were hanging from metal scaffolding overhead and more pots were on pallets raised up from the ground. Flats of flowers were stacked into racks, and against the chain-link fence in the back rested bags of potting soil and fertilizer.

"I'm going to have to have you load up a cart for me, because I don't know what I'm looking at," Sadie said, surveying the plant life.

"I'm more than willing to do that. And I will even give you my employee discount." Kate looked around, her expression shifty. "Just don't tell."

"Don't do it if you'll get in trouble. Otherwise, please and thank you, because I'm not *that* well-off."

"It'll be fine. It's for Garrett land, after all." She grabbed the handle of a flat metal cart and turned it, then stuck a flat of dark purple flowers onto it. "This will get you started. And…" She started hunting through the displays.

"So," Sadie said, feeling ridiculously adolescent for what she was about to say, but unable to stop herself from saying it, "what is your brother's deal?"

"Which one?" Kate asked.

She could always deflect now, and say it was about Connor, which should in no way make her feel less awkward, but it did. Probably because, as handsome as he was, in that grieving, several-weeks-old-beard kind of way, she just didn't want to look at Connor's butt. Eli's, on the other hand…

"Eli," she said, grimacing at her honesty and thankful that Kate was still eyeballing plants.

"Uh…" Kate straightened and flipped her braid over her shoulder. "I'm not sure he has a deal."

"He doesn't seem that happy to have me around. Furthermore, he got a little…testy when I suggested we might have some events on the ranch."

"Oh, well…he's private. I guess. I mean, I never really thought about it, but it's not like we have parties or anything at the ranch. Birthday stuff we do at Pappy's Pizza, and for stuff they don't include me in they go to Ace's. So…yeah, maybe that's it. Maybe he just doesn't like to have people out. I never do, but that's not really a choice. More of a happenstance. Because…you know, this town is really small and everyone knows

I have a brother with the power to arrest them. And one who would probably shoot and bury someone with no blip of conscience." She frowned. "Anyway, I'm sorry about Eli. Usually it's Connor we all have to apologize for."

"No, don't…apologize for him. But…is there, like, a plant I could get him?" she asked. Maybe a peace offering was the way to go. Right now she seemed to just be going the Purposefully Ruffle His Feathers Route, which was honestly really stupid and wasn't going to solve anything.

"Well, sure…you could get him an azalea," Kate said.

"An azalea?"

"Yeah, it's a flower, but they grow native here so it's less… groomed and more…manly. A manly flower."

"Okay," Sadie said. "A manly flower. I'm down with that. I'll get him an apology azalea. And then maybe we can try to talk again. Like adults instead of sniping children."

Kate winced. "Was it that bad?"

"I don't know. But some of it was my fault. We just…rub each other the wrong way." And she had a feeling that a lot of her annoyance boiled down to the strange tightening in her stomach whenever he was around.

Of course, putting it like that made it seem like she didn't know what that was, when she knew full well what it was. It was just…unusual in this context.

Usually she felt that level of excitement, that sort of low, giddy tug, when she was about to have sex. A brief little flash of anticipation. If she remembered right. It *had* been an awfully long time.

She was not used to it in regards to a man she wasn't interested in. Was not used to it being connected to a man she didn't like, much less a man she wasn't in a relationship with.

She was something of a serial monogamist. She'd meet a guy, they'd go on a few dates and they'd have fun while it lasted. And when things got…un-fun, they'd stop. There was no second-guessing, or yelling at each other. There were no question marks. She liked it straightforward and simple.

Her most recent ex, Marcus, was a classic example of that. They'd met at her gym. He was hot. He was fun. They'd gone on some dates, and then slipped easily into a physical relationship. And then, he'd gone and screwed it up by asking for a drawer. The man had never spent the night, and he wanted a *drawer in her dresser.*

It had been, to Sadie at least, a clear sign that they wanted two different things. And while her instinct had been to placate him or string him along, she knew that it wouldn't benefit either of them. And a lovely time in their lives would only be remembered for the discord in the end. She said a big no-thank-you to that.

It was always better to let someone go too soon than to hold on too long.

She liked it clear. And she liked it *simple.*

There was nothing simple about the way Eli made her feel. And there was nowhere for it to go. So, it could just stop.

But then, even when she'd been a teenage miscreant, loath to deal with his presence, she'd found him hot. So, if she knew anything about herself, it was that her body was die-hard stupid for Eli.

"Well, Eli really is a decent guy," Kate said, adding a plant with fuchsia flowers to the cart. "So I'm sure once you get on the same page he'll be reasonable."

"You think?"

"I don't know. But I'm just his sister. So often he's not reasonable with me, but I tend to think that's genetics at work."

"Right. Well, I'm an only child, so I'm not really up on the dynamic."

"That must have been lonely," Kate said.

For some reason, her words hit a sore spot. "Uh…" Sadie cleared her throat. "I had a lot of friends." Friends she hadn't spoken to in a decade. Were they here? Were they gone? She had no idea.

She didn't hold on. It wasn't healthy. And she was a bastion of positive mental health and good feelings. And stuff.

"Well, that's nice. I have...minimal friends, actually," Kate said. "But you know, the ones I have are good. People who love horses as much as I do."

"Hey, that's important. And it's better than lots of crappy friends anyway." Her friends hadn't really been crappy. Sure, they'd been terrible influences on each other, but they'd all had sucky lives. Smoking in the woods, drinking beer and making out were the best they could do since their homes were in such a sorry state.

"Yeah, I'm sure that's true," Kate said, putting a few leafy greens onto the cart. "Do you want some basil or mint or anything?"

"Oh, yeah!" she said. "Any. All. Can I put those in the windowsill in the kitchen?"

"Yep. I'll grab herbs on our way back inside and you can wait for me at the counter."

"Thank you," she said. "For your help and the discount and... not hating me."

"Eli doesn't hate you," Kate said, shoving the cart in through the door, her petite frame obviously a lot more muscled than it appeared at first glance. "He doesn't hate anyone. He's really very decent down to his core."

Sadie went to the front of the counter and set her coffee on the rough-hewn wooden top, digging in her back pocket for her credit card. "He seems like he is."

"He took care of me for most of my life. Our mom left when I was little. You probably knew that. Everyone knows that." She reached around and tugged on her braid, the gesture so childlike and sad it made Sadie ache a little bit. "Anyway..." She flipped her hair over her shoulder and went about grabbing the scanner and checking the plants. "Our dad... Things were hard

for him after that and someone had to take care of the ranch—
that was Connor. And someone had to take care of me and the
house. And... Eli did that."

Sadie cleared her throat, strange, aching emotion pressing in
and making it feel tight. "Well, then it's a good thing I plan on
extending an olive branch. Apology azalea. Whatever. I mean,
since he's such a good guy."

The total flashed up on the screen, and Kate tapped away
on the ten key, bringing the amount down by almost half, and
Sadie sighed in relief. "Really. Really, thank you."

"Really, no problem. Maybe...maybe we could hang out
sometime?"

"Yeah, maybe. I think... I probably won't get to plant these
until tomorrow. But if you're around, maybe we could work on
it together?"

Kate brightened. "Sure! And actually, if you don't need them
now, if you want I could put them in the bed of my truck and
bring them home tonight. Then you wouldn't get dirt in your
car."

Kate's offer gave Sadie serious feelings in the region of her
heart. She wasn't sure she deserved the other woman's friendliness. But she wanted it. She wanted a friend, darn it. "Thanks.
I'll take the apology azalea, though, since I need to talk to Eli
and I'm not doing it without reinforcement."

Kate grabbed the largish potted plant from the cart and
handed it to Sadie. "Here you go."

Sadie wrapped her arms around it, holding both her coffee
and the bag of knickknacks she'd purchased earlier. "Great.
Well. See you later." She turned and headed toward the door,
pausing when she realized she had no available hands.

"Sorry!" She heard Kate scurry around the counter, rushing
to hold the door for her.

"No problem," Sadie said. "I'll see you."

She walked out into the warm afternoon, wind kicking up
from the ocean, blowing her hair across her face and into her

mouth as she walked back up the sidewalk toward where she'd parked her car. She did a little cursory scan for Eli's patrol car but didn't see it.

And she tried not to think too much about the sinking, vague sense of disappointment she felt over that.

CHAPTER SIX

BY THE TIME Eli clocked out, he was ready to sink onto the couch and zone out. Maybe watch whatever sport was on. He wasn't picky. Hell, he'd take tennis at this point. Just something that didn't require thought.

But when he pulled his car into the dirt drive that led up to his house, it didn't take long for him to see that was not going to be in his future. There was a shiny black sedan in his space. Which meant there was a person here. Which meant he had to be on still. Which had him cursing internally in a variety of interesting combinations.

He groaned and pulled his car to the side, so that whoever owned the sedan could easily get out again once their business with him was done.

He put the car in Park and killed the engine, unbuckling and getting out, letting out a long-suffering breath as he did.

He took a few steps toward the house and saw the back of a dark-haired woman, long hair, shiny and curly, swinging down to a slim waist. She was facing...well, off into the vague distance as far as he could see.

He frowned and moved closer, then he noticed that there was another woman kneeling down in the dirt, her face partly blocked by a curtain of blond, straggly hair. He could see one pale, dirt-splattered arm. And for some reason, the sight of the bedraggled woman on her hands and knees gave him a jolt that the back of the glossy brunette hadn't.

Then the brunette turned, and revealed both her identity and that of the blonde. And suddenly everything, including his re-action, made very irritating sense.

Because Lydia Carpenter belonged to the glossy dark hair, and the gritty mess in his dirt was, of course, Sadie Miller. Of Course.

He and his dick needed to have a very serious conversation about appropriate reactions to women who were very annoying.

"What's going on here?" he asked, realizing, in some dim part of his brain, that this was not a socially acceptable way to greet people.

"Eli!" Lydia said, smiling broadly, taking a few steps toward him, her tan legs on display in a very short summer dress she had not been wearing earlier. She was also wearing red lipstick, which he didn't remember from earlier, either.

Sadie looked decidedly less happy to see him from her po-sition on the ground. She looked up, squinting against the sun, offering an approximation of a smile that looked a little bit like she was baring her teeth at him.

"Hi. Did we have a…meeting I forgot about?" he asked, look-ing from Lydia to Sadie.

Lydia's smile suddenly went a little snarly. "Uh. No. Great minds, I guess. Though I feel like I should have brought a plant."

"What?" He took that moment to look a little more specifi-cally at what Sadie was doing.

There was a mound of fresh dirt around an azalea plant, bright pink buds mocking him with their cheeriness on the ends of the branches.

"Surprise!" Sadie said weakly.

"Uh…" And he had nothing to say after that, so he just let it hang there.

"Eli," Lydia said, and he wondered, yet again, how they'd gotten all first-name basis all of a sudden, "I wanted to let you know that I ran the barbecue idea past everyone on the board and the response was massive. We're so thankful to have someone running for Logan County Sheriff who has such a vested interest in the well-being of Copper Ridge's economy."

Oh, dammit. This was like his worst nightmare come true. He was being railroaded. By two petite, smiling, *evil* women.

"Well… I… Of course I care," he said, and Lydia's expression changed to something else entirely. Something that he couldn't quite identify, but that terrified him down to his soul.

"I knew you did," she said, walking toward him and putting her hand over his. "And it's so greatly appreciated. By me. And…of course, the whole town. And county."

"Of course," he said, drawing back slowly. He looked down at Sadie, who seemed frozen, her eyes wide with a combination of amusement and horror.

"Well, I have to go," Lydia said, "but we should discuss this further. Over coffee." She reached into her purse and dug a card out, pressing it into his hand.

"Okay," he said, curling his fingers around it.

Lydia turned and smiled at Sadie, and again, he had a feeling it was a smile meant to convey something other than happiness. There was a lot of strange emotional subtlety happening here, and he basically needed to be bludgeoned over the head with feelings to have any idea of what was going on, so he resigned himself to confusion, and relief when Lydia walked back to her car and started the engine.

He turned back to Sadie, who was still on the ground. "What is happening here?"

"I brought you an azalea."

"Why?"

"To apologize," she said, blinking as if she was suddenly

realizing that her idea might not have been the best. "And to extend...goodwill."

"Some people just say they're sorry. They don't go planting unsolicited shrubbery in front of someone else's house."

"Yeah, well, some people lack imagination." She straightened and brushed her hands off on her jeans, leaving a trail of light dust streaked over the dark denim.

"Or have a greater grasp of social boundaries."

She made an indignant sound in the back of her throat. "That's also a possibility. I mean, maybe. But your sister assured me this was a manly plant. And also didn't seem to think it was a terrible idea."

"It has pink flowers."

"Honestly, the whole gendered colors thing is extremely ridiculous to me. Colors are colors. How can one be masculine and one be feminine?"

"I'm going to skip over this part of the conversation if it's all the same to you."

"It is."

"Great. What was Lydia doing here? Was she part of the plant installation?"

"No. Our missions were separate and coincidentally intertwined with each other."

"She's really into your barbecue idea. Congratulations on your evil plan working, by the way."

"I don't think it's the barbecue she's into."

"Are you still gnawing on that bone?"

"You don't need to whip out that much leg to talk community barbecue. Also, she was a little chilly to me."

"Why?"

Sadie rolled her eyes and crossed her arms. "She's threatened by me. Me and my azalea."

"She has no reason to be," he said.

"You like her that much?"

"I like you and your azalea that little."

"Dammit, Sheriff, right in my soft white underbelly. I'm trying to be nice to you."

"You've put me in a position I don't want to be in. Now I'm going to have to advocate for your little circus."

"Why?"

"Because. You heard her. The whole Chamber of Commerce is really excited, and it's an indicator of my commitment to the community. And my votes are riding on this stupid crap that I don't want to do."

"Oh. Ouch. Public opinion is a new concern for you, isn't it?" She didn't look at all sorry. She looked downright gleeful.

"Not exactly," he said.

"You have to join forces with me," she said. "Assimilate or die."

"You don't have to enjoy this so much."

"But I do!" she crowed. "I really do. And anyway, it's not going to be that bad. No one's going to make you participate or smile."

"I need boundaries," he said. "And a plan. If it's going to happen, I'm going to oversee it."

"Control freak much?"

"Yes," he said. "Much. And I'm fine with it. Now, if you're going to do something on my property you have to be okay with it, too. You don't have to like it, but the bottom line is, you will do as I say, or it doesn't happen at all."

"Oh, really? I thought you acknowledged that I had you over a barrel." She tucked a strand of blond hair behind her ear and arched her brow as if to say, *Gotcha*.

No. Way.

"Oh, no, baby," he said, not sure where the endearment had come from or why it had rolled off his tongue, but he didn't stop to try to figure it out. "You may have me in a position where I have to be willing to consider your idea, but make no mistake, it's you who has the most to lose. I don't *have* to do a damn thing, and I'm the one with his name on the title for this chunk of earth. So if you want to play, you'll play my way."

SADIE FELT AN UNFAMILIAR surge of raw, unmitigated anger course through her veins. This was not her style. It was not her game. She didn't do toe-to-toe shouting matches. Not with men, not with anyone. No. She did yoga. She meditated. She had a pottery wheel somewhere. That she never used, but still, she had outlets. Outlets that were not screaming like a child. Or hitting people with your fists until the anger beast cooled in your chest.

She didn't believe in giving free rein to negative emotions. It was healthy to acknowledge feelings, yes, and to talk about them in a safe space. But to let them explode out of your mouth and through your chest and let them take over all of everything? Which was what was happening right now, whether she wanted it to be happening or not.

She was...seething. And it was overflowing. Onto her, onto him, onto everything. And sure, maybe planting the azalea had been a step too far. But Lydia had shown up when she was dropping it off. And something about the other woman made her feel...competitive. Which was annoying.

But somehow she'd told Lydia that she was supposed to be there. Planting the azalea. And Lydia had lingered. Her mere presence a challenge. So plant it Sadie had.

And he was rejecting it. Honestly, even if her gesture was weird, it was nice. And he was being an ass.

"I bought you a motherfucking azalea!" she said, the words shooting out hard and short, intense like gunfire.

"And I didn't want it," he said, taking a step toward her. "I don't want it here. I don't want you here."

"Why?" she asked, moving nearer to him, compelled forward by the kind of deep, negative emotion she hadn't even known she possessed. "Because I'm getting my dirty, been-arrested, other-side-of-the-tracks, poor-girl filth all over your hallowed Garrett walkways?"

"Because," he said, "you are a mess. And I spent most of my life managing a giant-ass mess, and I don't see any reason why I should willingly subject myself to another one. I have things just the way I want them." He moved closer, a muscle in his square jaw ticking, the cords on his neck standing out. "And I do not need you coming in and ruining anything."

"Oh, really?" She moved nearer to him, so close she could feel the heat of his breath on her face. "I guess you are awfully neat and tidy," she said, her gaze flickering over his uniform, so perfectly pressed and…sexy, in spite of everything that was going on between them. "It would be a shame if I got my mess on you." And before she could police herself, she'd reached out and grabbed his tie, her dirt-encrusted hands sliding over the fabric, leaving a pale dust streak and tugging his face down closer to hers.

Her heart was pounding so hard it was making her light-headed. Her blood pumped to parts…more southerly. She had no idea what was happening to her. This was no sexual attraction as she knew it. It wasn't anything as she knew it. She was angrier than she'd been in recent memory, and a hell of a lot more turned on, and she genuinely didn't know how to process the two together.

She also didn't know how to process that she was inches from his face, his tie clutched tight in her hand, as his dark eyes blazed rage into hers. Rage and something else. Something hotter. Something that looked a lot like the fire burning in her belly felt.

And then…and then he dipped his head, his lips crashing into hers. And that's what it was. A collision. It wasn't a testing, or a tasting, or anything tentative at all. It wasn't nice, or fun, or easy. It was gasoline on a lit match. An instant conflagration that had gone from spark to out of control at the moment of contact.

She had no idea what was happening, only that she didn't want it to stop.

She tugged tighter on his tie and angled her head, parting his lips beneath hers and slipping her tongue into his mouth. He groaned, rough and raw and not anything like the good guy he seemed to want the world to think he was.

He locked one arm around her waist, drawing her tightly against his hard body. His lips were firm and sure. And everything about him, about this, was so much more intense than she'd imagined it could be.

She released her hold on his tie and cupped the back of his neck with her hands, holding him to her. She shifted, breaking some of the contact, and he growled—an honestly feral growl—and bit her lip, drawing her back in close.

Pleasure rocketed through her, her nipples tightening into hard points, desire settling low in her stomach, an iron fist gripping her inside and tugging hard, sending a shock wave of need straight down to her core.

She wanted... She wanted it to go on forever. This need that wrapped her up in a cocoon and held her to him. That blocked out everything. All the worry, all the anxiety, all the anger, and turned it into something... *Good* seemed too insipid a word. And she wasn't sure if this was good at all.

But it was necessary.

Suddenly, it was so very necessary.

She arched her hips against his and felt the very hard, irrefutable evidence of his own investment in this explosion of need. She wanted everything all at once with an intensity that defied anything she'd ever experienced. And she wanted it with all of herself.

Her heart seized tight, a painful spasm, and suddenly she felt herself move away from him, jumping back like a startled cat.

She was shaking. Her hands, her knees and everywhere in between. And kisses did not make her shake. And she didn't kiss men she didn't like. She didn't kiss men in uniforms who had a fetish for order and cleanliness.

She didn't yell at people, either, but right now the yelling was lower on her list of sins than the kissing.

"What did you… I don't even… I'm going to go." She turned, her shoulders stiff, her heart hammering in her ears.

"If I'd known a kiss would have gotten rid of you, I would have kissed you the moment I saw your car sitting on the side of the road."

Oh. That. Did it.

She whirled back around, anger gaining traction in her again. "Well, sure, your kiss got rid of me. Congratulations. Now who's going to help you get rid of the hard-on it gave you? Your right hand?"

He lifted a shoulder, his expression stone, the dull red color on his cheekbones the only indicator that he was affected at all. That the casual manner was a lie. "My right hand suits me just fine. And it's a hell of a lot quieter than you."

"Oh, sure, the masturbation reference you get. You must spend a lot of time alone."

A muscle in his jaw ticked, the color in his face deepening. Embarrassment or anger? For some reason, she felt compelled to find out.

"No comment on that?" she asked. "Hugely shocking to me that women aren't flocking to you." But honestly, his body was stupid sexy and there were, in fact, women who seemed to flock to him. Or at least, one woman. That she'd seen. But, whatever, she was trying to make him mad, so truth didn't have to come into it. Petty meanness was the only thing that mattered. "I mean, you're a jerk. And you don't like anyone in or around your house. You don't even like flowers."

He crossed his arms over his broad chest, and she had to fight to keep herself from looking below his thick utility belt down to where she was sure she would be able to see evidence of his arousal. She was so, so tempted. Because she'd felt it, and it had felt so good. And she was curious beyond reason about how it looked. How he would feel in her palm…

No. Stop it.

"I'm not fighting with you," he said. "But I'm not changing my stance. My way, or no way. It's up to you."

So he wasn't even going to acknowledge the kiss? He wasn't going to fight back and feed her anger and make her feel justified and...and... That bastard.

"Fine," she bit out. "I'll work with you. But if you kiss me again, I'll bite your tongue off."

"Don't worry," he said. "I don't think I'll be tempted again."

That stung. And she had no idea why. Because they shouldn't kiss again. They shouldn't have kissed once. So that meant there was no reason for her to feel upset about him not wanting to kiss her again.

But she was.

"We'll discuss this more tomorrow," she said, straightening her shoulders, trying to maintain dignity she knew she no longer had. "And if I come back tomorrow and my azalea is maimed, uprooted or otherwise denigrated I will vandalize something on your porch."

Then she turned and walked away, trying to calm her pulse, trying to calm the racing of her heart.

She just needed to go back to her place, calm down, and— now that the plumber had been in—get herself a cold shower to help recalibrate her stupid body.

And then everything would be fine. Tomorrow morning, she would be over this thing that had flared up inside her, and she and Eli could get on with planning the community barbecue.

Yeah, that was a very nice lie. And it was one she was going to keep on telling herself until she couldn't anymore.

"THAT WOMAN IS A MENACE," Eli said, pacing the length of his brother's living room, all the blood in his body still heated to boiling since he'd gone and done the most stupid thing imaginable and kissed Sadie Miller like she was oxygen and he was suffocating.

"I don't know, she hasn't caused much trouble other than bursting the pipes, but even with paying for that, her rent is bringing in enough that we're still coming out ahead on the agreement this month."

"Assuming she doesn't cause any more disasters," he said.

"Well, sure, assuming that," Connor conceded, sinking deeper into the couch, his legs sprawled out in front of him, his arms spread out across the back.

"Which is a big assumption, all things considered."

"Untwist your panties," Connor said. "You're just still pissed because I did this without consulting you. And you don't like change. And you don't like feeling out of control."

Well, dammit, was he that obvious?

"This isn't about me. It's about her."

"Sure," Connor said, resting his head on the back of the couch and drawing his hat down over his eyes.

"Will you stop that?" Eli asked.

"What?"

"Stop being so damned disengaged all the time."

Connor straightened, pushing his hat back. "Sure, Eli. You going to arrange to have my wife returned to me?"

Eli's chest seized up, his heart squeezed tight like it was locked in a vise. "You know I can't."

"Then maybe fuck off and stop commenting on how disengaged I am."

It was rare for Connor to acknowledge that he was still grieving Jessie. But then, it was rare for Eli to call Connor on his bullshit in a serious way.

"Fair enough," Eli said, his voice coming out tight.

"Now, I believe you were ranting about our tenant." Typical of Connor. Get really pissed, then pretend it hadn't happened.

"I was. She has plans. And dammit, Connor, I sort of have to side with her on them."

Now Connor's body registered some tension. "What kind of plans?"

"Community barbecue plans," he said.

"And how does this concern me?"

"Because she wants to host things here," he said. "Particularly, she's planning on having a county-wide Independence Day celebration here on our ranch."

Connor had the decency to look perturbed about that. "Here? On the ranch? I won't have to do anything, will I?"

Eli let the implosion happen internally. He hadn't imagined his brother would actually propose that he help out with things, but then, it would have been nice if everything that wasn't cows didn't fall to him.

Which was maybe really unfair of him, but at the moment he didn't care.

"We'll have to clear things with you and your schedule. And I would guess base some things around what fields you want your cows in at a given time. Also, if any barns are going to be used, that needs to be cleared with you."

"Right. Fine. Just…when plans get more advanced, run dates and things by me and I'll see what I can do."

The fact that it made Connor look so damn tired brought Eli back from annoyance to pity. "Great. Sounds like a plan."

Connor frowned. "What happened to your tie…and…all of you?"

"What?" Eli looked down and saw the streak of dirt on his tie. It screamed *feminine handprint* to him, but he was pretty sure that to the unknowing observer it looked like a streak of dirt. Still, it made him feel a lot more like a kid caught with his hand in the cookie jar than he would like. And it made him think about what had happened between him and Sadie, which, in all honesty, he hadn't stopped thinking about since he stepped onto Connor's porch, but now he just felt like his face was projecting the words so Connor could read them easily.

He tried to remind himself that Connor wasn't that perceptive. And then he wondered what was wrong with him because any normal man would feel some sense of pride over kissing a woman as pretty as Sadie.

But then again…what they'd shared wasn't exactly a kiss so much as an explosion that happened to be detonated by the meeting of their lips.

"You look like you rubbed up against the side of a barn."

Eli looked at the rest of his uniform, heat making his face sting. He could see where every inch of her had been pressed against every inch of him. "Something like that," he said.

Connor narrowed his eyes. "Something like that?"

"I wasn't paying attention."

"You pay attention to everything. Which means…you paid extra close attention to whatever happened to your uniform, because obviously you're lying."

"Why the hell have you chosen to get engaged with what's happening right this moment?"

Connor raised a brow. "I think this is the first time I've ever caught you doing something you weren't supposed to do."

"I'm an adult. As long as it's inside the law there's nothing I'm not supposed to do."

"But let's be honest, Eli, the laundry list of things you think you can't do is longer than your arm."

"You don't know everything I do."

"No, but I know everything you don't do. We live too close to keep secrets."

"Fine. I brushed up against the barn."

"Giving it a hug because you were so happy to see it?" Connor asked.

"Okay, you caught me," Eli said, keeping his tone dry. "I found two women mud-wrestling just outside town and when I went to make sure they had a permit for it, they couldn't keep their hands off me."

"Now I believe you hugging a barn before I believe that."

"Well, pick one. Because they're the only two stories you're going to get. Now, if you'll excuse me, I have to go and start organizing this disaster of a party, because frankly, I just didn't have enough to do."

"You know you don't have to do everything, Eli. There's a certain freedom in just giving the world the middle finger."

"Yeah, but since you do it so expertly, someone has to get in there and care." Eli turned and walked out the front door, feeling like a total ass.

Grab a woman who hates you and kiss her? Big fat check next to that box. Insult your grieving brother? Check.

He was on a roll today. There was no denying it.

He sort of wished the mud-wrestling story was true. That would have been fun at least. There was nothing fun about what had passed between him and Sadie. Hot, yes. But not fun. And certainly nothing he could strut around feeling proud of.

When she'd pulled away from him…*appalled* wasn't a strong enough word for the look on her face. She'd looked completely horrified that they'd touched. And he'd just wanted to grab her again. And kiss her more.

What the hell was wrong with him?

When he had…affairs, relationships…whatever you wanted to call them, he was careful about his selection. He found women out of town. He found women who weren't needy or close in proximity. He found women who wanted sex and some easy, occasional companionship.

With the notable exception of Brandy, the last woman he'd been seeing, they were all very casual and very nonintense. Brandy had turned out to be something of a secret badge bunny and about the time he found her naked in the back of his patrol car begging him to put her in handcuffs, he'd known that relationship had to end.

And one thing was certain—he didn't pursue women who didn't want him. Sex was easy. Attraction was easy. It wasn't… whatever this was.

And now he was officially too wound up to enjoy his downtime. Now he was on the verge of an extreme hard-on that would have to go unsatisfied. And now he was officially way past rest and relaxation, he realized during his walk through the property.

What he needed to do was focus on Sadie's event plans. Yes, that was what he needed. He needed the control. Which, when he thought about it, was probably what the kiss was about. Some unevolved part of himself was trying to seize control through sex.

It had nothing to do with reality. Or with Sadie. Or with him genuinely wanting to shove her top up and her bra down so he could get a look at her breasts.

No, that had nothing to do with it. It was the power struggle. But there was another way. He changed direction abruptly, heading toward the Catalog House as quickly as he could, determination making each step hit the ground harder than was strictly necessary.

He took the steps up the porch two at a time and then knocked on the door.

SADIE CHECKED THE REHEATING quiche in the oven and smiled. She'd put it in just before getting in the shower. It was looking perfect. And it had taken her only a few tries over the past few mornings.

She'd done it before, but she usually used a premade crust and she'd decided that wasn't going to cut it at Chez Sadie once she had guests. She took her oven mitts off the cabinet door and opened the oven, pulling the quiche out and putting it on the stove top.

Yes, it looked like heaven. And she was self-satisfied to a ridiculous degree. There was something she liked about all this. Building a business from scratch. Building...quiche from scratch. It was awesome any way.

There was a sudden, impatient pounding on the door that nearly made her jump out of her skin. But almost immediately, she knew who it had to be, without even looking. Because no

MAISEY YATES 233

one else seemed to have emotions strong enough to merit knocks that were quite that intense.

Unless someone had been involved in a terrible wood-chopping accident and was knocking on her door with what remained of their arm. In which case, she should hurry and answer it.

She felt bad for hoping it was someone with a bloody stump, but it seemed oh so infinitely preferable to Eli.

"Coming!" she shouted, pinning her damp hair back and reaching for the door handle, feeling her expression contort to one of horror when she saw who was behind it. "Oh, it's you."

"Who did you think it was?" he asked, his dark eyes intense and far too interesting for her own good.

"I was sort of hoping it was someone who'd been gravely injured and was in need of help."

"Sorry to tell you, it's just me."

"Are you in grave danger? Missing any appendages?"

"All body parts present, accounted for and attached," he said, his tone dry.

And now all she could think of was the body part that had most certainly been present and accounted for during their kiss. And she needed to think of anything else. "Well, damn."

He leaned in and for one moment, she had the fleeting thought that he was going to burst through that door, throw her onto the table and finish what they'd started earlier in the garden.

Which was ridiculous because she didn't want him to do that. And because she was not the kind of person who had crazy, throw-down-on-the-table sex. Because that required a certain amount of insanity that was just not a part of her physical relationships.

She was into relationships where you kept your head on straight and had sex at the end of a nice meal. She was well-adjusted about things. She wasn't an animal.

"I have to work for the next few days, so I don't have time to entertain you, or help you plan your little barbecue. But the minute that I'm off for the week? You and I have some talking to do."

So, he was not here to ravish her. Which was good. It really was. She was relieved. Almost as relieved as she would have been to see someone with a severe wound at the door.

"You make it sound like I'm in big trouble," she said, the words sounding a little softer and a whole lot more flirtatious than she intended.

Her body, it seemed, hadn't realized what her mind had—which was that the ravishment was off the table, so to speak—and had gone into Mae West mode accordingly.

She tried to tell her inner hussy that he could *not* come up and see her sometime, but her heart was still beating at hyperspeed.

"That all depends on your definition of trouble, Miss Miller," he said.

Oh, Lord, why did the way he said those words make a shiver of something rattle through her bones? *Why?* Why did she sort of wish she could go back to being in trouble with him?

She needed another shower. A colder one this time.

"Not really," she said, her words terse. "It kind of depends on yours since you have legal backing."

"I just want to give you a tour of the place. And discuss what is reasonable for the barbecue, and what isn't."

"Okay," she said, feeling a little blindsided by his darn reasonableness. "But I'm not really sure what inspired you to play nice."

"Must have been the azalea. And if you'll excuse me, it's my time off, and I'm going to go unwind."

She really wished she could stop herself from imagining what all him unwinding might entail. She remembered the presumptively thick erection from earlier and imagined him settling down and unzipping his pants…

No. Bad Sadie!

"Well, you go…do that," she said, forcing herself not to look down. Forcing herself to look only at his eyes and nowhere else, which, frankly, she felt she deserved a freaking medal for. His hardness had been pressed right up against her today and never—not once—had she given in to the urge to visually explore it.

"I will. And I'll be here on Thursday morning. Very early. Be ready."

"Bring coffee."

He arched a brow. "All right. I will."

And for some reason, that easy agreement before he walked down off the porch and into the fading light made her more nervous than any fight ever could have.

CHAPTER SEVEN

THE LAST TIME someone knocked on her door this emphatically, it wasn't because of an ax wound, and she had a terrible feeling it wasn't this morning, either.

Sadie wiped her hands on her apron and then untied it, draping it over a chair as she walked to the door. "Coming!"

She smoothed her hair, then jerked the door open with a smile pasted onto her face.

And there was the man himself, the cause of the past four sleepless nights, looking awake and far too sexy for a man in a simple pair of jeans and a black T-shirt. And far too tempting.

She looked down at the mug of coffee in his hand. "So thoughtful of you," she said, reaching out and snagging the bright blue-and-white-spotted tin mug and lifting it to her lips. "Mmm."

"That was mine," he said, pushing past her, "and are you going to invite me in?"

"You're in," she said, feeling warmed both by the coffee and by the implication that his lips had been on it. Which was juvenile in the extreme. She'd kissed him. What was the point of getting warm and sweaty over her lips touching a mug his lips had touched?

"So I am."

She took another sip of coffee, fully aware of the awkwardness that was building as they stood in the doorway, making eye contact and with her drinking his drink. Her nipples prickled and she shifted, the motion seeming to draw his eye right down to the place that was currently feeling quite perky and obvious.

"Do you want to come sit at the table?" she asked. "I actually have more coffee. Lucky thing, since you didn't bring any extra as instructed. And happily for you, my quiche of the day is ready."

"You have coffee and you took mine?"

"It's rude to turn down gifts, Eli. Didn't you ever hear not to look a gift azalea in the mouth? Oh, no…you must not have heard that."

"And gift quiche?"

"Same. It's spinach. And salmon."

He lifted a shoulder. "Well, I might be able to have some."

They moved into the kitchen and she fought to breathe right. She went to the counter and got a knife, slicing a generous piece of quiche for Eli, before getting him coffee, and delivering both to his seat.

"You're my guinea pig," she said, watching him expectantly.

"You're staring," he said, looking at the food, then at her.

"Yeah, I want to see if you like it."

"That's…disconcerting."

"Sorry. I'll look the other way." And she did. Obediently. Until he made a borderline orgasmic sound that sent a thrill straight down through to her midsection and…beyond. She looked back and watched his jaw working while he chewed. So weird, but she found the motion sexy. What the hell was wrong with her?

She wanted to make an excuse about needing to change her

top or something since she'd been cooking. Just so she didn't have to sit and eat with him. And stare at his weirdly sexy mouth motions. But that felt self-conscious. If she ran off before he was done, she would look like she was doing it because she was uncomfortable around him—which she was.

Oh, to hell with pride.

She stood up. "I'll be right back. I have to... I got flour on my top and I'm gonna...change."

She turned and scurried out of the kitchen, moving to the back room, where she'd just gotten all of her things organized last night.

It was part of an addition made to the house in more recent years. By which she meant the 1940s or so. The room was skinny and rectangular, set slightly lower than the rest of the house, matching the incline of the property, with windows covering the entire back wall and a slanted, wooden ceiling that had been painted white at some point.

It was weird, and quirky, and she was sure guests wouldn't like it very much. But it suited her just fine.

She opened the top drawer of her dresser and retrieved a new top. She tugged it over her head quickly, then hovered by the vanity, wondering if she should put makeup on. No, she shouldn't put makeup on. That was stupid. It was why she hadn't applied any after her shower this morning. They were just going out on the ranch, after all. And putting makeup on implied she cared about how she looked. And she totally didn't. At all.

While she was thinking, she picked up a blush brush and dashed it through the pink powder before swirling it over the apples of her cheeks. There. She looked awake now anyway.

She frowned and picked up her tube of mascara, brushing some over her lashes quickly. There. In the interest of looking awake.

She slicked some pink gloss over her lips next. That wasn't vain. That was just...upkeep.

She grabbed a rubber band from the little porcelain hand

statue on top of the bright yellow vanity and restrained her hair as best she could.

Okay. So that was done. And not to impress Eli but just because…it was basic hygiene. Right. She didn't care what he thought. At all.

She walked out of the bedroom and into the kitchen again, waiting to see the look on his face when he registered the change to her appearance. And…nothing. He just sat there drinking his coffee. She'd put makeup on and *nothing*.

Which was fine, because she didn't care. But…she'd expected a little better than that. From the guy who'd hate-kissed her once.

Okay, nothing about Eli and her attraction to him, her preoccupation with him, made sense. So maybe she should just stop trying to excuse the weird things she seemed to do in his presence.

She tried, for a second, to figure out what she would say to a patient in this situation, and couldn't find any readily available wisdom. Because when it came to attraction, her philosophy was simple. Pursue it and, if there was no returned interest, release it. If there was, continue on with it until it was no longer mutually satisfying.

But there was nothing about that philosophy that applied to this situation.

She didn't like him. She didn't want to be attracted to him. And he clearly didn't want to be attracted to her. If he even was.

Well, she knew he was, because boner.

But was that actual attraction or just some testosterone-fueled rage thing? And if it was, then why did the idea make her feel hot and twitchy and not angry?

Nothing about this man, or her response to him, made sense.

"So, what's the plan, then?" she asked, leaning against the door frame and staring down at him, where he had made himself very at home in one of her kitchen chairs.

"I'm going to show you around. We're going to talk about

your ideas, and I'm going to tell you which parts of those ideas are absolutely impossible."

"Or, to make it not sound dire and negative…you're going to tell me what will work?"

"Honestly, I have a feeling we'll be talking a lot more about what won't work."

"You are a ray of freaking sunshine, Eli. Has anyone ever told you that before?"

He looked over his mug and arched a dark brow. "No."

"Well, that's just shocking."

"You don't sound shocked."

She smiled. "That's because I'm not."

She reclaimed her coffee cup, but didn't rejoin him at the table. She hovered back, taking her caffeine hit before putting the mug back on the table. "Did you want to run this to your house or car or…?"

"I'll pick it up later." He tilted his cup back and finished his coffee in one deep drink before setting it back down and pushing himself into a standing position.

"Great. Then let's go tour." She turned and walked back out into the entryway and out the door, pausing just outside. "We're not taking the patrol car?"

"No," he said, walking past her. "I drive the truck around the ranch. And around town. I only drive the patrol car when I'm on duty. And today, I'm playing the part of cowboy, not the part of lawman."

Both of those things sounded so much hotter than they had a right to.

"Well, yee-haw," she said, following him over to the truck. It wasn't a new truck. It was one of those big, growly monsters with big tires and metal runners to assist in getting inside. It was square and boxy, a dull, faded red with mud splatter fanning out around the tires.

She pushed the button on the door handle and tugged it hard, before heaving herself up and onto the bench seat. There was a blanket over the original upholstery, and it made her wonder just what sort of things the man got up to in here.

She could certainly think of a few things that might be fun…

She was really starting to get concerned for her sanity. The mistake, she feared, was that she hadn't had a lover in…a while. Like, since pre-California, which put her at two years of celibacy and that was crazy.

She hadn't really accounted for needing sex when she'd moved to Copper Ridge, but she most certainly did, and the size of the town was going to make everything much more complicated.

Slow down, tiger.

Of course, she hadn't been worried about it at all until Eli. Now she was hyperworried about it.

She settled into the seat and closed the door, her elbow butting against the armrest, her shoulder against the window, anticipating just how intense it would be when Eli joined her in the enclosed space.

He climbed into the driver's side and, just as she'd feared, the moment he shut the door, she felt like all the oxygen had been sucked out, replaced by a heady mix of hormones and the scent of Eli's skin.

And yes, he most definitely had his own scent, one she was suddenly very keyed in to. It made her think of the kiss. Made her think of how he'd tasted. Salt, skin and man. And she really, really wanted more.

But that was crazy and she knew it.

He started the truck and it growled to life, vibrating beneath her in a way that was sort of perilous considering her current thought process.

"What is the first stop, then?" she asked.

"The largest barn seems like a good place to start," he said, putting his arm across the back of the seat as he put the truck in Reverse and backed out of her driveway, taking them to the main road that ran to the different houses and fields on the property.

"So you raise...?"

"Cows," he said. "And we have a hell of a lot of them. Connor deserves the credit for that. I give him a hard time, but if it weren't for him this place wouldn't exist."

"Why do you give Connor a hard time?" she asked, slipping into the easy, question-asking mode that she'd always used with patients.

"Because he's my older brother," Eli said, rolling his shoulders upward, his grip tightening on the steering wheel. "And it's what we do."

"Well, yes, but the way you said it implied something deeper than the natural brother-to-brother expression of affection via 'busting chops.'"

"Are you charging me for this session?"

"What?" she asked, like she was surprised, even though she was fully aware that she was both distracting herself and distancing herself by becoming Therapist Sadie, rather than being Sadie the bag of flail who was marinating in her own lustypants.

"You know. Don't play innocent. It doesn't suit you."

"Is that a value judgment based on the fact that I have a criminal past, albeit a very uncolorful one?"

"Yeah."

That was it. Just yeah. No apology. No attempt to explain. He didn't even seem at all apologetic for the fact that he was some kind of a relic from a bygone era. With his angry kissing and generally judgmental attitude, who even needed him or his kissing or his judging? She didn't. Well, for anything other than getting this whole community events thing started.

"Well, you know, some people might say that the way you judge other people says a lot more about you than it does about them," she said, sounding annoying to her own ears. Pious, even.

"Yeah," he said. "I'm sure it does. It says that I've spent so much time cleaning up the crap that other people just leave around that I'm short on patience for it. That I've spent my whole life being cleanup crew, which means I know people can do better than they do, because I do better. So yeah, it is about me. And I'm judgmental and I don't care to change it."

"Well," she said, "okay."

She was used to very postmodern men. Men who believed in the exploration and articulation of their feelings. Or men like Marcus, who had liked smoothies and telling her about his day over a light dinner.

She was not used to this kind of Neanderthal he-man thing. Well, scratch that, she was. And she'd walked away from it ten years ago. She wasn't going to willingly put up with it now.

She didn't say anything, though. Instead, she just let the silence grow between them until it filled in all the free spaces in the cab and pushed against her throat until she didn't think she could bear it anymore.

Because she didn't do the walking on eggshells thing now. She didn't take the path of least resistance, because she didn't have to. When people were asses, she walked away. No one got to insert their judgments into her life without her permission.

Not even when the person trying to do so was a badge-carrying, gun-toting deputy. Not. Even. Then.

"Listen, I don't care what you think," she said. "And I'm not going to let you try to put me down because of some kind of moralistic—"

"I know you don't care what I think," he said. "And none of this has anything to do with being moralistic. You know full well you were trying to psychoanalyze me, and then you went and played dumb about it. And now what? You're going to get all pissy because I said you weren't innocent? Because you're going to apply that statement way further than it was ever intended to go? And you're going to try to do it while feeling all self-righteous? Hell no, baby, that's not going to happen."

She sputtered. "I don't… You don't…"

"Tell me I'm wrong, Sadie."

"You're wrong."

"Liar," he said, putting the truck in Park in front of a giant barn that she wouldn't have even guessed was a barn at first glance. It had a dark brown tile roof and honey-colored wood siding, glass-paned windows and sliding doors of varying widths. It was more what she'd associate with a high-end stable, not a cattle ranch.

"I'm not a liar," she said, unbuckling and marveling at the se-vere...neatness of everything. Sure, it was dusty and there was hay all over the ground, but it was neat and tidy. There was no denying that. It was such a sharp contrast to Connor's house, and the lack of organization there.

"You are. And if you don't think you are, you're at least lying to yourself." He got out and slammed the door behind him. And she sat for a moment before scrambling out after him. "Thing is," he said, looking over his shoulder, "it's not that big of a deal. The original thing I called you on. I think you just like fighting with me."

"I don't like fighting," she said. "With anyone. And I went a very long time without doing it at all before you came back into my life."

"Correction, honey, you came back into mine."

"Call me honey one more time, and I'll dip your fist in honey and shove it in an anthill."

"My point stands."

"Okay, sweetie pie," she said, "the point is that except for you, I never fight with anyone. So I think it's pretty safe to say that you're the damn problem. Not me."

"Is it?" he asked.

"Yeah," she said, crossing her arms beneath her breasts. "It is."

"Or do you just not talk to anyone who dares to disagree with you?"

He strode toward the barn and left a hissing and spitting Sadie standing there, stunned for a full thirty seconds before she took off after him.

"Why don't we get back to business," he continued. "Since I don't really want to get to know you, and I'm betting you don't want to get to know me."

"Yeah," she said, "fine." She reached behind her head and tugged the end of her ponytail. "I don't want to know you. I want to know your barn."

"Get ready for the excitement," he said, his tone dry. "And I'm assuming *barn* isn't a euphemism for my...for anything."

"How could a barn be euphemistic?"

"I don't know. But you're always accusing me of missing those kinds of things so I figured I'd take preemptive measures."

"Right. Well. No. A barn is just a barn. Though, may I say, this is a particularly fantastic barn. Have you ever had weddings here?"

"No," he said.

"You should. Weddings and parties and—"

"No."

"You are the boringest man."

"I thought we were letting go of personal things and getting on with business?"

"Well, I was, but then you started talking about the possibility of barns being something dirty. Which made me think of your—" *don't say anything dirty* "—exasperating nature."

"Just look at the barn." He walked to the side door and released a wrought-iron latch, pushing it open, muscles in his thighs flexing, his biceps and forearms straining just enough to make everything in her tense up to match.

She stepped inside, the wood floor hollow-sounding beneath her feet, the expansive, empty section cleaner than most of her apartments had ever been. "Wow," she said. "I'm serious, you could host events here. And you could charge lots of money for them."

"It's nothing special. Just a place to keep equipment and hay."

"So...just a place to keep your entire livelihood? Yeah, you're right. It's not that special."

"Well, it's a serviceable barn. And it cost a hell of a lot of money. But the old one was run-down, and after we ended up with moldy hay one winter…it was pretty clear things had to change. After Dad died, we got a good chunk of change from his life insurance, and Kate and I gave our share to Connor to invest."

"Well, he did it in a very serious way," she said.

"Yeah, he did. But this place is our family legacy. Connor's the keeper of it, sure, but when…when there's another generation, I guess they'll all have a part of it. Though I'm sort of skeptical about any of us managing another generation."

"Okay," she said. "You, sure, because… I can see that you're not the open-your-home-up-to-chaos-and-crazy kind of guy. But Connor could find someone else."

"He doesn't want to. He seems to think cracking a smile's some kind of hanging offense."

"And Kate?"

"She's a kid."

"She has to be in her twenties."

"Twenty-one," he said. "She's way too damn young to be thinking about that stuff."

"Well, I agree on one level. A husband and kids? No way. Not at her age. But I assume she's dating and otherwise showing a normal interest in that sort of thing."

"Uh…not so much."

"Oh." Sadie's face heated, embarrassment washing through her. "Sorry, I was making assumptions. I should have said partner."

"What? Why?"

"Oh, just the way you said that I thought maybe I'd made a very broad assumption about her sexuality, is all."

He winced. "Can we please not talk about sexuality and my sister in the same sentence?"

"I just meant, if she's a lesbian I have no problem with that and I would hate for it to seem like I was passing judgm—"

"She's not," he said. "Considering the number of times I found torn-out magazine pages of...what's his name? Zac Efron?"

Sadie laughed. "Okay, but you realize that's an indication that she does have a sexuality."

"I refuse to have this discussion."

"All I'm saying is, don't give up on the next generation yet. You're such a cliché," she said, shaking her head and laughing.

"Maybe," he said. "But I sort of raised her from the time she was two years old, so I reserve the right to be a little insane."

The admission hit her somewhere around the heart. Which made her very uncomfortable. "Oh. Right. I wasn't...thinking."

"Our mom left before Kate turned two. Dad might as well have left. Someone had to work, someone had to take care of the baby. Connor and I were an old married couple before we could drive."

"Eli..."

"Hey, look, I'm over it." Except he so obviously wasn't. He wore it as sure as he wore his uniform. His need for order. His need for control. "But the thing is... I think that's why this place means so much. And why I'm an overprotective crazy person. Because it was all down to Connor and me. And when you have that much responsibility that early, it becomes a part of you in a way it never would otherwise."

She turned and looked at the barn, at the care that had so clearly gone into it. Evidence of money that could have taken them away from here. That could have taken the Garrett family on to other things. College, maybe. Had any of them gone? Kate was twenty-one and working, so she clearly wasn't in school.

They had given their all for this place. To hold it together. Because it was what they'd done all of their lives and it was what they continued to do.

For a woman who hadn't lived in one place for more than a couple of years, it was a level of commitment that was...hideously daunting. It was sticking something out through thick and thin, rain and shine. Old barns and new.

It was choosing to keep on staying even when there was an out. And suddenly all that history, all that intensity, made it feel as though the walls were closing in.

And you're here for five years.

"Wow," she said, taking a deep breath. "Anyway, this is great. I mean, if we could do tables, lots of tables in and around here, that would be...excellent. Just so very excellent." She started to walk back out, quickly, trying to escape the weird, oppressive weight that had settled onto her stomach.

"I'll have to clear it with Connor. Farmwork getting done is going to be the top priority. But I think we can arrange to have the field just over here cleared for parking, which should make things easy. It'll all have to be roped off and...well, it's going to be a big deal."

"I know," she said. "But the city is willing to kick in for some funds. And I think I might be able to entice some vendors. Local beers, wines, cheese. And you know, if you wanted to kick in some beef, I think it could end up being really great for the business side of the ranch."

"Again, I'll talk to Connor about it. I may need to get him drunk first."

"He doesn't have to hang out if people...bother him."

"Everything bothers him. To be honest, I'm not sure if he'd be any more miserable in a crowded bar than he is alone."

"I'm sad for him. Your brother seems like a nice guy."

"No, he doesn't."

Really, he didn't. But she'd been searching for something to say and the blanket, insincere words had rolled off her tongue easily. "Fine. He doesn't seem that nice. But I'm still sorry for him."

"That makes two of us."

"Anyway, it doesn't sound like the worst idea, does it? We'll get pies donated from the diner. We'll get…fried pickles from Ace's. We'll make it a whole thing!"

"You're really embracing this local spirit. Surprising, all things considered."

"Yeah, no one is more surprised than me. But I was ready for a change, and at this point, putting down roots is kind of the only way to feel like something's changed."

"And change is…"

"Good," she said, getting back into the truck. "Healthy. I mean, people should change things around them every so often. Especially when life isn't gelling the way it should." Practiced lines she'd told herself over and over. "So, why don't you take me to see that other field?"

"You want to see the potential parking lot?"

"Sure. And anyway, I thought you were supposed to tell me why all my harebrained schemes wouldn't work."

"Well, I haven't come up with a single damn reason why what you're asking for won't work," he said, slamming the truck door. "Do you have any idea how annoying that is?"

"I have a fair idea of how annoying that must be for you. It must really suck."

"It does."

But somehow, even he didn't seem unreasonable right now. He seemed…understandable. Here in this vast, wild place, so carefully tamed by the hands of his family, by him and Connor, she could see what a huge job it had been. Two boys who had been essentially alone in the world, with a sister to care for. She could easily see how much grit and strength it would have taken to hold things together. She wondered if that impossible task was what had built the solid man she saw in front of her. The man who was still doing the same thing. Still trying so hard to hold the pieces together.

Dammit. It made her heart all achy, and that was much more disconcerting than being horny.

They didn't get very far up the road before Eli stopped the

truck again. "Right there," he said, "we'll move the cows to another pasture and open up the gates."

She looked over to where he was pointing and shaded her eyes as she studied the bright green fields, dotted with glossy black animals, their heads down, the sun casting a ripple of light and shadow over muscle and sleek hair.

Yellow flowers popped like little sunbursts across the grass, standing in sharp contrast to the dark green and fading blue of the mountains beyond.

It took her breath away. It reminded her why this place was home.

Which was so strange, because she couldn't remember ever really feeling like it was before, but sitting in the truck, looking out at all this, she felt it. Not like something new, but even better and more rare for someone like her, it felt familiar.

"Parking lot doesn't really do this justice. Will it be okay to...drive on it?"

"Yeah, it's fine. We cycle the cows through the fields anyway and they're about done here for now."

"I can suddenly see why none of you ever left."

"It's beautiful," he said. "Some days I kind of forget to look at it. But the expression on your face just reminded me."

Something warm shot through her, across her face and down into the pit of her stomach. She swallowed hard, fought against it. It was a good feeling, but weird. Deeper than the kinds of feelings she was used to.

And she wasn't sure she liked it.

"Anyway, I have to get out and help Connor for a while, so I'll drive you back."

"I'm fine walking," she said, suddenly feeling the need to escape again. To feel a little sunshine on her face and some wind in her hair. "I mean, really, I want to walk."

He shrugged. "All right. Suit yourself. See you around."

She climbed out of the truck and tried to ignore the somewhat fuzzy feeling his casual, and not at all hostile, goodbye carved out in the pit of her stomach. Right in the middle of all the warmth.

"Yeah," she said, "see you."

She hopped out of the truck and breathed in deep, the air sweet from the flowers and salty from the nearby sea. She looked up and closed her eyes, letting the sunshine wash over her. And even though she wanted to, she didn't look back at Eli. Not even once.

CHAPTER EIGHT

NEVER HAD ELI been so glad for Jack to draw the short straw. That made him the designated driver for the evening, and it meant that Eli could drink some beers. Because he really, really wanted to drink some beer tonight.

Not that he would drink to the point of public drunkenness, since he had a reputation to uphold. And the legacy of being a worthless drunk's kid. But something to take the edge off the Sadie Miller knife that was digging into his gut would be nice.

Just a little haze. That was all he required.

Jack was still sulking because he had to stay sober, Connor had already gone to the bar to order beer and Eli was leaning back in his chair, enjoying being in town in plainclothes. Enjoying sitting back and watching people do things without feeling like he was on duty at a day care.

The bar was packed, but it was Saturday night and there were a limited amount of activities in town. There were average-quality restaurants, very expensive seafood restaurants, a movie theater with five screens and a local dinner theater. The bar was one of the more popular choices for obvious reasons.

Alcohol, darts and pool being some of the most obvious.

"Don't sulk, Jack," Eli said. "It's not a good look on you."

"Drunk isn't a good look on you," Jack returned, his arms crossed over his chest.

"I haven't been drunk since I was twenty-one. On my birthday. And never again."

"You're such a cliché."

Since this was the second time he'd been accused of this recently, he was starting to wonder if it was true.

"Aren't we all?" he asked. "We're in a bar on Saturday with nothing better to do."

"Looking to get laid," Jack said, turning and taking a Coke out of Connor's hand as he returned to the table with drinks.

"Speak for yourself," Eli said.

"Oh, right, you don't shit in your own yard."

Eli grimaced and took the pale ale Connor was offering him. "Not my favorite way of putting it, but the principle is sound."

"Liss isn't coming?" Jack asked Connor.

"Not tonight. She said something about painting her toenails and watching old movies. And that is where having me as her best friend tends to not pay off."

"You don't want to put the little toe separators in for her and blow on her feet until the polish dries?" Jack took a drink of soda to disguise his smile.

"I thought I'd come here and see if you wanted to throw darts at my balls instead," Connor said, tipping his beer bottle back and taking a long drink.

"If I were drinking, I would absolutely take you up on that," Jack said.

"Remember the time we were hanging out at the house," Connor asked, "and we thought we'd play darts? But there was nothing to hang the board we found…and you, you put the board in your lap? And told me to hit the bull's-eye?"

"I still have a scar on my thigh," Jack said. "So yeah, I remember."

"We did really dumb stuff."

"You two did dumb stuff," Eli corrected. "I mainly watched."

And told no one because there was no one who would have cared. Jack's mom was too exhausted from work to look his direction more than once a week, and the Garrett patriarch was usually passed out in his own vomit by 6:00 p.m.

They used to joke that if their parents got married they could be the world's most fucked-up version of the Brady Bunch.

That hadn't happened, because their individual parents had been too busy wallowing in their problems, but Jack basically lived at their house anyway, simply by virtue of the fact that it was bigger and there were more places to find trouble.

Jack liked trouble, and trouble liked him. Typically, female trouble.

He had no issue shitting where he lived, so to speak.

"We were badass," Connor said, a wistful look on his face. He took another sip of beer. "And you," he said, pointing at Eli, "were not blameless. You're the one who thought to build a ramp that went off the hayloft. And ride your bike down it."

"Ah…how did we not die?" Eli asked.

"Hell if I know," Connor said, tapping the side of his beer bottle. "But then, I'm sort of mystified by how those decisions are made." And just like that, the brief light on his face dimmed again.

Dammit. It was way too easy to say the wrong thing when someone had a ghost following them around.

"We all are," Jack said, slapping Connor twice on the back. "And when we're too mystified, we drink and talk crap at the bar."

"Damn straight," Eli agreed, knocking back another drink.

"With friends like you guys… I'll have a hangover in the morning," Connor said, making a weak attempt at a smile.

"You could have been painting Liss's toenails. You're paying for your own awesome choices," Jack told him.

"And you could have had beer," Connor said. "But you drew the short straw."

"It's a stupid tradition. We should just take turns."

"And you'd bail every time it was your turn," Eli said.

Jack smiled and shrugged in the boyish manner that got him out of situations that would have seen lesser men castrated. "Probably."

"And that's why we draw straws. Because one out of three men at this table is a piss-poor friend," Connor said.

"Guilty." Jack looked over Connor's shoulder and frowned. "Isn't that your hot new tenant?"

"What?" Connor asked, turning around completely unsubtly. The motion would have made a bull look graceful.

Eli looked up and saw that it was definitely Sadie, blonde, petite and, yeah, very hot, walking into the room and over to the bar. She leaned in, and he couldn't help but look, really look, at the way her jeans fit her rather fantastic ass.

"She really is hot," Jack said, his eyes getting that keen, focused look that he got when he was on the hunt.

"Not in this lifetime, Monaghan," Eli said, the words coming out a whole lot more threatening than he'd intended them to.

Jack sat back, dark brows shooting up. "Oh, really?"

"Damn straight," Eli said, hooking his hand around his beer and tugging it back, holding it against his chest.

"You're not for real," Jack said. "Sleeping with a woman who lives on your property is almost the same as marriage."

Marriage. That was the last thing he wanted. A little sex on the other hand...

Heat streaked through Eli's gut. He hated that his desire was that transparent, especially when he was still trying to pretend that he wasn't attracted to her at all.

He looked over at Sadie again. "I wasn't even thinking of it."

"Liar."

Connor was noticeably silent during the exchange. Eli managed to tear his eyes away from the view to look at his brother.

Connor looked up, his expression hostile. "What?"

Jack looked at him, too. "You're not commenting."

"Didn't notice she was hot," Connor said. "I was thinking about it, trying to decide if she was or not. Then I realized my dick is fucking broken."

Hell, maybe Eli's was, too. Because this was a total departure from his usual rules. He hadn't fully realized it until Sadie had pointed out the sheer volume of sexual innuendo he missed on a daily basis when he was with her, but his normal course of action was to just shut his libido down until he was ready to do something about it.

He had great luck with women—when he was pursuing one. Otherwise…otherwise he lived his life with blinders on. And it wasn't by accident.

He kept his life classified in very careful segments. And maybe the problem now was he'd left one segment neglected for too long. And now things were…intertwining that definitely shouldn't be intertwining.

And beyond the intersection of his personal life and his love life, the fact that it was Sadie whom he wanted when she was the most infuriating, irritating woman…well, that just proved that his dry spell had reached Saharan proportions.

"She is hot," Jack said. "But I have a feeling Eli is marking his territory."

"I am not," he said.

"You don't like her," Connor pointed out. "She's a criminal. You arrested her."

"She's not a criminal," Eli said, gritting his teeth. "And it was ten years ago."

"Yeah," Jack said. "Marking his territory."

"Don't say it like that. She's a woman, not territory. And she's definitely not mine. You sound like a jerk."

"I *am* a jerk," Jack said. "It's like you haven't known me since I was twelve."

"As you so eloquently put it, or…as you should have put it, I keep my sex life away from here. Far, far away. I'm not going to pursue a woman who has a five-year contract to live on my property. That's a degree too close to marriage for my taste."

Jack laughed. "Okay, I get that. So does that mean I can...?"

"No," Eli growled. "You can't. Mainly because I don't want to catch sight of your bare ass through any open windows. That is guaranteed to get you shot."

"You're not allowed to shoot my friend, Eli," Connor said. "I only have two of them. I can't afford to lose any."

Eli looked at Sadie and watched as she cocked her head to the side, blond hair spilling over her shoulder, the fluorescent lights from the Mirror Pond Ale sign behind the bar casting a yellow-and-blue glow over the pale strands.

Ace was behind the bar, big and bearded and wearing flannel, which women seemed to be giddy over these days. And Sadie was obviously no exception, with the way she was giggling and smiling and...dammit, touching the guy's forearm with her delicate hands. Hands that were, incidentally, not covered with soil from planting an azalea.

Annoyance coursed through him. She'd just kissed him last week, and now she was in here flirting with Ace.

And so what?

So, it pissed him off. Which made him even angrier. Because he shouldn't care. He wasn't jealous. He was never jealous because jealousy implied that he cared, and he never cared.

Not that he didn't like the women he had relationships with, but he didn't quite care what they did when he wasn't around.

This Sadie thing was messing with his head. Not only was wanting her simply a bad idea, he was sitting here pondering ways to remove Ace's arm.

"Excuse me," he said, getting up and pushing his chair back, leaving his beer on the table. He could feel Connor and Jack staring after him, and he knew that they were probably ready to discuss conspiracy theories about whether or not he'd been brainwashed or body-snatched.

And he didn't really care. Because right now he had Sadie in his sights and he was going to walk over to her and do…something. He would figure it out when he got there.

Hopefully.

His feet hit the wooden floor harder than necessary with each step and he knew that people were looking at him, because he was Eli Garrett, current candidate for county sheriff, walking across a bar like he had sex and murder on his mind.

Both of which were strictly true.

"What brings you into town, Sadie?" he asked, leaning against the bar next to her.

She jumped and turned, blue eyes wide. "What brings you here to talk to me voluntarily, Eli?" she asked, her expression schooled into something casual now, covering up the moment of shock.

Ace looked at them both and turned away from Sadie, pulling a drink from the tap and walking down to the other end of the bar.

"Curiosity," Eli said.

"It's not that weird that I'm at the bar," she said.

"But you're alone."

"Who would I be with? Anyway, I was just stopping by because I wanted to feel out the best local brews and find out if Ace had any contact info for me. For the Fourth of July thing."

"Right," he said. "You're on a first-name basis with Ace?"

"I remember him vaguely from school. Also, I called in earlier."

"Okay," he said, sounding a lot more uptight than he would like.

"Why do you care?" she asked, tilting her head to the side like he'd watched her do earlier.

"Honestly? I don't know," he said. *Honestly?* Why had he been honest? Honesty in this situation was a terrible idea. Because it was ceding the upper hand. It was admitting he was out of his depth and that was not acceptable.

Her expression changed. Not wide-eyed shock or practiced casualness. She lowered her lashes, her lips more relaxed, her gaze falling to his mouth. Each shift almost imperceptible, and quick. And yet, he saw it. Was so painfully aware of it, as if he could hear each change like the cocking of a gun. It was clear, it was intentional. And the only thing he wasn't sure of yet was if she was shooting to kill.

"Is it because you want to kiss me again?" she asked.

She was shooting to kill. This shot had hit square in his gut, radiating down to his groin. He'd only had a half a beer, so he couldn't even blame that.

"It's more because I don't want *him* to kiss you," he said, leaning in, his palm flat on the bar. "I don't want to kiss you. I wish I hadn't kissed you the first time and trust me, Sadie Miller, I sure as hell don't want to do it again." He angled his head and moved in closer, conscious that they were being watched by almost everyone in the bar. Aware that he had to be close enough to make his point, but far enough away that no one would be planning their wedding by tomorrow. "But I'm starting to wonder if I will. If it's inevitable."

She drew back, her breasts pitching sharply with the harsh breath she drew in. "I'm not sure how something like that could be inevitable. I mean, either you want to kiss someone or you don't. If you do, you do. If you don't, you don't."

"I thought it was that simple. Until you. You've completely screwed up my kissing theory." Damn, maybe he *was* drunk.

"That's more than thirty years of kissing theory messed up by one woman," she said, her voice sounding lower, thicker all of a sudden. "That's…a lot of power."

"It is," he said, his own voice following the same path hers had.

"Are you drunk?" she asked.

"I wish."

"Wow. You really, really know how to turn a girl on." Sarcasm tinged her tone, but the huskiness in her voice told him that he actually was turning her on, and he had no idea how to feel about that. "Telling me you don't want to kiss me and you wish you could excuse your being over here with your being drunk."

"That's because I'm not trying to turn you on," he said. And that at least was true.

"I wish I could say it was working."

"Me not turning you on?"

"Yes," she said, looking down at the bar.

"Are we flirting?"

She looked back at him, her pulse beating hard at the base of her throat, hard enough that he could see it. "I don't think so."

"You're probably right. I don't think I know how to flirt."

"You're just trying to keep me from getting flirted with."

"Sounds about right."

Ace came back over to their end of the bar and crossed his arms over his broad chest. "He's not bothering you, is he, Sadie?"

Oh, for God's sake.

Sadie looked at Ace, her lips quirked into a funny smile. "You know he's a deputy sheriff, right?"

"I know who he is," Ace said.

Oh, great, the jackass was in the mood to be tough, and Eli wasn't in the mood to compete for Sadie because he didn't even want Sadie. Or at least, he didn't want to want her.

But there was no way he was going to be able to let it slide. He knew that there was no way because he'd crossed the room to stake a claim on a woman he shouldn't want just because she'd put her hand on another man's arm.

He already knew he was too far gone for common sense. He already knew his head wasn't in charge of this one.

"Then you know that I'm more likely to protect her than drag her off and throw her into my trunk," Eli said.

"What is it they say about cops and the domestic abuse rate?" Ace asked.

"Cute. Did you take an online class?" Eli asked.

Sadie giggled and they both looked at her. "I'm sorry," she said, her smile barely suppressed. "Please go on. I'm enjoying the novelty of two men warring for my affections."

"Outside," Eli said.

"I'm sorry, are you ordering me around? Do you honestly think I'm going to obey like a lapdog? I, sir, am a cat person, and I'll probably just bite your hand."

"Out. Side," he repeated.

She arched a brow but slid away from the bar and started to walk toward the exit. He turned to Ace and shot him a look before he dared glance at Jack and Connor, who were staring at him openly. Connor looking a little annoyed. Jack looking annoyingly impressed.

Bastard.

He turned away from them and followed her out the front door, rounding on her as soon as it swung shut behind them. It was dark outside, the waves crashing against the shore nearby the only sound, the moon glinting on the water like silver fish swimming over the surface. Every pitch of the surf casting white light over Sadie's face.

She was so beautiful it hurt. A real ache that started in his head and pulsed through his teeth, all the way down through his gut and to his cock. Just from a little light across the bridge of her nose. The bridge of her *nose*. He needed his head examined.

But not by Sadie. Because the little therapist was the person causing all of his mental and physical unrest.

"What is going on?" she asked.

"I'm...not sure," he answered, pacing the sidewalk in front of her. "I'm really not sure. I came out to drink and maybe eat some fish-and-chips and definitely not to talk to you, or see you, or think about kissing you."

"Hey, I came down here to talk microbrews, not to deal with you and your chest-beating, rawr rawr, he-man routine!"

"Then why are you dealing with it?" he asked.

"Why are you talking to me?"

"Hell if I know," he said.

"Then consider that *my* answer. Hell if I know!"

He moved toward her and she backed up, the wood-shingled wall of the bar stopping her. Eli took a breath and pressed his palm flat to the wall, just by her head, his eyes locked with hers, heat arching between them. He couldn't have looked away if he wanted to. And he didn't want to. He wanted to keep looking at her. He wanted to kiss her.

And then some.

He wanted her more than he could remember ever wanting any woman. More even than his first, on a spring night after prom.

Right now he was beyond himself. Beyond control. And Eli Garrett was never beyond control.

Somewhere, in the depths of his thoroughly bent brain, it registered that that was a problem. That he shouldn't have ever let it get this far. That he needed to get a grip on things and stop it before it went further.

Dammit. He didn't want to.

He gritted his teeth against the rising tide of arousal. So intense it just hurt.

He took a breath through his nose and closed his eyes, lowering his head. If he just didn't look at her for a second…he could get a handle on things. On himself.

He breathed in again, slowly, and let it out through his mouth. Then he opened his eyes and looked back up at her. "Here's what we're going to do," he said, his voice almost unrecognizable.

"What?"

"We're going to go back in the bar. And you're going to go back and talk to Ace about local beer. And if he asks you on a date? I think you should go on it."

"What?"

"Yep. I'm going to go back to my table and drink at least two more beers, eat something fried and play darts. And I'm not going to look at you. I'm not going to talk to you. I'm not going to kiss you. We're going to start this night over, like I never walked over to you and opened my mouth."

"Eli…"

"And when we interact on the ranch it's going to be because we have tenant-landlord type business to deal with that Connor's pawning off onto me."

She bit her lip and nodded, a crease appearing between her eyebrows. "I'm even more confused now," she said.

"This ends one of two ways," he said, his throat getting tighter. "Either we keep this up," he said, thinking the *this* in the statement was fairly obvious, "and it goes too far. Or we stop it now. But I have a feeling if we keep it all accidental, then…"

"Right. And what would…be so bad about that?" she asked.

Her simple, nonexplicit words sent a slug of lust through him that was so intense he could hardly breathe around it. "Let me tell you something about me, Sadie. I'm a good man. I pride myself on that. But I'm not a very nice man. And I'm not the kind of man who does relationships. This is my town and I care about the people in it. When I want sex, I go outside the city limits for it because I know before I ever get in a woman's bed how it will end. Quickly. I don't want to bring that here. I don't want to run into old lovers while I'm crossing the street or when I'm making routine stops. And I sure as hell don't want to run into an old lover every time I cross my driveway." The very thought offended his sense of order in every way.

"I see," she said. "But…what makes you think I want any more than a little harmless sex?"

"Because sex is never harmless when it's this complicated. It's like setting fire in a barn instead of a fireplace."

She blinked and nodded. "Great. Fine. Whatever. I don't even see the point of banging a guy who wouldn't know fun if it got on its knees and sucked his…" She looked down, so pointedly that he felt it. "Well, you get the idea. Ace seems like he might be more the type I'm after. So I'll go in before you. I'll talk to him. Maybe I'll leave with him. We'll see."

You will not. His inner he-man, as she'd called it, growled.

"Sounds like a plan," he said instead. Because this was crazy. And it had to be stopped.

She forced a smile, her eyes meeting his quickly, a brief flash of electricity shooting straight through him before she turned away.

He watched Sadie walk back into the bar and waited for the tightness in his stomach to recede, for the ache to go away.

He had a feeling he was going to be waiting for a long time.

CHAPTER NINE

DRIVING INTO COPPER RIDGE the next day, Sadie decided to take a left instead of a right at the last minute. She'd been headed toward the main street of Old Town to visit Rona's Diner and see about pie, and something had pulled her the other way.

A ghost, maybe. The same one she'd been afraid she might find in a clearing. Or maybe just what normal people would call memories. She obviously wasn't normal.

But here she was, driving on the road that led away from the ocean. Away from the picturesque portion of the little town. This was where the other half lived. The poor half. The half who worked in the logging industry and at the mill, or didn't work at all.

The half she came from.

And on this road was her childhood home. Her throat tightened as she shifted her suddenly slick hands on the steering wheel.

She'd never imagined, ever, that she would come back here. In fact, she'd actively intended not to. What the hell was all this? Why was she here?

Who knew why she did anything these days? Coming back here, kissing Eli, almost kissing Eli again last night...

There was no point in thinking about that right now.

She took a deep breath and eased her car to the side of the road as she stopped in front of a blue house with shingle siding.

She took her hands off the wheel and looked out the window. The knot in her stomach eased. It looked different.

It was cleaner. The grass was cut. There was grass. When she'd been there, it had been nothing but a carpet of dandelions punctuated by groups of star thistle.

It was smaller, too. Brighter. She was sure it wasn't actually smaller, but it seemed that way.

A white minivan drove by her car and turned into the driveway of her old house. She watched as it parked and a woman got out. Gently taking her toddler from the backseat, along with a brown grocery bag.

They opened the front door and a small dog ran out to greet them. Sadie hadn't been allowed to have a pet.

Maybe this was what they meant when they said you couldn't go home again. The home that loomed large in her mind, *her* home, didn't exist. It hadn't since the Miller family moved out.

She thought of her patient Maryann, and how much she'd loved her home. How losing it had devastated her, because her memories had sunk into the wood. The love her family shared.

It wasn't like that for Sadie. Not for her family. Nothing of them was still here.

And thank God.

There was no power in this place.

She put her car in Drive and turned back around, shaking her hair out of her face. She felt like maybe things should seem momentous, but instead she just felt deflated.

Whatever she'd thought she might find there, she hadn't. Good or bad, really.

"You're getting weird," she said to herself as she turned onto

Old Town's main street and drove to the far end, pulling into the driveway at Rona's Diner before killing the engine.

She didn't have time to be sentimental about a pile of wood, bolts and insulation. She had a pie mission to see to.

Sadie took a deep breath and wrapped her sweater tightly around herself. It was June, but the Oregon Coast had no respect for summer. Even when the sun was shining, the wind had to undermine it with a chill that cut straight through the warmth, and her sweaters, apparently.

She clutched her paper coffee cup a little bit tighter and walked into the diner at the end of the main drag, out near the jetty. She'd been informed that they had the best pies in the county, and she wanted the best for the barbecue.

It was two in the afternoon and the diner wasn't very crowded, the lunch crowd long since dissipated, the dinner crowd not yet arrived. There were some middle-aged men sitting in the corner with cake and pie on plates and coffee all around. Fishermen, Sadie guessed by the look of them.

That was one of the unique things about this place. It was a coastal town, with deep traditions tied to the sea. With fishermen, and crab shacks, seagulls and amazing fish-and-chips. But just inland were the cowboys and ranchers. Sheep, cows and beautiful stables with high-priced horses.

Copper Ridge was the melting pot of everything good in Oregon. Trees and waves, forests and beaches. In that regard, her hometown was a lot more special than she'd realized until she'd been away from it for a decade.

Old Town had changed, too. Where before things had worn a coat of neglect and salt from the sea, they were repainted, revamped and attractive to tourists now. Which was a very good thing for her.

"Can I help you?" a waitress called to her from behind the counter.

There was a glass display case beneath the countertop, laden with the very same pies and cakes the fishermen in the corner were indulging in. There were also doughnuts, giant cinnamon rolls and cupcakes that Sadie was thinking needed to go with her coffee right now.

"I'd like a cupcake. And to talk to whoever does the baked goods."

The woman blinked and something about her expression sent a flash of memory through Sadie. "That's me."

"Oh, well, great."

"What kind of cupcake?"

"Your favorite. I'm not picky."

"I like the chocolate peanut butter."

"Sounds perfect." Sadie watched as the other woman bent to get the cupcake from the bottom of the display case.

Familiarity nagged at Sadie, but she still couldn't quite place her. Obviously she had to be someone she'd known here. Someone from school?

When the waitress rose back up, the motion stiff, a grimace on her face, it hit her. "Alison?" Sadie asked. "Sadie! Sadie Miller. From school. And other things that weren't school-related."

The other woman's eyes widened for a moment and something sad passed through them before there was recognition and then, finally, a small smile. "Oh…oh, Sadie. I didn't recognize you."

"Well, I wear less black eyeliner these days. Clearly, so do you."

She laughed nervously. "Yeah. A bit."

"So, what have you been up to?" Sadie asked, dimly realizing that there was something uniquely wonderful in seeing faces from your past.

"Nothing much, really. Working here. Baking. I got married."

"Congratulations."

"Yeah," she said, forcing another smile that looked distinctly sad.

Alison had been part of her tight-knit crew. They'd caused a bit of trouble together—the barn incident being one of them—and mainly spent time in the woods near the Garrett ranch or on the beach, because for them it had been better than being at home.

They were the misfits of Copper Ridge, and even if no one else had fully realized it, they had. They knew they were different. They knew they were wrong. Broken families, poverty. Abuse.

There was only one elementary school, one junior high and a high school that sat squarely between Copper Ridge and Tolowa, making the most out of the shared student population. That meant they'd spent a lot of years circling each other like wary strays, slowly forming a group. A bond that had been, at the time, thicker and stronger than the bond with their families.

Alison, Damian, Matthew, Kelly, Sarah, Josh and Brooke. A few other people rotated in and out, but that was the core.

And she'd left them behind. She'd never contacted them.

In that moment, she felt ashamed.

"Not married," Sadie said, holding up her bare left hand for emphasis. "I've been…moving a lot. Being a crisis counselor. And now a proprietress at a bed-and-breakfast. So… I still don't make a whole lot of sense."

"Sounds nice to me. You escaped," Alison said.

That was how she'd felt at the time. Now she wasn't so sure.

"I'm back. This place has that way about it. It even called *me* back eventually, and I like moving on a lot more than looking back. Historically speaking."

There was a disconnect happening. Something so fundamentally defeated in Alison's eyes, something so familiar, that it hurt Sadie to look at it. And she couldn't nail down what it was or why. Maybe just fatigue from a long shift.

"Do you ever… Do you talk to anyone else from school?" Sadie asked.

Alison looked down. "Not really. Matt's still here. He fishes. Brooke owns a shop up the road, but we don't… I don't have a lot of time. Everyone else moved like you. Josh went on and made all kinds of money... I'm just still here."

"Oh." She made a mental note to track Brooke down later.

"Yeah."

"Well," Sadie said, filling in the silence, which she was professionally good at. "I heard that you had the best baked goods in town. And the thing is I'm organizing a community Independence Day barbecue on the Garrett ranch, which is, not incidentally, where my B and B is. And I wanted to have a dessert booth. Possibly a pie eating contest. So I wanted to talk to you about what you have, what is possible production-wise and if the owner of the diner might be interested in donating a certain number of pies for the contest in exchange for advertising space."

"These are the best pies!" one of the men shouted from the corner. "Alison makes the best everything." There was a round of agreement from the other men at the table and that pulled another smile out of Alison.

Getting a smile out of her, Sadie was coming to realize, was as difficult as pulling Toby out from the back of the lazy Susan cupboard when he was annoyed about the vacuum cleaner.

"There, that's all the validation I need," Sadie said. "So if you're up to it, I'd really like to involve you. And if the diner owner isn't super into it, I'm happy to purchase pies directly from you. Or maybe you'd be interested in manning the dessert booth? You could sell pie by the slice. It'll be a great bit of advertising for you. And hey, since I think you're probably a million times better than me at baking, pies might be a great thing for me to have in the B and B anyway."

Sadie wished she could stop the tumble of words now, because Alison looked wary, and it hit a warning button deep inside Sadie. But the ideas were rolling off her tongue now without her permission. Possibly because of that internal warning signal.

For a therapist she was awfully useless in out-of-office people situations.

"I'll have to check with Jared. If he can spare me for that much time," Alison said.

"The diner owner?"

"My husband," she said, blinking rapidly. "He may not want me getting so involved in something like that. It's already hard with how much I do here."

"Right. Well, I mean, only if you want to. Don't feel an obligation to me or anything."

"I do want to," she said.

"Then I'm sure your husband will be happy for you. It'll be good for you and all."

Alison didn't look so sure and that right there sent Sadie's instincts from warning bells to the desire to maim the guy in the testicular region.

"Right. Yeah. Just the cupcake?" she asked.

"A marionberry pie, too, actually. I'll have it after dinner."

Alison bent and pulled a pie out and put it in a white box before ringing both items up.

"Great," Sadie said. "And now I know where to get my goody fix, and where to see an old friend. So all in all, this was a productive day." Sadie reached into her purse and pulled out a crumpled receipt from the coffee stand she'd gone to earlier, and wrote her cell phone number across the back. "Call me. If you ever need anything, or want to hang out, or have questions about the barbecue."

"Sure," Alison said, taking the receipt. "I will."

Sadie had the feeling the other woman was lying. And again, she couldn't quite place why. But everything seemed wrong. Well, the statement about the husband not wanting her to be gone too much seemed off to Sadie, but then, Sadie knew there might be other factors. Even though her gut response was that it sounded awfully controlling.

"Thanks for the goodies. If I slip into a sugar coma, don't be too surprised." Sadie waved and walked out the door, back down the sidewalk toward where she'd parked her car.

She was happy about the pie, but uneasy about everything else.

And this was the problem with coming home. There were so many emotions tied up in things. She didn't like it. Before leaving Copper Ridge she'd had a whole lifetime of heavy. Of bad feelings and worry and outright terrifying crap, and she just didn't like to feel things that were even close to that anymore. It wasn't healthy to dwell, after all.

But Copper Ridge made her dwell, dammit.

And just like that, the magic of returning home was gone.

IT WAS DECK DAY. And Sadie had a bevy of shirtless construction workers off the back of her house, putting down posts and cement blocks in preparation for the building of the massive deck she'd designed for the B and B.

She had big plans for it. Tables. A barbecue. No, a barbecue wouldn't strictly be breakfast, but she could fix other meals.

Her one serious question, though, was whether or not a group of construction workers was a bevy.

Perhaps they were more an assemblage. Or a herd. A pack. That sounded nice and manly. Very sexy. She sipped on her lemonade and watched them from her living room window, privately pleased that she was perving on them rather than the other way around.

"Yeah, baby," she said, tilting her glass back and catching an ice cube between her teeth. "Show me what your mama gave you."

She was determined to get some visual enjoyment out of these guys. It was a way better idea than thinking about Eli and how much she would rather see him shirtless and sweaty.

There was a knock at the front door and she jumped, splashing lemonade onto her hand. She shook her head, walking to the door. She supposed it served her right. Getting caught being a dirty peeping Tom. She still didn't feel guilty, though.

She tugged the door open and saw Kate standing there,

schooling her expression into something almost comically casual. "There are a lot of work trucks out here."

"There are indeed," Sadie said. "Because I'm having a deck built. And the guys are doing it without shirts on if you want to come in and watch."

"That was what I was hoping," Kate said, her cheeks flushing pink.

"Never apologize for being a connoisseur of the male form, Kate. And never blush about it."

Kate blushed deeper and followed Sadie into the living room.

"Dear Lord," she said, and Sadie had the feeling that only the barest hint of decorum was keeping her from pressing her face to the glass like a frustrated window-shopper.

She recalled what Eli had said about feeling protective of Kate, or rather, being content to deny she had a sexuality altogether, and she wondered if Kate ever got to do anything more than window-shop.

"Not bad at all," Sadie said. "Makes me feel like a lady of leisure. Sipping cool beverages and ogling the slick sweaty men. And I'm not sorry about it."

"My female intuition told me that this might be happening over here."

"The force is strong with you. Would you also like a cool beverage? Lady of leisure status could be yours, too."

Kate smiled. "Sure. That sounds great."

Sadie went into the kitchen, humming as she did, and took a glass out of the cabinet before pouring some lemonade from the pitcher on the counter.

She returned a moment later and handed it to Kate. "Get your leisure on."

Kate took a sip and let out a long sigh, her eyes glued to the activities outside. "It's too bad this isn't a transferable skill."

"Not so much a big market for ogling while indulging in cold drinks, no."

"My goal is to make money doing things with horseflesh. Not manflesh."

"Doing what?"

"I barrel race. I'm looking to turn pro, but I haven't quite earned enough points to get my card. I didn't get to compete as much this year because I needed to work more hours at the Farm and Garden. Focus on saving. I won a decent-sized pot a while back, but not much since and I need money if I'm going to travel with the rodeo."

"That's incredible. You really barrel race? Like…you ride horses around barrels and wear sequined jackets and things?"

"I'm light on the sequins, but yeah."

"And you're good enough to go pro."

Kate took another sip of lemonade and smiled broadly. "I think I am. And my winning streak concurs. But it's just getting everything to line up. And feeling like Eli won't implode when I leave."

"Ah. Eli."

"He's a nervous hen."

"I can definitely see that," she said, thinking of him and his do-gooder complex.

I'm a good man but I'm not a nice man.

Oh, no, she didn't need to replay that scene.

Because it made her shivery in…places. Which was silly because that should be off-putting. She liked nice men. She did not like scoundrels. Or men in uniform with hella-bad attitudes and control-freak tendencies.

She could not be controlled or contained. She was the mothereffing wind.

"And he needs me more than he thinks," Kate said.

Sadie had a feeling that was a lot more insightful than Eli would think it was. "Sure," Sadie said slowly. "But you can't live your life for other people, Kate." She knew she was playing therapist again. But she was licensed, so it wasn't really *playing*. She was unsolicited, but she was a professional at least. "It only builds resentment, and in the end it destroys more bonds than honesty will. If you want to go, then you should be free to go."

"You make it sound really simple."

"It is," Sadie said. "It's what I do." She realized dimly that insinuating anyone should do what she had done was edging into bad-advice territory, so she attempted a redirect. "But it isn't as though you'll stay gone. It's just that you may need a bit more independence."

"And more shirtless men in my life that I don't share genetic material with," Kate said. "We're country, but not that country."

Sadie laughed. "Uh, I don't suppose you are."

"But yeah. I need to get away. Small town. Same places. Same jobs. Same guys. Take those guys, for example. I either went to high school with them, and they showed no interest in me. Or they went to high school with my brothers and wouldn't dare touch me."

Sadie figured it was better not to mention she hadn't had that problem with guys in high school. But then, she hadn't given off the salt-of-the-earth vibe Kate did. And she also didn't have two giant older brothers.

There was also the fact she doubted Kate had the knack for finding trouble that Sadie did. Which was probably for the best since Sadie had managed to find serious, life-threatening trouble thanks to the smaller trouble she'd found.

Not that anyone in Kate's family would ever hurt her. She could say that for Eli and Connor. She knew they would never hurt women, or anyone who didn't really deserve it.

And she was thinking about unpleasant things again. Ugh.

This place had a way about it. Good and bad. And both a little more intense than she'd been prepared for.

Though, if she was totally honest, she was never really prepared for intensity.

"That is a problem," Sadie said, keeping an eye on the guys. "Which ones did you go to school with? I feel like they're probably off-limits to me."

"Are you really going to…talk to them?" Kate asked, sounding awed.

She should. She should offer them cold beverages while wearing a bikini top. And get numbers. But she wasn't going to.

And she had a horrible feeling it was stupid Eli's fault.

Why she was still thinking about him in those terms was a mystery to her because he'd made it very clear he didn't want to find her hot. Even though he obviously did find her hot. And he'd turned down her very clumsy, ill-advised, sort-of offer of casual sex, too.

In that moment, if he'd agreed, she really would have hopped into the nearest bush with him and ridden him until she was saddle sore.

Had she ever wanted a man this much?

She didn't think she had, and that made her feel relieved he'd put a stop to it. Well, maybe not relieved. She felt twitchy and annoyed, and super horny.

She scowled and looked more determinedly out the window, trying to decide which guy had the nicest butt, and from there trying to decide if she would enjoy smacking it.

She could not decide. And she did not want to smack *any* of the denim-clad asses, truth be told.

She was broken, and it was Eli Garrett's fault.

There was a knock on the front door, which was still slightly open since she'd let Kate in. "Come in," she shouted.

The door opened and she heard footsteps on the hardwood in the entry, and then in walked the man himself. The new owner of her libido. Who had rendered her mainly useless when it came to ogling. It was all very upsetting.

"Hello, Eli," she said. "Is this your version of avoiding me?"

"Why were you avoiding her?" Kate asked.

"I'm not," Eli said, lying neatly for a man with an honor complex. "I came looking for you."

"How did you know I was here?" Kate asked.

"Your truck is in your driveway, but you weren't, and your

horse was in his paddock. You weren't with Connor, so I thought I would see if you were here, and lo…" He looked past them both and out the window. "Are you kidding me?"

"We're learning how to build a deck," Sadie said, arching a brow and swilling her lemonade, the ice clinking against the glass. "By observation."

Eli looked at Kate.

"The human mind is an amazing thing," she said, on the verge of giggles.

"Just watching all the nailing and screwing," Sadie said. "It's so sweaty." She took the glass and pressed it to her cheek, giving Eli a very meaningful look.

He swallowed visibly and shifted. Well, he'd obviously taken *that* innuendo on board. Good. He deserved to suffer. He deserved to suffer as she was suffering. He deserved to watch beach volleyball and get no joy from the bouncing. Which was mean-spirited, she knew. But she didn't care.

"I was looking for Kate," he said, his words very pointed as he turned back to his sister. "Carl Ames came by and was looking for someone who could possibly board a horse for his daughter. I said we had the space, but the thing is they might need someone to ride him on days they can't make it out. And I didn't want to volunteer you without asking. Of course, you would get the boarding money."

"All of it?" she asked.

"Yeah. I mean, if you took responsibility for the horse, I don't see why you shouldn't get paid."

"Paid to ride a horse. You know I have no problem with that."

"Great. Well, here's his number if you want to call. They'll probably have him by next week." Eli handed her a card and Kate smiled, set her lemonade on the sideboard, then waved at Sadie and dashed out of the house. Obviously construction workers still ran second to horses in Kate's world.

Eli probably loved that.

"That's going to leave a ring," Eli said, indicating the glass Kate had just discarded.

Sadie picked it up. "How did she turn out to be thoughtless of coasters with you in charge?"

"I blame the missing coaster gene on Connor. Anyway, I see you're being a bad influence on my sister," Eli said, but there was no venom in his words.

"Your sister heard the work trucks a mile away and came running for her chance to gaze upon some prime, Grade A man muscle. Don't blame me for her actions."

"I don't really," he said.

He should leave because there was no reason for him to be there. Not when they were avoiding each other.

"So, you're having a deck built?" he went on.

She nodded. "Yes. Connor approved that plan before I moved in. I'd seen pictures of the place in the online ad and knew I wanted something more than just the front porch."

"Online ad. Liss must have helped him with that."

"Was she the woman who answered the phone call I made?"

Eli lifted a shoulder. "I would guess so."

"His...girlfriend?" Sadie asked, knowing it was nosy but not really caring.

"Friend. You met her at the poker game," Eli said. "She's one of the only people he listens to. Incidentally about the only person who can put up with his bullshit for more than a very short amount of time."

"I see. And who puts up with yours?"

"No one. I put up with everyone else's."

"Right," she said, looking back at the construction workers. "Men and tools are a marvel."

"What about you? Ace putting up with yours?"

She laughed. "Uh...not currently."

"Interesting."

"Why?"

"I'm surprised he didn't ask you out."

Dammit. "He did," she said. "But flannel isn't really my thing. Beards are so…scratchy. You have testosterone, we get it. So much that hair is growing from your face!" She waved her hands, the ice clanking against the glass again. "Just so… obvious."

"You prefer nonobvious men?"

"Just, you know, maybe I don't prefer any man right now. Or any one man. I have a fine assortment right out there. Why would I tie myself down to a date with one bartender, when I could stand here and look at the variety behind the glass, so to speak."

"You're making an awful lot of excuses about turning down a date. To a man you profess not to like."

"I don't like you," she said. "And may I say, you're loitering a lot in the house of a woman that you profess to be avoiding." She looked pointedly at him.

"I guess I am."

"And so…"

"Nothing. I'll go." He turned and she felt instant regret, which was more annoying than anything else. More annoying than not being able to enjoy checking out other guys. More annoying than all the darn emotions this place made her feel.

"I just… I ran into Alison," she said, not really sure why she was prolonging the conversation. He turned back toward her. "Used to be Brown. At the diner. She's the one who makes the baked goods there. I was just wondering if you knew anything about her. Like…if she's okay. I knew her in school and she seems… I don't know. Something felt off."

He nodded slowly, a shadow passing over his face. "Yeah. I know her. From the diner mostly. Her husband, Jared, is a logger. I know him because I've arrested him once or twice for after-work fights with coworkers. And yeah, I think something seems off. But she's never said a thing to me, and I've never seen anything… There's only so much you can do."

Her stomach tightened painfully. The memories from ten

years ago were way too close to surfacing. Such familiar words. Familiar regret.

Only so much we can do. If you weren't an adult we could send child services in. But you're eighteen. Your mother is telling a different story. You could always call the police in…

She shook it off. Forcing the memory back into dark, dusty, unused corners of her mind.

She didn't need this. Not any of it.

"Right," Sadie said. "That…sucks. That sucks."

"I'm sorry for her."

Anger built up in her, more familiar now than she would like it to be, and all connected to Eli Freaking Garrett.

"If you were sorry, if you were paying attention, you would do something instead of just apologizing to me."

"What?" he asked.

"That's all people like you do in situations like this. Talk about how it's sad and unfortunate and regrettable—that's when you're not acting like you just don't see it at all." She ignored the guilt that lodged in her chest because that had been the first thing she'd done. Her first instinct. To think she was paranoid, and that it could be other things.

And sure, it still could be. But in the interest of her own comfort she'd been completely dismissive, and she knew the kind of pain that caused. Knew that that attitude could be utterly devastating to the people being shoved into the shadows for the convenience of others.

"The thing is, Sadie, I haven't seen anything. Except that I know the guy is a dick. On the job site and off. But being a dick isn't a crime. Now, when he has committed crimes? It's been handled. But he hasn't recently, and I swear to you I have nothing but supposition about how he treats her."

"But can't you investigate—"

"No," he said. "I can't. Because as much as I would like to sometimes, adults have a right to privacy. If there has not been a crime, then there's nothing I can do. I can't assume someone has committed a crime and go in after them. There are lines, and I can't cross them."

"Whatever. You're a chronic do-gooder. You're all up in your family's life. You feel like you're all up in mine, because here you are in my house again, and you're talking to me about boundaries?"

"I'm sorry, but the girl who runs from everything is going to talk to me about getting involved in people's lives? When was the last time you were involved in anyone's life besides your own, Sadie? When was the last time you took the time to help someone with their problems?"

"I did it for a living, jackass."

"And that helps you sleep at night, doesn't it? It helps you feel like you talk to people and like you've done something, but you never have to stay around, day in and day out and see the same people. See the same struggle. Know that all the help you've offered has meant nothing in the end."

"What are you talking about?" she asked, crossing her arms under her breasts.

Eli turned away from her and stalked toward the entryway and she followed him, her heart raging. "Hey, you just impugned my character, now stick around and explain it," she said.

"People don't change, Sadie. If I've seen one thing in my life, it's that. But to realize it you have to stick around. You got to sit in an office and listen to people talk, for money, but I won't even go too deep into that because, yeah, I take care of this community for money and I don't think a paycheck negates caring. But the thing is, I'm here. Year in, year out. I arrest the same kids over and over again. The same street people, the same addicts. The same abusers. And I wish to God they would get it. That something would reach them, but nine times out of ten, it just doesn't."

"I try, Eli. Even if I don't stay for twenty years, it doesn't mean I don't try," she said, the ball of fury growing hotter, bigger.

"You get to feel superior," he said, "and that's damn convenient. Because you get to judge me for what you think is me refusing to make a difference, and the view from your high horse tells you that you have made one. But it's only because you're all wrapped up in this fuzzy, fake reality blanket you knitted for yourself. You get to say that it's real, that what you do is real, and you get to look around this place that hasn't changed and say that what I do isn't. But it's because you've never bothered to look behind you."

"That is…" she said, searching for words. But it was hard when they were all mired in anger. "That is completely unfair."

"Is it? You're standing here telling me I don't care when, honestly, the thing is, I do. But caring doesn't do a damn thing. You have to act. I act according to the law. I keep things in order, using real rules and guidelines. I don't deal in the subjective, because I can't afford to make irrational mistakes."

"I see. So emotions are irrational."

"Hell yes," he said. "Emotions are damned irrational."

He took a step toward her, the tight space of the entryway growing smaller. "You know what else is irrational?" he asked.

"What?" She shouldn't ask what. Because she shouldn't want to know. Because the answer was going to lead to something stupid, and she knew that better than she knew just about anything at this point.

"Attraction," he said, his voice getting deeper.

Oh, no. That was definitely the wrong topic.

Everything slowed down, except her pulse, which sped up, beating hard in her neck, her wrists and, noticeably, at the apex of her thighs.

"Sure," she said. "Attraction is…you know, not logical, because it originates in your pants and not your brain. Which is not strictly true, actually. Your brain definitely plays a part in attraction…" Which begged the question why her brain and body were conspiring against her.

"It's a nuisance," he said.

"Get off my lawn, sexy feelings," she said, shaking her fist and trying to laugh.

But before she could finish the fake giggle, it was cut off by Eli's mouth over hers, by the fierce strength of his body propelling them both backward until they hit the wall. She dropped her lemonade, hearing it hit the floor, hearing it splash upward and spill the ice. It would be sticky and slippery and she just didn't care right now.

He pushed his pelvis against hers, the hard ridge of his erection evident against her softness. She rolled her hips against him and he groaned, the sound reverberating through her.

She didn't know why anger and lust were all tied into one thing with this man. She didn't know why she couldn't control her emotions or her body around him. She didn't know why she wanted him even when he drove her crazy.

Even when she didn't like him. At least, she was pretty sure she didn't like him.

It was hard to parse the finer feelings just at the moment.

He growled, a kind of deep, low sound. A sound that spoke of both satisfaction and hunger as he moved his hands to her waist to hold her, slid them down to her hips and held her tight.

She wrapped her arms around his neck and pressed herself more firmly against his body, and she found herself backed more tightly against the wall, the kiss intensifying.

She bit his lip and he returned it, his teeth leaving behind a stinging impression that burned all the way down. She was past thinking. She was past anger. She was past caring whether or not they could ever go out to dinner together without fighting.

Because what did that matter when there was this? Nothing else mattered. Not the construction workers outside, not her pride, not anything. Not in comparison with the heat that was burning between them, white-hot and insistent. Perfect.

This was sexual need in its purest form. Undiluted. A straight shot of alcohol that buzzed right through the brain and turned everything on the periphery gauzy. Consequences didn't matter.

Eli mattered. While the rest of the world faded, he remained. Sharp and present, perfect. Necessary.

She released her hold on him and ran her hands down his chest, over the thin black T-shirt that seemed to be his out-of-work uniform. She could feel the muscles underneath, the hard ridges, defined peaks and valleys.

And she couldn't stop herself from dragging her fingertips all the way down to the edge of his shirt and pushing her hands beneath the hem. She hissed when her fingers made contact with hot skin and rough hair.

This might kill her. He might kill her.

She didn't know if she had the fortitude for this. Because it was definitely like nothing she'd ever experienced before.

This wasn't a pleasant tightening in her stomach and a bit of slickness between her thighs. It was all-over need. Warmth that bloomed low and spread to all of her extremities, that infiltrated her veins and heated her blood, making it flow hotter, faster, went straight to her heart and sent it into overdrive. Left her shaking and weak and *needy* in a way that should terrify her.

Scratch that, it *did* terrify her. But the arousal drowned out the fear. Mayhem was crashing around her, but it didn't matter because lust was a giant hand holding her head down beneath the waves. Where she was insulated, and at the same time in terrible danger.

But that only made it better. More exciting. More desperate.

She moved her fingertips up over his stomach, over abs that could be played like a washboard in a country band and toward that broad, perfect chest.

"Oh, just take your shirt off," she muttered against his lips, pushing upward while he tugged the end and hauled it over his head.

Her heart stuttered for a second before racing ahead again as she took in the overwhelming hotness that was Eli Garrett. She'd thought of him as Officer Hottie on first sight, but she'd had no. Freaking. Idea.

Tanned and toned with just a smattering of body hair over his chest and down the center of his abs. Like the path on a map, leading to buried treasure. And she could tell, based on the feeling of his hardness against her, that he was packing some serious treasure.

He pushed the straps on her dress down, exposing the thin, peach-colored bra she was wearing. He swore, harsh, breathless, and moved to cup her, sliding his thumbs over her nipples. She leaned her head back, banging it on the wall. And she didn't even care.

He lowered his head, pressing a hot, openmouthed kiss to her cleavage, the desperation in his actions spurring her on, bringing her closer to orgasm with each touch of his lips, his tongue, his teeth on her tender flesh.

Kissing, touching, had never brought her so close. He hadn't even put his hands between her legs—where she was wet and aching for him—and she was still right on the edge, ready to go over with the slightest touch. Another flick of his thumb over her cloth-covered nipple, another calculated slide of his tongue against hers.

He didn't do either. He lifted his head and looked at her, dark eyes meeting hers. His brows were locked together, his lips pressed into a line. He looked like a man trying with everything he had to cling to his control. A man who was losing. The moment jarred her, gave her body just enough of a reprieve that she didn't feel so close to the end.

She moved her hands behind her back, shaking, and unclasped her bra, throwing it onto the ground.

A flame burned hot and dark in his eyes and she could see the moment that all that control snapped. As sexy as it was to see Eli Garrett in full command, seeing him unleashed was even better.

He moved back to her, lowering his head and sliding his tongue around the center of her nipple before sucking it in deep as he moved his hands around her back, slipping them beneath her dress and cupping her butt.

He inched one hand lower, his finger dipping between her thighs. She gritted her teeth in a futile attempt to hold back a hoarse moan as his fingers slipped under her panties, over her wetness, and one pushed deep inside her.

She moved her hands to his back, nails digging in deep as she arched into his touch. Between his hands and his mouth, she was going to lose her ever-loving mind before this was over.

You already have. Might as well enjoy the ride.

That was the truth. But it was hard to regret losing her mind when it had led to the discovery of *this*.

He shifted his attentions to her other breast while he withdrew his finger, then slipped two fingers across her slick folds, over her clit.

She dug her nails into his skin, and she was pretty sure she might be drawing blood, and she didn't even care.

He slipped his fingers back, teasing her entrance with partial penetration before he pushed both inside of her. A ragged curse word escaped her lips as her orgasm crashed through her, as she held tight to him and rode out the storm.

When the waves stopped moving through her, he withdrew, shoving his pants and underwear down his thighs, revealing his body to her.

"Damn," she said, the word tinged with awe.

He smiled for a second, before the expression was replaced with one of total intensity and concentration. Then he bent and grabbed his jeans, fumbling through the pockets for his wallet, and then fumbling through the wallet for a plastic packet that was a more welcome sight than water in the desert.

"I will never mock your sense of responsibility again."

He opened the condom and rolled it onto his beautiful, considerable length, then he closed the distance between them. "Sadie?"

"Yes?"

"Shut up." He bent his head and kissed her, pushing his hand back between her legs and tugging her panties to the side before gripping her thigh with his other hand and tugging her up against him, the thick, blunt head of his cock testing her.

Then he thrust in fully, a raw sound escaping his lips, the sudden, intense invasion leaving her breathless, leaving her on the verge of begging for more. On the verge of coming again, even though she'd just had an orgasm strong enough to render her whole two-year man hiatus forgotten.

She held tight to his shoulders and lifted her other leg up over his hips, her ankles locked behind him as he pushed her back hard against the wall, his hands holding her hips tight as he withdrew and thrust deep inside her.

"Yes," she breathed against his ear, biting his neck gently, then licking it as he pounded into her. Driving her back toward orgasm so much faster than she would have imagined possible.

He captured her mouth again as he thrust in deep and she felt the first ripple of a new climax starting to move through her.

Then he put one hand on her breast again, squeezing gently and flicking his thumb across the tightened bud at the center, and she was consumed by it. Pleasure tore through her, and on its heels was a rough, feral growl from Eli as he lowered his head and gave himself up to his own climax, his erection pulsing inside her as he came.

He collapsed against her and her legs slipped down his lean hips, her feet making contact with the floor, her shaky knees making it impossible to stand straight.

She pressed her shoulder blades against the wall, suddenly very aware that her sundress was tugged down beneath her breasts and pushed partway up her hips, her undies askew. And her lemonade had spilled all over the floor, the ice cubes melting on the hardwood.

So many bad choices made in such a short period of time. And it was hard to regret them when her body was still buzzing, her breath was still MIA and she just felt so thoroughly satisfied that for the first time in her life she didn't feel on the verge of running somewhere else and never returning.

But all of that lasted only a moment.

"Fuck," he said, straightening and pushing off from the wall, walking back and forth for a second, looking down at the condom, which he was still wearing, a crease appearing between his brows.

"The bathroom upstairs," she said. "You can use it without walking by open windows."

He bent gingerly and grabbed his jeans, picking them up and climbing the stairs, and in spite of encroaching regret, she paused to admire his muscular calves, thighs and butt as he made his way to the bathroom.

She was high. On pleasure. On him. And with every step he took away from her, she sank a bit lower. Until her stomach was in her feet.

She wasn't needy after sex. It was not her thing. But she needed something more than this. Something more than a curse and his naked back as he left her.

The bastard. He was post-orgasmically uptight, which was a commitment to crabbiness that seemed almost impossible to maintain.

But Eli was incredible that way.

And in other ways.

The man was built. He'd just proved that the size of the boat had a lot to do with how the motion of the ocean felt, that was for sure.

Under normal circumstances she would feel...triumphant. He was, without a doubt, the single hottest guy she'd ever been with. Not that there had been a lot, but she'd never been too worried about it. It was all casual.

The trade-off with Eli seemed to be that nothing about it felt casual. Amazing, cataclysmic sex, with a side of angst.

Gah, and no thank you.

She preferred no angst to multiple orgasms.

Lie, lie, you lie. That was the best sex of all time. It'd be worth waxing both your eyebrows off in their entirety to experience that again.

Meh. Why did her internal voice have to know her so well? She heard footsteps on the stairs again about the time she realized she was still standing there half-dressed. She scrambled to get her dress pulled into place, kicking her bra into the corner.

Then she reached beneath her skirt and adjusted her panties and straightened, hoping she looked a little less epically tumbled.

Sadly, she didn't feel less epically tumbled. She was hypersensitive and tingly, and her mouth felt like she'd gotten it too close to a flame.

She turned, and all those feelings got worse. He was walking toward her, down the staircase, jeans low on his hips, very low, no underwear band visible because his underwear was still on the floor and not on his fine body. His chest was bare, his ab muscles rippling with each step.

His mouth was grim. And it still looked kissable. His lips looked extra kissable when they were grim, which was some sort of sick joke her hormones were playing. Because everything in her took it as a challenge. To soften his mouth. To make him relax. To make him groan.

To make him shake and sweat and come.

Bad road. Her mind had gone down a bad road.

"So, that was...fun," she said, clearing her throat.

He shot her a glare that could only be described as evil and bent to get his T-shirt, tugging it over his head, and over her happy fun times ab show.

"I take it *fun* isn't your adjective of choice," she said, knowing she was making it worse, unable to stop herself from warding off the awkward silence with even more awkward words.

He took his underwear off the floor and stuffed them in his pocket. She would have laughed if it wasn't all so horrible. Actually, she might have laughed anyway because anything so singularly hideous had to be a little bit funny.

But she didn't laugh because she didn't want Eli to kill her with those very angry brown eyes of his.

Though, they were starting to make her angry, since it wasn't like she'd assaulted him. He was the one who had kissed her.

He had kissed her and now he was glaring.

And just like that she went from tingly to uncontainable rage.

"Please don't stalk around here like I compromised your maidenly virtue. You kissed me. You pushed me against the wall. You were complicit in the screwing. So get over yourself."

His nostrils flared and a muscle jumped in his jaw. "I am well aware that I'm at fault here."

And that made her bristle, too. "At fault? You make it sound like we had a fender bender. It was sex, Eli. There doesn't have to be a guilty party."

Color slashed over his cheekbones and she knew that he felt... ashamed. Of her. Of wanting her. And that just made her feel like garbage. All the glow was gone. All the good everything. And the anger, too.

It just left her with a sharp sinking sensation, a feeling of aching uncertainty. And just like that, the fear, the knot of terror that seemed to be a constant companion, was back in her chest.

And she wanted to run.

Not just from the room, or the house. But from the town. The state. She just wanted to leave it all so far in the rearview mirror that she couldn't see it. That she wouldn't be able to remember this regret.

"Why don't you just go," she said.

He nodded once and walked out the door, closing it firmly behind him. And she realized they hadn't even locked it. They'd screwed in the entryway of a place that seemed to have revolving doors on every structure and they hadn't even locked up.

"I wish I could go," she said, pressure building in her chest, tears stinging her eyes.

She cried. Of course she did. At the end of books, during commercials for life insurance and movies with intense acts of bravery that were sure to end in death but were performed anyway.

But she didn't cry over real-life things. Because she kept negative space, negative emotion, out of her life. And she didn't feel it. She didn't let it get down beneath the surface when it did run out to confront her.

But Eli had managed to get inside her, and not just in a sexual way. It was…terrible. She leaned against the wall, her heart slowed down to a dull thud that resonated in her ears, her stomach turning, making her feel sick.

Okay, she was not going to wallow. She was *not*. Wallowing didn't solve anything. And repeating the same mistakes twice didn't solve anything, either.

One good thing about growing up with her abusive asshole of a father: she'd learned about human nature in a harsh and real way. Had seen what happened to the optimistic when they believed a bad situation could change with love. With lying to yourself.

She'd come out of that with eyes wide-open. And with a ruptured spleen, but that was another matter entirely.

She sucked in a deep breath and managed to hold back the tears. She wasn't going to cry over Eli. It was a spilled-milk situation. Or rather, spilled lemonade. She just needed to wipe up the mess and carry on.

She heard the soft thump of four paws hitting the kitchen tile, and then Toby wandered into the room, rubbing against her bare legs, his gray tail twitching up above his head.

She bent down and scratched him between his ears. "I messed up," she whispered, because her voice didn't seem to want to function on any other level. "But I guess that's par for the course, right?"

Toby meowed and pushed his head harder against her hand, angling so that she hit a particular spot just behind his left ear.

"How do you put up with me?" she asked, and was met with nothing but a request for more head petting. Which in many ways was just fine. "Kitty before mantitty," she said, moving her hand beneath his chin and scratching.

This was just a onetime thing. A moment of insanity. She should be grateful it had happened. Yes, grateful. Because the intensity brewing between them wasn't healthy. And it had needed some diffusing. That was what today had been. She could draw a line under it and call it good.

What was sex like with Eli? Question answered. What did he look like naked? Question very much answered. There was no more burning curiosity. None.

And that meant the tension between them should be somewhat relieved. So there.

She took another breath, some of the tightness in her chest easing. There was no reason to be upset. They were adults, and they could handle this. Eli would be fine next time she saw him. He'd just been suffering orgasm hangover and hadn't handled things well.

But everything would be fine.

It had to be.

CHAPTER TEN

IT WAS PIZZA NIGHT for the Garrett family, and it should have been somewhat enjoyable. Usually, Eli liked the routine of them assembling in the main house for an evening.

Even though there weren't a whole lot of sunnier times for their family to be reminded of, they'd always had each other.

The three of them, and sometimes Jack, against the world.

But tonight he wasn't enjoying it to the degree that he should, and all because of Sadie. Because of Sadie and the fact that, only four hours ago, they'd had sex against a wall, which he'd never, ever done in his life.

Because that spoke of a lack of control he didn't even think he was capable of. Never before had a kiss just turned into sex.

When he had sex with a woman, they both knew it was on the agenda and things followed careful steps. Living room couch to bedroom. And then out the door again because he didn't spend the night, but it was okay, because they didn't expect him to.

It did not just…happen like that. Almost against his will, and certainly against his better judgment. But one minute they'd been shouting at each other, the next they'd been kissing, and then...then he'd been about knocked on his ass by the intensity of his orgasm.

Before he knew it he'd been upstairs in her bathroom, totally naked, pouring cold water down his neck so that he could get back downstairs and out the door again without popping wood when he saw her.

He'd spent the rest of the day riding his horse around the pastures, doing essentially nothing but trying to pound his balls into submission with tight jeans and a punishing day in the saddle.

Unfortunately, he'd just ended up replaying the scene in Sadie's house over and over.

"Why are you scowling?" Connor asked from his position at the counter, where he was sitting on a bar stool and inhaling his pizza. "Scowling is kind of my thing, and I feel like you're edging in on my territory."

"Scowling is your thing? I thought the Robinson Crusoe look was your thing," he said, indicating Connor's beard and hair, which were both starting to get a little long.

"I can have more than one thing."

"What's my thing?" Kate asked, leaning forward on the counter, speaking around a mouthful of cheese.

"Bad table manners and objectifying construction workers, apparently," he said, his words a little testy since, in fairness, it was Kate's fault that he'd gone looking for her in Sadie's house. It was his sister's damn *sex drive* that had put him in this position.

Her cheeks turned pink and she looked down. "Thanks for ratting me out, bastard."

"Objectifying construction workers?" Connor said in mock horror. "That's shocking. Did you whistle at them and say, 'Hey, baby! Why don't you drop that hammer so I can watch the view'?"

"I did not," she said, looking like she was about to fold in on herself.

"Missed opportunity," Connor said.

"Whatever," Kate said, pulling a piece of pepperoni off her pizza and putting it in her mouth. "You would lock me in my room if I ever did that." She stuck her thumb in her mouth and sucked the grease off it loudly.

"Honestly," Connor said. "I don't worry much about you and men."

Kate looked genuinely offended by that. "Why not?"

"I have my reasons," Connor said.

Relationships, or hookups, which was the veiled content of the conversation, were not Eli's favorite topic just now, so he was keeping his mouth shut.

"So what happened the other night?" Connor asked, his focus on Eli now. As if his older-brother sense told him that Eli was clamming up to avoid talking about something.

"Which night?" Eli asked.

"You dragged Sadie out of the bar and returned ten minutes later. She looked like she'd been scolded. You looked like you'd accidentally branded your own ass instead of a calf's. What happened?"

"Why are you choosing this moment to start paying attention to what I do?"

"I always pay attention. It's just you don't usually have anything happening. And I want to know what's happening with Sadie."

He thought about earlier. Soft skin under his hands, her full breasts...what it had been like to take one of those perfect nipples into his mouth. How wet she'd been.

Mind-blowing, cock-busting sex.

"Nothing," he said.

"Yeah, I don't believe you."

"They're avoiding each other," Kate said, looking at him almost apologetically. "Well," she continued defensively when he shot back a mean glare, "it's what she said when you were at the house earlier. When you busted us creeping on those guys."

"I'm avoiding her because she's a pain," he said.

"And yet you told Jack to keep his hands off."

Kate's head whipped around to Connor. "Jack is interested in her?"

"Jack," Connor said, "is interested in tits. Whether they're attached to Sadie or not is immaterial. They are the new breasts in town, and therein lies the attraction."

Kate lowered her head and mumbled something that Eli didn't understand.

"What was that, pumpkin?" Connor asked.

"Gross," she said, a little louder, and a little crisper.

"Men are. Your life lesson for the day," Connor said.

Seemed like it was Eli's lesson for the day, too. Since he'd done a fantastic impersonation of a pig today.

"To be fair, Connor," Kate said. "I appreciate a man's ass in a pair of Wranglers."

Connor looked like Kate had hauled off and slapped him with her meat-greasy fingers. "Sure," he said.

"I just meant Jack's attitude is gross. Sex isn't gross at all." Kate was looking mutinous now, and Eli's blood pressure was rising because he didn't need sex talk just at the moment. And he needed sex talk from Kate never.

"That's enough," Connor said.

"I mean, if a guy wants to look at my tits I'm not going to—"

"Did someone spike your Diet Coke?" Eli asked.

"I'm just sick of this overprotective crap you guys always pull. 'Boys are gross,'" she said, in a bad imitation of Connor's voice. "'You'll get cooties if you touch them.'"

"I *never* said that," Connor said.

"You told me penises had teeth," she said, deadpan.

Eli's head whipped around to face Connor. "Did you really?"

"I don't remember," Connor said.

"You did," Kate said. "I spent the next two years concerned for the health and safety of the inner thighs of every boy I knew."

In spite of his mood, Eli laughed. "I'm sorry, that's just funny."

"Brothers are horrible," she said.

"I know, but we're also the best you have," Eli said. Poor Kate. They were all she had, and they fell short in so many ways it verged on tragic.

"You're good for some things," Kate said. "Not as much for others."

"The same could be said for anything," Connor pointed out. "Badgers. Great for being kickass in the woods. Bad for sharing a shower."

"Connor..." Kate groaned.

"Krazy Glue. Good for sticking things together. Bad for personal lubricant."

Kate scrunched her eyes shut and stuck out her tongue.

"I rest my case," Connor said. "Men are gross."

"*You're* gross," Kate said.

"Your mom is gross."

"My mom's hygiene is open to interpretation because no one has seen her in nineteen years."

"Sorry," Connor said. "Bad joke."

"Sure," Kate said, looking dismissive, "but she's your mom, too."

"Barely," Eli said.

She was the woman who had left them all to drown in chaos. His father slipping away on a wave of alcohol while the kids were left to pull themselves up from the wreckage of glass bottles, unwashed clothes and garbage.

To say that Eli had come out of it a little bit of a neat freak was an understatement. Order and control had become essential to survival, and bleach had been a weapon he'd employed early on.

If Connor had become the man of the house, Eli had become the housewife. No thirteen-year-old boy wanted that job. But they had Kate to worry about. And dammit all, worry didn't even begin to cover it.

But Eli and Connor were both old enough to realize that if rumors about their dad's drinking got passed around, there was a high likelihood CPS would step in. There had been too much loss for them to be split up. For Kate to be taken away from them. For them to be taken from the ranch.

And so they'd done whatever they'd had to.

School days had been torture for a while. He'd been in hell wondering if his sister was being cared for while he was trapped in a classroom, Kate in a crib while his father drank the day away.

Fortunately, Connor did more with the ranch as a fifteen-year-old than their father had ever done, and they'd earned enough money to put Kate in full-time day care.

So Connor would get up before school and do what needed to be done on the ranch, and Eli would get up and wake Kate. Give her a bath, wash and braid her hair. There was too much to do for him to allow chaos, too much at stake to ever let Kate look like she was less than lovingly cared for.

Connor and Eli had kept up appearances until the old bastard had driven off one of the winding Copper Ridge roads five years ago, drunk as hell, and nobody had been in the dark after that.

In so many ways, it was easier with their dad dead. At least they didn't have to take care of him now, too.

Well, you did a terrible job of taking care of him in the end.

He shook that thought off. What the hell was wrong with him today? Sex against a wall and this stupid stuff.

He didn't like reflecting on the past, and he wasn't really sure why he was doing it now. Maybe just because today sucked like that.

But did it really suck? Because, be honest, you've never had sex that good.

No, he hadn't. And that made it even worse.

Because no matter how bad of an idea he thought it was, he

wanted more. The temptation to shove her down onto the floor, hook her legs over his shoulders and have his way with her had been way too big, which was why he'd stormed out of there as quickly as he could.

Because he didn't trust himself. He almost didn't know himself, and for a guy like him, that was a terrifying admission.

"Well, genetically," Connor said, "I think we can all agree that other than in the looks department, we lost the parental lottery."

Eli almost laughed at that since Connor was currently looking shaggy enough that it would take a very close inspection to decide whether or not he was good-looking.

"But seriously," Kate said, "brothers are actually good for a lot of things. So… I've never felt like it was so bad."

Eli cleared his throat. "Dammit, Kate, why'd you have to get all sincere?"

"You have to warn a guy, Katie," Connor added.

"Call me Katie again, and I won't say anything nice to you for the foreseeable future." And it was all back to normal already.

Okay, he'd screwed up earlier. No denying that. And things were going to be weird for a while. And hard for a while, which was a potential double entendre Sadie would have enjoyed. But he still had Kate and Connor. And his run for sheriff. So most areas of his life were fine. He was just going to rope off that little disaster labeled Sadie and avoid it for the time being. Pay attention to the good and ignore the wreckage.

The incredible, mind-blowing wreckage.

He took a bite of pizza, even though he wasn't hungry. Tomorrow he was back to work. And with any luck, that would help keep his mind off things he had no business thinking about.

CAMPAIGN SIGNS AND POSTERS weren't enough, it seemed. Not for the general election. TV ads and radio spots were needed. According to Lydia at least.

He knew those things were probably necessary, and he'd

done some checking into it already, but there was something about the way Lydia talked about the election, filled with spark and enthusiasm, that made it seem like a very daunting reality.

Made him fear it was just too damn much to take on. The feeling he was sinking beneath a pile of endless work was one he'd had for most of his life, so it wasn't new. But it didn't mean he had to like it.

He ought to slap a campaign manager button on her chest and hire her right here in the coffee shop. But that would mean constant exposure to this level of energy and ideas, and he wasn't sure he could handle that now.

Not with hurricane Sadie encroaching on his borders.

Eli was starting to think he needed to buy coffee somewhere else. But other than The Grind the closest place with decent caffeine was fifteen miles away and it wasn't his usual assignment. And he basically had no reason ever to drive there for a latte, even when it meant avoiding Lydia's too-keen eyes.

After what had happened with Sadie it felt exposing, and made him feel a little guilty. Which was stupid, because if Lydia was interested in him, he'd never given her a reason to be. And he shouldn't feel at all like he'd somehow led her on.

But he did. And he felt even worse because she was helping with the Independence Day Community Whatever and because she seemed so invested in his campaign.

And if she found out he'd slept with Sadie…well, the help would likely be withdrawn from both endeavors. Which, when he thought about it, was more tempting than it should be.

"I think you should do a full-color spread," Lydia was saying now.

"Excuse me?"

"Like…put your picture on the posters and the signs. I feel like you have the looks to really grab voters."

"Is that…a thing?" he asked.

She smiled. "It's always a thing. I mean, when you're as kind and dedicated as you are, handsomeness shouldn't matter. But it certainly enhances things. It's part of charisma."

He was so rarely accused of having that.

"Well, the other guy running certainly has a lot of good qualities, and has years more experience than I do."

"He isn't from Copper Ridge, though. And since this is the largest town in the county, that matters. They just work here. It's different."

It was in his mind, too. Man, it would be so much easier if he found Lydia attractive. Ferret-like levels of energy aside, she was pretty amazing. They could work together on his campaign, and hell, in spite of his gut opposition to a wife and family, he could eventually settle down with someone like her and they could be the unofficial king and queen of Logan County.

Too bad a stick in the eye sounded more appealing.

He looked away from Lydia, across the street, and saw a messy blond bun bobbing on the far side of the cars parked against the curb. And he knew, instantly, who the bun belonged to.

He'd avoided her for three days. Three days without seeing her and kissing her, or putting her up against the wall and banging her.

It had been a successful, if not entirely fun, three days.

The identity of his visual target was confirmed when she appeared through a gap in the parked cars, turning away from the street and facing the wall of one of the shops. She set a stack of papers on the ground and held a staple gun up. Pressing one sheet of paper to a bulletin board and holding the gun against it, she efficiently shot a staple into each corner, before bending and picking up the flyers again and moving on to the next shop.

They were maybe fifteen feet apart, but that didn't stop her from adding a flyer to that board, too.

"Sorry," he said to Lydia. "I have to…law enforcement business."

He walked to the end of the sidewalk, to the crosswalk, and moved quickly across to where Sadie was.

"What are you doing?" he asked.

She turned, her expression fierce as she pressed the trigger on the gun and shot a staple through the paper and cork board. "Posting posters," she said.

She lowered her hand to her side and lifted her eyebrow, the staple gun menacing in her dainty hold.

"I can see that."

He looked behind her head and read the words.

> *Logan County Community Barbecue*
> *Independence Day*
> *Come to the Garrett Ranch for food, fun and games.*
> *Horseshoes, pie eating contest, live music*
> *and a barbecue battle.*

"Well, this is…firming up."

She looked down below his belt pointedly, raising her arm, and the staple gun with it. "Is it?"

He frowned. "Sadie…"

"Give the guy a little sex and suddenly he gets the dick jokes."

"Are you mad at me?" he asked.

"Did you expect me to be super thrilled with you?"

"I expected you to do the socially acceptable thing and pretend nothing happened while you brooded silently. That was my plan."

"Too bad for you, I've never excelled at the socially acceptable."

"Look, let's talk about this," he said, indicating the poster. "Not…the other thing. This is good. The other is bad."

"The other was actually *quite good*, if I say so myself. I am apparently not only good in bed, but good against the wall. Adding it to my résumé."

"Why are you so difficult?" he asked.

"I don't know. Character flaw? Asset? You be the judge."

"And I'm trying to be nice."

"Not doing a very good job." She propped her chin on the staple gun handle.

"So why don't you try to play nice for two seconds. Why don't you go ahead and not keep bringing up what I think is sort of an awkward moment for both of us."

"I don't think *awkward* is the word I would use," she said, frowning.

"It's not?"

"It was actually really athletic. I thought we were kind of awesome."

"Yeah, I guess we were," he said, taking a sip of his latte as an involuntary smile tugged at the corners of his mouth.

"Ah, the male ego," she said, giving him the squinty eye. "So susceptible to praise. Now suddenly The Sex exists."

"I know it exists. I just don't see the point of doing a post-mortem on something that we both know can't happen again."

"Why not?" she asked.

"Because. Because it can't," he said, feeling the conviction leak out of his words as he spoke them.

"Because why?"

"Because we don't get along. And I'm busy running for sheriff."

"Yeah, well, I'm busy, too."

"And I'm busy with cows."

"Moo," she said.

"That is absurd."

"Yep."

"And cute," he said, trying to get a handle on the heat firing through his veins.

Then her cheeks turned pink, a smile curving her lips. "Aw, you think I'm cute."

"I think puppies are cute, too. Don't go getting a big head."

"And cats?"

He shook his head. "You know I don't think cats are cute."

"Which is another reason we shouldn't have sex, is that right? Because I love cats. Not just Toby. I love every kind of cat."

"Yeah, no."

"Also, you're humorless."

"Untrue."

She crossed her arms beneath her breasts and leaned back on her heels. "Is it? Tell me a joke."

"I'm not going to tell you a joke."

"So you are humorless."

He paused for a second, genuinely considering telling her one just to get her off his back and prove that he had humor, dammit. But then for some reason, he could think of only one joke. And it was…well, not the kind of joke he should tell.

"Well?" she asked, cocking her head to the side.

"Fine," he said through gritted teeth. "What's the difference between snow boys and snow girls?"

"What?" she asked, smiling wide.

He sighed heavily. "Snowballs."

"Ha! You said balls. Also, that is a terrible joke."

"It's the only one I could think of."

"I don't think that counts toward proving your point."

"Of course you don't, because if it does, I win."

"I don't think a bad joke constitutes as a win for any involved. Are you going to stand here all day? Because I have posters to hang."

He frowned. "And I have a job to do."

"Are you not patrolling the streets?"

"I should be out doing traffic stops."

"Doesn't that just make you feel like a dick?"

"No," he said. "I've lost too many people to road accidents. If I make someone mad because I pull them over or give them a ticket, that's not really my problem. Or my concern. My concern is that they live to drive another day, as do the other people they share the highway with."

He was annoying himself with how obnoxious he sounded, how serious and in general downbeat. Especially when talking to Sadie, who seemed to be all smiles and laughter, except when he messed with things. He was the bad guy in this scenario and he didn't particularly like it.

"Fair enough," she said, her voice softening. "I'm sorry, that was kind of insensitive of me."

"Why would you ever connect doing traffic stops with the people I've lost? It's my own particular issue. It has nothing to do with you."

"We all have issues, right? And I get that you want to take care of everyone," she said, biting her lip. "It's pretty obvious that you really do care a lot for the people in your life. And the people here, which I think I owe you an apology about, but more on that later."

"When later?"

"When I feel like eating dirt. Right now I don't really want to because I'm hanging posters and I feel bad enough for saying what I did about the traffic stops."

"Don't feel bad," he said, and he meant it.

She looked at him expectantly.

"What?" he asked.

She blinked. "What do you mean, what? I said I owed you an apology for saying bad things about you. Don't you owe me one?"

"I think you've said a lot worse things to me than I have to you," he said, frowning.

"Oh, really?"

"Yeah, and anyway, most of what I said was true."

She blinked rapidly. "Excuse me?" And she was pointing the staple gun in his direction, with what appeared to be intent.

"Sadie..."

"You said that I ran from things. And that I was on my high

horse. And that the work that I do is worthless. And you're going to stand by all of that being true?"

"That's not exactly what I said."

"It's pretty much what you said."

"I'm sorry," he said. And he was feeling pretty sorry for most everything that had happened since Sadie had come to town. He'd screwed up with her. Way more times than he wanted to count. And now she was standing here calling him on it. All of it.

She huffed out a growl. "You're just saying it now."

"So?"

"So it doesn't mean anything now."

"I give up, Sadie," he said, turning away from her and walking back in the direction of the crosswalk.

"Wait," she said.

He stopped. "What?"

"Don't leave. I'm mad at you. And I feel like we haven't resolved anything."

"Do we need to?"

"I'd like to."

He turned to face her again. "Okay, what is it you want resolved?"

"I was wondering something."

"What?"

"Do you want to keep having sex?"

CHAPTER ELEVEN

SADIE COULD HAVE immediately bitten her own tongue off. Where the heck had that come from? Oh, okay, she knew where it had come from.

Sleepless nights, endless erotic dreams about his strong body, his hands, his lips, his...well, his everything. She couldn't forget him. Couldn't forget how amazing it was to be with him. How much she wanted him.

She was so annoyed with herself, too.

She didn't do the physical obsession thing. She just didn't. And here she was basically burning up her sheets alone, waking up all sweaty and tangled up in the bedding like a dolphin in a tuna net.

On the verge of orgasm and with no desire to finish the job herself. And now this. This had come out of her mouth. On a public street, during a lovely sunny day. With children most likely playing at a nearby park.

Eli had been walking away, she'd looked at his butt, a butt that was so perfect and masculine and muscular and begging for her to touch it, and the words had just fallen out of her mouth.

He was just standing there, his expression stone, his lips pressed into a firm line.

Now she was filled with regret. Swollen with it. And she was still holding a staple gun.

It was a weird moment. There was no denying it.

"What did you say?" he asked.

"Oh, you know what I said. Why do people do that? Ask you to repeat something they heard but was totally crazy. Do you think I actually want to repeat that?"

"I have to be sure you said it," he said. "Because honestly? My mind could be playing tricks on me. It's entirely possible."

"Yeah, I said it."

"Then I have to be sure you meant it."

He was frozen, every line in his body hard and firm, on high alert. Was he interested? All of his talk about how crazy it was—and it was—and the way he'd stormed out after... But maybe it was just because it was all making him feel as insane as she did.

Maybe it was because he wanted it but didn't want to want it.

Well, he could join the club.

He just kept staring at her, waiting for her answer. And dammit, she didn't know the answer. She wanted it, yes, but was she willing to engage in a purely sexual, no-strings fling with a man who made her want to pull her hair out?

"Yes." Apparently she was. "I meant it."

She could see his hard swallow, his teeth grinding as his jaw shifted. And she hoped, a good portion of her *really* hoped, that he would say no. That he would make her angry. Walk away again and say something insulting on his way down the street that would be so vile all the lust she felt for him would be knocked out of her system.

"Okay," he said. "But I need rules."

"I..." She couldn't believe he'd agreed. She'd been counting on him to be the voice of reason. That was what he did, who he was, except for that time against the wall. And she'd been counting on him to make the smart choices here, since she was very obviously not going to do it. "What kind of rules?" she asked.

If he couldn't be the voice of reason, maybe, just maybe, there was still time for him to piss her off so she'd change her mind.

He looked to each side and then walked toward her, apparently satisfied that there were no prying eyes. "Just sex," he said.

"Yeah, that's what I said."

"And no one knows about it."

She rolled her eyes. "Well, obviously. I'm not going to print it in the paper. Or march over to your brother's place like, 'Hey! Been banging Eli. Here's your rent.'"

"I'm serious. I don't like complications. This is more complicated than I like it already, so it needs to stay clean."

"You don't strike me as a player."

"I'm not."

"But these are player rules."

"They're the rules of a man who generally doesn't date women who live within walking distance of his house. Or even the same town. Or really…a man who doesn't date much at all. But I'm still not a player. I'm just a guy who has too much to do. I don't want a wife, kids or exes all over where I have to patrol every day, so that means I do the best I can to keep things separate."

She hadn't really thought of it like that. Eli moved around town, around the whole area, all the time. Talked to random people, responded to calls. Having exes right in town had the potential to be a mess. She tended to move states away from hers, and she was never all that attached to any of them, so it wouldn't have much mattered anyway.

"Okay," she said. "And ultimately it doesn't really matter to me one way or the other. I like it casual, and no, I don't normally go in for sex only. In fact, I never do. But my relationships have all been very…nonserious."

"I just don't want you to get hurt," he said.

"Pfft. Eli, I've yet to fall in love with any man who touched me. Good in bed or not. Even if the guy is prone to giving me flowers and taking me out, I tend to remain fairly distant. It's hardly going to change with you. Remember? I don't even like you. I just want your body. And that means that this will be the best sex-only relationship ever. Plus, we live close. Late-night booty calls will be a breeze and there will be no temptation at all to develop finer feelings."

He lifted his coffee cup and took a drink. "Okay, I have to get back to work. Then I have to bring Connor food to ensure he does more than ingest alcohol today."

"Sure," she said, feeling a little like shrieking or scurrying in circles or something. Not with joy or anything, but with... panic, excitement and a pulse of adrenaline that seemed more appropriate for scaling a mountain than propositioning a guy for no-strings sex.

"I'll see you after."

"My place?" she asked, her throat dry.

"Probably for the best."

"Bring condoms," she said, looking around, suddenly concerned people might have started milling around since Eli last looked. "I am lacking, currently. And that would be a shame."

He nodded. "I'll come prepared." The black radio on his shoulder buzzed and he put his hand up over the top of it. "I have to go. See you tonight. Good luck with the posters."

Then he turned and walked away. Like some badass action movie star with a surprisingly poor exit line.

Oh, dear Lord, what had she done?

She bent and picked up her stack of posters again, holding them to her chest, the staple gun braced against the back of them.

There was no reason to panic. None at all. She'd propositioned Eli Garrett. And he'd said yes. They were going to have a no-strings fling that would result in many orgasms for both of them.

Putting it like that, it didn't seem like a big deal at all.

No, it sounded awesome.

A slow grin spread across her face and she turned and started walking down the sidewalk, beneath the covered walkway that ran along the row of little shops.

She paused at the next bulletin board, her heart beating fast, excitement building now.

Things had just gotten a whole lot more interesting.

"Dammit, Eli. There's mustard on this."

"What?" Eli looked at his brother for a full ten seconds before he processed what he was saying.

"My burger. There's mustard. You know I don't like mustard."

"Sorry," he said, taking a French fry out of his carton and eating it, looking across the kitchen counter at his brother, who was looking grumpier than normal.

"How the hell do you forget something like that?"

Oh, good, Connor was hell-bent on being an ass. This would be fun.

"I just did," Eli said.

Because his mind was on Sadie. Because his brother could starve for all he cared, except he couldn't really let that happen.

So he was here, pretending like he was invested in the meal he'd brought in for the two of them, listening to Connor bitch about condiments.

"Ace knows I don't like mustard," Connor said, glaring and getting up from his seat, going to the counter to get paper towels and a knife.

"He didn't ask if the burger was for you."

"Who else would it have been for?"

Fair question. "Kate. She likes mustard."

"And you remember that, apparently," he said.

"Shut up, Connor," Eli said, watching him flick the bulk of the mustard off the top bun with a knife before wiping it, seriously wiping it, with the paper towel, then scraping it thoroughly with the knife.

"You don't normally forget."

"If you want a flawless hamburger order, have Liss do it, since she actually likes taking care of you. Or better yet, why don't you go and order your own damn food."

Connor took a bite of the hamburger. "Because you do it for me," he said.

"I should stop," he said, putting another fry in his mouth.

He heard footsteps in the doorway and for a moment, his heart leaped up into his throat, his body tensing as he wondered if it was Sadie with a disaster of some kind, or… Sadie for any reason, really.

But it was Liss, speaking of, walking around the corner, holding a big white box. "Pie," she said, smiling.

Connor looked at Eli. "See, I bet she got it without mustard."

"If you put that pie down in front of me I'm going to squirt mustard all over it, Liss," Eli told her.

"Connor doesn't like mustard," she said, setting it down on the counter.

"Yes. We know."

She dropped her purse onto the counter and her keys with it, sighing heavily. "Is there anything for me?" she asked, turning and facing the fridge, jerking the door open.

Liss had a tendency to act like she lived here, which didn't seem to bother Connor at all. But then, Liss had been a fixture during his marriage, since she'd been close to him and Jessie both. "Dear Lord, Connor, you need to go grocery shopping."

"Still?" Eli asked. "I told him to go two weeks ago."

"I did. I went out to fill up my truck and stopped and bought beanie weenies and beer."

Liss gave him the evil eye. "That doesn't count."

"Why not?"

"I'm eating your fries."

"That's healthy."

"Fries before pies," she said, reaching over and snagging a handful of them out of the container.

And now that Liss was here, and would probably manage to keep Connor from drinking himself into a coma before bed, it was time for Eli to leave.

"I'm going to take off," Eli said, standing, shoving another French fry in his mouth and pushing the carton forward.

"Are you going to finish your burger?" Liss asked.

"No."

She reached out and pulled the carton over to another stool and sat down. "Thank you."

"You're welcome."

"Where are you taking off to?" Connor asked.

"Tired," he said, lying his ass off.

Connor gave him some serious side eye. "Okay. If, say, I were to send our younger sister to your house on a random errand in about an hour she wouldn't be emotionally scarred by activities conducted with female visitors, would she?"

No, because he wouldn't be at his house.

"No, but she'll wake me up and I'd be forced to come over here and shove your head in a toilet."

Connor smiled. "Interesting. Well, fine, I won't send her over. And I won't bug you."

Eli grunted and walked out of the house, feeling very much like he'd already been caught with his hand in the cookie jar. But he didn't care. He was going to go eat his damn cookies anyway.

SADIE WAS A BALL of nervous energy. Adrenaline pumping through her veins, heat pooling in her stomach, arousal throbbing between her legs.

She was expecting him soon. And she'd been waiting all day. No, she'd been waiting for this all week. This was what she wanted, and now that she was finally embracing it she was free to appreciate how much she truly craved him.

She wanted more than against the wall. She wanted him

naked. All the way naked. In bed. For hours. Subject to her exploration and any twisted desires she might have. She didn't usually have desires she'd consider twisted, but she hadn't ruled anything out with Eli.

Because he made her feel like a giant ball of want. Like a ticking time bomb of need that was ready to explode all over her living room—which was currently spotless, because after she'd done any and all planning she could do for the barbecue alone, and after she'd ordered bedding online for all of the bedrooms in the house, she'd had nothing better to do but clean.

You know. The floor, the wall, the kitchen counter. Just in case he wanted to bang her on unconventional surfaces. She did not need a nasty kernel of cat food right by her head while Eli was trying to satisfy her on the living room rug.

"Oh…cat," she said aloud.

Toby might not allow for sexual spontaneity.

He was currently sprawled over the blue armchair in the living room, looking like the tragic victim of a train collision, his paws out straight, head cocked back and to the side, his back legs up and spread.

"You're a sophisticated beast, Toby."

He didn't move. But of course, it was because it didn't suit him to move. If Eli started making out with her on the couch Toby would probably wake up and decide the only place in the world he wanted to be was on Eli's lap.

And she wasn't going to go locking him in the bathroom or anything just so she could have a good time in the room of her choice. The thing with Eli was physical. Toby, though he couldn't speak actual words, was her friend. Who had stuck with her through it all, mainly because his other choice was a life on the streets as a mouser and he wouldn't engage in anything so gauche.

Either way, she wasn't prioritizing her hookup over her cat's comfort.

Besides, she was having soft, luxurious bed fantasies. And that was better anyway.

The heavy knock on her front door had her scrambling toward the entryway, her heart bouncing around in her chest like a rubber ball that had been thrown at a wall as hard as possible.

She stopped for a second and looked down at the scoop-neck dress she was wearing. Then she leaned forward, reached down the front of the dress and cupped her breast, tugging it up in her bra before doing the same to the other one.

She took a breath and examined her improved cleavage. "Okay. We're good. We can do this."

She shook her head, her hair falling over her shoulders, then walked to the door, grabbing the handle and opening it.

"Hi," she said, going for casual.

"Can we not do the talking thing?" he asked. "You just get mad at me when we talk." He shifted, the bag he was holding rustling with the motion.

"I'm okay with that."

He walked into the house without waiting for her to invite him in, his presence dominating the entryway, filling it. He was a solid wall of man, and now that she'd been naked with him, she knew just how solid.

Knew how his skin felt beneath her hands, how his lips felt on hers, how his stubble felt against soft skin.

And she didn't want to talk, either.

"I want you naked," he said. "Now."

"Should we go into the bedroom…?"

"No," he said, slamming the door shut, shrugging off his jacket and hanging it on the peg.

That made her smile, because even in his dark intensity he couldn't bring himself to make a mess. Even now, he was still conscious of order.

But that was okay, because it was part of what made him him.

And no matter what she said about not liking him, she had to like him at least a little bit, or any male body would do.

There was something special about this male body that went past muscles and body hair and…well…generous physical attributes down below the belt.

And that was the soul that was in the body.

The thought made her chest feel tight. Made it hard to breathe. But then, that could just be because he was looking at her like a starving man might eye a piece of very chocolaty cake.

She took a breath, banished the nerves and made eye contact with him as she reached around behind her back and tugged the zipper on her dress down.

She folded her shoulders in slightly and let it fall to the floor, left herself standing there in nothing but a lacy black bra and matching panties.

She'd never been insecure about her body. She had one small scar from her laparoscopic surgery, but nothing too noticeable. Which was good, because she rarely had to explain it, and she barely thought about it, since it was so close to invisible.

Also, she'd never seen the point in being inhibited. If a man had shown interest when she had clothes on, he wouldn't get less interested once her clothes were off. And if he did, that was about him, not her.

But right now, she cared. She really, really wanted to see interest flare in Eli's eyes. Wanted him to be crazy with desire because she felt that way about him.

Because he wasn't another naked man, as good as any other. He was the best-looking man she'd ever seen. Because just looking at him got her hotter than twenty minutes of foreplay with any of her exes. So it felt much more important that he find her more than passable.

She watched him closely, watched the color across his cheekbones heighten, watched his chest pitch with hard breath, his hands clenched into fists at his sides.

It was safe to say she had a captive audience.

She arched her back and reached behind her, putting her hands on her bra clasp and carefully separating the hooks and eyes before letting the garment drop to the floor, her black lace flag of surrender.

He kept his gaze on hers. He didn't look down at her breasts, not right away, and for some reason, that was unspeakably hot. Watching the tension increase in his frame, watching his dark eyes burning with heat, determinedly fixed on her face.

She smiled. "Are you trying to earn an award for not being too obvious?" she asked, sliding one hand up her stomach, just beneath the curve of one breast, before drawing her fingertips over her nipple, a small gasp escaping her lips.

That broke his concentration.

His eyes dropped then and she ran her hand over her other breast, pausing to tease the tightened bud. His jaw was clenched tight, his arousal pushing aggressively against the zipper of his pants.

Oh, yes, she had nothing to worry about.

"You aren't done," he bit out.

"Am I not?" she asked, stilling her hands and glancing at him, trying to look innocent. Knowing she was failing, because she wasn't innocent at all. She was a woman who knew exactly what she wanted. And she knew how to get it.

Knew she was going to get it.

"The rest," he said, the words a hard command that sent a shiver through her.

She pressed her palms against her body and slid her hands down to the waistband of her panties. Then she pushed her fingers below the lace, in the front, cupping herself as she pushed them down, watching as his breathing increased, the pulse beating so hard in his neck she could see it.

She shoved them down her legs and kicked them to the side, leaving one hand where it was, sliding her fingertip over her clit. She gasped, white-hot pleasure firing through her. She was a whole lot more sensitive than she expected to be. But a day of anticipation, combined with how it felt to have his attention, was a hell of a lot more intoxicating than she'd anticipated.

"I'm wet," she said. "If you were curious."

"Bedroom," he said. "Now."

She turned away from him and walked slowly through the house, through the living room, casting a quick glance at Toby, who was still asleep, because obviously he couldn't be bothered to care about humans and their shenanigans.

She could hear Eli's heavy footsteps behind her. And she fought the urge to look back. But not looking was so much better than looking. Feeling his hot gaze on her without seeing him. Knowing he was watching her butt as she walked. That he was as tense with need as she was.

She led him to her bedroom. "Watch your step," she said, taking the small stair that dropped down at the entrance to the room.

She heard his boot hit the carpet behind her and she turned, her heart kicking hard against her breastbone as she looked at him.

"Can you close the door?" she asked.

"Why?"

"Trying to avoid Cattus Interruptus," she said.

"Right." He turned and shut the door behind them, setting the bag, which she assumed contained contraception, on the dresser. "This is another point in favor of keeping animals outside," he said.

"Yeah, yeah. Your anti-cat platform has no momentum here, might as well drop it. And while you're at it, drop your pants, Sheriff."

"Deputy sheriff."

"Why is that hot?" she asked, sitting on the edge of the bed and leaning back, propping herself up with her elbows. "Why is you being obnoxiously pedantic sexy? I don't even get it."

"Hell if I know."

"I mean, I know why the rest of you is sexy. Dayum."

He smiled as his hands went to his shirt collar. "Sorry about this," he said, tugging his tie from his shirt collar in one easy snap, the whole thing intact.

"Clip-on?" she asked.

"Standard issue. You can't take it off without looking like an idiot."

"All right, I'll let the tie go. But only because I'm already naked over here. And very, very horny."

"Points for me," he said, setting the tie on the edge of her vanity. Then he moved his hands to the first button on his shirt and released it, undoing it quickly, revealing a plain T-shirt the same color as his uniform underneath. "This is less of a strip show than bachelorette parties might have led you to believe," he said. "Didn't have time to go home and change."

"Are you embarrassed?" she asked.

He stilled with his hands on his belt. "No. But you went to a lot of... You had on matching underwear."

She nodded. "I did, it's true. But I am way less interested in your clothes than I am in the removal of them. So carry on."

He undid his belt and shrugged the tan T-shirt over his head. Beneath that was a thin black vest. Kevlar, she assumed. And something hit her in the stomach, a sharp pang. A realization of who he was and what it was he did on a whole new level. He wasn't just a man who cared about his town. He was a man who put his life on the line. He was a man who backed up his word.

And tonight? He was all hers.

He took the vest off, laying it neatly with everything else.

"Oh, yesss," she said, the breath hissing through her teeth. "That's what I'm here to see."

He looked at her, one dark brow arched.

"What?" she asked. "Women don't usually sing the praises of your body?"

"In my experience, it's expected for me to sing the praises of theirs." He turned to face her, working at the clasp on his pants, the muscles in his chest shifting, his abs rippling with the motion.

"Well, by all means, sing my praises. But it has to be said that you are one hell of a man."

He shoved his pants down and proved her point and then some, his erection thick and enticing and, right now, just for her. He folded his pants carefully on top of the rest of his clothes.

"Come here," she said.

"You think you're giving the orders?" he asked.

"If you want to play," she said, raising a brow, "you might want to follow them."

"What sort of game do you want to play?" he asked, his voice rough.

"One we're both going to like. I want to taste you." His eyes darkened, his expression getting tense.

"Come on, Deputy Sheriff," she said.

He walked over to the bed and wrapped his hand around her head, gripping her hair tight and leaning down, kissing her hard on the mouth before straightening, putting all of *himself* right at eye level.

She licked her lips and looked up at him, bracing her hands on his lean hips. She wanted this. Had wanted it since well before the first time they'd been together. They'd only had urgency then. No thought, no finesse and very little time for exploration.

Now she wanted to explore.

She leaned in, gripping his shaft in her palm and squeezing tight. He groaned, his head falling back, his hand returning to her hair, tugging slightly, the stinging sensation sending a shot of pleasure down between her thighs. Making her hotter. Wetter.

Then she leaned in, blazing a trail over his hard length with the tip of her tongue, her heart hammering fast as she explored him from tip to base and back again before taking him deep inside her mouth.

He was beautiful. He was incredible. And he made this a pleasure. A gift that was truly more blessed to give. Though based on the shivering of his thigh muscles he was very happy to receive.

She pleasured him with her hands, her lips, her tongue, reveling in this strong, solid man's loss of control as he cursed and shook beneath her touch.

She'd never felt more powerful.

She'd never felt more wanted.

Such a dangerous game, but she wanted to play as long as she possibly could. To hold her hand near the flame until it burned her.

She shifted and took him in deeper and he tugged her hair hard, pulling her head up. "Not like that," he said, his words a growl.

She looked at him, at the fierce, untamed light in his eyes. Eli Garrett was never anything less than civil. He'd once put her in handcuffs while she'd clawed and spit like a mad cat, and he'd never been less than a gentleman.

That was probably where some of the strange conflicting anger-desire had come from back then. Even when she was angry at him, she'd sensed somehow that he was the closest thing to a real-life superhero. Truth, justice, the American way and all that.

Yes, civility was second nature to him, and now it was stripped away. And he was reduced to nothing more than a man who desired a woman. Desired her. Restraint folded up on the floor with his uniform.

"What do you want?" she asked, moving away from him, leaning back on the bed, conscious of how her posture displayed her breasts, of how her relaxed thighs gave him a view of everything else.

"I need to be inside you," he said, moving to the dresser and getting the bag, tugging out a box of condoms. He opened it, took out one condom, then threw the box to the bed, where it landed next to her. "You can put those in your nightstand."

"Generous of you."

"They're only for me," he said.

And she knew then that she'd only teased him at all to hear

him say something like that. To hear him get proprietary and possessive and all the things she usually hated.

But being with Eli seemed to be an exploration of everything she'd previously labeled off-limits. Everything she'd always called a bad idea.

This was her chance to dip her toe into some fantasies she'd never given breath before. A man who would take charge. A man who would give as good as he got. A man who wouldn't shrug and say, "Yeah, whatever," if she called it off.

She put the box in the nightstand, not wanting to push him now. Someday she would. Just for fun. Just to see what would happen. But not now.

He tore open the packet and she watched, rapt, while he rolled the condom onto his thick length. She liked seeing that big, masculine hand wrapped around his cock. She'd love to watch him bring himself off sometime. And she'd never wanted to do that before, because what would be in it for her?

But with Eli…watching him was one of the best things she could think to do with her time.

He moved to the bed and she smiled, kissing his lips, then pushing against him with all of her weight so that he was on his back and she was straddling him, the slick entrance to her body touching his hard length.

"What are you doing?" he asked.

"Going for a ride," she said, smiling.

"Not just yet."

He angled his head up and took one nipple deep in his mouth, sucking hard. A sharp groan volunteered to be the soundtrack to her pleasure, and there was nothing she could do to stop it as his hand teased her other nipple, while he slid his other palm down over her ass, his fingertips delving into the elegant line there, sending a shock wave of sensation through her.

Then he gripped her butt hard, tugging her into position, lowering her down onto his arousal, every thick inch filling her slowly. Perfectly.

"I'm supposed to be in charge here," she said, when he was buried in her to the hilt.

"Sorry," he said, his voice rough. "Missed that memo."

"No, you didn't."

He slid his hand over her bottom again, squeezing her. "What are you going to do about it?"

"Ride you until you can't speak anymore. Until you don't have the energy to challenge me."

"We could be here all night," he said.

"Oh, I hope so."

He gripped her face, tugging her head down so he could kiss her hard, his other hand still firm on her bottom, keeping her pressed tightly against him as he flexed his hips upward, stealing her control, stealing her breath.

He was amazing. Perfect. Everything.

And never before had she assigned those adjectives to a man.

But they fit him, just like he fit her.

She pushed her hips forward, butting up against his, sensation rocketing through her. He released his hold on her chin, his head falling back, his hands moving to a more relaxed position on her hips as he let her take the lead.

She braced her hands on his shoulders, moving in time with his breathing. Slow and measured at first, then faster, harder, more intense. Her orgasm started to build, a low ball of pleasure and intensity in the pit of her stomach, pulsing down to her core, her internal muscles tightening around his hard length.

She squeezed his shoulders tight, her nails digging into his skin. She hoped he felt it. The pain and pleasure. She hoped she marked him, because he was damn well marking her. This didn't feel like a game now. Not the light power struggle it had been. The fun flirtation. This was something raw. Pleasure walking a knife's edge. One wrong slip and it would cut deep. Wound. Destroy. And scar forever.

She closed her eyes, her heartbeat pounding against the backs of them, blood roaring through her ears. "Oh… Eli…"

"Not yet," he said, his voice harsh, pulling her through the haze, pushing her climax back.

He removed his hand from her hip and put it between her legs, just near where their bodies were joined, his fingers tracing her clit, sharp, hot need assaulting her as he did.

"I want to give it to you," he said, his eyes intense on hers as he continued to stroke her. The combination of his touch along with the feeling of him inside her was almost too much to bear, but now she was fighting her orgasm.

Because she wanted to stay like this. On the edge. In this moment of beautiful torture.

He took his hand away and she gasped, then lifted his fingers, the tips touching the edge of her lips. Then she looked at him, leaned forward and sucked both deep into her mouth.

He swore, short and hard, never looking away. She ran her tongue along the edge of his forefinger and he pulled her down, hard, thrusting up inside of her as he did. That was enough. To push her from the edge into the abyss.

She shuddered, leaning forward, palms braced on the bedspread as she rode out the climax, waves rolling through her, leaving her breathless, shaking and on the verge of the kind of emotional breakdown she never allowed herself. Ever.

He let out a harsh breath, his grip on her tightening, his muscles shivering as he found his own release, his stomach muscles contracting and expanding beneath her.

She waited until it was over. Until he was relaxed. Then she rolled away from him, lying on her back, her arm over her face, her eyes shut tight behind it, trying to gain her balance. Trying to find her center or whatever. But she was firmly…off center, so that just wasn't going to happen.

He'd tromped all over her center. Left his big, standard-issue boot prints all over it.

She was wrecked.

He wrapped his arm around her and pulled her close and she moved her arm, blinking, shocked by the fact that he was touching her, that he wasn't halfway out the door. But no, he was leaning in, his head pressed to her breasts, his breath hot against her skin.

She lifted her hand and traced his jaw with the tip of her finger, his stubble rough. There was something undeniably male about it. Undeniably sexy.

What was it about him? Why did he make her feel so *much*?

She shook all that off, trying to catch her breath. Trying to pull herself out of the emotional well she'd fallen into. This wasn't like her. She didn't get moony and weird. And she didn't sleep with guys after sex. She was too busy getting dressed, saying goodbyes and getting back to her own space. Or pushing them back to theirs.

Well, she wasn't going to sleep with Eli. She was just going to rest for a second while she got her bearings, and then she would remind him that he needed to get back to his place stat.

He moved his hands over her curves until she could feel herself melting into the sheets like a candle pressed into a flame.

Man, she was pathetic.

And all she wanted to do was sleep. Or turn over and lick him. All over. Oh, yes, that was what she wanted to do. Lick every inch of Eli Garrett until he was shaking. Until he was hard again. Until…

There was a fearsome-sounding scratch and a sound that was closer to a caterwaul than a meow at the door.

She jumped, the sound breaking hard through her fantasies.

There was more scratching, this time on the carpet beneath the door, followed by more angry feline noises.

"Oh, you damn cat!" she growled, wiggling out of Eli's hold and sitting up. And she was almost grateful Toby had come to the rescue then, because it had saved her from revealing her fairly intense neediness.

She stood and looked down at Eli, who was staring at the ceiling, all naked and muscle-y and as hot as ever. Then she turned and went to the door, flinging it open. "What?"

Toby sauntered in, and his eyes seemed to go straight to Eli. "Don't judge," she said to Toby. "You don't have balls. You don't know what this kind of drive does to a person."

Eli laughed, a deep, male sound that was much more relaxed than he generally was. "Do you always talk to your cat?" He sat up and swung his legs over the side of the bed and she was sort of struck dumb by the whole display.

His body in motion, regardless of the motion, was a beautiful thing. And naked? It was mouth-dryingly, pantie-dampeningly beautiful.

"Yes, yes, Eli, I do talk to my cat. And please be advised," she said, crossing her arms beneath her bare breasts, "that I won't allow for anti-cat speech in this house."

"Anti-cat thoughts?"

"Forbidden. The thought police are here. Assimilate or be destroyed."

"I didn't understand any of that."

"It's a good thing you're nice to look at."

"Nice to touch, too, I hope," he said, standing and walking toward her.

Her heart stuttered. "Do you have to ask?"

"Doesn't hurt to be told."

"Touch. Taste. All of the above. I very much enjoy the many attractions your body has to offer."

"Possibly the strangest compliment I've ever received."

"Well, that gives me a new target to aim for. Something weirder than that."

"I look forward to it." He bent down and picked up his clothes, shaking them out, tugging his underwear and pants on.

Her heart sank. She was so much more disappointed by the fact that he was leaving than she should be. She'd just been thinking she needed to get rid of him. Reclamation of space and all that.

But now he was vacating her space. And that was different.

At least it felt different for some reason.

He tugged the tan shirt on over his head and collected the overshirt and tie, and put them into the bag the condoms had come from. Then he went for his boots. And she just stood there naked and watched, which was hugely stupid but she couldn't really bring herself to stop watching him. Or to move and get dressed. She didn't want her lacy underthings or her dress back anyway.

She wanted jammies. And she wanted to cry a little bit.

She felt like an alien being with way too many feelings had crawled into her ear and then chewed his way from her brain stem, down her neck and into her chest, where he'd made a comfy home and decided to force his emotions on her.

Yes, that was what she felt like. Foreign, and completely out of her depth. And she just wasn't used to feeling that way. She kept herself out of situations that made her feel this way for a reason.

"See you tomorrow," he said, all casual and like his skull hadn't been cracked by the thundering pleasure that had just rolled through them both.

"Uh…okay."

"I can't stay," he said, not looking at her.

"No," she said. "No, I know. I mean, I wasn't going to ask you to. I was going to ask you to leave, actually. But I didn't have to because of the cat, and then you got up, and now you're going so I didn't have to."

Sure, Sadie, ramble. That's convincing and doesn't sound at all weird.

"Okay," he said slowly.

"Don't say it like that. I'm fine. I don't sleep with guys. I like my space, just like you do. And we made rules. Rules on the street corner. In front of God and everyone."

"I'll see you tomorrow, Sadie."

Two days in a row. That was intense. It was, she realized in that moment, a violation of her usual relationship conduct. She'd never been in a relationship where she felt the need to have sex that often. It was healthy and good to have nights alone, and to have time to herself and…and…he was talking sex tomorrow. Probably the next day, too.

And she was going to say yes.

"Okay. Tomorrow. Do you work?" she asked.

He nodded. "Yeah. I'll be patrolling the highway mainly, but I always come to town for coffee and lunch."

"I was going to stop in on Alison again. So I'll be in town tomorrow, too."

"Maybe we can run into each other when I get coffee," he said.

"Elevenish, right?"

He nodded.

She shouldn't be making a coffee date with the guy. She shouldn't even have made an immediate follow-up sex date with him. And now there would be an additional meet-up. But she wasn't going to tell him no. She might not show up to coffee, though. She might not.

Toby started rubbing against her legs and she looked down at him. "What?" she asked, and got nothing but a blank cat stare in return.

"See you," Eli said.

"Yeah, bye."

He walked out of her bedroom without even kissing her goodbye, and she stood there, naked, until she heard the front door shut behind him. And she became acutely aware that she was standing naked in a room with a cat leaning against her legs, watching the blank space where Eli had been.

She shuffled to the bed and flopped onto her stomach, then shrieked when Toby followed, jumping onto the bed and walking across her back, the pads of his feet cold on her skin.

"Boundaries!" she shouted, mainly at Toby but also partly at herself.

If this Eli thing was going to work there would have to be boundaries. Because he'd left her feeling hollow and emotional.

She rolled to her side and curled her knees up to her chest, her heart thudding dully.

It was all because she'd been celibate for too long. She was out of practice. The sex had been easy. More than easy, it had been so much better than she'd ever remembered it being. But the surrounding stuff all seemed harder. Deeper. Weirder.

But she would work it out. They would work it out. Because this was way too good to give up.

But she was not meeting him for coffee tomorrow.

SHE COULD NOT BELIEVE she was meeting Eli for coffee. Sadie frowned deeply so that she would appear as angry with herself as she felt and tugged on her sweater sleeves, crossing her arms beneath her breasts as she stormed across the street and into the coffee shop.

Where he was not.

Well, eff him and his effing coffee break. Was he not coming? Was that the game? Make Sadie think you were coming to coffee and then not come to coffee the day after you banged her senseless and left her curled up alone in bed with a cat?

As if he could make her feel more pathetic.

No, she wasn't pathetic. And he wasn't allowed to make her feel pathetic because she forbade it. She withdrew permission. She was the keeper of her own life, blah blah blah.

She leaned against the counter, tapping her fingertips together while she looked over her shoulder at the closed door, then into the empty dining room.

There was a girl who had to be in high school working behind the counter, pulling espresso shots and chatting with another boy who really was no more than an infant. Or…sixteen, but whatever.

They were flirting. Ugh. Well, someday he would leave her standing in an empty coffee shop. So flirt away, little children.

Bah.

Sadie didn't know how Cassie, the owner of The Grind, could

stand to be around the heady teenage hormones all day. But there she was, smiling away at the register and seemingly un-annoyed by her employees.

It was because Cassie was in love herself, probably, as Sadie had learned during her frequent visits to get coffee. Because Cassie was so in love, she radiated joy and spent much of her time talking about her man, Jake. That love nonsense seemed to blind otherwise rational people to related stupidity.

The door behind her opened, the wind rushing in. She turned and the breath rushed out of her. Eli. He was here. He hadn't stood her up.

And it shouldn't matter.

Feeling a bond with him post-sex is okay. It's not like you've ever done it quite like this before.

Ah, yes, her running internal monologue had a point.

Before him she'd always been in an actual dating relationship with the men she slept with. And with that had come compan-ionship and coffee dates and nice talks. And it had all gone a long way in reinforcing her and her ego.

But this was different and so the fact that she didn't have a firm handle on it really was understandable.

There, pep talk managed. And now she would just enjoy her coffee.

"You came," she said.

"I'm on time."

Yes, dammit, he was. And she had been flailing around for no reason at all.

"Of course," she said. "Coffee?"

"That's what we're here for." He walked to the counter and Cassie smiled.

"Deputy Garrett, the usual?"

"Yep," he said. "And whatever Sadie would like."

Her eyebrows shot upward but she didn't say anything. He was buying her coffee in public. That seemed like a...thing.

Like a public declaration, even. Or maybe it was just coffee. Probably it was.

"I'll have just a coffee. Room for cream. Two raw sugars," she said.

Eli pulled out his wallet and paid with cash and she almost laughed. He, and everything about the town, was about eight years behind everything else. In fact, now that she looked, she didn't think the store was set up to take a debit or credit card. Good thing he'd treated, because she didn't have any cash.

"And how has your day been?" she asked.

"Good. Gave out some speeding tickets, so the answers of those I've encountered could be different."

"I would say," she said. "I've gotten a lot of speeding tickets."

"Have you?" he asked.

"What can I say? I'm a rebel." Too late she realized she was making jokes about not driving safe again. Bah. She should have gotten a biscotti to gnaw on so her stupid mouth would be occupied. Talking to Eli wasn't safe.

And why was that? Why was she such a mess with him? She was usually really good with men. All small talky and light and flirty like the barista babies behind the counter.

But not now. And not with him.

"Here you go," Cassie said, handing the cups to Eli. "Have a nice day, Deputy Garrett. You, too, Sadie." The other woman's expression was far too meaningful for Sadie's liking.

"Same to you, Cassie. Tell Jake hi." He turned and started to walk out of the shop, her coffee in his hand.

"Wait! I need my cream." He stopped and handed her the cup, which she took from him before turning to face the little bar, popping the white lid off and picking up the thermos to dump a healthy amount of half-and-half into her drink.

She put the lid back on, managing to avoid spilling and looking like a total dork, which, with her shaky sweaty hands, had been a distinct possibility. "Okay, now we can go."

He shook his head slightly and pushed the door open, holding it for her. It should not have made her stomach feel warm and fuzzy, but it did. She had a serious fuzziness issue where that man was concerned.

"So," she said, once the door closed behind them. "How did *you* sleep last night?"

He turned, his shoulder stiff, his cup paused midsip. "Fine," he said.

Fine. Well. Fine. She'd been fine. Totally fine. Not at all shivery or lonely or horny. "Oh, good. Me, too."

"The way you said it made it seem like maybe *you* didn't sleep well."

"That's a lot of…meaning you read into my very simple question."

"Your very simple question with what sounded like specific emphasis."

"Fine," she said. "It had emphasis. Specific emphasis. But you're lying."

He raised a brow and stopped walking, the wind ruffling his short dark hair. "Really?"

She wasn't going to stand there and wallow in indignation. She was going to take a chance. To take a chance on the fact that last night had been as amazing for him as it had been for her.

"Uh-huh. Lying. You didn't sleep well." She leaned in. "You slept terrible. Naked. Sweaty and tangled up in your blankets. Wishing I was there to touch you. Wishing it was me putting my hand around your cock instead of you."

She could see the tension work its way through his body, tightening his shoulders, tightening his jaw. The gamble had paid off.

"That's enough," he said.

"Oh, no, it's not nearly enough."

"I am on patrol."

She winked. "Yeah, you are."

"Euphemism?"

She lifted her shoulders. "Could be."

"For what?"

"Just messing with you."

"Don't you have somewhere to be?"

"Well, sort of," she said. "I was going to swing by the diner to talk to Alison about pie."

And also kind of to check in on Alison, since Sadie was feeling twitchy about the entire situation. Unless someone came into her office to talk touchy situations, she didn't normally seek them out. But Alison used to be a friend. And this was different.

Though she felt she could be talked out of involvement very easily since it sorely tested her comfort zone.

But then, just about everything she'd done for the past couple of months—signing a long-term lease, sleeping with a man who gave her feelings and dealing with spiderwebs in a house that had been long empty—had tested her comfort zone.

So why not continue the theme?

"Right. You were going to, but…?"

"What is your stance on ride-alongs?" she asked, looking at his patrol car parked down the street.

"It depends on who the person is."

"Me. Me is the person."

"Heavily against."

"Why?" she asked, knowing she sounded whiny, knowing she was using him to help her avoid the Alison thing.

"Because. I'm not going to let a known criminal sit in the front seat of my car."

"Ha-ha-ha," she said drily, "you are a clever, clever man. And fine. I'll go off and do my actual stuff instead of forcing you to spend any more of your precious time in the presence of my adorableness."

He let out a long breath. "Fine. Come on."

"I can go?"

"If you promise not to mess with things."

"I can't promise that, Eli."

"Why?" he asked, looking long-suffering now.

"Because if there are buttons, I may not be able to resist the urge to push them."

"I'll dump your ass on the roadside and leave you to hitch-hike back to town."

"No, you won't," she said, breezing past him. "You're too nice."

"I am not."

"Sure you are," she said, waiting by the passenger-side door of the car. "You're so nice you're letting me come on a ride-along."

He opened his door and unlocked hers from that side, then got in without waiting for her. She opened the door and climbed in. There was a laptop mounted to the dash, and in the center console were all the buttons, radios and things she generally wanted to mess with, but didn't, because the car wasn't moving yet, and at this point he probably would still kick her out.

"That is not evidence of any particular niceness," he said, starting the car and putting his drink in the cup holder.

"You don't like it that I think you're nice?"

"I don't want you to get the wrong idea," he said.

"You're just annoyed because I have the right idea."

He pulled the car away from the curb and onto the mostly va-cant streets. It wasn't quite lunchtime and it wasn't peak tourist season, so the main street of Copper Ridge was quiet.

"So how did you sleep?" he asked. "Real answer this time."

"Like a baby."

"So you woke up every few hours crying?"

"Meh," she said, taking a sip of her coffee.

"Or maybe just…wet and aching and wishing it was my hand between your legs instead of your own."

She snorted, coffee spurting over the hole in the cup lid and down her chin. She lowered the cup and wiped at her face.

"What?" he asked. "Was that not a nice question?"

She was wet and throbbing now. And not just from the slight dribble of hot coffee on her chin.

"No, it was not nice. Or polite. Or gentlemanly."

"I warned you. Good, sure. Nice, no. Also, not a gentleman."

"I feel like I'm learning a lesson about still waters running deep. And a little dirtier than expected, to be honest."

"Are you sad about that?"

She thought back to last night. To his much-better-than-average bedroom skills. "Uh, no. Can't say that I am."

"I thought you seemed to enjoy it."

"Are we allowed to talk about this on a ride-along? Shouldn't we be talking official sheriff's department business?"

"We could. Do you have questions?"

"Funniest call you've ever gotten?"

"Concerning piglets who scattered in the elementary school."

"Wow. That is…way to break small-town stereotypes, Copper Ridge."

He laughed. "A student had brought them in for show-and-tell. And I happened to be there for a Say No to Drugs assembly. So when all hell broke loose I took the call over the radio. So I was the official first responder to the pig debacle."

"Legend," she said.

"Pretty much."

"Did you always know you wanted to do this?"

"Sort of. I mean, at first I thought maybe I'd do state police. Or head up to Portland and work there. Do something in the city. But I always had my eye on law enforcement because I liked the idea that I could…make people follow the rules." His voice halted a little on the last part.

"You wanted everyone to behave?" she asked.

He cleared his throat. "When I was a teenager I thought… I thought maybe if I were a cop I could make my mom come back. Make my dad quit drinking. It was power to me. Authority that I didn't have. I mean, I got over the fantasy really quick, but the desire to be able to change things stayed with me."

She clutched her coffee to her chest, her eyes on the thinning buildings and the increasing trees, the waves in the distance. Something about his words had made her feel raw. Like the admittance of his own childhood fantasies, of change and control, had scratched against hers.

Interesting how those two desires had put them on such different paths. She'd thrown up her hands and let it all go. Walked away and never looked back because when she'd realized that nothing in her family would change, she'd realized that she couldn't stay. That she couldn't even tempt herself to try.

And yet Eli had stayed. And he'd made changes here that were concrete. He'd done what he'd always dreamed, in many ways. Even though he still hadn't saved his family. It made her feel like the flake she'd been accused of being more than once.

Especially next to this solid man who had dug his heels in and stayed, even when it was hard. Even when it seemed like there was no point.

But then, she had no brothers and sisters. She'd had no one to stay and fight for.

What about your friends? Alison?

But then they would have known. They would have known what had happened to her and the simple fact was, she hadn't been able to take the humiliation.

She'd lost her spleen and her family, so it had seemed a bit much to also lose her pride by letting everyone know that her dad had beaten the shit out of her and her mother had sided with him.

No, thank you. Internal bleeding was enough.

Man, what a massively horrible train of thought that was. She was done with it in three, two...

"I think it's amazing you did what you set out to do," she said.

"And what about you?" he asked.

Well, darn. She wasn't in the market to talk about her.

"What about me?"

"Did you always want to be a therapist?"

"No," she said. "I'm not even sure I wanted to be one when I was one. Which is why I typically did other things on the side. Painting, working part-time in coffeehouses, that kind of thing."

"Then why did you do it?"

"I was able to get financial aid for school with the help of a guidance counselor." That counselor and Jenny, her therapist, were the only two people she'd ever talked to about her dad. "And then from there it was recommended I see a therapist. And it was part of being a student at the school, so I went. Jenny listened to me. It made me feel good. I realized that having someone to listen was important."

She'd never spoken with honesty before. Not even to her high school friends. They'd spoken in veiled terms about how bad it was. Some had unexplained bruises. Some had drugs they'd stolen from their parents' dresser drawers. They were all escaping, supporting each other, but none of them had ever wanted to detail what their home life was like. If they spent their time away doing that, what was the point of leaving?

She cleared her throat. "Anyway, it was different with Jenny. She made me feel like my words had value. Like I mattered. Like my experiences mattered and like I'd solved something by talking about them. I wanted to do that. And I had to choose a course of study so… I ended up getting a master's in social work. I figured I would find a way to help people."

"And you chose crisis counseling."

"That's partly because I move so often. It makes more sense for me to work with people who are dealing with a sudden, isolated event, rather than people who need long-term care. I like to help people. But it's not an easy job. I mean, people in crisis are…well, they're in crisis. And hearing about those problems isn't always the most fun." She drummed her fingers on the door handle. "Though I imagine I'm preaching to the choir."

"Yeah," he said. "Law enforcement isn't all locking up bad guys and being the hero. It's a whole lot of sad reality."

"Reality is lame. It's basically my least favorite."

"Too bad there's so much of it around."

"Man, I feel like you *get* me," she said, laughing and letting her head fall back against the seat. She was happy being with him. And she didn't want to examine that too closely.

"We're going to park up here," he said.

She sat up straighter, her heart thundering. "And make out?"

"And wait for speeding cars to go by."

"Uh. Boo. I like mine better."

"This," he said, waving his hand between them, "has to stay in your bedroom."

"Then why did you meet me for coffee?"

"Why did you meet me?" he asked, pulling over and turning to look at her.

"Because it seems like I should know you a little. And that we should talk without fighting. If we're going to sleep together."

"I thought the same thing."

"Well, so then this makes sense," she said, biting her lip.

"Yep."

"And we're not making out in the patrol car."

"No," he said. "Please tell me you aren't a badge bunny."

"A badge bunny?" She turned to face him. "Is that a thing? Tell me that is not a thing."

"It's a thing."

"Wow. You sound so regretful about it. It's like a badge-related groupie, right?"

"Yes, yes, it is."

"And you don't sound thrilled."

He let out a sigh. "It's weird. I'm not a rock star or anything. Women who are hyper into the whole uniform thing... it's weird."

"Most guys wouldn't question it."

"Jack wouldn't. Jack doesn't," Eli said. "The other bunny we get is the buckle bunny. They like cowboys. They go after Jack and Connor."

"Connor obviously doesn't go back."

"No. He was never much of a player. And he's less of one now. Jack, on the other hand…"

"That's your friend. The one I met briefly the night I burst the pipes. And he was with you in the bar, too, right?"

"Yeah. That's him. He's more like a degenerate brother. But he's never taken anything half as seriously as Connor or I do. Which is probably why he's happier."

"If more sex is equal to more happiness, then sure. Though you should be bucking up by now."

"We've only had sex twice," he said.

"We probably could have doubled that if you would have stuck around for a while last night."

"Not the best time to have this conversation."

"Well, just don't go scuttling off into the cold tonight and you're likely to get a little more action."

He cleared his throat. "I didn't want to assume."

"Oh, I can go all night, buddy," she said. Which wasn't a theory she'd tested. Because usually one and done for the evening was fine with her. One orgasm basically put her under the table. She was a sexual lightweight in that way.

"Good to know," he said, sounding a little strained.

She liked that she could affect him this way. Because he was so solid. So stoic and serious and *good*. She liked that a little naughtiness got him hot under the uniform collar. And clip-on tie.

"So now we wait in semi-camouflage," she mused, looking into the woods on the passenger side of the car, "for an unsuspecting speeder to go by?"

"Basically," he said.

"I'm drunk with power," she said. "And I don't even have ticket-writing powers. How the hell do you do this without succumbing to the urge to abuse your authority?" She wiggled her eyebrows.

"Humorless response coming, beware."

"I expected nothing less," she said, rolling her eyes.

"If I abused my power, my entire reason for wanting it wouldn't be the same. I want to fix things, remember?"

"So you're not going to go breaking them further."

"Not exactly."

The radio buzzed and Eli held up his hand, putting his hand on the black button. A woman's voice filled the car, along with a decent amount of feedback. "Disturbance at Oak and Scotch-broom. Suspect appears to be unarmed but is threatening diner patrons."

"Copy. En route."

He put his hand back on the shifter and put the car in Drive, flipping a U-turn before turning on the lights and heading back toward town. "More than you bargained for?" he asked.

"Yes," she said, hanging on to the door handle. "The diner."

"Yep."

"We would have been meeting up even if I hadn't gone with you," she said, suddenly very glad she was on this end of the call, and not the other. Because men—violent men—did scare her. There was a place down in her soul that went cold when she saw violence in a man's eyes. That same part curled up in a ball and cried like a little girl getting kicked, over and over again, by her father.

A memory that was never buried as deep as she wished it were.

Suddenly she felt tense. Tense and transparent. He would know that she was afraid. That heading toward whatever was happening was like walking back into a fractured memory she never wanted to revisit.

Calm the hell down, Sadie. It's a man creating a disturbance and you're with a man who has a gun.

She took a deep breath and let her internal pep talk bolster her a little.

"Everything will be okay, right?" she asked, in spite of herself, looking over at him.

"I have a 100 percent success rate on making it through the day. I don't expect today to be any different."

She didn't argue with him about how everyone on earth had the same success rate he did, right up until they didn't. Because it was too nice to hear him say that. Too encouraging. And it made her warm all the way through. Banished that ice-cold fear. And for now she was going to let it, because it was so much better than being afraid.

They entered the town and her tension rose, metallic fear flooding her mouth, like her internal thermometer had broken, poisoning her with a wave of mercury. Or possibly she was being overdramatic. Hard to tell, what with the fact that she was panicking.

He pulled into the lot of the diner and she saw a group of men standing in the parking lot, and Alison on the fringes, wringing her hands.

"Stay in the car," Eli said.

"But Alison—"

"Stay. In. The. Car," he repeated, his words terse as he got out, his hand resting on the top of his gun.

ELI SURVEYED THE CROWD, assessing exactly what was happening. It was what he suspected—a late-morning drunken dispute, which was something that shouldn't happen, but did—and he doubted anyone's life was in danger today.

But then, those kinds of thoughts got people killed, and he well knew it, which meant his hand was staying on his gun. He didn't want to come in looking like a threat, but he wasn't going to be passive, either.

He knew these guys. Loggers mainly, and unsurprisingly, at the center, Alison's husband, Jared. He was the drunk one from the looks of things, and the one causing trouble.

"What's going on here?" he asked, walking over to the knot of men.

"Jared being an asshole," said Randy, a middle-aged man

with a long beard and a tobacco habit that had taken a toll on his teeth.

"Typical day, then," Mark, a fisherman, added.

"I'm just defending what's mine," Jared growled, his expression mutinous and unfocused.

"Jared..." Alison said.

"Shut up. Shut the fuck up," Jared spat in his wife's direction. "I wouldn't have to be down here if you weren't acting like a slut. So shut your whore mouth."

Eli let out a long slow breath. Because otherwise he would be tempted to get violent. And that wasn't what he was here for. But the temptation to move in and shut Jared's mouth with his fist was a lot stronger than he'd expected.

"There's no need to talk like that," he said, his tone hard.

"Free speech, Deputy," he said.

"We could take a vote on whether or not we like your kind of speech," Bud, not the one from the gas station, said. "I, for one, would cast my vote with my fist."

"That's enough," Eli said. "Is anyone hurt?"

He looked around the group. There was no blood or visible bruising. But there was no way he could say there was no harm done. Alison was ashen. Terrified. And it churned his gut.

"Is anyone wanting to press charges?" he asked.

"Nah," Mark said. "No one got hurt."

Dammit.

He could escort Jared home, but that was about it. State laws regarding public drunkenness were essentially nonexistent. A public health concern, not a misdemeanor. And given that no punches had been thrown, he was back at sending Jared back to his house, where Alison would be later. And that gave him no small amount of concern.

"Jared, I'm going to make sure you get home okay."

"No, thank you, Deputy," he spat.

"Oh, well, see, that's not your choice. Get in on your own, or get in in handcuffs." He turned back to his car and opened the passenger door. "Out, Sadie, I have to make a delivery, and I'd rather you weren't with me."

She looked at him with big worried eyes and it made something in his chest twist. She'd been afraid on the way to this call, and he'd dismissed it as normal, civilian fear, but right now he had a feeling it was something different.

Especially when she got out of the car without argument and headed to the side, not approaching the crowd.

"Stay here and eat pie, I'll be back for you," he said.

"I... I could walk to my car."

"Wait for me," he said. "You'll be fine."

He looked pointedly at Jared, who chose that moment to obey him. "Backseat," Eli said, then he walked over to Alison. "Call me," he said. "Call someone if he gives you any trouble, do you understand me?"

She shook her head. "He doesn't."

"You're lying to me," Eli said, his voice low and soft.

"I'm not." She met his gaze, her brown eyes defiant.

And he wanted to punch something again. A wall. Jared's face. Why did she protect him? Why did they always protect them?

"Well, even so..." He reached into his jacket and took out his card. "Call me."

He walked back to the patrol car, back to his drunken, asshole backseat tenant. He would drive Jared home. The guy would sober up for a while. And the cycle would go on and on.

He knew it would. It was what he saw in a town this size, over and over.

Times like this he could understand why Sadie didn't stay.

CHAPTER TWELVE

SADIE SAT IN THE BOOTH, a cup of coffee and a piece of pie in front of her. The fishermen were back in their corner booth, and Alison was pacing behind the counter.

She took a bite of the lemon meringue. "It really is good pie," she said, loud enough for Alison to hear.

Alison tried to smile. "Thank you."

"Could I get more coffee?" She didn't need more coffee, but she needed Alison to come to where she was sitting, and to stop hiding.

So yeah, this wasn't her favorite thing, but obviously she wasn't avoiding Alison, or the facts about Alison's life today. Fate had handily intervened even when she was trying to jump ship.

She felt a little like Jonah. Thrown overboard, swallowed by a giant fish and vomited into the diner, the very diner she'd been avoiding. Yes, it was an analogy of Biblical proportions, but appropriate, she felt.

Alison walked across the diner and looked into Sadie's full cup. "Just kidding. I lied. Sit down."

"I'm working," Alison said.

"Yeah, and I'm eating pie. Sit."

Alison did, her hands folded tightly in her lap, the carafe placed in front of her on the table.

"So, hi," Sadie said. "It's been a while. Or since last week. But you know."

"Yeah," Alison said.

"I feel… I feel like I should apologize."

Alison looked startled by that.

"For dropping off the earth after high school. For never calling. For never coming back. Because we were a team, in some ways. We laughed together, and I don't think we laughed very much when we were apart. You spent all those years sticking by me. All of you did. Josh Grayson was my first kiss. Hell, my first…everything. And I just left you all. Without looking back. I had to leave… I had to. But I should have thought of you."

"Sadie…we never knew what happened to you really. Your mom just said you'd run off. And…"

"You believed her because I used to say I would," Sadie finished. "And I did run off. It's true. I mean, I ran off to college. And a career and things. It's not like I was pole dancing, not that there's anything wrong with that. It's just…the long and the short of it is, I ran."

"We missed you," Alison said.

She looked so tired and sad. A sharp contrast to the Alison whom Sadie remembered. A girl in black clothes, with a fierce light of determination in her eyes.

A girl who'd looked ready to fight.

The fight was gone from her now. Drained out of her slowly over the years. Years when Sadie had been gone.

But if Sadie had stayed…the same thing might have happened to her. She and Alison had started out in the same place. A couple of teenage girls who'd never had innocence. Who'd always seen the hard, ugly side of life. Neither of them had illusions about love.

And still Alison had ended up with that man. Sadie was very aware that it could very well have been her sitting there, sad-eyed and defeated.

Sadie sucked in a sharp breath, feeling like something had cracked in her chest. "I... I didn't expect to be missed."

"I don't think any of us would have," Alison said.

"That's a problem," Sadie said. "It's not...healthy, that's for sure. So... Josh left?"

"Yeah, he's doing business somewhere. Washington first, and I haven't heard anything about him in a while."

"Hmm." Sadie allowed herself a brief, nice memory of him. He'd been hot, at least in her teenage estimation. But the memory of him didn't make her shiver or anything. Not like Eli.

"You stayed," she said, turning her focus back to Alison.

"I thought about leaving, but my mom's health wasn't good. Then right after she died, I met Jared."

"Ah, yes," Sadie said, the ache in her chest inverting, splintering and sinking down to her stomach. "I believe I met him today."

Alison cleared her throat and looked determinedly at the carafe. "I know it looks bad."

"It is bad," Sadie said. "Don't BS me. I'm a therapist by trade, when I'm not renovating bed-and-breakfasts. I see women who have come out of abusive relationships all the time. I see men who are afraid they might be abusers. And more than that, I lived with a man who solved problems with violence for my entire childhood. So, I repeat, do not BS me. I am the wrong person to try that on."

"He's not that bad."

"We can skip that part. We can skip the part where you tell me why you make him do it. And he's a good guy. And his past was hard. Because I've heard it. Just...five months ago maybe, I saw a woman who was in the hospital. Recovering from the wounds her husband had inflicted on her. I've seen where it ends, Alison. Unless you make the decision to leave."

Alison grabbed the napkin to her left and started twisting it, her hands shaking.

"I'm not talking to you as a therapist," Sadie said. "I'm talking to you as an old friend. As someone who knew you before him. You're not the only one. And you don't have to be embarrassed."

"I don't have to be embarrassed?" Alison asked. "I think I do, actually. Because…because I think you have to be pretty stupid to get pulled into something like this."

"That's not true," she said. "It's not. It doesn't matter how smart you are. It's not your brain making these decisions. It's your emotions. It's the things he's done to you. The things he's told you. The stuff he's twisted all up so slowly over the years you barely realized what was happening."

The other woman shook her head. "It's too late for me," she said. "I don't have anyone else. I don't have anything else. Just this job. And that man."

"Then get more," Sadie said, frustration burning through her. "Want more."

Alison stood up. "I don't remember how. Coffee and pie are on me. Thank you," she said. "Just…thank you."

Alison turned, slight shoulders hunched, and walked back to the counter, just as Eli walked through the door.

Sadie stood, not having any of the appetite to finish her pie, even if it was free pie, and walked toward him, shepherding him back out the door before he could ask why.

"Did you get him home?" she asked, barely meeting Eli's eyes when they were out in the parking lot.

"Yeah," Eli said. "Do you see what it's like?"

"He deserved to be hit. He deserved to have his head shoved into the pavement."

"Yeah, and I can't do that, Sadie. The minute I act like I can, I'm not a whole lot better than he is. Because I have authority and I have to be careful never to abuse that. But I might have let

Mark and the other guys off with a warning if they would have done it. Or if someone would have...said anything."

"Given you a reason to arrest him," she said.

"That's the problem with situations like this," Eli said, putting his hands on his lean hips and looking back toward the diner. "She's an adult. I can't drag her out of that house any more than I can put handcuffs on him for something I suspect but have never seen." He turned and hit the top of his patrol car with his open palm, a rough growl escaping his lips. "Sometimes the more power you have the less powerful you feel."

"She won't... I tried to talk to her," Sadie said. "But..."

"I know." He took a deep breath. "Listen, I'm on for a while longer. I'll take you to your car."

"Okay. We'll see each other tonight?"

He nodded slowly. "Yeah. I think I need to."

SHE WASN'T LESS NERVOUS than she'd been the night before. If anything, she was more nervous. Because now she knew for a fact the intensity between Eli and herself wasn't a fluke.

Because she was kind of going all in tonight, knowing full well what she was getting herself into. It was a dangerous game and she liked it. That surprised her more than anything.

But today had been beyond upsetting and she was looking forward to something just as strong to help take away some of the unsettled feelings that remained.

At least for a while.

You can't fix things for people when they don't want them fixed.

She'd reminded herself of that countless times over the years. Every time she hadn't called her mother. Checked in on her to see if her father was still ruling the house with a fist of iron. Because she'd tried to help. And her mother had chosen to stay. Her mother had chosen the man who'd put her daughter in the hospital. So Sadie had accepted that she couldn't change things for her mom and had set about changing them for herself.

She was going to have to let this go, too. Even though it sucked. It was a lot harder when you couldn't physically let it go by driving into another city and never looking back.

"Bah." She stalked into the kitchen and hauled herself up onto the counter, her knees planted firmly on the granite surface as she rummaged through one of the cabinets for a bottle of wine. Probably she would have to get a real fancy-ass wine rack for when guests were here. Luckily, she had a little time.

She took two glasses down, along with the wine, because in all honesty, Eli probably needed a drink, too.

She wondered if he would get more relaxed if he had a glass or two. If she could get him to smile. If his lips would taste like merlot and sin and the *smile* that was the rarest thing she could think of.

She licked her own lips in anticipation and carried the objects she now considered her fantasy aids into the living room.

She was still in the same clothes she'd been wearing earlier—sad for Eli, no matching bra and panties for him today. But after the incident at the diner, she'd thrown herself into B and B things, including looking at website proofs, which were fan-freaking-tastic, and choosing the stain for her deck, which was very nearly done because a whole team of burly men could handle decks like no one's business.

She hummed as she set the glasses on the old-fashioned captain's trunk she was using for a coffee table and sat on the couch, her feet tucked up under her.

And for one heart-crinkling moment she really wanted Eli to just come and sit next to her. To release his stress while she let go of hers. To share in a calm moment.

She blinked. No. That wasn't what this was about. It wasn't supposed to be about sharing emotions. It was supposed to be about sharing nakedness and orgasms.

The heavy knock on her front door saved her from her thoughts. "It's open!" she shouted.

She heard the door open, then close, the heavy shoes on the

wood floor, and finally Eli appeared in the living room entryway.

"Hiya," she said, surveying his tall, lean frame. He'd changed.
Dark jeans conforming to muscular thighs, a tight black T-shirt
giving hints of all the fun that lay beneath the fabric.

"Hi," he said.

"You can come in," she said, patting the empty spot beside
her.

"Right." He cast a long look at a sleeping Toby, who was in
the chair he'd claimed as his own, before walking across the
room and joining her on the couch, keeping a healthy distance
between them.

"Wine?" she asked.

"I don't really care for it."

Well, dammit. There went her merlot-flavored fantasy. She'd
just drink enough for both of them. "Well, I hope you don't mind
if I drink," she said, tugging the already-popped cork out. She
poured herself a generous amount, then picked the glass up and
clinked the edge against the empty one still sitting on the trunk.
"Cheers to me, then." She took a sip and sat back, feeling distinctly broody now. Because she'd gotten a picture in her head
that shouldn't have been there, and now she was disappointed
for him not conforming to said ill-advised picture.

"Are you mad at me now?" he asked.

She looked up over her glass and at him, at serious brown
eyes that made her stomach do tricks. "A little."

"Why?" he asked, the corners of his mouth turning up.

There was her smile. A small one, but she'd gotten it. "Because you were supposed to drink wine and be cozy with me."

"That doesn't sound like what we agreed on," he said, his
tone gentle. Why was he being so nice? She was trying to be
peeved.

"No, I know it doesn't. But I was sort of hoping for it. Because I am a fickle and difficult creature."

"Yeah, you are."

"You weren't supposed to agree so readily."

"Sadie," he said, his dark eyes burning hotter now. He reached out and gently touched her glass, lowering it. "You know what this is."

"I know," she said. "You don't need to worry about me."

"Then why are you angry?"

"Because," she said, setting her wineglass down on the trunk and standing, moving over to where Eli sat and standing in front of him, "I had a little fantasy."

"Did you?" he asked, his focus sharpening.

"Mmm-hmm." She put her knee on the couch, next to his thigh, and then the other one, straddling his lap. "It had to do with getting you to relax a little."

"This is not the way to relax me," he said, putting his hands on her hips. "You realize that, right?"

"I was going to relax you," she said. "Lick the wine flavor off your lips." She leaned in and traced the outline of his top lip with the tip of her tongue. "But I have to say you taste pretty good all on your own."

He took a deep breath, his hold on her tightening, his head falling back. "You're dangerous. Do you know that?"

"I've never been accused of being dangerous." She planted her hands on his chest and leaned forward, kissing him hard. "Flaky. Fun. Fluttery. Lots of *F* words, none too naughty. Never dangerous."

"Then the men you've been with before were blind."

"Or maybe we just didn't have this kind of chemistry. It's definitely a little bit more combustible than the norm."

"True," he said, sliding his hand upward, forking his fingers through her hair, his thumb teasing the edge of her lips. "You still mad at me?"

"Not really," she said.

"Good. Because I didn't come here to fight."

"I'm hoping you came for another one of those *F* words."

"Yep," he said, "and I stand by my original statement. You, Sadie Miller, are dangerous as hell."

"You're not exactly a kitten, Deputy Garrett." She arched her hips forward and gasped as she came into contact with his erection, rock-hard and obviously ready for her.

Really, she was becoming less and less disappointed in the loss of her brief domestic fantasy.

He tightened his hold on her hair and tugged her face down to his, kissing her deep and long. Leaving her gasping for breath. "Not exactly," he said.

Just like that the intensity was back. The need that hit hard like a punch to the stomach and made it hard to breathe. The desire that verged on pain, her core already so slick with need for him, so sensitized, one more calculated move against his cock would send her straight over the edge.

But the releases Eli offered weren't easy. Not a sweet relief like the opening of a flower, they were like going through a storm. And she was charging in willingly, knowing full well how it would be. Knowing that this time might be the time that saw her washed overboard, completely adrift.

It was worth the risk. Every time it was worth the risk.

She kissed him back, bit his lower lip as she tugged his T-shirt up over his head. Then she put her hands on his chest, all that hard, hot muscle for her to explore. Just for her.

"You, too," he growled.

And she hastened to obey, tugging her shirt up over her head, undoing the front clasp on her bra. She leaned forward, a short, sharp sound escaping her lips when her nipples came into contact with all that hot bare skin.

He moved his hands over her back, his touch firm and sure. He touched her with the kind of authority she had no issue with at all.

He tightened his hold on her and picked her up, switching their positions so that she was lying sideways on the couch, on her back, with him over her, his hands on the snap of his jeans.

Heat flooded her face, her body, anticipation coursing along her veins as she waited for him to get his pants off.

She undid her jeans and pushed them and her underwear down her legs. "Come on," she said, "you're going to kill me."

"I don't think you're going to die," he said, leaning in, tracing the outline of her nipple with his tongue.

"Yes," she said, the breath rushing from her lungs, "I really think I might."

"I didn't realize you were so fragile," he said, kissing her lightly on the breast before moving downward, pressing another kiss to her stomach.

"I am not fragile."

"You sure, baby? Another one of those *F* words."

"You turn into such a bad man when your dick is hard," she said, her voice shaky.

"And you like it," he said.

"Hell yes, I like it."

"Then we don't have a problem." He took hold of her leg, his fingertips sliding along her inner thigh, her muscles quivering in response.

"Except the little problem where I die because you won't give me what I want."

"What do you want?" he asked, pressing his lips along the path his fingers had just traced.

"Oh… I… You know."

"You want this," he said, leaning in, hot breath blowing across her clit.

"Oh…yes. Please."

"You're going to have to ask me by name."

"Please, Eli," she said. She wasn't above taking orders. Hell, at this point, she was so desperate for release she wasn't above begging. "Oh, please."

"Please what?"

"Please do…you know."

"You want me to lick you until you scream?"

Heat shot through her, her face burning hot. She was not a prude, but she'd never had a man talk to her like this before, either. And the fact that it was Eli, straight-arrow Eli Garrett who didn't get double entendres and who'd once put her in handcuffs in an un-fun way, made it feel all the more illicit and shocking.

"Eli…"

"Do you?" he asked.

"Yes," she said.

He curved his hands around both of her thighs and tugged her down hard, his lips meeting her tender flesh, his tongue stroking her clit. She threw one arm over the back of the couch, putting the other one on his shoulder as he teased her, as he pushed her, mercilessly, straight over the edge into a climax she wasn't even remotely prepared for.

Pleasure poured through her, threatening to drown her, and all she could do was cling to Eli. Cling to him and hope she survived the storm.

"Turn over," he said, his voice rough.

"What?"

"On your knees, babe," he said.

She sat up and obeyed, resting part of her body against the arm of the couch, her knees pressing into the cushions.

She could hear him getting his wallet out, tearing the condom packet. Her throat was dry, her body throbbing. She could not need to come again this bad less than a minute after that last orgasm. It wasn't even possible.

But it was happening.

She was shaking, she needed him so bad. And shaking with fear because this level of need was terrifying. But she couldn't stop him. Which only made it scarier. Because she didn't want to. She should be running. She should be in her Toyota and halfway to the Washington border. But she was here, bracing herself on the couch, waiting for Eli. Needing Eli.

She didn't have to wait long.

He pushed inside her, and she lowered her head, her forehead pressing against the arm of the couch, the brocade pattern biting into her skin.

He gripped her hips and established a steady rhythm, his hand drifting between her thighs, stroking her clit, making her shiver. She was powerless in this position, at his mercy. And she loved it.

It was so different from the last time they'd been together, when she'd ridden him until they both lost their minds. This was his game. He set the pace, and he had total control. She'd never liked this, submitting to a guy like this. But she liked it with him.

She more than liked it.

He pulled her back against him and increased the intensity, her whole body tightening up, pleasure twisting around her, reaching that unbearable point where she knew something had to give.

He pressed down hard between her thighs, the added pressure the final straw that snapped the tension, sending waves of release pounding through her.

He put both hands on her hips, his fingers digging into her skin as he rode her hard, chasing his own release. He found it on a harsh growl as he stiffened against her, then relaxed, his head resting against the curve of her back.

He moved away from her, her skin prickling in the cool air after he removed his warmth. "I'll be right back," he said.

She lay flat on her stomach, her knees and arms like wilted kale. She tried to catch her breath, to catch a thought, before he came back. So she didn't do something dumb and needy like crawl into his lap and bury her head in his chest.

But she kind of felt dumb and needy. Which was really aggravating.

She pushed herself into a sitting position so that she would look a little less pathetic upon his return.

He walked back into the room, beautifully naked, his eyes most definitely focused on her breasts. "Hi," he said.

"I'm having déjà vu. Except you were wearing clothes last time you walked in and said that."

"So were you."

"Yes, well. Not now."

"Obviously."

"Don't leave," she said, and she could have bitten her tongue off.

"I won't," he said. "Just yet."

"Yeah, that's what I meant. Just not…right now. We could… We could go into the bedroom, and…"

Toby chose that moment to jump onto the floor between them and look at them both, judgment gleaming in his golden cat eyes.

"Oh, you," she said, "go make yourself useful. Catch vermin!"

"You said he didn't catch vermin," Eli said, a smile curving his lips.

"He needs a hobby. One that is not staring at us after we have sex. Over it, cat. I'm over it."

Toby meowed and walked over to Eli, rubbing against his bare legs and winding his tail around his calf. Eli looked pointedly at Sadie, his eyebrows arched.

"He can smell your disdain. It's…well, it's like catnip to him. He feeds off hatred."

"Why do you like him again?"

"Don't take this the wrong way, but I think for reasons similar to the ones I like you for."

He looked back down at the cat, who was winding himself around his ankles, then back at her. "Excuse me?"

"We don't always get along. You can be grumpy. Standoffish. Judge-y as hell. But there is just something about you."

"You're really selling my personality."

"Hey, I know what I like. Grumpy, judgmental cats and… grumpy, judgmental men in uniform."

"I'm not judgmental," he said.

"Sure you're not."

"I'm not."

"You seem upset. Are you going to punish me to the fullest extent of the law?" She wiggled her brows and stood up, her legs wobbling beneath her.

"I might," he said, his voice getting deeper, huskier.

Oh, yes, this was better than the alternative. Desire was better than that other stuff. The intense aftershocks of sex with him. The deep need that it seemed to expose, without ever satisfying it.

"I think it's time for us to go to bed."

And for once, he didn't argue with her.

CHAPTER THIRTEEN

IT WAS EARLY. It was cold. And it was fence repairing time.

All things that, in many ways, Eli found enjoyable. All right, so fence repair wasn't the most fun thing he could think of to do on a Saturday, but it was quiet work. And he and Connor had thermoses of coffee set on the fence posts, their breath putting out bursts of condensation in the cold air, and there was something about it that was familiar. Constant.

Of course, his brain was back in bed with Sadie. He'd gone to her place every night that week. He hadn't slept there any of the nights, but last night he'd stayed until the sky had started to lighten, slept for an hour, and now, here he was out in the field.

It was jarring. To go from this sort of out-of-reality experience with Sadie, in her arms, in her bed. He had the kind of sex with her he'd barely even fantasized about. Because he hadn't thought it was real. Or even a possibility.

What they had was hot, on a level he hadn't known existed. He wasn't used to sex consuming him like this, but he sure as hell wasn't arguing.

But yeah, the transition from there, to sleep, to this had him a little off his game.

"Hand me the wire cutters," Connor said, his voice still rough from sleep.

"Sure," Eli said, reaching out and taking the cutters from the ground, and placing them in Connor's outstretched hand.

"You're quiet this morning," Connor said.

"And you appear to have woken up with an estrogen surge."

"What the hell?" Connor asked.

"Seriously, what was that? 'You're quiet this morning.'" Eli knew he was being a jackass, because he *was* tired, because he'd been up all night having sex. Which he felt kind of smug about, but also which he didn't want his brother to know about. "Only women say crap like that."

"You seem to have woken up on the asshole side of the bed this morning and stepped in a pile of sexist on your way out to the barn," Connor said.

"You make a similar trek every morning. Why should it bother you if I'm trying to speak your language?"

"Because you don't normally. You are normally very well-adjusted, which actually kind of pisses me off, because you're my younger brother and your shit is way more together than mine. In fact, no matter what's going on, it all seems together for you. Which makes me very suspicious of why you're acting this way." Connor straightened and tugged off his glove, leaning against the wooden fence post and picking up his thermos, unscrewing the cap. "Yeah, very suspicious." He poured himself a cup, black, no sugar. "Either you're still mad because you want to screw Sadie, or…oh, no," he said, a smile curving his lips. Eli groaned internally. "No, that's not it. You said you weren't going to sleep with her, so even if you were in full monk vow of celibacy mode you wouldn't be grumpy like this. You did sleep with her. And you're mad because you broke your little vow."

Wrong. He was not mad about sleeping with Sadie. He loved

every minute of it. He was, however, more than a little pissed that his brother had guessed so close to the truth.

"Shut up, Connor," he said, reaching for his own thermos and pouring himself a cup, with cream and sugar.

"You did. You slept with her."

"I *am* sleeping with her," he corrected, his tone hard. He hadn't intended to admit it, because it just wasn't Connor's damn business. It felt like something that was just for him and Sadie. And it felt wrong to talk about it. Like it violated what they had. Like it violated her.

"Well," Connor said, pushing his hat back on his forehead. "I did not expect that."

"What?"

"To be right, for you to admit it if I was, and for it to have happened more than once."

"I can't even count how many times it's happened." And there he was putting male ego over decency, which he rarely did, but he was only human.

Connor shook his head and took another sip of his coffee. "For a second, I was jealous of you," he said.

"Only for a second?" Eli asked.

"Yeah, then I remembered how much I don't want to screw with any of that stuff ever again."

Eli let out a long, slow breath. He didn't want to have this conversation with Connor, but they were apparently having it. "You're never going to sleep with anyone again?" he asked.

"Not planning on it." He took another sip of coffee.

"That's not… You're thirty-four years old, Connor. That's not healthy."

"You don't still believe in blue balls, do you?" Connor asked.

"No. Look, I just…" He swallowed. "I don't like to tell you how to deal with this. To deal with Jessie, and the loss of her, because who am I? I've never loved a woman, Connor. I don't plan on ever marrying one. It's just not in the cards for me. But *you* have to move on."

Connor shook his head, his jaw tight. "No, Eli, I don't. I don't have to move on. I don't have to do anything I don't want to do."

"So you're going to be like this forever?"

"Maybe. I run my ranch. I get the work done. What the hell else do I need to do?"

"Be okay?" Eli asked.

Connor laughed. "I'm not okay," he said. "Why should I bother acting like I am?"

Eli looked down. "It's been three years," he said, his tone soft.

"And it was supposed to be a lifetime." Connor put the lid back on his thermos. "When is the appropriate time to get over the loss of your whole life? Answer that question, Deputy."

"I can't," Eli said.

"Yeah, I didn't think so. You don't want to get married."

"Give me one reason why I should," Eli said, leaning forward on the fence, propping his boot up on the bottom slat. "Love comes here to die." It seemed a weird thing to say, with the pine trees in the distance tipped in gold from the sun, and the breeze coming in from the sea, mixing with the scent of earth, trees and livestock. With all these things that made the ranch look like heaven, it was hard to see it for what it was.

But the simple fact was, no one in his family had ever managed to hold on to love. The house, the Catalog House that he was starting to think of as Sadie's, was the original monument to that. A gift for a woman who wouldn't stay.

And on it had gone, all the way to Connor.

No, Eli had no plans to get married. He'd never seen a good reason to want love, and he'd seen plenty of reasons to avoid it.

"Yeah," Connor said. "Sometimes it feels that way. But my point is, you already don't want marriage. With the way things were for Dad after Mom left... I did, and look where it got me? Don't you think I have enough of a reason to not want to get married again?"

"Sure, but not to never have sex again."

"Let me worry about that."

"Yeah, I promise I'll never think about it again. Or ask you about it again."

"Sounds like a plan. So there. You had the talk with me. You said the thing that's been brewing. And I spoke my piece. You can call your brotherly duty done."

"Good," Eli said, but none of it felt good.

"The sex good?" Connor asked.

"What?"

"With Sadie. Is the sex good? Tell me that at least."

"Damn good."

Connor groaned. "Okay, well, we got that out of the way, too. World's most awkward conversation?"

"Very."

"Did you want to talk about religion or politics next?"

"I'll pass," Eli said.

"I guess we just fix the fence and mind our own business, then."

"I'm okay with that."

Eli went back to work, his eyes on the pale blue sky extending above lush green mountains. He tried not to replay the conversation he'd had with Connor. Tried not to remember the bleakness in his brother's eyes. It was everything he'd had been afraid was in him, said out loud. That Connor wasn't okay at all.

And he couldn't fix it. Dammit, he hated when he couldn't fix it.

It was like his dad all over again. Watching somebody drown in sorrow, doing their best to manage their addiction until just once…just once you weren't there to stop them. To care for them.

At least Connor wasn't drinking as much as their father used to. But Eli worried. His brother sure as hell drank more now than he had before Jessie's death.

The thought gave him heartburn. More than that, it made him want to get back into Sadie's bed. At least there things were good.

Mind-bendingly good.

There, he didn't think so much about the things he needed to fix that couldn't be fixed. He could just think about himself. Just a hell of a lot more length of fence to fix, some calf vaccinations to deal with, and he'd be back with her.

That would be his happy thought for the day. It was rare he had a happy thought, and no one was more surprised than he was that today Sadie Miller was his.

"THANK YOU FOR COMING, KATE," Sadie said, standing with one hand outstretched, an apron dangling from her fingertips.

Kate looked from side to side. "I see no half-naked deck builders."

"You're not here to ogle, sweetheart. You're here to bake."

Kate crossed her arms beneath her breasts, her dark eyebrows shooting upward. "I am?"

"Yep. We're going to make dinner rolls. I mean, if you want to. I thought we could hang out. And since I'm trying to learn how to get some recipes perfected I thought this might be fun." Sadie really hoped this might be Kate's idea of fun. Otherwise she feared hanging out with Kate might involve intensive horseback riding, or something equally outdoorsy. Not that Sadie was opposed. She just needed to work up to it.

Much to her relief, Kate brightened and took the apron. "Sounds great." She started putting the apron on. "Not that I really need to protect my clothes," she said, indicating her plain white T-shirt and high-waisted jeans.

"Better than wearing flour for the rest of the day."

Sadie started getting out mixing bowls and ingredients while Kate stood in the center of the kitchen, obviously slightly out of place in the environment.

"Let me guess," Sadie said. "You don't have much cooking experience."

"Not really. Eli's always done that. Throw meat on the grill, bring home pizza or whatever. Why are you cooking rolls for a bed-and-breakfast?"

"Well, I have to eat so I thought I would offer additional meals for an additional price a few days a week," Sadie said. "Anyway, I like cooking."

"Oh." Kate moved in closer and stood at the counter.

"You sound surprised."

"Eli never seemed to like it. But, I mean, he did it. And his food is edible. Unlike Connor's…"

"So Eli did all the cooking for you guys?" Sadie asked, unbearably curious and slightly guilty. She should not be interrogating Kate about her brother. Especially because Kate's brother was her secret lover. And if Kate knew that Sadie and Eli were sleeping together, she would probably make a horror face and run screaming from the room and never speak to Sadie again.

And thus, Sadie would lose one of the very few friends she had.

"Yeah. He did. Connor kept the money coming in, and, I mean, Lord knows that was important, but… Eli was the one who made sure I was ready for school. He learned to braid my hair," she said, her hand going to the hairstyle she still wore.

Sadie's stomach squeezed tight, her eyes stinging. Eli's strength was sexy, no question, but this? This was even sexier. It was a part of the strength, really. A part that most people wouldn't see.

Braiding a little girl's hair.

Sadie saw it, though. An older brother, a teenager, getting his little sister ready for school. Cooking meals. All things that would never be public, but that had shaped Kate into the woman she was.

Eli was all that had stood between Kate growing up to feel safe and secure…and growing up feeling like Sadie had. Like no one cared. Like she was better off cutting ties and leaving parents who didn't want her anyway.

It was Eli who'd protected Kate's trust. Her openness. Eli who'd given her her strength.

Sadie couldn't help but be envious. And she realized then

that the little fascination she'd had for him when she was a teenager hadn't been about a bad girl wanting a cop. It had been about wanting a man with that kind of strength to protect her. Care for her.

Well, he didn't. No one did. Deal with it.

"That's…really sweet," she said, grabbing a measuring cup and pushing it down into the flour bag, a white cloud rising up around them.

Kate smiled. "Well, don't let him hear you say that. But then, if he's still avoiding you, that shouldn't be a problem."

Sadie felt a twinge of guilt, which made a sucky companion to the envy. "Yeah," she said. "Not sure when I'll see him again. So, let's make rolls."

"POTATO SACK RACING."

"Lame," he said, lying back on the bed, keeping his focus on Sadie, who was sitting next to him, completely naked, her hair tumbling over her shoulders.

"It is not lame. Not for kids."

"Three-legged race is better."

"Unless you have to run with a boy who is stupid, doesn't listen and stinks."

"But what if you get to run with the cute girl that you have a crush on?" he asked, leaning in and kissing her shoulder.

"Did you have crushes?" she asked, cocking her head to the side.

"Sure, didn't everyone?"

"I don't know. Sometimes I kind of picture you like you sprang out of the ground wearing your uniform and a frown."

"Your flattery is almost embarrassing."

"Sorry if it didn't sound complimentary," she said. "I wouldn't be here if I didn't like you. Scratch that, I would be here, you wouldn't be. And I would be alone."

"Well, I wasn't born in uniform."

"And I wasn't born running," she said, smiling faintly.

"Life has a lot to answer for."

"Sure does."

She flopped backward, raising her arms above her head, and his eyes fell to the little silver scar on her side. A surgical scar. Sometimes he wanted to ask her about it, but ultimately, her medical history wasn't really his business. So he didn't ask.

"Where are you at on your big barbecue plans in terms of booths? We'll put three-legged races to the side for now," he said, shifting so that he was lying on his side.

"I've got pony rides. Cookie decorating. Face painting. John from the Farm and Garden is going to bring over one of those mini-sheds that looks like a playhouse for the kids. And the pie eating. There will be pie eating."

She ran her fingers through her hair and the temptation for him to do the same was too much. He wanted to pull her close. Play with the silky blond strands. Braid it. Which was not something he'd ever done for his lovers, but something about the idea appealed to him.

He wanted to take care of her.

He wrapped his hand around her hair, about to separate it into three separate sections, but she turned her head. He dropped his hands back down to his sides, the strange tightness in his chest dissipating a little.

He'd had a moment of temporary insanity. Sadie was good at doing that to him.

"What are you going to do about Alison?" he asked.

"Nothing," she said, chewing her lip. "What can I do? I can buy pie from her. Hope she feels proud of her accomplishment. Hope she wants something different for herself, but really, there is nothing else I can do."

He moved his hand over her breast, down over her stomach, his conscience tugging at him. "I told Connor," he said.

"About Alison?" she asked, frowning.

"About you and me."

She sat up, blinking. "Why?"

A damn good question. A weird impulse, as weird as the one he'd just had to braid her hair.

"I just… He sort of asked. Well, he tried guessing. He guessed I slept with you once, and I…corrected him. I'm not a very good liar."

She leaned forward, covering her mouth, a giggle trapped behind it. "Oh, my gosh. No, I bet you aren't." She looked down at him, her hair sliding over her shoulders, over her breasts, covering pale pink nipples. She was such a tempting picture. Naughtier because she was smiling, because she was covered. He wanted her again. So soon. And it didn't even shock him anymore. "You're way too straitlaced."

"I'm straitlaced?" he asked.

"Yeah, you kind of are."

He pushed her onto her back and she shrieked, then he kissed her neck, feeling her pulse quicken beneath his lips. "How many straitlaced men do you know who can make you come so hard?"

He never talked to his lovers like this. Ever. Hell, he never really talked in bed at all. But she brought it out in him. He didn't worry. He didn't overthink. He told her what he wanted. And she loved it. And that did things to him. Things he hadn't known he wanted to have done to him.

In truth, he'd never been this consumed by sex. Because his mind was always somewhere else. Because taking care of things was still in the forefront, but here, there wasn't room for anyone but her and him.

"None. But then, I think this might be colored by the fact that I haven't exactly tested the sexual prowess of every strait-laced man I've known."

"Fair point."

"I like that you don't lie," she said, her blue eyes on his. "I like that when I look at you, I feel like I really see *you*. Not just the man you want the world to see."

That made him feel a little guilty. Since, in so many ways, he felt like he did just put on a good front. The man who seemed unruffled on the surface, hiding the festering pool of worry beneath. The gut-churning terror all the responsibility he took on built in him.

"Sadie…"

"No. If you're going to tell me you have secrets, just don't. Because I want to think I know. What's the harm in thinking that for now? It's not like this is forever."

"No," he said. "It's not."

For some reason, her words and the agreement made his chest feel like it was full of lead.

"So let's have the fantasy. You be the straitlaced badass who rocks my world. I'll be comfortable here with you, trusting you. All well-adjusted and stuff." She smiled and kissed his chin, wrapped her legs around his calves.

"Are you saying you aren't well-adjusted?"

"Shh. In the fantasy, I am."

"Are you drunk?"

"A little," she said. "You won't share the wine with me so it's not my fault I have to drink more than normal."

"Connor won't tell anyone," he said. He was sure of that. Because the information Connor had given in exchange was too precious. Connor wouldn't want anyone to know how bad he was hurting. How hopeless he felt.

Eli didn't even really want to know, but he did. And now he had to try to fix it. Make it right.

He could never escape that feeling.

He pushed it aside, though, because Sadie was beneath him, and devoting everything to that sensation was, right now, more important.

"It's for the best. We don't need everyone all up in our business. And besides, Lydia is a good ally. She keeps the Chamber of Commerce on my side. And I have a feeling she might cut me if she knew I was sleeping with you."

"Really?"

"She's very smiley. I find that concerning."

"Maybe she's friendly."

"Maybe," Sadie said. "You are just something else."

"Am I?"

"How have you seen so much of the crap you have, and still… How are you so good, Eli Garrett?"

"I have to be," he said, the words slipping out before he had a chance to think them through.

"Why?" she asked, pushing his hair off his forehead.

"If I'm not…who will be?"

"Not enough people," she said.

"You are," he said.

"Me? You mean me, who runs away from everything and everyone?"

"I should never have said that to you. I'm sorry." Regret tightened his stomach.

She shook her head. "You weren't wrong. And the more I see you here, the more I realize how much harder it is to deal with people when you have to watch them not learn. And not listen."

"Regardless, it doesn't mean that you haven't helped people. You listen to people."

"For money," she said.

"So? Some people would pay to *not* listen to people's problems."

She laughed. "Okay, so maybe we're both okay?"

"Sure. We're both okay."

"Right now anyway." She arched against him, sending a shock of pleasure down his spine.

"Right now I'm more than okay."

SADIE CLOSED HER LAPTOP and looked out the window at the row of buildings across the street. The sky was bright blue, clear, the breeze pushing waves over the American flag that rose up from the two-story restaurant behind the main street, just off the harbor. She imagined it was creating matching waves on the sea beyond the buildings, too.

She'd managed to touch base with Alison, awkwardly, about the pies and confirmed that she would make some for the contest and sell some in the booth. But it didn't really make her feel much better about the situation as a whole.

She'd spent most of the day in the coffee shop approving the mock-up of the B and B's website. She'd ventured out briefly to go to the Wagon Wheel, a local home store, and special order curtains for the house, and some quilts. Then she'd stopped in at the glass studio Brooke, her old friend from school, now owned.

Brooke's life seemed to be going better than Alison's. So that was a comfort at least. She'd been enthusiastic about the barbecue and had asked for brochures for it, and for the B and B, to put in her shop. They'd parted with plans to do lunch, and unlike most times vague lunch plans were made, Sadie had a feeling they really would get together.

She tapped her fingers across the top of the computer. Eli was off today. Well, working on the ranch. Putting in his part-time cowboy hours. Which was his definition of a day off. And she'd decided to leave the ranch and come to town because it was better and less embarrassing than hanging out and hoping to catch glimpses of him walking around all sweaty and sexy and *everything* that a man should be.

Yeah, she needed an Eli hiatus. Which was why she'd asked Kate to drop her off at the coffee shop this morning, so she could do all her online work for the B and B from a remote location.

She wouldn't be taking a hiatus from him at night, of course, because heaven knew how many nights they had left together. And she would not be skipping a single night of orgasmic bliss. Apparently, pleasure was the price she'd willingly pay for her sanity. And she couldn't even be bothered to feel bad about it.

Nope. All she felt was pleasantly aroused, thank you very much.

But the issue with being around him all day was that he made things other than her lady parts fluttery. He made her chest area feel fluttery. And that was not something that needed to be indulged.

In fact, quite the opposite.

It was harder still after nights like last night. Where they'd sort of wound around each other, naked, and talked, and laughed. And he'd told Connor about them.

That had made her breath hitch. Made all the questions about what that could possibly mean float to the forefront of her brain. The logical part of her knew it meant that he was too honest to lie to Connor. But then there was this weird, previously dormant girlie part of her that seemed to want to pull it apart further to assign labels and meaning to every little piece and part of what he'd said.

This was not a good time to get all freaky about that stuff. Well, okay, there was never a time for that. She sighed and stood up, tucking her laptop into her purse, chucking her cup into the trash can and waving at Baby Barista Number One before stepping outside.

She shook her head and lifted her face toward the sun, taking a deep breath before crossing the street and cutting through two buildings on her way down to the wharf.

The water was a deep gray blue, pitching and rolling against the rocks on the jetty. She turned and looked down toward the bar, and saw a patrol car, parked across the narrow street in the do-it-yourself car wash.

"He's at the ranch," she said to herself. "And not on duty, so that isn't him." She was already walking toward the car, her internal commentary not doing anything at all to deter her.

She got closer, and her view shifted, and then she saw him. In blue jeans and a T-shirt, washing the patrol car in one of those do-it-yourself car wash spots. It was like some sort of fantasy delivered to her at a very unexpected time.

All that was left was for him to spray his chest with the water so the shirt stuck to his muscles...

"Hello, stranger," she said, feeling like a total dork the moment it left her mouth. "I mean, hi, Eli." She knew the amendment hadn't done much to cover up the original silliness, but oh well.

His eyebrows shot up. "What are you doing here?"

"I am a hallucination," she said. "Your subconscious mind brought me to you."

"Oh, really?" he asked.

"Yes. Don't you want to know what I mean?"

"I suppose you're going to tell me."

"I mean that you're extremely—" she wiggled her brows "—randy. And you're feeling sexually frustrated. Taking it out on your car, too. Wax on, wax off. Very suggestive."

"Is that all, hallucination Sadie?"

"No. I'm also here to warn you. You're in graaaave danger."

"Is that all?"

"And I would like a sandwich?"

"Do you evaporate soon?" he asked.

"Nope." She approached the car and him, her heartbeat speeding up a bit when she got near him. "Because I'm real. Surprise."

He smiled then, and her heart did a full turn in her chest. "In that case, what are you doing here?"

"I was in town working. Your sister dropped me off."

"Are you ready to head back?"

"Sure. Are there sandwiches?"

"There could be sandwiches," he said.

"What kind?"

"Get in the car."

There was something about that authoritative tone that made her shiver all the way down to her toes. He was magic like that.

"Only because you asked so nicely." She opened the door and got in, and he did the same. "So, you wash your car on your days off?"

"Yes," he said. "It's either that or leave for shift early, or leave late. And I keep the car parked at the house, so it gets a lot of stuff dropped onto it from the trees."

"You are so cute," she said.

"I'm not sure how I feel about that."

"What? I like that you don't lie and you take care of your things. My gosh, except for your lack of inhibition in bed, you're like a flashback to a black-and-white film."

"And what is my lack of inhibition like?"

"A flashback to spam emails often found in my inbox. But, like, in a good way."

He smiled, started the car engine and pulled forward through the car wash, and around, out toward the street. "I haven't really been to the beach since I've been back," she said, looking out at the ocean.

"Do you want to go?"

"Eh. Sand has its place. It also gets in *places*, so there's that."

He snorted. "What the hell sort of things do you do on the beach?"

"Not *that*. *That* we saved for the woods. It's more private. Actually most of my teenage shenanigans were saved for the woods. We conducted very few on the beaches."

"Likely why you got away with them. Especially back when I worked nights, I did a lot of drive-by spotlighting on the beaches."

"Oh, man, that would have been awkward."

They needed to change the conversation topic since she was starting to get a bit hot around the shirt collar talking sex with him in an enclosed space.

Something about the car turned her on. And granted, she'd been existing in a perpetual state of arousal since Eli had first kissed her, but this was different. It had an edge to it. Maybe it was the fact that, while she was sure it wasn't this exact car, he'd put her in the backseat of one very similar to it ten years ago, her hands in cuffs.

And maybe it had something to do with the fact that the

memory had morphed into something sexy since she'd begun sleeping with him.

Strange, since before it had been such a horrible one. Not because of what he'd done, but because of what had happened after.

Something about the car fantasy seemed like a reclamation of that night. And maybe that was assigning too high of a purpose to her sexual fantasies, but she kind of liked it.

"So you've never had sex in your car?" So much for changing the subject.

He whipped his head to the side to look at her. "What? That's…random."

"Not really. We were talking about my sex life…in the woods, not on the beach, thanks. And I was wondering about you."

"No. That's edging into… Like I was saying, I was with a woman once who was a badge bunny. Which was fine in some ways, but in others got really weird. And…no, I haven't."

"So it only seems *weird* to you?" she asked, biting her lip, feeling disappointed. "Not even a little hot?"

"I feel like you're leading me somewhere."

"I want you to do it with me in the back of your car."

He applied the brakes, hard, sending her jerking forward, the belt catching her. "Ow. Glad to know I succeeded in shocking."

"I didn't expect that."

"I guess not." She looked over at him, his jaw clenched tight, his knuckles white on the steering wheel. "What are you doing?"

"Thinking of all the places I could pull over and not get caught. I know where I have caught people having sex in cars before, so I'm trying to be original."

"Are you serious?" she asked, eyes wide.

He took his hand off the wheel and curved it around her arm, drawing it over to his lap, to his erection, hard and thick beneath his jeans.

She moved her palm over him. "Serious indeed."

That he was doing this for her, that he wanted to do it when it had put him off before, was a thrill she hadn't realized it would be.

"You have that effect on me."

He turned away from town, onto a service road that led out into the forest. It wasn't the preferred location she and her friends had used, but it was similar, she imagined. A pocket deep enough in the woods that people rarely bothered to drive in, especially when it wasn't hunting season.

Her stomach tightened and she squeezed his cock through his jeans.

"It'll be over before it starts if you keep doing that," he said, his teeth gritted.

"Well, we can't have that. I want my reward."

"Your reward?"

"I was arrested by you, and put in the back of a car. And it was one of the least fun backseat experiences I've ever had." They were driving over dirt and pine needles now, the pavement ending abruptly as the trees thickened. "Scratch that, it was the worst backseat experience I've ever had. Given all that, don't you think you owe me a better one?"

"I damn well think I do," he said, pulling into an alcove of trees just off the road. "Get in the backseat."

She unbuckled slowly, keeping her eyes on him as she did, before opening the door and getting out of the car. It was so quiet the silence seemed to close in around her, around them. It was a strange, intimate openness. Somehow much more public than being in a bedroom, but also much more secluded.

She closed her door, then opened the back door, climbing inside before closing herself in.

He got out of the car and she watched him through the windows as he moved to the back and opened the door, his hands on his belt, sliding it through the loops before joining her inside, closing the door.

"This is way more like it," she said, leaning back, resting her head on the window.

"Yeah?" He moved over her, leaning in and kissing her deep.

"Mmm. Yeah. Much better than being back here all by myself."

"I'm surprised you remember it," he said, and this time, there was no judgment in his voice. No disdain.

"I was pretty drunk, right?"

"Yeah, you and everyone else. They kind of scattered and left you to it." He brushed his knuckles over her cheeks. "I never thought that was very fair."

"I survived," she said. "The charges didn't stick anyway. My rap sheet remains somewhat mythical."

"Well, you left town anyway. Probably would have ended up getting charged with failure to appear."

"I needed to leave," she said, her heart tightening.

His dark eyes turned serious. "I'm sure you did."

She looked over to the side and saw a glint of silver in the center console of the car. She knew what they were, remembered what it had been like to wear them in the back of the patrol car. Feeling trapped. At his mercy. How different that thought was now. How different it was with Eli, the man as she knew him now.

"Are those handcuffs?" she asked, reaching out and snagging them. "Well, indeed. You just leave these lying around?"

He took them out of her hand. "Not usually."

"You put these on me that night."

Emotion passed over his face. Something like regret wrapped in horror. "I had to."

She smiled. "I know. But in the interest of re-creating things…"

ELI LOOKED DOWN AT SADIE, his heart thudding dully in his throat, making him feel like he might choke. He was so turned on he couldn't see straight, and somewhere, in the middle of just trying to remember to breathe, he was trying to parse exactly why when his ex had done this, it had turned him off.

And why now, with Sadie, it didn't just seem sexy, it seemed impossible to resist. And heavy with some kind of meaning he was having trouble guessing.

That again had to do with body parts shifting. Heart to throat, blood to cock. Things like that.

And then the handcuffs.

"You really want me to handcuff you?" he asked.

She bit her lips, the action so unconsciously sexy it sent a jolt through his body and down to his dick. "I really do."

"Why?"

"Do I have to know why something turns me on?" she asked. "If so, I like the idea of putting myself here, of my own free will. Letting you keep me, because I want you to. Because that first time I didn't have a choice...well, I didn't have a choice once I'd made the several bad ones I made that got me arrested in the first place."

"That's a little twisted," he said, even as his gut tightened.

"And what's your point? Isn't it a little twisted that I came back to town and fell into your arms?" She traced his jawline with her forefinger, a wicked smile on her face. "To tell you the truth, I think you like twisted a little bit."

He wrapped his arm around her waist and tugged her down so that she was lying flat on the seat, then he gripped her hands, deftly putting the cuffs on. In many ways, he was more confident in his ability to handcuff a woman than he was in seducing her. He'd just never wanted to combine the two.

"Maybe I do," he said, his words rough.

She saw things in him. The dark things. The secret things. And he couldn't deny, something in him liked it. Because it meant he didn't have to hide. Didn't have to try so hard to be upstanding.

Very few people would call what he was doing now upstanding, and he knew that. But they didn't matter. Nothing mattered but her.

"Now what?" he asked.

"I think you're the one in charge," she said, blue eyes wide.

"I guess I am." He traced her lower lip with the edge of his thumb, his eyes intent on hers, watching to make sure she wasn't nervous or afraid. "You okay with that?"

Her mouth curved upward beneath his thumb. "It's kinda what I asked for, right?"

"I promise to make it worth it."

He lowered his hand to her stomach, pushing her shirt upward, watching the muscles contract as she took a short, sharp breath. He pushed it up higher, his fingers brushing the rounded underside of her breast before sliding up farther, the fabric of her T-shirt folding over his hand as he moved his thumb across her tightened nipple, barely covered by her whisper-thin bra.

Her head fell back, her hands lifted upward, bound by the cuffs.

"Good?" he asked.

"Mmm."

"I'll take that as a yes."

He moved his hands to her jeans, unsnapped them, cursing the stiff denim as he hauled it down her thighs and pushed it, and her shoes and socks, off her legs.

"This was just an excuse to get me to do all the work, wasn't it?" he asked.

"Ah, darn," she said. "You're onto me."

He looked at her, her top pushed up, barely covering her breasts, bright blue panties low on her hips, standing out against her pale skin. "I'm finding it hard to be too upset about it."

He slipped his finger beneath the waistband of her panties, his breath hissing through his teeth as he felt the soft hair beneath the silken fabric. As he moved lower and felt how wet she was for him. How much she liked this game.

Well, he liked it, too. It was everything he never thought he'd do, things he'd never thought he'd want, and now he was all in, shaking with need. Unable to turn back.

He didn't even want to.

He leaned in and pressed a kiss to her stomach, her skin soft beneath his lips. He breathed in deep, taking in the scent of her arousal, the scent of *her*.

He lifted his head and looked at her, at her flushed cheeks, her blond hair tumbling over her shoulders. This was not his life. This was not the kind of thing that happened to him. Not the kind of beauty he was allowed to indulge in.

He almost couldn't breathe. Everything in him was bound up, suspended in the moment.

He reached into his pocket and took out a condom, shrugging his pants and underwear down his legs while holding tight to the plastic condom packet. "I did this out of order." He tugged his T-shirt up over his head, fighting with the tight space of the car.

She giggled. "I'm suddenly remembering why, since becoming an adult with my own bed, I haven't revisited my backseat days."

"I never had to use one."

"Oh, am I your first?" she asked.

"You are. My first for quite a few things in this particular instance. And now, my first woman in handcuffs in more than one way."

He tore open the condom and rolled it over his cock, his chest muscles seizing up as his fist squeezed his aching flesh tight.

She arched her hips upward and he positioned himself, pressing his arousal against her cloth-covered sex, heat shooting up through his teeth when he made contact with her. He rocked against her and she gasped, arching upward, pressing her breasts to his chest, the metal handcuffs clanking against the window.

"Oh...please," she said.

He didn't need any encouragement, not when he felt like he needed to be inside her five minutes ago. But he loved to hear her beg. Loved that she was at his mercy.

Who the hell was he?

Right now, he didn't know, and he didn't care.

All he knew was that watching her, seeing how much she

wanted him, making her wait, was the best damn feeling he'd ever had. This was for him. It wouldn't fix anyone, it wouldn't save a damn thing. But it would feel good. And he wanted it.

Wanted her.

"Take my panties off," she said, her words coming out short, harsh.

"Not yet," he said, rocking against her, watching the color in her cheeks deepen.

"You bastard," she said, and wrapped her legs around his hips, tugging him down harder.

"I think you called me that last time I had you in handcuffs."

"It was true then, it's true now." She shifted. "And you didn't make me come either time."

"We still have time." He slipped his hand around beneath her and cupped her ass, tugging her hard against him.

She whimpered, her breath hot on his neck. "Please… I need you."

He shifted his hand and tugged her panties to the side, positioning himself at her entrance and sliding in slowly. He cursed, short and sharp. She was so slick and tight, he thought he might go over the edge the moment he was buried inside her to the hilt.

"Eli," she whispered, his name broken on her breath, the splinters lodging deep inside him, burning his soul. Branding him.

"I've got you, baby." Her eyes clashed with his, wide and… shocked? Almost afraid? It made his stomach clench tight. "Hey, hey, I've got you."

She nodded wordlessly, her eyes never leaving his. He leaned in and kissed her lips, long and slow, withdrawing from her body, just an inch, before pushing back inside.

Then he was lost completely, chasing the liquid heat that was raging through him, building, bringing him closer to the edge. His blood roaring through his ears, canceling out everything, his vision going dark, nothing remaining but the hot, hard bite of pleasure, twisting and turning in his gut, ready to savage him, ready to squeeze everything inside of him into dust, the pressure building, threatening destruction if he didn't find release soon.

"Come for me, Sadie," he said, the words hard-won, almost impossible to push through his tightened throat. "Baby, I'm on the edge. Come for me."

She arched against him, flexing her hips, the motion twisting everything in him even tighter. He tightened his hold on her ass, his other hand braced flat on the window behind her head as he circled his hips slowly, grinding against her clit.

Finally, he felt her give, heard the hoarse cry escape her lips, felt her internal muscles squeezing him tight. And he let himself go.

His release roared through him like a wildfire, scorching everything that had been contorted inside him, hollowing him out completely and leaving him devastated in its wake.

He tried to catch his breath, his muscles shaking, sweat rolling between his shoulder blades. He felt like he'd just run five miles in the desert. And found an oasis at the end of the race.

Sadie.

He let out a harsh breath and moved away from her. "Well," he said, leaning back against the seat, dimly aware that sitting bare-assed in his patrol car was probably not the most professional thing, but he didn't think he could move much farther right at the moment. "I didn't think the condom thing through," he said, looking down, feeling vaguely embarrassed that he hadn't quickly dealt with it out of her sight, like he would normally do.

"Oh, dear," she said, wiggling slightly then giving him a hard stare. "I need releasing."

"Oh, sorry," he said, leaning forward and pulling the key out of the cup holder, undoing the handcuffs as quickly as possible.

She smiled, almost shyly, which was unusual, if not unheard of, for Sadie. She rubbed her wrists, looking around. "Yeah, I think you have to bury it."

He let out a long breath. "This is more complicated than I thought."

"Well, you can't litter. That's a crime and you're, like...running for sheriff. Can you imagine the scandal?"

"You're right. We can't have that," he said, opening the passenger door, one bare foot hitting the pine-needle-covered ground. "This is the most awkward thing I've ever experienced."

He heard a giggle behind him and turned and gave her a hard look.

"The view is good anyway," she said.

He rolled his eyes and shut the door, hurrying, naked and in broad daylight, into the trees, where he dug a small hole in the soft dirt and disposed of the condom. Then walked as quickly as he could back to the car, taking light steps, trying to avoid majorly sharp rocks and any particularly crunchy sticks.

When he returned to the car, Sadie was sitting there with the door open, her legs sticking out, jeans back on and T-shirt tugged back down. And she was smiling. Far too broadly.

"You look all back to normal," he said.

She stood, her legs wobbling. "Looks can be deceiving. Are you ready to head back?"

"Well, I'd like to get dressed."

She swallowed visibly and nodded slowly, moving to the side so that he could reach in and grab his clothes. He shrugged his underwear on, making sure none of the pine needles that were sticking to his feet flaked off inside the underwear, then grabbed his jeans, tugging them on as quickly as possible.

And now he felt at least marginally less ridiculous. He turned back to Sadie, who wasn't smiling anymore. She had her arms folded beneath her breasts, a blank stare on her face, her lower lips trembling.

He flashed back to that moment she'd looked at him. That calm before the storm when she'd looked almost terrified in his arms.

"Sadie? Did I… Did I hurt you?" he asked, regret slamming into him, making his face feel numb and his stomach sick.

"No," she said, shaking her head, "I'm fine." A tear trailed down her cheek, leaving a streak of glitter on her skin.

"You are not fine," he said. "What did I do?"

"Nothing," she bit out. "It's just… I don't know, it was more intense than I anticipated, is all."

"I should never have agreed to this. To the handcuffs and…"

"No, it's not that. Well, it is that. It's just… I can't stop thinking about what happened that night."

"I'm sure it's scary to get arrested," he said, feeling like he was treading on thin ice, unsure of what to say next. "I'm sure…"

"Not the arrest," she said. "It's what… Eli, that night after I left the police station…my father picked me up." She leaned against the patrol car and picked up a twig that had fallen onto the trunk. She gripped it, pushed on it with her thumb and snapped it in half, the sound echoing in the dense silence around them. "And when we got home…he beat me so badly I ended up in the hospital."

CHAPTER FOURTEEN

OH, DAMMIT, SHE WAS CRYING. And not just a few tears, but the honest-to-God beginnings of a flash flood. She could feel the dams eroding, so much emotion building, pressing against the already-compromised structure, and she knew the minute it gave way, she was going to cry until she was dry inside.

Because it had been building for years. And now it was all falling apart in front of the man she...the man she'd spent a long time blaming in so many ways. The man who'd just taken her to heaven and back in his car, with what could very well be the same handcuffs on her wrists.

It was fitting he was the one to witness this. When he hadn't witnessed it then.

Why didn't you protect me, Eli? You protect everyone. Why couldn't you see I needed it?

But she didn't say that out loud. Instead, she continued on, ignoring the tears that slid down her cheeks.

"He was angry at me. For the arrest. And...oh, he said I'd been daring him for a long time. And he wasn't wrong about that," she said, swallowing hard, imagining how her father had looked that night. His face red, the vein in his forehead standing out as he'd screamed at her. As he'd landed his first blow, knocking her to the ground. And after that she hadn't seen him at all. She'd just wound herself into a ball while it continued. Unable to defend herself. Unable to move. While she heard nothing. Nothing but the sound of his knees, boots and fists hitting her body.

When she'd imagined him doing this, she'd heard her mother screaming for him to stop.

But in reality, she hadn't. In reality, her mother had been silent.

"Anyway," she said. "It was the last straw. I'd finally set him on me. After years of watching him go after my mother I finally managed to turn it onto myself. She didn't call 911. So you would never have heard it over dispatch. She drove me to the hospital in Tolowa. We were far enough out that it was just as close as the one on the other end of Copper Ridge."

"Sadie," he said, his voice rough. "I had no idea…"

"I know," she said. "But please let me finish. I had to go into surgery. I know you've seen the little scar." So funny that it was so small, when the scars beneath were so massive. "My spleen had ruptured."

"Shit," he said, the word harsh in the silence of the forest, so much heavier with emotion than her own blank retelling.

"My mother told them I had gotten into a fight. She didn't tell them my father had done it. When I was alone with the nurse she said that I could press charges. But that it was going to be difficult because my mother was adamant I'd gotten into a fight with a group of boys," she snorted. "She said if I were a minor I could be removed while investigations were done, but I was eighteen and that meant there was nothing they could do. So she asked me what I wanted. My father had come to pick my mother up. My car was in the parking lot. My mother had left the keys. And that was when I realized that people don't change. So I figured… I'd just change everything around me."

He covered his mouth with his hand and took a step back, his complexion waxen. "Sadie, I don't—" He dropped his hands to his sides. "That happened because I arrested you?"

"Don't," she said. "Don't do that. I've done that. I… I do it still sometimes. It was my choice that got me arrested. It was his choice to beat me. It was…"

Suddenly she was pulled tight against his chest, all of the resistance pulled from her by his tight embrace, all of the emotion wringing out of her, tears falling down her cheeks.

He moved his hand over her back, warm and comforting. And way too much.

She buried her face in his chest, the tears hot now, angry. "Why didn't you protect me?" she asked, the words slipping out before she could process them. Before she could analyze just how unfair they were. He didn't know. He couldn't have known. But it was the question that had screamed inside of her for ten years, even when the pain was buried so far beneath years of rocks and rubble and dirt she'd thrown on top of it in an effort to keep it quiet. In an effort to blot it out.

He tightened his hold on her and she curled her hands into fists, pressed against his bare chest as she let him hold her. Her shoulders jerked upward on the sob that filled her throat, forcing her to suck a sharp breath of air.

"You said it's your job to protect everyone," she said, the words muffled by his chest. "Everyone in your town. But you didn't protect me."

He gripped her shoulders tight, tugging her backward and looking down at her face, his dark eyes sincere, intense. She wanted to look away from him. Hide her weakness, her emotion. Every insecurity and stupid thought.

"Never mind, it's not your fault…" she began again.

"Sadie, listen to me," he said. "I would never have given you to him. Ever. I would never have let you go home. If I'd had any idea..." He shook his head. "I should have seen it."

"Why would you?" she asked, stepping back, feeling so embarrassed she wanted to crawl under the patrol car and curl up into a ball.

"It's my job. And...sometimes I think I don't look long enough or hard enough. Because...well, like with Alison. My hands are tied because she won't tell. She won't ask for help. She won't leave. I hate knowing that. That, no matter what, I can't help. But I could have helped you. If I had asked...you would have told me, wouldn't you?"

She studied his handsome face, the deep grooves around his mouth that spoke of years of frowns. The lines between his brows that told the story of just how many nights he'd sat up worrying. "I was angry, drunk and belligerent. There was no reason for you to offer me anything. I deserved to be arrested and I—"

"You said something to me when you first came to town," he said, interrupting her.

"What?" she asked, feeling gritty and watery at the same time, and not really enjoying either sensation.

"You said that...that there were people like me who just put people away, and people like you who listen, and try to change things. You're right. I wouldn't have listened, not then. I didn't listen. I figured I was doing the right thing. The legal thing was all the protection that was needed, but it wasn't."

"Eli, don't. Don't take it on yourself. You wouldn't have listened, but I wouldn't have told you. I wanted him to do it. For years... For years and years I watched him hit her. And then I finally decided I was sick of walking on eggshells. That I was going to go ahead and dare him to do the same to me. Because in my head I figured I could take it. Because I figured she would stop it. Well, it turns out I'm not as tough as I thought. And it turns out she didn't care as much as I thought, either."

"Sadie, you said—"

"I shouldn't have said it. But I needed to say it," she said. "I don't… I've thought it before. I… Look, I really hate talking about this but I needed to tell you because, well…hello, post-sex emotional breakdown, and you did need to know why. I've… I was hammered that night, okay? But when you grabbed me and put me in the car, all I could think was you were really strong. The kind of guy who could put a jackass like my dad in his place. The kind of guy who would. You were good, Eli, and I knew it then. I know it now."

"I'm sorry I didn't stop him."

"I'm sorry I ever blamed you."

"Don't apologize to me," he said. "Not for that." He looked grim, and she knew she'd pushed the worst button she could have ever pushed.

Other men might have shouted and said there was nothing they could have done, and they would have had a right. She'd given Eli a new sin that didn't belong to him, to add to the long list of other people's transgressions he seemed to be trying to atone for.

He released his hold on her and turned back toward the car and she just stared at his broad back, his strong shoulders.

All the better to carry the weight of the world on them.

She moved over to him and wrapped her arms around him, resting her head against his bare skin. "Don't carry this," she said, kissing the deep groove beneath his shoulder blade. "Please don't."

He lifted his hand and covered hers with it, pressing it against his chest. "No one's going to hurt you again," he said. "I promise."

Another tear trailed down her cheek. Because it was everything she'd ever wanted to hear from someone, and it terrified her how much it meant to hear from him now.

Even more terrifying was just how much the words meant, and how cold she felt in her chest when she had to acknowledge that the only person who really had the power to hurt her was him.

No matter how much she'd wanted to keep her feelings for him neutral, he'd burrowed beneath her protective layer. At some point "just sex" had become a hell of a lot more. And she had no idea how that was possible.

She'd had relationships with men, whole relationships based on more than just sex, that hadn't been like this.

At least, she thought that was what they'd been. They'd gone on dates and chatted, and some nights they hadn't even slept together, which proved that they had a deeper connection than just the physical. Or that's what it was supposed to prove.

But this was supposed to be sex. Hot, sweaty, ill-advised cop-cowboy sex. Like some kind of alpha-male female fantasy on steroids. With handcuffs. On a horse.

So why hadn't it stayed that way? Why did she feel like things were changing? How in the hell had a romp in the backseat of a patrol car turned into the most exposing, soul-baring experience of her life?

"I guess we should get back," she said, stepping away from him, wishing that separating the feelings that she had for him from her heart was as easy as breaking contact with his skin.

"Yeah," he said, bending down and retrieving his shirt from the backseat of the car and tugging it on.

Something had changed between them. It was good and bad. She could feel it. He was all tension now, and she couldn't blame him. But at the same time she felt like the bond had tightened between them.

Because he was the only person who knew. The only one who knew the whole story. Who knew that she wished, more than anything, she'd had someone to protect her.

She hadn't even let herself in on that, not really, until the moment she'd told him.

"That was fun," she said, wiping the moisture from beneath her eyes.

"Yeah," he said, slamming the back door shut before jerking open the front door. "Fun."

ELI SLAMMED THE MAUL down on the splitter and two pieces of wood went flying onto the dirt, the physical energy doing very little to relieve the raging…whatever the hell these feelings were that were roaring through his veins.

He didn't know what he was feeling. So he was chopping wood instead of feeling. Or at least, that was the plan. And if that didn't work, eventually he would be exhausted enough that he would just forget he had feelings that didn't involve his screaming muscles.

Barring that, he'd drink them away, but considering that was the way most other men in his family handled Unpleasant Things No One Wanted to Handle, he was averse. But not entirely opposed. Desperate times, et cetera.

"You have enough wood to keep all of Copper Ridge toasty through the wet season. Why are you chopping more?"

Eli turned and saw Kate standing just behind him, her hands on her hips, her weight resting on one leg. "Because," he said, bending over and picking up one of the log halves, "I'm expecting it to be a cold year."

"Oh, okay. Hey, have you talked to Sadie lately?"

Oh, good, that was what he needed. To talk about Sadie with his sister when he was trying to forget the woman via manual labor. In that way that he just wanted to forget about her for long enough to make himself feel comfortable again.

Enough to make himself forget the look on her face. The way she'd shivered in his arms.

Why didn't you protect me?

He bent and picked up the other log half, scowling deeply. "I talked to her this morning. Why?"

"I wanted to tell her that I made rolls."

"What?"

"I made rolls by myself. And they're edible. She showed me how yesterday, so I was… Hey, how are you?"

"Fine," he said, gritting his teeth and walking over to the wood pile to stack the pieces on top.

"You don't seem fine," she said, frowning. "Is this about the people coming for the barbecue next week?"

Weirdly, that bothered him a hell of a lot less than it had in the beginning. In fact, in a very strange way he was looking forward to it. Looking forward to seeing Sadie's vision come to life. To seeing her hard work become a real, tangible thing.

He shouldn't care. He did.

Don't carry this.

Too damn late, Sadiepants.

"Nope," he said. "I am fine."

"You are growly."

"And?"

"That's Connor's job. What is up?"

"Just thinking about things," he said, putting another log on the stump. "Dad."

"Oh," she said, looking down.

He positioned the splitter, then lifted the maul again, bringing it down hard. "It's that time of the year."

"Yeah, I guess it is." She bit her lip and looked down, then back up, her dark eyes fierce. "I don't think about him very much."

"You don't?"

"No."

He looked at Kate and fully realized—maybe for the first time—that she had never, ever known the good parts of their mother or father. And they had existed. Their mother hadn't always been despondent and unable to cope. Their father hadn't always been a man viewing life through an alcohol haze.

He'd gotten to know the people they were. So had Connor.

"He was a good man at one time, Katie," he said.

"That's fine," she said. "For him. For you and Connor. But I never knew that man. I never saw him any way but falling on his ass drunk. You and Connor loved me. Then Jessie, when she married Connor. Jack was there, and Liss, our friends who always made our house feel less empty. But I can't miss the person who made the house seem sad."

She didn't understand, because she didn't realize what really made him think of their father. She didn't know that he was trying to cope with the feelings Sadie's words had triggered.

That they had brought to mind all he'd failed to protect.

And that was the crux of the problem. He wanted to protect the people he loved, the people of Copper Ridge. And his track record was hit or miss at best.

"Hello." He turned and saw Sadie standing in the driveway, her hands in her back pockets, tugging the T-shirt she was wearing tight across her breasts, her expression sheepish. "Hopefully I'm not interrupting anything."

"Not anything important," Kate said, forcing a smile.

She looked a whole lot like him when she faked okay, and he wasn't sure what he thought about that.

"How is everything, Kate?" Sadie asked, smiling. Sadie's smile, regardless of her feelings, always seemed genuine. And that was even more concerning. He was starting to realize that everything about Sadie, all of her ease and lightness, wasn't what it seemed.

Ruptured spleen. Hospitalization. Her mother wouldn't defend her...

He couldn't imagine it. Couldn't believe this bright, amazing woman had been subjected to horrors that topped the Garrett Ranch's Greatest Hits by a mile. He hadn't even guessed at her pain, and today she'd poured it out onto his chest.

And he felt it now. The weight of it. Of what he hadn't done. Of what he always left undone.

"Good," Kate said. "I was actually just asking about you."

"Well, here I am! Things are really moving along for the barbecue. Though I wanted to ask you, and I know it's really last minute, but are you interested in doing any type of rodeo demonstration?"

Kate brightened visibly. "Yes. I'd love to. I could do some barrel racing in the arena, or even some calf roping."

"Both if you want."

"Maybe Jack will be interested in helping out," she said.

"That would be great."

"I'll go and call him," Kate said. "See you." She waved and then bounded off in the direction of her little cabin.

"She is quite something," Sadie said, moving in closer to him.

"She is. Sometimes I'm afraid she really lost out having to be raised by us. We're not exactly a soft touch."

"No," Sadie said, "but you're a pretty darn satisfying touch if I say so myself."

"Well, thanks for that."

"Actually, that's what I'm here to talk to you about."

"Oh?" he asked, feeling the scowl forming from the inside out. He'd come to cut wood and escape her and here she was.

Wanting to talk about the feelings he was pretending not to have.

"I'm sorry about what I said. I wanted to make sure we were okay."

She didn't meet his eyes when she said any of that. And he knew she really was sorry, and that she was afraid that she'd overstepped. But he also knew she'd meant it all. And it had hit its mark.

"We're fine," he told her, because it was the thing he had to say to get sex. And whatever he felt, he knew he still wanted that.

"Good. I don't normally spill my guts like that. Normally I listen to other people do it. That's kind of why I do it. Did it."

"Therapy?"

"Yes. Because I got to give it to other people and sort of turn over their own issues and never think of mine. I mean…it hurts. That memory hurts. I think it always will. And I'm projecting. I know that. I…wished someone would have seen, Eli, and in my head, because you were so tangled up in that night, something in me made that person you. My patients do the same thing and I know better. But you know…it's a 'doctors are terrible patients' kind of a thing."

He could hear what she was saying, and he even believed her to an extent. But it didn't change the way that heavy mass of emotion felt in his chest. Didn't make breathing easier or his throat less tight.

"Let's forget that it happened," she said. "You know. You're basically the only person who knows. And… I think we should just…go to bed."

"It's six o'clock."

"So?" she asked.

They were standing outside his house. And he'd never had her in his house before. But he'd had her in his patrol car. And that was, in some ways, more intimate.

"I guess I can't think of a reason." Mainly because the blood had all rushed down south of his belt. A chronic, Sadie-related issue.

"Oh, good," she said, looking relieved. "I don't want things to change."

Neither did he, but he was afraid that they had.

"We're on the same page, then."

"Your house or the car?"

"House," he said.

"Probably for the best. In hindsight, it was a pretty poor use of the people's property. Doing it in a county-owned vehicle."

"Excuse me," he said, the tension in his chest easing slightly, though not the tension in his cock, "you started it."

"True. But then," she said, putting her hand on his chest, a smile curving her lips, "I am a criminal. A very bad girl. And you are so good."

He wrapped his hand around her wrist and drew her fingertips up to his lips, sucking one into his mouth, swirling his tongue around the tip. Then he closed his teeth lightly over her skin and released her. "Am I?" he asked.

He didn't feel good. He felt like a failure. Like a man who'd let another man beat this woman near to death. Like a man who couldn't protect the weaker people around him, even though he tried with everything in him.

There were tons of people who never let their fathers drive off in a drunken stupor and die. And those people probably didn't try half as hard as he did.

Sometimes he wondered if he was destined to fail everyone around him, no matter how hard he tried to be acceptable. To be good enough.

So if he was going to be bad, maybe he should just embrace it.

"I think you're underestimating me," he said. "Still. And I've had you in handcuffs."

"I don't know, Eli."

"Sadie," he said, gripping her chin, kissing her firmly on the lips. "Get your ass in my bed."

CHAPTER FIFTEEN

SADIE WASN'T SURE what was happening, or why it felt so different. It wasn't about sex. She knew that much. Well, it was about sex, but it was about something more, too. Something deeper. Something she really didn't want to guess at.

Eli had only let her in his house that night she'd used his shower when she'd burst the pipes. Never since.

They had sex at her house. And then he returned to his space. His neat and ordered space.

She walked through the front door, her heart hammering hard. Everything was like she remembered, identical, really, to the only other time she'd ever been here.

Neat, clean. Verging on shiny.

For a man who worked with farm animals and criminals, he sure kept his space spotless.

Maybe that was why.

"You know where my bedroom is," he said.

"Yes."

"Get upstairs." There was a hard, determined light in his

dark eyes. Like a switch had been flipped. There was so much electricity arching between them. So much heat. And so much intense meaning.

Things had changed. She'd changed them by telling him her story. By telling him he should have protected her.

She wasn't sure yet if she'd made things better or ruined them, but she was sure she'd changed them. She'd felt it then, standing isolated in the woods with him, and she felt it now.

"Okay," she said, because whatever was happening she wasn't going to tell him no.

She turned and headed up the stairs, her footsteps loud on the wooden floor, her heart hammering louder in her ears, sounding over her feet.

"I like to watch you walk," he said. "Though I like it better when you aren't wearing anything."

She heard him behind her, following her, his voice rough. "Well, I'm hardly going to walk through your kitchen naked," she said.

"I walked through the woods naked for you," he said. "And that's not my usual thing."

"No," she said, tossing a look over her shoulder, her stomach knotting tighter as she saw the hungry look on his face. "I don't suppose."

"But I don't do any of the usual things with you," he said.

She pushed open his bedroom door and tugged her shirt over her head, ditching her bra just as quickly before crossing one arm over her breasts and turning, giving him her best saucy smile. "Oh, really?"

"No," he said, his voice lowering. "I don't."

"Well," she said, spreading her fingers, giving him a slight peek at her nipple, knowing that she was driving him crazy, "maybe we can see what else I might tempt you to do."

He advanced on her, his expression dark. He extended his hands and cupped her face, tilting her head backward, his fingers forked through her hair. "Don't make this a joke, Sadie."

"I'm not," she said, her heart tightening, like he'd grabbed hold of that instead of her face and squeezed tight.

"You're trying to make light of it so you don't feel it. I can't do that. As you pointed out, I'm a pretty humorless bastard." He traced the edge of her lower lip with his thumb. "So no more talking. Don't try to make it funny. I have to feel it. So you damn well have to feel it, too."

Her heart lurched into her throat, made a response impossible. But it didn't matter because then he was kissing her, his lips hard and firm on hers, stubble scraping her chin, her cheeks, as things intensified between them.

Their little love scene in the car had been intense, driven by her need to wash something out of the past. To make it different. But this was different still. He was different.

And he was right. She wanted to do exactly what he had accused her of. She wanted to do a striptease and laugh and make it fun. She wanted it to be the kind of sex she knew, the kind she could control.

But Eli was in charge now. And for some reason, she felt more helpless now than when her wrists had been in handcuffs.

Because that had been her idea, her plan. But this was about his demons, not hers.

He pushed her back onto the bed, stripping her jeans, underwear and shoes from her body before he shoved his jeans down his hips, leaving him naked, bare for her.

"I'll be right back." He turned and walked into the bathroom and returned a moment later, rolling the condom onto his length as he moved back to the bed.

He positioned himself between her thighs, kissing her deep. There was no foreplay, no preamble at all, but she didn't care. She was ready. She'd been ready since the last time he was inside her.

There was just something about him.

He pushed inside of her, deep, thick, filling her completely. A sharp gasp escaped her lips as he pushed his hips forward, going impossibly deeper. She wrapped her legs around his thighs, opening herself to him, allowing him better access.

She smoothed her hands over his hair, down his shoulders and back, her eyes never leaving his, the impact hitting her deep, sparking off the protective shields she'd built up around her chest, making her burn. Making her feel like she was on the verge of an attack that might bring the walls down forever.

He ground himself against her, pleasure rushing through her, her orgasm taking her by surprise, taking her over completely. Rushing through her and eclipsing all of the emotions that had been knotting up in her chest, leaving her feeling clean, new.

Relieved.

Above her, Eli lowered his head, his body shaking as he shuddered out his own release. He let out a hard breath and moved away from her, rolling onto his back. She just stayed where she was, staring at the ceiling, at the slats of wood, knotted and imperfect, but somehow orderly. Like the man himself.

The only sound was his harsh breathing. Probably hers, too, but for some reason she was much more aware of him than of herself. Possibly because she didn't want to be aware of herself, all things considered.

The things considered being the fact that it felt like there was a potential avalanche of feelings about to crash down inside of her. A veritable rock slide of emotions.

No, thank you, sir.

She closed her eyes and tried to capture the post-orgasmic warmth that she was counting on coming to the rescue. She felt decidedly less glowy than normal.

She was far too aware of everything. The burn on her cheeks from his whiskers, the blood still throbbing hot through her body, her heart beating unevenly. How cold her breasts felt now that he'd moved away from her.

The shifting of the mattress as he got up and the sound of his feet slapping on the wood floor as he headed back into the bathroom. She shivered, then looked around the room, pushing herself into a sitting position.

He didn't have pictures on the walls. The wood-paneled walls were broken up by large windows that overlooked the dense trees that backed the house. The sun was sinking outside, golden rays filtering through the green, casting everything in a hazy filtered light.

She suddenly felt completely exhausted, her eyelids ready to sink like the sun. She crawled up to the head of the bed and slipped beneath the covers, lying on her side, watching the tree branches outside wave in the breeze. She heard Eli walking back through the room, felt the mattress sink just across from her.

The covers slipped down and she felt his warmth beneath the covers. Wordlessly, he wrapped his arms around her and pulled her close. She relaxed, head resting against the solid wall of his chest.

She would just close her eyes for a second.

Then she would go.

WHEN SADIE OPENED HER EYES, gray light was bathing the bedroom, and Eli's arms were still wrapped tightly around her.

She scrubbed her eyes, rolling onto her back, his hands drifting over her breasts as she did. Then she craned her neck to look over him, and at the bedside clock.

It was five-thirty, and she sure as hell knew she hadn't gone back in time, which meant she'd slept here all night.

She sat up, pulling the covers up to her chest. Eli made a deep noise, then rolled over.

Her heart was hammering, her hands a little sweaty. She'd never done that before. Never slept beside another person like that. There was something so impossibly intimate about it. Something sort of terrifying.

She waited for her muscles to spring into action, for her legs to get her out of bed and her feet to run her out the door.

But it didn't happen.

She breathed in deep, and the panic started to subside, her breath normalizing. She didn't want to leave. That was the most startling revelation that came from her subsiding panic. Other startling revelations included that she actually felt happy that he'd let her stay the night. That he'd invited her into his home and his bedroom.

He'd shared something with her last night. Like she'd shared with him after they'd made love in the car. But he'd done it wordlessly, and she had no idea what exactly she was supposed to extrapolate from it, but she still felt it.

She slipped out of bed and hunted for her clothes, tugging them on before she went downstairs and helped herself to Eli's mugs and his coffeemaker, humming absently as she did.

She remembered that he ordered lattes and pulled some milk out of the fridge, nuking it in the microwave, then whisking it while the coffee brewed. Then she added a generous helping to his coffee, along with some sugar. Leaving her own coffee fairly underdressed with a dollop of warm milk and a little sugar. When she got back upstairs, Eli was out of bed, standing in the center of the room, naked and looking a little lost.

"You're still here," he said, when she walked in.

"Yes, I am. And I come bearing caffeine."

"Well, then, I'm very glad you stayed," he said.

"Is that the only reason?"

"No."

"Well, good. A woman hates to be wanted only for her bean-brewing skills. Though mine are legend. And no man has ever benefited from them. But they will at the B and B."

Eli frowned and set his mug on the nightstand, grabbing his black boxer briefs and T-shirt from the ground, throwing both on, then retrieving his mug. "What do you mean no man has ever benefited from your skills?"

"I'm not into sleepovers," she said, smiling, trying to keep it a little lighter than things had been between them. She turned away from him, and he caught her arm, turning her back.

"What does that mean?"

Oh, damn Eli. Why did he always want to know what something meant?

"It means that I like to sleep alone, which I've told you before. And it means that I've always slept alone. Whiz, whir, thank you, sir, if you will."

"Why, Sadie?"

"Because I don't do close, okay?" she said, realizing as the words slipped out of her mouth, cranky, curt and very pre-coffee in attitude, that they were true.

It was easy to pretend she was fine. That she had normal relationships and let them go when they weren't working because she didn't need conflict, because she wasn't going to submit to a life of unhappiness and violence under the guise of sick, twisted love, like her mother had done.

But the simple truth was, she didn't do heavy, because she didn't want to get close to anyone. She didn't let her boyfriends spend the night for the same reason she lived in a place for only a couple of years at a time.

She didn't want to bond with anything. She didn't want to need anyone.

She blinked, standing there frozen in the middle of Eli's bedroom having an epiphany. "I don't like to let people get close to me," she repeated, the words making the back of her neck prickle.

"Why?" he asked.

"Because people hurt you." That was true, too. She was filled with truth. She needed to be filled with coffee, so her truth could stay in. In and buried, like it normally was.

He nodded slowly and walked toward the French doors, undoing the latch on one and opening it out, and onto the deck that wrapped around the second floor of the house.

"Care to take your unheard-of morning-after coffee out on the deck?"

"Oh, why not?" she said, lifting a shoulder and following him outside. He set his mug on the railing, and she did the same, resting her elbows on the rough wood and looking out at the view.

She tried to see through the trees, past the closest branches, to see what was beyond, but they were like a dark blot of green ink, bleeding together to cover the blankness.

"I'm sort of mad at you," she said, looking down into her coffee, listening to the wind rustle through the trees, to the birds that were just starting to wake up.

"Why?"

"I thought I was really well-adjusted before I met you."

"Did I...maladjust you?"

"No, you just had the balls to point out that I'm a total head case. No man before you has dared."

"Every man before me got the boot out the door too quickly."

She waved her hand. "Eh. Granted. All right," she said. "Why is your house so clean?"

"Because otherwise it gets chaotic. And out of control. And I've lived that way before. I won't live that way again."

"Your dad?"

"Yes. He was a mess, Sadie. I took care of Kate, but my dad was like another child at a certain point. He made bad decisions, and it was up to me to clean it up. Cover it up. Before my mom left he was okay."

"He never got over your mom?"

He lifted a shoulder. "Probably at some point he was just an alcoholic who liked booze. Probably there was a point where he'd forgotten why he ever started drinking. But that's just a theory. There was always so much to take care of."

"It explains you."

He looked at her, his eyes blank. "I failed him, though. In the end."

"What?"

"The night he died. Whenever Dad got drunk, I used to take his keys and hide them. That was my routine. Dad was drunk every night, for the record, so I knew to hide his keys every night."

"Eli, you should have never had to deal with all that."

"But I did. We don't get to choose our lot, we choose what we do with it. Except…the night my dad died I decided not to go home after my shift. I was out. Connor and Jessie lived in the cabin Kate lives in now. My dad and I were in the main house. I hadn't moved out because he needed someone. And I knew he needed someone. But that night, I figured he was probably passed out so I didn't need to go home. Went out with a bunch of guys from the department instead. And a call came in over the radio."

"Oh… Eli."

"Yeah, well…it's been a long time. And my dad was not a father to me, not really. But that doesn't change the fact that I let him down. He was impaired, always. And he needed someone to help manage his decisions. I wasn't there and he died."

"You can't honestly blame yourself…"

"You blame me for not saving you from abuse I didn't even know about. Of course I blame myself for this."

"Eli, I don't really blame you…"

"You do," he said. "And I understand. It's because I've promised to protect people. If I just said screw it like…like Connor does, then I wouldn't expect better. And no one else would, either. But if I say I'll take care of it, I better. And I haven't always. I've failed a lot of people."

"I'm sure you've helped more people," she said, her stomach clenching.

"But I failed where it really matters."

"But it was his fault."

"Does it matter?" he asked, turning his back to the view, leaning against the railing. "Does it matter if you know you should feel a different way about it?"

She thought about how she'd felt when her blame had poured

out of her back in the woods. About how she'd been carrying that feeling around, buried deep and low, for years.

"I guess not," she said. "But…you shouldn't feel that way."

He lifted a shoulder. "Sure."

"Do we get some sort of…accolades for exposing just how screwed up we both are?" she asked. "Because I figured this just-sex thing would involve a lot less talking."

"Then why are we talking?" he asked.

"Because. I spent a lot of years listening for a living and never met anyone I wanted to talk to. And… I want to talk to you. But I don't always like the things that get said."

"Neither do I."

"Maybe we should stop talking, then," she said, moving to him and curling her hand around his neck, kissing him.

"I have to be at work in an hour."

"I can get a lot done with twenty minutes. Just you wait and see."

SADIE WAS ACTUALLY NERVOUS. Like…upchucking nervous. The barbecue was today. Booths were being set up. Volunteers were on hand, paid workers were on hand, individual vendors were on hand.

Over the past week she'd finalized everything for the barbecue, bought new linens for the B and B, and perfected her menu, and also during that past week, she'd been sleeping with Eli, either at his place or hers.

She liked to think that had something to do with how well things were going. If for no other reason than being with him made her feel very good.

She paced the open field area where everything was being set up. The good thing about getting local businesses to participate was that everyone basically saw to their own booth once she directed them.

Barbecues were already being fired up for the cook-off, very large pots of beans and potato salad were either heating or chilling. Beer on tap was at hand. Kate and Jack were in the large uncovered arena ready to do some rodeo work and to show some basic roping techniques.

And Jack was even coordinating a round of mutton busting, with prizes donated from the Farm and Garden. She wondered if Connor had checked with his insurance about that. She imagined not.

Jack and Kate had proven to be enthusiastic additions, and their passion for the events was contagious. It was also enticing a whole new segment of the county to the barbecue.

The only booth that was empty was Alison's. And it was starting to make Sadie wring her hands in despair. Well, she could get pies from the grocery store for the contest if she had to. But she doubted it would make for as special a dessert booth as she'd planned. In fact, without the homemade stuff, it felt like a "why bother."

But considering what had happened the last time she'd seen Alison, she wasn't that surprised.

"Sadie!"

Sadie turned and saw Lydia, her favorite intrepid Chamber of Commerce representative and fellow admirer of Eli's butt. "Hi, Lydia. You're out early."

The other woman smiled. "Yes, I am. I thought I would see how it was all shaping up."

"Nicely," Sadie said, surveying the grounds. "It just might not fail."

"Eli would never let it fail," Lydia said. "Not to say you would," she quickly amended. "Only that I've known Eli for the past six years and he's always been so stable and organized. Just one of the many reasons I'm wholeheartedly endorsing his bid for sheriff."

Sadie scanned the field, looking for Eli. She didn't see him. "Yeah, I definitely think he's the man for the job," she said.

She thought back to last week's conversation on his porch.

About how he felt like he failed when it came to caring for people.

She couldn't understand it.

Maybe because you suck and you threw a bunch of your issues at him?

Maybe because I really feel that way, she argued back with herself. *Because maybe…if I ever thought there was such a thing as a knight in shining armor, it would have been him.*

She didn't even bother to push the thought away.

Didn't bother to pretend there wasn't more swirling around inside of her than simple lust.

Somehow, in the space of a month and a half, she'd gone from disliking Eli immensely to…well, whatever this thing was where she felt like the sun hadn't really risen until she saw his face.

Whatever you called that.

"Sadie." Lydia interrupted her train of thought. "I was wondering if you wanted to get brochures for the B and B down to the Chamber. And also, I was wondering if we could put some brochures in the B and B for some other businesses. Tourist attractions, whale-watching excursions, things like that."

"That would be great!" Sadie said, feeling strangely warm toward Lydia at the moment. Not that she was cold toward her normally, but it was a little awkward to talk to the woman you knew had a thing for the guy you were semi-secretly sleeping with.

"Beneficial for all," Lydia said. "Oh, there he is!" Her smile broadened when she saw Eli, and Sadie felt a sliver of guilt push its way beneath her skin. Lydia was more Eli's type. They made sense. She was organized, passionate about the community. Caring.

She wasn't terrified of interpersonal connection and more likely than your average startled house cat to tear off and hide under the furniture than forge any kind of meaningful relationship with someone.

Except…she and Eli did have a meaningful relationship. She

could feel it. She was carrying it around in her chest, and it weighed a ton. And it was effing inconvenient.

"Eli!" Lydia called, waving.

Oh, man. Like it couldn't get more awkward. Because she and Eli were not a couple, and when she stood near him in front of the general public she didn't know what to do with her hands. Because they were itching to touch him but she knew she couldn't.

He walked over to them, looking generally awkward, as awkward as you would expect the guy to feel in the situation.

"Hi," she said, shoving her hands into her back pockets so they wouldn't get all feelsy with him.

"Sadie," he said. "Lydia. How are things going?"

"Great," Sadie said. "And on your end?"

"Parking area is set. Connor is sober. I consider that a win."

Sadie winced. "Is Connor going to come?"

Eli shrugged. "I don't know. I kind of doubt it. Families and things...he doesn't handle this stuff well."

"Man," Sadie said. "I didn't think of it from that angle. I feel like crap now."

"Don't," he said. "Connor objectively realizes the value in this. Okay, he didn't say that, but I know he does. He'll hide away. It's his deal. Though Liss might be able to draw him out for a while when Jack and Kate ride."

"I can't wait to see them," Lydia said. "Really exciting. It'll be very fun. We've had a lot of calls about this down at the Chamber."

"That's great," Sadie said. "And goes a long way in eliminating my deep fear that I will end up here alone, eating all of the food myself. Which is, in many ways, not a bad fantasy, but... you know. People are investing a lot of time and money in this, and there has to be a good turnout or it just won't be worth it."

Eli surprised her by putting his hand on her shoulder. "There will be a big turnout. Because you've done an amazing job. And I know I was kind of grumpy about it for a while, but this is great. You did great. And people have already started pouring in." He slid his palm down her arm, the gesture going from casual encouragement to something that revealed a deeper level of intimacy between them.

And Lydia noticed. Her smile faltered for a moment, and Sadie inwardly cringed.

"Thank you," Sadie said. "Thank you both for all your help and thanks… Eli, for saying that. I really…tried." And in spite of herself, she had bonded with this place.

She looked around the picnic area, at the people there. Bud from the gas station sitting with his wife and smiling. Cassie from The Grind was with a very nice-looking man Sadie assumed was the same Jake she talked about with a dreamy smile on her face.

The group of fishermen from Rona's were there with their families, and their beer. Her old high school friend Brooke with a group of women dressed in cutoff shorts and American-flag T-shirts.

It wasn't just this place. It was these people.

This man.

And if she was going to do this, be here, she wanted to do it right. She wanted to do it all well.

She sort of hated the pressure that came with it all. The crushing need. So different than a life that wasn't tied to anything. No anchors holding you back. Nothing to entice you to try. She missed it, in a way. But then, going back to it seemed impossible.

Because…big, cowboy-in-a-uniform-shaped anchor. No matter what looked better or easier, it would never really be easy again. Cutting ties with Eli would be something she regretted. But being with him was damn hard. Because he called her on her BS and made her be serious, made her look in his eyes when she climaxed. Forced her not to joke about her pain, but to speak about it honestly.

He added an uncomfortable level of depth to her life. Discomfiting when she'd tried for so long to stay in the shallows. Bastard.

"You did more than try," he said. "You succeeded. Now we just need to wait for the place to fill up."

And it did fill up. It was unbelievable. By the early afternoon they had people everywhere. Eating, laughing, talking. There was a band playing. Ace, the sexy bartender, was serving beer from the portable tap. The barbecues were going strong and adults were laughing while kids danced in the grass with bare feet.

Eli's three-legged race was a serious hit, and everyone was anxiously awaiting the official barbecue judging, and Jack and Kate's demonstration.

She noticed Eli standing on the perimeter and walked over to where he was, jabbing him lightly with her elbow. Since, you know, she probably couldn't kiss him in public.

"You hungry yet?" she asked.

"Starving."

"Let's get food. There's obviously enough. And we earned it."

"We did," he said. "Well, you did."

"Stop it," she said, leaning into him again and shoving him with her shoulder. "This is your place. And you've been a big support. Stop being so nice to me. It's freaking me out."

"Am I not nice to you?" he asked.

"You are," she said. "I think you've officially crossed over into being mainly nice to me. Which, considering where we came from, is kind of a huge deal."

"Well, I know you now. Instead of just thinking I know about you."

"Same," she said. "Shall we get our barbecue on?"

They walked through the crowd, Eli periodically smiling and waving at those who called out a greeting, and all she could do was just walk next to him in awe of all that he was to these people. He was a cornerstone, her man. The kind of guy who did good all the time. The kind of guy who'd affected many of the people here in amazing ways.

It was daunting. Daunting that a man like him could have clearly done so much and still feel like he hadn't done enough.

It was extra daunting because she wasn't sure if she'd ever made half that impact, even if you cobbled together the things she'd done across all the places she'd lived.

"Chicken or beef?" she asked, when they approached the barbecue line.

"Any," he said. "Any and all."

"All right, we'll fill your plate with meats."

He smiled and right then she didn't really care about impact and other deep things like that. Because Eli was smiling right at her, and that meant a hell of a lot.

"What about you?" he asked.

"I want steak, and I hear it's fantastic because it's Garrett beef. And I want copious amounts of potato salad because who doesn't love a mayonnaise and starch party in their mouth?"

"Well, you obviously do," he said.

She smiled at him, then had to look away to avoid kissing him. She noticed that Alison was at her pie booth, looking harassed and serving pieces of pie onto plates as quickly as possible. Then she noticed that Jared was standing right next to her, his large arms folded over his chest, looking every inch the threatening, Neanderthal jackass he was.

"Uh-oh," she said, "I think we might have a problem."

Eli frowned, then followed her line of sight over to the pie booth. "Oh. That asshole."

"Yeah."

A muscle in Eli's jaw ticked. "I'm feeling pretty short on patience with him."

"I know. But I do understand that there's..." Suddenly Eli was moving out of line and heading toward the booth. "Oh," she said, hurrying after him.

Jared was leaning in near Alison, saying something, and

Alison was looking increasingly distressed. And Eli was starting to walk faster.

"Do we have a problem here?" Eli asked.

Jared was a big guy, and scary enough if you were a woman. But Eli stood about four inches taller and had to outweigh him by thirty pounds of pure muscle. Even without the badge and the gun, Eli was an intimidating sight.

In many ways he was more terrifying without the uniform than he was with it on. Because in the uniform, you could see his boundaries. Clearly. Deputy Garrett was a lawman. He was a man who would see justice done in accordance with the legal system.

Right now in his cowboy hat, tight black T-shirt and jeans he looked more likely to dispense a different kind of justice entirely.

And she didn't really know what he might do.

And that was funny because he was predictable and good. Except…except he wasn't all that predictable, not really. When they were in bed, he was a different man, a dangerous man.

When they were together he was something a lot more authentic.

Just now, as he was standing there ready to do God knew what, she realized that the man he was in bed wasn't an anomaly. It was him.

"No problem, Deputy Garrett," Jared said, not drunk today, just hella mean, apparently. "Just talking to my wife." Alison's shoulders shrunk in when he said the word. "That's not a problem, is it?"

"It depends on what words were being used."

"Eli…" Alison said. "It's okay…"

"You on a first-name basis with him?" Jared asked, his tone hard. "Is that why he always seems so worried about you? Are you sleeping with him, you stupid whore?"

And that was when Eli moved.

He leaned in and grabbed Jared by the back of his neck at the same time he brought his fist in to meet the other man's nose. Then he shoved him downward, bending him at the waist while he brought his knee up into Jared's stomach.

Before stepping back and letting the other man fall to the ground at his feet.

People were looking now, craning their necks, wide-eyed. Sadie just stood frozen, almost unable to believe that Eli had done it. And yet, at the same time…she wasn't shocked. No, she wasn't shocked at all.

But she was proud.

"I don't take kindly to the words *bitch* and *whore*," Eli said, keeping his voice low so that the families nearby couldn't hear him. "Especially not when you're talking to your wife. Now stand the fuck up." He gripped the back of Jared's neck and brought him to his feet. "You want to hit someone, why don't you hit me? Or is it not as much fun to go toe-to-toe with someone who outweighs you? I'll bet you're okay with hitting women. But that's not going to play today, so why don't you go ahead and hit me instead?"

Jared spat and blood dribbled down his chin. He wiped it with the back of his hand. "You prick," he said, his eyes blazing.

"Yep," Eli said, "and let me tell you something, this prick is not on duty today. Today, I'm just the owner of this property, and you're the bottom-feeder who isn't welcome on it. You're not welcome in my town, either, but there's nothing I can do about that. But I'll tell you this. I'm going to be looking for you to make a mistake. And then I'll lock your ass up. You put one finger out of line?" He gestured to Alison. "You touch her again? I will see that you stay in a jail cell for a very, very long time. So step carefully. And right now? Step. The hell. Off my property."

Jared stumbled forward and headed away from the stand. Then he turned to Eli, shouting obscenities that all ran together in a blur, before he stopped, like he intended to come back. Until Connor walked into view, from the direction of the main house.

He wrapped his hand around the back of Jared's neck, holding him steady. Eli was pretty big. Eli was threatening. But bearded Connor, who was broad and thick, every bit of him heavily muscled and with rage pouring off him, was terrifying. "I think my brother asked you to go," he said. If Eli hadn't been deterrent enough, Connor was there for backup.

Jared looked back at Eli one more time before turning and walking away, spitting profanities as he went.

Connor moved forward and joined the group. "Well, what an asshole. Sorry." He directed the apology to Alison, who was wide-eyed and shaking. "But seriously."

"Are you okay?" Sadie asked Alison.

Alison nodded, then shook her head, closing her eyes. "I don't know."

"Fair enough," Sadie said.

"I'm embarrassed. I'm so embarrassed that I'm still married to him," she said, her voice breaking. "But it's…"

"I know," Sadie said. "And trust me, I have spoken to a lot of women who've dealt with this, professionally. And unprofessionally…my mother has never left, Alison. She's stayed and stayed. For more than thirty years. I've seen what it does to someone. I've seen what they can make you think about yourself. But you have to know, whatever he's said, it's a lie."

She nodded. "I know. I do."

"Please don't go back to him. Don't go home tonight."

Connor shifted his stance. "Especially don't go home tonight. He's a coward with us, and that means he'll take it out on you."

"Is there somewhere you can go?" Eli asked.

She nodded. "My…my mom and dad live in Tolowa. I can go there. Not sure what they'll think when I show up, since I don't really… I've been so embarrassed."

"You can call them if you like," Sadie said.

Alison shook her head. "Right now? I just want to serve pie. Because that's what I'm here for. And now that… I have a feeling I'm going to need this. This business. The pie."

"Well, I'll buy a few a week at least for my B and B," Sadie said, determined. No matter how good her cooking skills were, she wasn't going to produce a pie as amazing as Alison's. "And I'll be around. Whatever you need."

"And if he ever comes near you again," Eli said, "if he hits you or threatens you…"

"I'll report him," she said. "I promise I will." She took a deep breath and straightened, and for the first time, Sadie saw an echo of the girl she'd known in the woman who stood before her. Someone a little scrappy. A lot angry. Someone who was ready to fight. "Now, I have pie to serve."

She turned and went back to slicing her pies and Eli, Connor and Sadie moved away.

"What are you doing out?" Eli asked Connor.

Connor shrugged. "Liss is going to meet me to watch Kate ride. You know I like to watch her do her thing."

"Yeah," Eli said. "She's great."

Sadie looked behind Connor's shoulder and saw red waves bouncing just before Liss came into view, jogging up behind him. "I made it. I'm late but I made it."

"You're chronically late," Connor said, turning to face her. "It's an illness."

"I'm bizay, Connor," she said, poking him in the side. "You don't know anything about that, obviously."

"No," Connor said, "I just run a whole fricking ranch, Liss. I know nothing of your busyness. I bet all that paperwork is a real strain. Wanna trade?"

"Eff no. I am not roping cows."

The ghost of a smile touched Connor's lips when he looked at his friend. "The cows don't like you much, either, honey."

"Glad to know it's mutual. The cows and I can go on giving each other the evil eye. Then I'll eat a burger because I'm human and I win."

"Come on, then, let's go," Connor said, putting his hands in his pockets and jerking his head in the direction of the arena.

"We haven't eaten yet," Eli said, and his referring to them as a "we" made Sadie feel a little warm and fuzzy.

"Go get some food, then. We'll see you over there," Connor said, eyeing them both, and Sadie felt her cheeks heat a little.

"So that was Connor in a good mood?" Sadie asked, when he and Liss were out of earshot.

"Pretty much. He got to threaten bodily harm to someone so I fail to see how he could have had a better day."

She started back over to the barbecue line, chewing on her lip. "Are you worried?" she asked. "About how all that might affect your campaign?"

He frowned. "I didn't even think of that. Which is…weird. I usually think of everything."

"Well, I don't want to add concerns that you don't really need."

"No," he said, "I think it's interesting. I don't care," he said, meeting her gaze. "I just don't care. Because I still want to be sheriff. I still think I'd do a damn good job, but I do a good job at what I do now. And…whether or not it was a popular thing or easy thing or good thing…punching that asshole in the face was the right thing to do."

She wrapped her arms around his neck and hugged him, then quickly stepped back, embarrassed by her public demonstration. "It was," she said.

"Somehow, knowing that, believing that, makes me not care very much what the consequences are."

"I think you're amazing," she said, looking ahead, smiling. "I mean, if that matters."

"It does," he said.

"And…thank you. Because she's my friend. Because she reminded me too much of my mom. And… I'm always afraid people like that will never leave."

"A lot of times they go back," he said, his voice rough.

"I know. But we'll help her."

"Yes," he said, "we will."

Yet again, she didn't know what to do with him. She felt so close to him right now, and she couldn't kiss him here. She wanted to ask him to hold her. She wanted to tell him something about herself. Wanted him to decide that, much like punching a guy in front of the whole town, she was okay, too.

And right then, she thought of the one place she hadn't been yet. She'd driven by the house where she'd grown up, but she hadn't been back to her clearing. Even though it was within walking distance of the B and B. She'd avoided serious thoughts of it since the first day back.

Again, a prickling sensation dotted the back of her neck.

There are no ghosts there. And if there are…maybe this will put some of them to rest.

She let out a long, slow breath, trying to gather her nerve. "Can I show you something?"

"My mom warned me about girls like you," he said, a smile teasing the corners of his lips.

"Did she?"

"No, my mom wasn't here."

"That's a dire punch line."

He lifted a shoulder. "Sometimes life is so dire you have to make a joke about it, right?"

"I think you've learned too much from me."

"Or not enough," he said.

"Hey, I'll get our food. Can you get a blanket for us to sit on?" she asked.

"Yeah."

She finished waiting through the line and got small portions of everything on offer, making small talk with the men and women manning the grills and scooping up sides. It was hard to do, though, since she was all jittery and fluttery inside over what she was about to do.

And there was no real logical reason why. Just that it seemed like a big deal. Bigger in some ways than what she'd shared about her father.

Because this was something she'd avoided. The last bit of Copper Ridge she hadn't revisited. And she wasn't going to test it alone to be sure she was okay. To be certain she could visit it without betraying her emotions.

She was going to let him see. All of it.

She wandered over to where he stood on the edge of the lawn, where people were sitting at the tables that had been set up, and on blankets spread out like a rainbow patchwork over the green grass.

"Okay," he said, "what do you have to show me?"

"I hope you're ready for a hike."

IT WAS ONLY a five-minute walk, through the trees behind the B and B, just over the Garretts' property line. But the path was thick with brush and branches, the narrow trail overgrown in the years since Sadie and her friends had used it.

She and Eli wound through the evergreens, needles reaching out and grabbing her T-shirt. Then the grove thinned out, and beyond that was her clearing.

It was overgrown now, moss covering the ground, ferns encroaching. There was still a fire ring. Stumps, some on their sides, some still positioned like stools.

It had definitely been used by other people in the past decade, but not, it appeared, very recently.

"This," she said, "was my home away from home."

Her chest swelled up with emotion just looking at it, being in it. She wasn't sure why. She wasn't sure why this felt so big. Why she felt so naked.

But, like all her big feelings concerning Eli, the flip side was that as much as it hurt, she wanted him to know this part of her.

She wanted him to know her. There wasn't, she realized, another person on the whole planet—except Toby—who did.

"Alison, Matt, Josh, Brooke and a few others and I all hung out here in the afternoons. Sometimes when we were supposed to be in school. Usually on weekends."

"Doing what?" he asked.

"Drinking. Smoking…things of varying degrees of legality. Like you do. Well, not like *you* do, but like a lot of teenage ne'er-do-wells do."

He looked up at the canopy of trees overheard, then back at her. "I bet it was a great place for that."

'Perfect," she said. "You never arrested me here."

"I didn't."

"But then, in fairness, I never lit the woods on fire."

"That is true enough."

He set the blanket down in the middle of the clearing and they sat, putting their food in front of them. Sadie sat on her knees and started to poke at her potato salad.

"I lost my virginity here." Next to her Eli made a choking sound and she laughed. "Sorry," she said, "just a Sadie fun fact." It wasn't, though. She was minimizing it again. Minimizing why she'd told him. She always did that. So that if what she'd offered was rejected, she could pretend it didn't hurt.

She shoved her plate to the side and took a deep breath. "Sorry." She started over. "I told you because it seemed… This is where I learned to run," she said. "Where I learned to escape. None of us could handle the things that were happening at home and so we came here. Did a bunch of things that made us feel good. Sex was just another thing to do. But that's changing for me. All the way until I met you, sex was just a part of the logical steps in a relationship. A way to pretend that I was intimate with someone without ever really having to be. And this? Telling you this, showing you this, it's more intimate than anything I've ever done. But that's fitting, because when we're together…when we… It was never part of a logical step. It was just a thing we couldn't *not* do. And that's different, too."

"You're…different for me, too," he said.

She wanted him to say more. And she didn't know what more, but she did. She wanted to say more, but again, she wasn't sure what else. Wasn't sure what she could say that wouldn't scare her off.

She was a flight risk of the highest order, putting herself in a situation that scared her to death.

"Eli… I…" She wanted to say something big. She wanted to try to express what she was feeling but she couldn't even quantify it to herself.

The thing she wanted to say was the thing she couldn't say. Because to say it was too much. And way more than this was ever supposed to be.

The one thing she knew for sure, and the thing that terrified her to her bones, was that she wanted to have him here. In this place. The moments of weighted silence, punctuated by heavy sighs and long drags on cigarettes. Days when they'd come and sat in the rain and talked and swore as loud as they wanted, because screw the world. They were in their own world. When she'd come alone with Josh and kissed him and, eventually, taken things further because they'd both just needed someone to touch.

In this place where she'd been with her first guy, she wanted to be with Eli. The last one.

Shock skittered over her skin in an electric current. At the weight of the thought, the depth of it, the truth of it.

So she just said what she could.

"I want you."

"I thought you wanted potato salad."

She tried to laugh, shaking from the inside out. "No. Just you."

He seemed to sense the shift in tone. Another luxury of being with him. Of having him know her. He seemed to know what was happening inside her without her having to say it.

He set his plate off the blanket, too, cupping her cheek and leaning in for a kiss. She returned it, her chest filling, swelling, making it impossible to breathe. But breathing seemed secondary at the moment. Because of Eli.

She wrapped her arms around his neck and he slipped one hand down her back, holding her waist tight as he lowered her to the blanket, his body solid and warm above her. They sat together, his hands stroking her face, her hair.

He kissed her deeper and she laced her fingers through his hair. She felt everything happening on the surface of her skin. The scrape of his stubble against her neck as he kissed her there. As his hands moved over her T-shirt, the warmth of his touch seeping through to her skin.

But it was the echo beneath the surface that really hit. That anchored her to him, to the world. It was like a deep bass note that resonated through her, vibrating along every vein, moving deep to the core of her being.

They broke the kiss, looking at each other, and her eyes met his, emotion building in her chest, bigger and stronger than any sexual climax.

It was painful and beautiful. She didn't think she could stand it for another moment, and she didn't want it to end. In that moment, she felt it all, the good, bad and scary, bound together, inescapable.

She was drowning in it, drowning in *him*. In what he made her feel. She couldn't run from it, couldn't make light of it. Couldn't shove it to the side.

All she could do was embrace it.

She held on to him, hoping his strength would hold her together because at this point, she didn't trust her own. And that was a damn scary place to be. But she was with Eli, so it had to be safe, too.

"When I'm with you, I don't want to be anywhere else," he said, moving his hand over her hair, sliding his fingers through the strands.

"Me, either," she said.

It was true. And for a woman who was always so keen to move on to the next place, the next thing, it was a huge and frightening admission.

He shifted their positions so that she was sitting between his thighs, her back to his chest, his fingers gentle as he laced them through her hair. She closed her eyes, a tightening moving from her chest, up her throat, making it hard to breathe. Making her ache.

"Is this what you used to do here?" he asked.

She laughed, a shaky sound that didn't do anything to loosen the knot of emotion inside her. "Not exactly. I've never done anything quite like this."

"Me, either."

He tugged lightly on her hair, once, then again. She turned and looked at him, and he kept hold of her. "What are you doing?" she asked.

He cocked his head to the side, a rueful smile on his face. "Braiding your hair." He kept his eyes on hers as he wove another section together. "Is that okay?"

She looked at his face, at the sincerity in his eyes. Sincerity and caring she'd never had directed at her before, and that she'd never hoped to deserve. The walls inside her cracked and she had to fight to keep the tears that welled up in her eyes from spilling down her cheeks.

Because when he said that, what she heard was *I'm taking care of you.*

"Yeah," she said, the word a whisper. "It's okay."

She closed her eyes while he finished, focusing on breathing. On not breaking down completely over this moment. On not betraying everything she felt.

He slid his thumb down the side of her neck, his touch gentle. "Done."

She turned back to him again. She wanted to say so much. And nothing, and everything.

He leaned in slowly, his breath fanning across her cheek. Then he kissed her, and she let herself get lost in it. In a kiss that wasn't meant to start anything, wasn't meant to arouse. A kiss that was meant to forge a connection. An outpouring of all the emotion their joining had brought to the surface.

Panic clawed at her as she realized the kiss would have to end. This moment would have to end.

She didn't want the kiss to end, because when it did, they would have to deal with what happened next. And part of her was already panicking about that. Part of her was feeling the need to run.

This was deep. And it was real. And the most terrifying four-letter word she could think of was pushing into her conscious-ness, hovering on the edge of her lips, burrowing into her heart.

And that was the one thing she hadn't wanted. The thing she feared more than anything.

But the kiss had to end. And it did. When they parted he slid his thumb over the edge of her lip. "Sadie..."

"We should go," she said, terror gnawing at her. Terror that he was going to say what she was trying not to think. That he wouldn't say it. That he would never say it. Or that he would now when she wasn't sure she could deal with hearing it.

She reached back and touched her hair, ran her fingertips over the imperfect braid. "We really should go," she repeated.

"Uh...yeah," he said, letting out a big gust of air. "You're right. The barbecue. It's your baby. You...you should be there for it."

"Well, yeah," she said, wrapping her arms around her mid-section. "I kind of should. Sorry about... Not much of a seduc-tion, I guess."

He met her gaze, his eyes intense. "I don't know if I'd say that."

She breathed in deeply through her nose, smoke burning her nostrils, and frowned. "I would have thought they'd be power-ing down the grills about now. It's getting dark."

"Maybe that many more people showed up," he said, sound-ing slightly grim and serious, and it was probably her fault. For cutting him off. For bringing him out here and spilling her guts and then basically telling him nothing of what she was feeling because it all scared her too much.

"We can hope," she said, rounding up the blanket and holding it tight against her chest. Like she was trying to apply pressure to a wound, and in some ways, she felt like that's exactly what she was doing.

Eli picked up the uneaten food, and Sadie mourned it slightly, because she didn't feel like eating at all now. She was too full. Of feelings she didn't want to sort through. Emotions she didn't want to have.

They headed back toward the ranch, cutting through the trees, Sadie taking the lead and not walking hand in hand with Eli, like she sort of wished she could.

You can't bolt if he's holding on to you.

The smoke got thicker as they got closer to the ranch, the wind bringing a wall of it their direction. "What the hell?" he asked.

"I don't know," she said. "That's not... That's not normal."

Eli picked up the pace, passing her, before he moved into a dead run. She followed after him, clutching the blanket against her pounding heart.

She was saying things. Worried things. Things with swearing. But she couldn't really make sense of them. They were just pouring out of her mouth without any kind of specific order or reason. Fear, irrational at this point, but intuitively driving her on.

She knew something had gone wrong. She knew it as certainly as anything she'd seen with her own eyes.

And she knew it was bad.

They crossed the dirt road and back into the Garrett property line to see flames rising up above the trees.

"Oh, no. Oh, no," she said, running after Eli, releasing her hold on the blanket and letting it fall to the ground as she picked up her pace.

They ran back to the main area to find the picnickers standing facing the barn. The beautiful barn that Connor had poured his money into. Now on fire. A wicked blaze that was eating through the beautifully stained wood, the newly shingled roof.

"The horses," she said, gasping for air. "Animals?" She couldn't think. She couldn't remember the layout of things, not now. Her brain was just swimming.

"No animals in there," Eli said, his brow creased, his mouth turned down. "Just the equipment. The feed. All Connor's equipment," he repeated. "Did someone call the fire department?" Eli asked.

"Yeah." Sadie turned and saw Liss standing there, a tear rolling down her cheek. "I did."

"Is there anyone inside?"

"Not as far as we know," Liss said, her eyes not on Eli, but on Connor, who was standing nearer to the blaze than anyone else, his posture stiff, staring right at it. Watching so much of his livelihood burn.

"There's insurance," Eli said.

"Of course," Liss said. "It'll be okay." She didn't sound convinced, not at all.

A group of boys, who must have been twelve, walked up to Eli, their faces ashen, their eyes wide. "We didn't mean to, Deputy Garrett," the smallest one said. "But it's a Fourth of July thing and we were messing with fireworks…"

"In the barn?" Eli asked, his tone hard.

"Well, yeah, because we didn't want our moms to see. And we didn't think…"

"About the hay," Eli said.

"We thought," one of the other boys said, "that we'd gotten all the sparks doused and we left…"

And they'd left a smoldering firework in the hay, to burn it all from the inside out so that by the time anyone realized, the blaze inside had consumed the fuel and moved on to the structure.

Sadie was starting to shake. It was too similar to her last night in Copper Ridge. Too close to sins she'd already committed.

Eli hadn't wanted this on his property, Connor hadn't wanted it and she'd pushed. She'd come onto their property, into their lives and destroyed their order.

And this was the result.

This is what happens when you try. You can't fix it. You never could.

She was watching the Garretts' world burn in front of her. Her handiwork. No, she wasn't going to fall prostrate to the ground and take total fault. She wasn't an idiot. It had been little boys with firecrackers, not her with a match. Not her at a party knocking over a lantern.

But it didn't change how horrible she felt. Didn't change the way it was unfolding. Or the fact that the boys were only here because of her.

"Eli..."

"Not now, Sadie," he said, his voice rough.

"I'm so sorry... I..."

"I said not fucking now, Sadie," he bit out, forking his fingers through his hair, his eyes on the scene in front of them. Sadie's heart curled in tight around the edges, like it had been set on fire, too.

She took a step back from him, her head swimming. She wondered if she should do something with the crowd? Try to manage? But everyone was frozen, staring at what was happening, and she just felt useless. Helpless. Like she'd been as a child in her home growing up. Watching sick, unending horror playing out before her eyes while she cowered, powerless to stop it.

The fire department came, en masse, sirens rising up over the sound of the blaze. And when it was over, there was no question as to what was left: nothing.

Nothing but a charred husk. Unusable, unsalvageable. The crowd had thinned by then, families with small children taking them away from the upsetting scene. They'd all moved on to the main fireworks display down at the beach. Though mainly they'd left so quickly to escape the smoke and debris. Sadie wished she could get carried away from it, too, but she had to watch, her own eyes gritty with ashes. She felt honor bound in so many ways.

Finally, all that remained were Liss, Jack, Kate, Eli, Lydia, Ace, Bud and the fishermen.

And Connor. Who stood alone, silent and in sharp contrast to the blackened ruins in front of him. Unmoving.

Liss was the one who broke from the small crowd and went to him, her hand going to his shoulder. He jerked away from her and walked back toward the main house, leaving Liss standing there with her arms folded beneath her breasts.

A moment later she took a deep breath and marched after him, a stubborn set to her jaw and shoulders, and for a moment, Sadie could only admire the other woman's strength. Liss was a woman who stayed. A woman who went the tough rounds.

It made Sadie feel painfully inadequate, standing there in the semi-darkness, with cooling ashes just in front of her.

"Whatever you need, Eli," Ace said. "You know we're here to help out."

"I know," Eli said.

"Anything," Lydia said. And Sadie knew she was ready to offer comfort as well, and Sadie couldn't even be mad because she felt so unequal to the task.

"Probably we all just need sleep right now," Eli said, forcing a smile.

Kate was standing silent, tears streaming down her cheeks, her shoulders shaking. Sadie moved nearer to her and put her arm around her. Feeling so inadequate to do anything to stanch the flow of grief around her.

"Of course," Ace said. "We'll get out of your hair. I'll come by tomorrow if you want, help assess the damage?"

"Thanks. I imagine we'll just be making an insurance claim. And they'll have to send someone out. Best we leave it untouched for now."

"Fair point. Come by for a drink, though," Ace said, touching the brim of his ball cap before walking away.

"Guess I better let you get rest, too," Lydia said, putting her hand on Eli's shoulder in a decidedly nonsisterly way. "I'll come by and check in on you tomorrow."

Eli didn't protest.

Lydia squeezed Sadie's shoulder, too, as she walked by her. "I'm happy to check in on you, too."

That tipped her over into utter misery. Because she didn't deserve that kindness. Not at all. "Thanks," she said, her throat raw.

"I'll go talk to the firemen," Jack said, "see if there's anything we need to know. I'll report back."

"I'm going to go find Connor," Kate said, her voice thick as she pulled away from Sadie and walked in the direction of the main house.

That left Sadie and Eli, and a pile of glowing, charred wood, alone in the darkness.

She swallowed and tried again. "Eli, I…"

"We have to be done," Eli said, cutting her off.

"What?"

"This. Us. It has to… I can't do this," he said.

ELI'S HEART TWISTED into a knot in his chest, but it had to be said. It had to be done. Because yet again, while he'd been out enjoying himself, the whole world had fallen apart. All of this, the time spent with Sadie, had been an illusion.

When he didn't keep control, the world burned. In this case, literally.

It was just too damn close to his other failures. Too damn close.

"When I'm with you, I forget what I'm doing. I forget other people. I forget myself. No, I don't forget myself, because myself is all I think of. Myself and my dick, and it can't happen like this. There is a reason that I've lived my life the way that I have. A reason that I can't ignore for good sex."

Sadie blinked rapidly, her eyes glossy in the dim light. And his stomach twisted, sick regret forming. But there was nothing else he could do. He needed to stay on top of this stuff and he wasn't doing it.

His sister had just stood there in tears, his brother watching the one thing he'd held on to since losing his wife burn to nothing.

It was all way too reminiscent of the night when he hadn't taken the keys. Of the last time Eli had let himself become distracted.

And it didn't matter what Sadie said, because in the end, this was the result. It didn't matter if he shouldn't feel at fault. He did. And it didn't change the fact that when he wasn't holding up the world around him, it all seemed to fall apart.

For a second today, he'd thought he could be something different, have something different. And then all this had swooped in and reminded him just why that wasn't possible.

Why he had to forget their moment in the woods, and every moment before. Why he had to stop wanting more, when more would never be in the cards for him. He knew that. He'd known that before Sadie Miller had blown into his life like a windstorm and rearranged his existence. Made him think that maybe everything he'd believed about his life, about himself, had been a lie.

Which was a whole lot crueler than never having hope had ever been.

For one moment, he'd thought he could do it. Thought he could punch the hell out of a guy who deserved it, thought he could sneak into the woods for a moment alone with the only woman who'd ever driven him that crazy.

Thought he could go to sleep with her every night and wake up with her every morning.

"Good sex, Eli?" she asked. "Really? Good sex? Because I think, I mean, I pretty freaking well think what we have is a

lot more than that. I mean, I think we'd both had good sex before we ever met each other, and that…this is something else
entirely. What we share is something else."

"It doesn't matter," he said. "It can't happen." He wanted to
lash out. To blame someone other than himself. He was so tired
of carrying it all. And this was just another failure. "It seems
like when you're around barns tend to burn down," he said.
"You have a knack for spreading disaster, I guess."

"Eli, please don't do this. Not now, not… Please."

"Sadie, I can't afford any more distractions," he said, the
words scraping his throat raw. "And that's all this was. All you
are to me is a distraction."

She stumbled backward and he felt like his heart lurched
through his chest to follow her, leaving nothing but a bloody,
vacant hole behind. This felt like he thought dying might. But
he couldn't take the words back now.

He wouldn't.

It was the right thing to do. Other men could have wives and
kids. Other men with other lives.

Not him. Never him.

"Well," she said, her voice thick as she put distance between
them. "Don't let me distract you any longer."

She turned and walked back in the direction of the B and
B, which he only thought of as hers now. What a difference a
few weeks made.

But he couldn't afford the difference, and neither could any
of the people who depended on him.

CHAPTER SIXTEEN

SADIE DIDN'T SLEEP AT ALL. She spent the whole night out on her newly stained deck, a mug of coffee clutched tightly in her hand, tears rolling down her face as she slowly accepted what had happened. As she slowly accepted what she'd let herself do.

She loved Eli Garrett.

He was the first person she'd loved since she'd lost hope in her family a decade ago and run out of town.

He was the first person she'd been close to in as many years, if not more. If not ever.

She stayed on the deck, wrapped in her blanket and her misery, Toby snuggled in her lap, until pink started to bleed into the sky, extending up above the tree line.

Well, damn. There went her theory about the world stopping because she was devastated.

She deposited Toby gently onto the deck, then went into the house with him following behind her. She went upstairs, undressed and stepped into the shower, letting the hot water wash away the stiffness, the misery.

In the end, some of the stiffness got worked out, but the misery remained.

She brushed her teeth, which were fuzzy after an evening of nursing coffees, then made herself another in her single-serving brewer, bought especially so that her guests could have a fresh cup at any point in the day.

She let out a heavy sigh. Her guests. She'd had several people get in touch since the night before, inquiring about availability through her website. So soon there would be guests. She had a five-year contract.

She lowered her head, feeling very much like she was sinking into the mire. A mire she couldn't just cut and run from.

And suddenly she felt claustrophobic. She wanted to claw her clothes off, claw her skin off, step out of her body and just run from all of it.

Get away and start fresh. Away from that man, away from the feelings he made her feel.

She looked around the B and B, at her attempt to build something permanent. To make something stable. She should have known it was never about her surroundings. It was about her. It always had been.

She couldn't sign a five-year lease and expect it to make her different.

The simple truth was, she'd never been important enough for anyone to change for her. That was the painful heart of it. Her mother would rather spend her life being beaten by a man, the same man who beat her child, than leave him for the good of them both.

Her love for a husband who dealt out pain and misery was stronger than her love for Sadie. And that made it impossible to imagine anyone changing their life drastically for the sake of her love.

And Eli was proving that no one would.

This was why she always left. Because if she left first, if she never let anyone close, if she never asked anyone to know her and accept her anyway, she couldn't get hurt.

But she'd come back to Copper Ridge. She'd given of herself. She'd fallen in love and dared to hope for it back.

And now she was broken. And she had no idea how long it would take to glue the pieces back together.

One thing was for sure. She couldn't do it here.

"Toby," she said, looking at her little gray friend, the only friend she really had, "I think it's time for us to go."

ELI PACED THE LENGTH of the living room, eyeing his brother, who was passed out on the couch. He was going to hate life a whole hell of a lot when Eli woke him up.

Which was going to be now, because Eli hated life, so Connor might as well join the living.

In hell.

"Wake up, Connor," he said, clapping his hands and watching his brother go from blissfully conked out to awake and in a world of pain in an instant.

"Dammit all!" he said, then winced, his hand on his forehead. "Ow."

"Yeah, I would think *ow*. You drank roughly the amount of alcohol it would take to cleanse all the wounds on a frontier battlefield."

"Oh…shut up, Eli. Honestly."

"We have things to do."

"Like?" he asked. "Work? Because I think all my tools are gone."

"You have animals that might want to get fed."

"I don't have hay," Connor mumbled.

"So get off your ass and get some," Eli said, feeling angry. At himself, mainly, but yelling at Connor was more convenient than dealing with that.

"What the hell is your issue this morning?" Connor asked, moving into a sitting position, running his hands over his beard.

"Maybe I'm tired of watching you wallow while I take care of you," Eli said, resentment flaring up, rage burning hot in his chest.

He'd resigned himself to this last night.

To caring for other people and putting himself on hold. But this morning? This morning he'd woken up alone. And it hurt worse than he'd imagined it could. Thirty-two years of it. He should be used to it. But this morning his bed had felt so empty it had mimicked the damn hole in his chest.

And he was forgetting already why a burned-out barn had mattered more than Sadie next to him.

"What?" Connor asked.

"You are my older brother. You're a grown man."

"I never asked you to take care of me," Connor said.

"You expect it," Eli bit out.

Connor shook his head. "Look, man, I don't know what the hell your problem is, but I've never asked you for anything. I'm glad you're here, I won't lie, but if you weren't? I would be happy to just stay drunk and live in filth. You're the one who—"

"And it's things like that, Connor, that mean I can't leave you to it. Because you don't think I know you'd sink in it? I do, and I won't let it happen."

"And so what, Eli? I'm supposed to get myself together the way you see fit so you don't have to deal?"

"Yeah," Eli said. "Yeah. Just…could you? Because I can't work a job, and work on the ranch, and run for sheriff, and file your insurance claim and not lose my fucking mind. I can't… I can't do it all."

That was the first time he'd ever admitted that. To himself. To anyone else. That he couldn't shoulder everything. That he didn't even want to.

"I didn't know, Eli," Connor said, looking straight ahead. "I've had a hard time caring about anything other than myself. For the record, I mostly still don't care about anything else, but… I'm damn sorry you felt that way."

"It wasn't ever just you," Eli said. "But you know you've added to it."

"Well," Connor drawled. "I do what I can."

"You make me feel like a dick for complaining since you've been through hell."

"Yeah. Still in it most days," he mumbled. "But I guess I don't have to bring you with me."

"Sometimes I think I brought myself on purpose."

"Well, stop," Connor said.

"What?"

"Stop. Being unhappy is stupid. If there's any way you can fix it? Fix it. I can't bring my wife back. I can't...fix anything that happened. I can't make my life better just by making a different choice."

"I'm not sure I can, either," Eli said.

"Does it have to do with Sadie?"

Eli breathed in deep. "Yeah."

"She's not dead, is she?"

"No," Eli said, his voice rough.

"Then there's still hope."

CHAPTER SEVENTEEN

SADIE FINISHED PILING her personal belongings into the car. She was violating her lease agreement and she knew it. It sucked, but she just… She couldn't stay. She didn't know much about what would happen next, but she knew that much.

She sighed and put Toby's cat carrier in the backseat, safely on the floorboards, before shutting the back door.

She heard a car driving up the driveway and swore copiously under her breath. She didn't want to deal with a crestfallen Kate, a pissed-off Connor or…worse than them all, an Eli, in whatever form he chose to present.

But instead of a Garrett vehicle, it was a shiny black car making its way down the driveway.

"Lydia," she grumbled, leaning against her car and looking down. Oh, well, the other woman could give her a send-off. Hell, she'd probably be thrilled to do it.

Lydia stopped her car and got out, a stack of brochures in her hand and a frown crossing her fine features. "What's going on?" she asked.

"I'm heading out," Sadie said. "It's…kind of what I do. Don't be alarmed."

"Too late," Lydia said. "I am. Eli didn't tell you to—"

"Oh, no, he's too much of a gentleman for that." Not too much of one to break her heart and say she wasn't important, but he'd never ask her to violate a lease agreement. That shit was legally binding.

"Does he know you're leaving?" she asked.

"No, I didn't tell him. Though it's really more relevant to Connor since he's the one who sort of headed up the lease thingy…"

"Oh, what a bunch of baloney," Lydia said. "It is not more relevant to Connor than it is to Eli if you go. And I think you know it."

She averted her eyes. "Do you know it?"

Lydia sighed. "I'm not stupid. Possibly a little bit…mmm… too hopeful? But yeah, not stupid. I've seen the way you look at each other."

Sadie cleared her throat. "But have you heard the way we talk to each other? Because that might be a better indicator of where we're at."

"Do you love him?" she asked.

Sadie's heart squeezed tight. "It doesn't matter."

"It matters. Eli Garrett is the best man I know. The best man I've ever known. And you know, I realized he's not that into me. Sure, it's sort of been a die-hard crush, even with that in mind, but, pretty much the minute you showed up I knew I was screwed." She smiled, the expression tinged with sadness. "Not in a fun way, either. But ultimately, I know I won't be happy with a guy I have to coerce into a relationship. And I have a sneaking suspicion he won't be happy *without* you."

Sadie laughed. "Tell him that. He told me he didn't want me."

"He's lying," she said. "You realize that, right?"

"I don't think Eli knows how to lie."

"Well, maybe not on purpose. But he's lying even if he

doesn't know he is. One benefit of watching someone more closely than you should, you get to know them. The way he looks at you? That's special. If I were you? I wouldn't walk away from that. I'd fight for it. And I'll be honest, Sadie, I took you for kind of a badass, so...if you run now, I'm going to have to retract that."

"I'm not a badass," Sadie said. "I'm basically whatever is the opposite of that. And I've never pretended to be much more. I'm a runner. And it's my cue to go."

"That sucks, because I think if you stayed, and if we weren't competing for the same guy, we could be friends. And I think if you stayed, and you married him, eventually, we would be friends. You know, after I got over my seething jealousy."

"You don't seem to be seething all that much," Sadie said.

"It's a quiet seethe. Like I said, I know he's not mine." She smiled a little more genuinely now. "Kind of bummed I never got to..."

Sadie coughed. "Yeah...that's kind of... He's good at the sex."

Lydia cleared her throat, her cheeks turning pink. "I was going to say kiss him. But sure."

Sadie winced. "Well, he's good at that, too."

"I can't decide if it sucks to know that or if it's gratifying to realize my fantasies were on track."

"It sucks to know. Because I know it sucks that I know. Because it's over. And I wish it weren't."

"So fight for it, badass," Lydia said. "Fight for *him*."

"I don't think there's anything to fight for."

"Well, then, maybe you should go. Because I happen to think he deserves someone who will fight. I thought that might be you."

"Maybe you should fight for him," Sadie said, feeling mean, small and not at all in the mood to watch another woman fight for the man she loved. But not brave enough to go and get him herself.

Lydia looked at her sadly. "It was nice to meet you, Sadie. I hope you find whatever you're looking for. And I really hope that you don't realize it was here when it's too late for you to come back."

Sadie watched Lydia toss the brochures on her passenger seat and drive away and felt a whole hot ball of rage grow in her chest. Who was Lydia to tell her what she should do? Seriously. She hadn't been there. She hadn't heard the way Eli talked to her. What he'd said.

Lydia probably had no idea what it was like to be certain that the only way attachment could end was rejection.

And hell, he'd rejected her. Why subject herself to it twice?

Because for the first time, you felt complete. Because for the first time you want to stay. Really, really.

Well, it didn't really matter. Because he'd pushed her away. *You're just too pathetic to fight for him. Too afraid.*

Yeah, well, because what if she was wrong? Sure, maybe Eli was as afraid as she was. Maybe that was half of why he'd pushed her away. Maybe.

She jerked the backseat door open and pulled out the pet carrier, depositing it on the porch, checking to make sure Toby's food, water and litter weren't disturbed.

Then she looked out into the forest.

The place she'd always gone to escape, before she'd run for real.

She took a deep breath of the pine and salt air. And then she ran.

THE WAY ELI SAW IT, he had two options. The Connor option—really, the Garrett option—that meant drinking until you couldn't remember why you were sad.

Or the handle-your-shit option, which was a lot harder.

He stared at the bottle of Jack on the counter and placed his palms flat on the marble surface, looking at the bottle. As if it might tell him what to do.

"Drink it and it might," he said.

Then he shoved off from the counter and started pacing the room. What was he doing? He felt like hell. Or something worse than hell, whatever that was.

But he had order. He didn't have a blonde whirlwind with a strange emotional connection to a cat. He didn't have distractions. He had what he'd spent a lifetime cultivating.

"Loneliness," he said to the empty room. "You have loneliness. Give the man a prize."

And it was all he ever had to look forward to. An orderly life and an empty bed. All because he was too afraid to let someone in.

All because it was so much easier to keep everyone out and to never lose anyone or anything again. All because it was easier to blame himself so he could pretend he had some control in the universe when the simple fact was he didn't have control over any of it.

Mothers left. People died. Barns burned. And no amount of diligence on his part would ever stop it.

He slammed his fist down onto the counter and swore as pain shot up his arm, straight through to his heart.

What a terrible realization. And too late. Dammit, if he was going to have to deal with the fact that he had no control over his life, over anything, the least he could have done was grasped the concept before he'd lost her.

Sadie...

He looked at the spotless counter, where she'd once put her damned tennis shoes. Who did shit like that? And even though the shoes were gone, and there was not a speck of dust from the tread left behind, the memory lingered so strongly there might as well have been a muddy footprint there.

It would have been easier to erase.

He turned away from the counter and looked out the front window, and his heart about burst. Her azalea. Her apology azalea with its pink flowers. Another Sadie invasion that had been obnoxious at first, but that he couldn't imagine life without now.

She was everywhere in his house. At the counter, drinking a beer. In his bed. His shower. His yard. His heart.

Dammit, she was in his heart.

He loved her.

The realization sent warmth blooming through him. Like a burst blood vessel around his heart, flooding his chest and making him feel weak.

He *loved her.*

He hadn't loved anyone but Kate and Connor in...ever. Hadn't wanted to because he'd been so busy trying to hold the world together. Trying to make sense of things that just didn't make sense.

Trying to keep his family from falling apart, so that no one else would leave. So that he would matter.

But Sadie had always acted like he mattered, even when he was screwing things up. Sadie had held him, stripped him of his inhibitions in a way nothing and no one else ever had, accepted him when he confessed his shortcomings. Sadie, who had shared herself with him when she hadn't shared with anyone else.

An offering of herself, but also a demonstration of the trust she put in him.

And he had turned her away to keep wandering through life, holding on with an iron fist, trying desperately to earn the trust of strangers. To be seen as good enough.

When she'd already seen him that way.

"Probably not now, asshole," he said into the empty room.

No, probably not now.

And he couldn't blame her.

But he had to ask. He had to try. He had to beg forgiveness.

He had to tell her he loved her.

And damn the consequences.

Order meant nothing without her, control meant nothing without her. And the only acceptance that mattered was hers.

He shoved the Jack Daniel's bottle back into its place in the cupboard and walked out of his house. He strode toward the B and B, his heart in his throat, his hands honest-to-God shaking. Everything in him was shaking.

He'd never loved anyone. And he'd never asked anyone to love him back.

He'd tried to earn it, every day. But he'd never asked.

Today he had to ask.

He walked across the driveway and into the clearing in front of her house, and saw her car, the back door open, suitcases inside.

"What the hell?"

Just then, Sadie came down the stairs, a couple of pine needles stuck in her hair, tears on her cheeks, her face pale. Her eyes widened and she froze, staring at him like he was some kind of ghost. He walked toward her.

She was packed. She was leaving.

She was leaving him.

Hell no.

He reached out and wrapped his arm around her waist, tugging her to him, his lips crashing down on hers. He tried to make her feel what he did. To understand what he'd just started to understand. That he loved her. That she'd changed him.

She clung to him, grabbing his T-shirt and holding it tight, holding him tight.

When they parted, they were both breathing hard, and her cheeks were wet, tears tracking down her pale skin.

"Don't leave me," he said, his tone a command. "Don't go."

"Eli…"

"I am an idiot. You *are* distracting. And you did change things. But dammit, Sadie, I want to be distracted by you. I want to be changed by you. Hell, baby, I need it. And I was just about to drink a whole bottle of liquor to try to forget how much of an ass I am. But then I saw my counter."

"Your counter?"

"It's clean. Your shoes aren't sitting on it. Everything's in order. Everything. You're not there saying some…sexual innuendo I barely understand, and you know what? I hate it. I hate the order if it means I can't have you. I love you, Sadie."

"I'm not leaving," she said, her voice trembling.

"Then why are you packed?"

"Because. Because I was going to leave but I went and did some thinking. And now I'm not," she said.

"Why?" he asked.

"You know…it's hard to say. Because leaving is what I do. And even when I knew I would miss you like hell it seemed easier than this. Easier than standing in front of you and telling you I want more. But I'm going to do it anyway. I went back to my clearing. It was where I used to go when things got to be too much. When I needed to escape. But I didn't find oblivion there. I found you instead. And whatever power there was in escape, whatever I used to enjoy about it…it was gone. I don't want to run anymore. I want to stand and fight. I want to stay. I want more. Because I want you. I want everything. Good and bad and stick up your ass. I love you and I want to fight for that love like I've never fought for anything."

He felt like he'd been punched in the chest. It was one thing to confess his love to her, but he didn't think for a damn minute he deserved to have it returned. Not after the things he'd said to her.

"How can you love *me*?" he asked. "I failed you."

"That's the thing, though, Eli, you didn't. I wished that someone would have stepped in and saved me. Of course I did. And I think…it was easy to wish it had been you. But what I really needed was to save myself."

"You did, Sadie," he said, his chest tightening. "You left."

She shook her head. "No. That's not when I saved myself.

That's when I learned to run. Which is the first step sometimes. But I realized something today, when I was ready to leave this place, to leave you. I realized it's not enough to have a life. You have to have all of life. And I haven't let myself do that."

"Sadie…" His throat closed up. "I haven't, either. I wanted to believe that I could control things. That somehow I could stop bad things from happening. But the problem with that is that… I can't. I thought if I could, if I got things in order… But it's not in my power. And admitting that is one of the scariest damn things I can think of because control is everything to me. Being the one taking care of things is everything to me. So that…" He felt like an ass even thinking this, much less admitting it. But it was time to say it. And it was time to let it go. "People leave me, Sadie. I thought someday I'd make myself so important it wouldn't happen again."

"Well—" Sadie wiped the tears from her cheeks and smiled "—Eli Garrett, future sheriff of Copper Ridge, you have made yourself so important to me that this woman, who always has her running shoes on hand, can't leave you."

SADIE LOOKED UP AT ELI, at the deep concern in his dark eyes, at the sincerity. And the insecurity. And any remaining walls around her heart crumbled completely.

She threw her arms around his neck and held him close, stroking her fingers through his hair. "You're the best reason in the world to stop running. And you don't have to work to get me to stay. I'm offering to. Because you're the best man there is. And anyone who made you feel like less deserves to be dragged behind a horse."

"I love you, Sadie. More than a clean house, more than stability. If you kept running, I'd run after you. Even if I had to leave all this behind. Because it doesn't mean a thing without you. And I'm sorry. Sorry for all the crap I said to you. Everything I put us through. I couldn't run, so I guess the best I could do was try to make you run. Because you scare the hell out of me, woman. But I'm even more scared of living without you."

A tear rolled down Sadie's cheek, emotion filling her, so full she thought she might break with it. "Then it's a good thing I'm staying."

"Oh, hell, does this mean I'm part of the bed-and-breakfast?"

"Only if you spend the night."

"Yeah," he said, "about that… Do you think you could run it if you mainly slept at my place?"

"Mainly?"

"Always."

"I have a cat," she reminded him. "And he sleeps indoors. He basically lives indoors."

"I will give him his own bedroom."

"Holy crap, you do love me!" she said, laughing, another tear sliding down her cheek.

"I really do," he said, leaning in to kiss her. "I really, really do."

Sadie kissed him back, the feeling of completion when their lips touched unlike anything she'd ever experienced.

Whoever said you couldn't go home again had never been to Copper Ridge. The place hadn't changed at all.

But Sadie had. And for the first time, she was home, and she was ready to stay.

* * * * *

ACKNOWLEDGMENTS

They say it takes a village to raise a child. Sometimes I feel like it takes a village to create a book. A huge thank-you to Margo Lipschultz, who encouraged me to send this series to HQN and who has put in so many tireless hours to make it the best it can be. Kate Dresser, my fantastic editor on this book, I only wish we could have done more together. You're amazing. I always owe thanks to my wonderful agent, Helen Breitwieser, who has believed in me from the beginning. To Jackie Ashenden for reading every word I write and serving up hard truths wrapped in encouragement. Many thanks to Nicole Helm for her insider knowledge on police uniforms and how they are removed, velcro belts, clip-on ties and all. And I owe the biggest thank-you of all to Victoria Austin for the snowballs joke that Eli tells in the book. You are a goddess of the corny joke, and for that I am grateful.

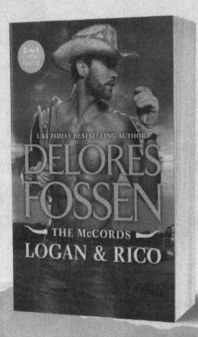

Subscribe and fall in love with a Mills & Boon series today!

You'll be among the first to read stories delivered to your door monthly and enjoy great savings.

WE
SIMPLY
LOVE
ROMANCE